The Way Down Is Shorter…

A Hank Cassidy Novel

By
Dean Drabin

All rights reserved

Copyright © 2012 by Dean Drabin

This is a work of fiction. Names, characters, places, and incidents either are the product of the author's imagination or are used fictitiously. Any resemblance to actual persons, living or dead, events, or locales, is entirely coincidental.

ISBN-13: 978-1475102956

ISBN-10: 147510295X

Visit the author at: deandrabin.com

Books by **Dean Drabin**

The Way Down is Shorter
Blue Lady

Dedicated to E.A.P.

Long is the way and hard that out of Hell leads up to light

John Milton,
Paradise Lost

Chapter One

"Son, are you right with Jesus?" the voice thundered.

Pronounced it "Jay'-zuss" with an accent straight out of Biloxi—though the rest of his words argued that he'd never been south of Reno.

Oh, brother...

I deliberately sipped from my coffee mug to mask my reaction.

His name was Reverend J.T. Sayles, pastor of the Church of the Holy Messenger; and when Kelly greeted him on the way out the front door with our dog, Satchmo, he'd pointedly ignored her and then proceeded to march into my house like a tribune at the head of his legions. Planting himself squarely in front of my dining room table (actually, dining room table when there's food involved; for business purposes it's my reception desk), he'd then fixed me with a miles-holier-than-thou look as he issued the aforementioned lofty challenge to my spiritual bona fides.

Lowering my mug halfway, I briefly studied him. With no legions in sight the man looked considerably less than imperial: average height (might just make it to five-eight and a half if he wore lifts); average weight—one-sixty, tops; beige pants, light-brown long-sleeved shirt, no tie; nondescript nose, small, humorless brown eyes under pencil brows; paper-thin lips habitually frozen into a cipher; pasty, unlined forehead surmounted by a ridiculous comb-over of stringy black hair.

An average guy; an actuary's dream—five minutes after he left the room, you'd probably have a hard time picking him out of a two-man line up.

The only feature which appeared to distinguish him, in fact, was that grotesquely oversized voice; something he evidently took great pride in flourishing, bouncing each word majestically—and unnecessarily—off of the log trusses and knotty pine planking of my vaulted ceiling. He might have made a dandy public address announcer at pro sporting events, but as there were currently no pro teams playing in Central Oregon, I guess that the default position for those pipes was evangelical minister.

There are times when I think that the good lord invented these guys so that he could have a few laughs on his day off.

Given this admittedly jaundiced attitude towards pushy religionists, the strident tone of the preacher's obnoxious preamble and his rudeness toward my girlfriend—not to mention my usual morning irritability—; I was immediately possessed of a profound urge to kick the man's sanctimonious butt out onto my gravel driveway. But as, unfortunately, my investigative business was at that moment gasping for air, I decided that a little discretion might make better philosophical—not to mention economic—sense, and so with some effort I choked back the bile and said, politely, "I beg your pardon?"

"I *said,*" he repeated impatiently, drawing himself up to every bit of 5'7 ½" (no lifts) and managing to squeeze out a few additional decibels; "are you right with the *Lord*? You see, in order to consider enlisting your services, we need first to establish that we are dealing with a proper, upright *Christian* man. We must never allow ourselves to traffic with the unworthy." Evidently pleased with this choice of words—and, especially, with his delivery of them—the man beamed at me, expectantly.

Must've missed that whole thing about pride being a sin.

"Was that the royal 'we'?" I asked, quietly.

"What?" he said.

"Just wondering if this was a solo act."

Puzzlement creased his putty face. "Huh? I don't—"

"Are you here on *personal* or *congregational* business?" I asked, a little more crisply. Probably could have put it that way a few sentences sooner, but pompous self-righteousness tends to bring out the obtuse in me.

"It's a personal matter," he said, his voice at last knocked down to a somewhat more conversational timbre.

"So, what's with all this 'we' crap, Reverend?" I asked.

Sometimes bile can really be quite tasty...

"Young man," he said, brusquely, "I dislike being spoken to in that manner."

I could feel my eyebrows lifting. "And I dislike being called 'son,' and 'young man' by someone obviously younger than me."

"Oh that," he replied dismissively, his thin lips reforming into a tight, humorless smile. "It's nothing, really; just a force of habit—an affectation, if you will. It happens to be how I tend to address all of the members of my flock."

"That's mighty ovine of them," I said.

"Excuse me?"

"I'm not one of your sheep, Reverend."

"What you are, I think, is rude."

"So take a hike," I said.

So much for good philosophical and economic sense.

This curt dismissal clearly took the man by surprise, and he didn't immediately respond to it; instead he stood there simmering, silently and uncertainly, as I picked up the Bulletin sports section and even more deliberately took another sip of my coffee. The conflict being waged on his face suggested that I was probably a last resort—something which resonated with a calculation I'd already made before he showed up. I live at least eighteen miles south of town. Add to this the fact that my business had not as yet accumulated much in the way of word of mouth, and further, that my modest, quarter-page ad in the yellow pages could hardly have been described as magnetic, and the obvious conclusion was that if this man had driven all the way out here to the boonies to consult with me, it must have meant that he'd done so only after having already exhausted the list of far better-known and much more conveniently located investigators to be found well within Bend's city limits.

Seeing that the preacher was continuing to fidget in what for him must surely have been an unaccustomed shortage of words, I decided to cut him a little slack—but only a little.

"Look, Reverend," I said, "let's you and me keep things simple here. I'm a private investigator, not an acolyte. If you want to hire me, fine; this is how it works: you tell me your problem; I tell you whether I can help, and how much you're going to have to pay for my services."

"But what my beliefs—or lack of them, for that matter—might happen to be; that will be none of your damned business. And I am neither your 'young man,' your 'child,' nor any of your barnyard animals. My name is Mr. Cassidy—or Hank, if you prefer to be informal. Now, if these are concepts you can't quite get your head around, then don't let the door hit you where the dog bit you."

"Are you always this gruff?"

"If the situation calls for it."

"As it does now, apparently."

"You set the table, Padre."

He struggled with that for just a few moments; and then his shoulders sagged, and he sighed.

"All right...um, Mr. Cassidy. Do you...could we...do you think, perhaps, that we might start over?"

"Absolutely," I said, magnanimously, and pointed to the nearest dining room—I mean, *office*—chair. "Please; have a seat."

He sat.

We were silent for a few moments, and his head swiveled this way and that as he took in the noticeably luxurious appointments of my custom log home. We were seated in the dining portion of the great room, vast and majestic with its eighteen foot ceiling, floor-to-roof stone fireplace and massive glass wall offering a panoramic western view of the Deschutes River, now shimmering under a cloudless, late-summer's sky. The house had cost me nearly eight-hundred large to build two years ago, and I was sure that at the moment the good Reverend was puzzling over exactly how a bottom-of-the-barrel PI could afford to live in such rustic splendor. Of course, that my house had in fact been born of the fruits of a previous, completely unrelated career was something of which he was currently unaware. And as far as I was concerned there was no particular need to enlighten him.

Nor was I inclined to broadcast how much my financial condition had deteriorated since I'd moved into this house. A large portion of this decline, of course, was due to the ice-water-like shrinkage in the value of my mutual funds during the last year and a half, the direct product of the by now extensively-documented exploits of those greedy, reckless scoundrels on Wall Street. Additionally, I'd been experiencing a rather uncomfortable, concurrent decrease in the status of my more liquid assets––this condition owing, primarily, to an absolutely jaw-dropping run of gambling reversals—a streak of shitty luck which had begun with a substantial, ill-fated wager on last February's Super Bowl.

The net result of this financial double-whammy was that way too much yolk had been sucked from my nest egg, leaving me, if not exactly panicky about my situation, then at least queasy enough to negotiate a fairly hefty first mortgage on my house, so that I could continue to keep body and soul in the same area code while I waited for the economic pendulum to swing back in my direction.

As I watched the Reverend continue, with flinty, judgmental eyes, to inventory my house and its contents, I was tempted, somewhat subversively, to direct his attention towards my trilobite fossil, three hundred-fifty million years young, which was prominently displayed on a small, wooden easel on the fireplace mantel. But, in the end I held back, deciding that such an evolutionary reference would have just been the gratuitous needling of a helpless, hidebound fundamentalist.

Instead, I asked, "What does the 'J.T.' stand for?"

"Jeremiah Tayback," he announced, grandly, his baritone pipes making something of a minor comeback.

"Tayback?" I said, feigning confusion. "That some sort of biblical name?"

His look accused me of acute scriptural duncery. "No, of course not. It was my mother's maiden name."

"Ah…" I said. "Of course. Coffee?"

"No, thank you."

"Okay." I leaned back. "So, what's your problem?"

He hesitated, looked away and then said, "My son is missing. I want you to find him, Mr. Cassidy."

"How old is he?"

"Sixteen." He paused, then added as if it mattered: "and a half." He pulled a photo from his shirt pocket, unfolded it and then passed it to me, saying as he did so that I could keep it. The photo, a five-by-seven, had evidently been taken in front of the giant, double doors of a church entrance and showed the preacher, dressed in a somber, black suit, standing next to a striking adolescent male, similarly clad. The young man was taller by three inches than his father, with a full head of black hair and dark, piercing eyes, and only resembled the Reverend in the thinness of his lips and the color of his hair. Neither was smiling, and their uncomfortable, stiff postures clearly indicated a reluctance to stand close enough to each other to fit in the same frame.

"Nice-looking kid," I said. I looked up from the photo, just in time to catch a sharp look which suggested that I'd somehow insulted the preacher. He must've realized this: the look passed quickly, and he managed a strangled "Thank-you."

"Name?"

"Joshua."

"Tell me about him."

He paused, apparently again constipated in the word department by my simple request. Finally, with some effort he managed to get his lips in gear. "He's a...a fine young man...yes, a fine young man; perhaps not quite as disciplined as I might like—you might even say a trifle wild—and not nearly as respectful to his elders as he ought to be, but...a fine young man just the same. He's no scholar, mind you—unfortunately takes after his mother in that respect—but he does have some aptitude, and I do wish he'd apply himself more diligently to his schoolwork, and, in particular, to the Scriptures...and to his service to the Lord—"

"But he's a fine young man," I intoned.

"Yes," he agreed, evidently not catching onto my sarcasm. Clearly this was a father coming up short on his supply of positive opinions about his offspring.

"I suppose," he said, his voice abruptly shifting into a kindly, patronizing, and to my ear, entirely bullshit tone, "that the boy has been doing the best he could, under the circumstances..."

"Circumstances?"

"Yes," he said. "You know, it can't be easy, growing up as the child of one of the community's most prominent religious leaders."

I was tempted to toss my mug at him; instead I sipped from it, nodded and said, "Right; kid's certainly got a lot to live up to, doesn't he?"

"Yes, yes," he agreed, enthusiastically. "There are times when I almost feel sorry for the boy."

"Sorry for him..." I said.

"Yes," he said; "given his many failings, I think that the boy might have been more comfortable growing up in a slightly more…um, *prosaic* environment."

"The boy;" never *"Joshua or Josh;"* always *"the boy."*

This was getting tedious, so I switched gears. "How long has he been missing?"

"Two months."

"Has he ever disappeared before?"

"Run away? My son? Never!" he replied, crisply. "He knows all too well the consequences, both practically, as well as spiritually, of such a rash and selfish action. 'Honor thy father and thy mother,' sayeth the law. Believe me, Mr. Cassidy, there's no leeway in that commandment; no child of mine would ever show *me,* of all people, such profound disrespect. The Lord himself would never permit such a blasphemy."

"That is, apparently," I pointed out, "until two months ago."

"What? Oh well, yes, of course, yes," he said, suddenly deflated, as if in the midst of his oratory he'd completely forgotten the circumstances of his visit. His pale face reddening somewhat, he said: "Yes, Mr. Cassidy, and now, despite all of my best efforts, all of my prayers, all of my good *work,* my son has disappeared. Which makes this whole thing all the more incomprehensible— unless, of course, something has…happened to him. It's impossible to think otherwise, in fact; impossible to believe that the boy could have done something like this of his own volition."

"So you think he was taken."

"Have you not been listening? He *must* have been. Taken, coerced—tempted, perhaps; but I am sure that he would never have simply gone off on his own."

"Was there a ransom note?"

"No. There has been no contact of any kind."

"Uh-huh. What do the police say?"

"The police," he said, huffily, "are not quite prepared to concur with my assessment of the situation. But after all, these are people who are, at their hearts, politicians; as such it is simply not in their nature to hazard any sort of opinion until such time as the evidence to support it becomes too overwhelming for them to ignore. I do forgive them their timidity though, and at any rate I can hardly accuse them of any lack of effort on their part. It is obvious to me that the authorities have been *more* than diligent, and that they've been devoting considerable hours and manpower to my problem." Apparently unable to restrain himself, he added: "I am, after all, a man of some significant influence in this town."

Again with the pride.

I did my best to ignore it. "So, as you say, the police are all over this. You know, those folks are really pretty thorough when it comes to this sort of thing. What makes you think I could add anything?"

"Oh," he said, shifting slightly in his chair, "I'm sure the police are competent enough in their fashion." His thin lips curled slightly. "But…well, perhaps there could be some things a private investigator can accomplish that the authorities might not be able to? Besides, I must satisfy myself that I have covered all the bases. He *is,* after all, my son…"

I studied him a little more closely. These last words were certainly appropriate, but the attitude was off. There was something particularly *pro forma* about his presentation; a stiffness and formality which tended, strongly, to remind me of the man's posture in the photograph I was holding.

"Yes, as you say, Reverend, Joshua is your son," I said. "Do you have any other children?"

"No," he said, unemotionally, "he is my only child. There are just the three of us: myself, the boy...and my wife."

"Okay." Interesting: seemingly listed in order of importance, with the wife bringing up what sounded like a very distant rear.

"So," he said, "will you take my case?"

I was sorely tempted not to. I really didn't like the man. He was pompous, colossally self-centered, and loud. I hate loud. Not to mention that everything he'd said so far indicated far less parental worry for a missing son than it did egocentric concern for his own public image. It was curious, this apparent lack of affection for his own family. Not to mention ironic, considering the emotional support and counseling he must have been expected to routinely provide, as a spiritual leader, to various members of his "flock" concerning their own familial problems.

But as I sat there I was reminded of what a veteran PI had told me while I was down at the county offices filing for my license: *"You don't gotta like your clients,"* he'd said. *"Hell; you should count yourself blessed if even half the assholes you work for don't make you wanna puke your socks."*

Colorful, yet instructive.

That this particular morning's asshole appeared to be one who came packing a healthy bank account—unfortunately an all too rare species to be found out in the

Cassidy neck of the woods—was in itself no small argument, in light of that hefty new monthly house payment I was saddled with.

And if the mercenary angle wasn't quite sufficient to sway me (which it was, let's face it), there was also something in the Reverend's decidedly off-kilter comments regarding his son which kind of piqued my interest and played, to be frank, to the iconoclast in me—to a perverse curiosity about what sorts of cracks were to be found in the pedestal of this morally upright, "prominent" Christian minister.

As I deliberated, a high-pitched cry caused us both to look out the window. Circling slowly above, in the sparkling, bright blue sky, a large osprey was scanning the river below, searching for the silhouette, just beneath the surface, of a likely candidate for breakfast. I watched him for a few seconds, then turned back before he made his move.

The Reverend's eyes remained fixed on the fish eagle, however, and from him I could tell the moment of its attack by watching his face as he followed the rapid descent, fascinated, until the bird disappeared from view below the line of the river bank. Then his gaze shifted back to me.

"Well?" he demanded.

Did I mention that I could *really* use the dough?

"Alright. I'll take it," I said, intentionally not disguising my reluctance, and then immediately recited my standard terms, to which he nodded, pulled out his checkbook and filled in my retainer without complaint. And when you come down to it; that's always a good thing—piqued interest or no.

"So, what's your first step?" he asked, as he handed me the check.

"Oh," I said, trying to sound casual; "the usual." Which of course was as lame an answer as could be. The bald fact was that I had absolutely no idea what "the usual" was, this being my first missing-persons case. Closest thing previous had been a couple of skip-traces on behalf of local creditors, but there hadn't been all that much to either of them—mostly a matter of surveilling known friends and relatives until the targeted deadbeats ran low on beer and cigarettes and broke cover. I felt pretty sure that this particular case was going to prove considerably more complicated than that.

Anticipating a challenge to my inadequate response, I was mentally conjuring some hasty, plausible nonsense to follow it up with, when the preacher surprised me by merely nodding. "Fine," he said, sliding his chair back and rising, while extracting a card from his pants pocket and dropping it on my desk/table. "All of my numbers are there," he said; "feel free to call any time—any *reasonable* time, of course. If I am not available right away, it's probably because I am busy tending to my church duties. But I will try to get back to you as quickly as I am able."

"All in God's good time, eh?"

He stared at me, quizzically, but I kept my face noncommittal.

"Yes," he said, uncertainly. "Well, I really must be going…" He turned to leave.

"Oh, Reverend," I called out, causing him to pause. "I'll need a list, as complete as you can make it, of friends, relatives and acquaintances of your son."

The blank look he gave me at this request spoke even more eloquently about his relationship with his son than his words had, and I guessed that his version of a "list" probably wouldn't require much more than a three-by-five index card and a minimum of ink. "Okay," he said, and continued toward the door.

"And of course I'll need to speak to your wife."

That also stopped him for a moment; but then he quickly recovered, and mumbled over his shoulder, in his first truly *sotto voce* utterance of the morning: "Certainly. I'll have her contact you."

Chapter Two

The usual

The first thing I did was to call my friend, Detective Sal Denove, of the Deschutes County Sheriffs, to find out what "the usual" might mean to the police. Not that I expected him to know much about this case; the kid's disappearance would certainly have been handled by the Bend police department rather than the county boys. But I didn't as yet know anybody there, and I figured that, if nothing else, Sal might be able school me a bit on the subject, and, possibly, hook me up with someone downtown.

Denove answered his cell phone quickly, coughing out what for him amounted to a chuckle as he recognized my voice. "Well, I'll be—Hank Cassidy," he deadpanned; "now my morning is complete."

"Hey, Denove," I said.

"What's up?"

"I need a favor."

"Aha," he muttered sardonically, "a favor; *quelle surprise*. More PI 101 instruction, I presume."

"Of a sort," I replied, discounting the detective's all-too familiar tone of sarcastic condescension. This practiced, scornful attitude towards private investigators seems to be imprinted in every cop's DNA. But I knew that at least in my case it was an entirely artificial construct, since, aside from Kelly, Denove had been the one who'd most encouraged my jumping into this business in the first place, even taking the trouble to personally walk me through the Oregon licensing process.

"No problem," he said, dryly; "I'll just put my entire life on hold. How can I help you, Citizen?"

"Missing persons case."

There was a pause. "What...you're not talking about the preacher's kid—"

"You know about that one?"

"It's our case."

Surprised, I said, "No kidding. I thought for sure that this thing would have belonged to the Bend Police."

He grunted. "Yeah; two blocks further west and it *would* have been—and welcome to it. Unfortunately, the preacher's house and adjacent church sit just outside current city boundaries, and that makes this one a County matter."

"I take it you're not thrilled."

"You met Reverend Sayles yet?"

"He just left."

"Well?"

"Saints preserve us."

Denove snorted. "Amen."

"I almost tossed him out."

A heavy sigh leaked from the earpiece. "Unfortunately, we civil servants don't have that option."

"Is it your case, specifically?"

"No. It's Frank Whalen's. But I've been assisting. We all have, as a matter of fact. The Reverend's a bit of a public figure, as I'm sure he told you—a particularly noisy one, too—so anybody with loose time has been dragooned into this thing."

"And no luck, so far?"

"No luck."

"Care to give me a run-down?"

He barked out another tubercular laugh. "Ah, of course; and that request translates to: exactly what steps does a fledgling private investigator take in order to locate a runaway teenager, and, incidentally, how many of those steps have the cops already covered so that said fledgling private investigator can avoid having to duplicate the effort."

"Something like that," I said; "although I really wish that you'd leave off the 'fledgling' part."

"Oh, I *am* sorry," he replied; "how about 'green,' 'inexperienced,' 'floundering—'"

"Fledgling will do nicely, thanks."

"You're welcome. Let's see...not much to it, really. First thing we did, of course, was to have the parents seal off the kid's bedroom to preserve it as a possible crime scene, which we then had processed by the forensics crew. Next, we conducted extensive interviews—parents first, then everyone else in the neighborhood. Finally, we talked to all of the kids from his school who'd known him."

"What'd the parents have to say?"

"*Parent,* actually. The mother was the only one to have seen him the day he disappeared."

"Where was the preacher?"

"Left early, well before the kid got up. Had some errands to run; building materials to pick up for repairs to the chapel. Took the ministry's pickup truck. Later he headed out to Prineville to do some family counseling. We checked with the local lumber yard and a nearby Ace

Hardware store, and verified his purchases. We also confirmed his mid-afternoon arrival at the home in Prineville."

"Okay, so what about the mom?"

"The mom. According to her, Joshua Sayles left home shortly after breakfast—tennish on Tuesday, just over two months ago, sixth of July. Was wearing jeans, hiking boots, t-shirt and light club jacket; nothing out of the ordinary."

"Drove?"

"Uh-uh; doesn't own a car."

"Bicycle?"

"Left it in the garage."

"Walking. Backpack?" I asked.

"No. We checked his room, and found a closet full of clothes, bed neatly made, two empty daypacks hung up on the closet door, nothing missing from his bathroom—not even a toothbrush."

"No plans for a trip, then."

"At least that's the way it appeared at first," he said, "until we checked his bank account. It was drained—almost twelve hundred taken out. So, at least at the beginning, the kid would have had plenty of traveling money; could have bought everything he needed on the way, and still had enough left over to keep him in Quarter Pounders for a couple of months."

"And by not packing anything, he doesn't arouse anyone's suspicion until well after he's out the door."

"Yeah; if that was his plan. Just a typical kid running out to enjoy a nice, warm, summer's day."

"Any suspicious phone calls in the logs?"

"No. Records from the house phone going back several months show nothing out of the ordinary. In fact, they don't show many calls at all—sent or received. And the kid didn't own a cell phone, so nothing there, either."

"No kidding," I said; "a teenager without a cell phone?"

"Yeah," said Denove; "possibly the only adolescent in Central Oregon without one."

"Sounds almost medieval."

"Make that *evangelical*. The way the mother put it when we asked her, the reverend wouldn't allow it."

That was hardly a surprise. "All right; so phone calls are a dead-end. Did anyone see him after he left that morning?"

"Nobody. As I said, we canvassed the area, interviewed neighbors, friends, postal workers and delivery people, got nothing. Outside of his mother, no one saw him at all that day. So, what we've got here is a kid, walks down the front path from his house and disappears into thin air as soon as his feet hit the asphalt."

"Someone pick him up?"

"Accomplice? Kidnapper? Maybe. But if the boy got help running away, it wasn't from anybody we talked to; alibis galore and they all panned out. On the other hand if it was an abduction, it wasn't witnessed. And I've got more problems than that with the idea of abduction—like for instance, how come no ransom demand? And how does sudden abduction square with the kid's having withdrawn all of his money prior to that day?"

"Did he pull the cash all at once?"

"No, he didn't," Denove answered, his tone approving my question. "Took him just over a week, chunks of a hundred to two hundred at a time; always from an ATM machine, always after banking hours."

"Interesting," I said; "seems to have taken care not to interact with anyone. So maybe it wasn't Josh doing the withdrawing."

"Maybe not, but we really don't have much to tell us either way," he replied, sounding aggravated. "When we checked the videos at the three ATM locations that were accessed, we found that at one of them the camera wasn't working, and at the other two, covering five separate withdrawals, whoever was getting the cash was doing a very deliberate, very successful job of concealing himself: heavy jacket, wool cap pulled low, face turned away from the lens; tough even to get a read on the guy's height because of the extreme overhead placement of both cameras. One thing, though: the jacket he was wearing did appear to match up with one we found in Josh's closet, and the knit cap was also one that his mother recognized."

"So it probably *was* the kid."

"Probably," he said, not sounding entirely convinced. "But if it was, why would he be so careful to conceal his face? And anyway, why all this secrecy about withdrawing money from his own account?"

I had no answer to that one. "Any sudden changes in the kid's behavior leading up to his disappearance?"

"He was moody," said Denove. "Problem is, according to both parents moody was the rule."

My eyes strayed to the father-son photo lying on the table in front of me. While using a finger to smooth out the crease in it I said, "I get the feeling that the preacher and his boy weren't exactly the best of pals."

The detective snorted. "Yeah, but so what? I'd think you'd have to say that's hardly an unusual situation for most teenagers and their parents—particularly when we're talking about a teenager whose father happens to be a religious paragon."

"Yeah," I agreed; "heavy on the holy starch."

"Indeed; kid probably felt like he was walking around in a strait-jacket."

"Tell me about him," I said.

"Who?"

"The dad."

"Right; hang on…" There was the rustling of paper. "Reverend J.T. Sayles, founder and sole proprietor of the Church of the Holy Messenger. Born forty-three years ago, just outside of Coeur d' Alene, original first name William. Moved his young wife and child to Bend from northern Idaho about thirteen years ago. Worked various jobs, mostly in retail, apparently without much success despite the made-to-order last name."

"Let's see"—more paper shuffling—"ah yes: the preacher started his church about six years ago, after having first legally changed his 'Christian' name to Jeremiah. It was a modest venture at first—congregation met in somebody's garage—but then it grew pretty quickly; apparently this is a fellow who's got a real gift for purple oratory. After a couple of years he was able to attract enough followers—make that 'contributors'—to come up with a down payment for his own home on a sizeable parcel, complete with a large, sturdy horse barn, which he then immediately slapped a big white cross on and topped with a steeple, thereby converting it into a gen-you-wine house of worship."

"From there the whole thing really took off: new converts showing up every week, word spreading like a fungus throughout the community, so that by today his barn—excuse me, *house of worship*—is practically bursting at the seams. Toss in that the preacher's been a frequent sermonizer on AM radio for the past year, and that his church is planning its gala inaugural broadcast on local television next month, and what you have here is a serious up-and-coming religious phenom, and a major regional celebrity to boot."

I nodded to myself. Deschutes County, though an increasingly diverse region with sensibilities spanning the entire spectrum of political, cultural, philosophical and social perspectives, nevertheless seems—at least, to me, anyway—to be fairly top-heavy in the number and variety of Christian denominations it supports. And, as a good number of these congregations tend to fall solidly into the category of evangelical theology, the fact that among evangelicals Reverend Sayles' church had been taking an increasingly dominant position would certainly be difficult to ignore.

Thus, considering the rapid ascendancy and influence of this guy in the community, it was no great surprise that the county cops felt compelled to devote so much extra time and effort to the missing teenager's case; and it was also not hard to imagine their distress at the inevitable bad publicity stemming from what had been the lack of a quick resolution. This thought led me to wonder how much ink the Bulletin's reporters had spilled on the matter, and I privately chastised myself for not having gotten in the habit of paying closer, more regular attention to the local news. I made a mental note to look into the paper's archives.

"'Holy Messenger,' I said; "What sort of name *is* that, anyway? Something from scripture?"

"Not exactly," he said, then paused. "Hey, don't you get it?" The detective's voice betrayed uncharacteristic amusement. "This guy Sayles *is* The Holy Messenger."

"Wow," I laughed, trying to visualize the nonentity who'd just left my home as some sort of divine prophet. Failed, utterly—couldn't quite get past the comb-over. "That's some kind of chutzpah," I said. "Anyway, isn't J.C. always supposed to get top billing?"

"Yeah," he responded; "Him or his dad. But I suppose if you're trying to develop a stand-out spiritual franchise you've got to cook up something particularly catchy to differentiate you from the rest of the hucksters."

"Hucksters? Pretty cynical attitude there, Detective."

"I'm a cop," he said; "*cynical* comes with the uniform."

"What's the mom like?" I asked.

"Josh's mother. From appearances, a typical preacher's wife: shy, innocuous, quiet; keeps herself pretty much in the background. Although I did get the impression that there might be a bit more to her than meets the eye…or ear."

"How's she dealing with this?"

"Oh, I'd say she's properly distraught—"

"Sounds like you're not quite buying it."

"It's not that, exactly. I am, to an extent. She appears genuine: real tears, anxious face, choked voice. But, well, it feels like there's also a significant component of relief in it; like her son's disappearance has removed something uncomfortable from her life. My guess is that with whatever conflict he was having with his father, things are probably a lot more peaceful around the old homestead these days. I get the feeling that if she could be assured that the kid were safe and had good prospects for a new life, she'd be okay with it." He paused. "Just a feeling, anyway," he repeated, uncomfortably. As a cop, Denove was not prone to wading into the amorphous waters of speculation. At least, not out loud.

"I should be speaking with her soon," I said. "Let's see if my feeling matches your feeling."

He sighed. "You might actually get more out of her than we did. This is one lady who really doesn't like talking to cops."

"Who does?"

"Aw, gee whiz, Cassidy, so nice of you to put it that way. Anyway, this particular woman was unforthcoming in the extreme: a whole lot of one-word responses, and the few complete sentences she did manage to put together appeared to come only with massive effort. Said her son was a good boy, etc, etc; but quiet, withdrawn—like I said: moody. Claimed she had no idea what might have been bothering him enough to split; kept punctuating everything with, 'but you know how kids are'—standard line for parents who have absolutely no clue what's going on with their children's lives."

"What's her first name?"

"Nadine." He paused again. "Word to the wise: when you sit down with her, make sure you do it as far away from the preacher as possible; maybe then you might be able to get the lady to open up. We had her in a separate room in their house that first day, but I got the distinct impression that just the fact of the man's presence in the vicinity—even out of earshot—was enough to shut her down."

"You haven't spoken to her since?"

"Oh come on now, Cassidy, of *course* we have," he barked, annoyed. "Several times, in fact, and in all these cases we made sure that her husband wasn't around. But we never got anything further from her; in fact we got less––just a bunch of worry, knitted brows, wringing hands, etc. No contact with the boy, no idea where he went, nothing at all."

"And no ransom note."

"No, and this late in the game, we're no longer expecting one. Around here, most of us think we've got a classic runaway situation. But if it's not; if we're talking about an abduction, then without the for-profit element the prognosis at this point is hardly a good one."

"Any chance of faxing me the case file?"

"I'll talk to Whalen. Honestly I don't think he'll have a problem with it. Fact is we're stumped. We've contacted all of the relevant agencies, entered Joshua's description in the FBI's NCIC computer, notified the press coast to coast. So unless someone comes forward, or something unexpected pops up locally or on the wire—like maybe the kid showing up somewhere at a shelter—we're basically on watch and wait. Case like this, two months is an awfully long time. At this point anything you could come up with would be more than welcome."

"Thanks Sal. Anything else?"

"No, you'll find everything in the file. One thing though…"

"What?"

"Get yourself online, do a little research. You need to become familiarized with the whole subject of teen runaways."

"I'll do that."

Chapter Three

Kelly walked in just as I was hanging up the phone. Satchmo, my shepherd/coyote mix, bounded noisily across the hardwood floor, put her paws up on the arm of my chair, and planted manic, sloppy kisses on my face as if we'd been separated for years, rather than less than an hour. And that's why we love our dogs.

Kelly approached at a much more leisurely pace, which allowed me time to savor her graceful, Mediterranean features, enticingly obvious despite the camouflage of baggy sweats and my favorite Ducati baseball cap. When she reached me, her own kisses were neither as manic nor sloppy as Satch's, but just as welcome. Maybe even more so.

"What a beautiful morning," she exclaimed. "I think fall has to be my favorite time of year up here."

"It's not fall yet."

"Just a matter of days, Cassidy. Don't nit-pick."

After bathing for a moment in the glory of her clear, olive-complexioned face and bottomless dark eyes, I asked: "So, where'd you take Satch?"

"Oh," she said, "along the river, out by the Bridge."

"The Bridge" referred to the former site of the General Patch foot-bridge, a quarter mile up the Deschutes River from my house. Early last year Satch and I had discovered a body floating in the shallow water at the river's edge, not far from the ancient span which at the time was still up and in use. That the body had turned out to be an ex-girlfriend of mine had forced me to return to Los Angeles, my former home, in a quest to find her killer, where, in the course of my search, I'd had the unbelievable good fortune to encounter Kelly Wilhoit; smart, witty, beautiful, sexy, unattached, and sufficiently dissatisfied with her circumstances at the time to be willing to pull up stakes and join me in my home in Central Oregon.

Ironically, my quest would eventually lead me full circle to that same, rustic bridge—where, on a moonless, frigid night nearly two weeks after it had begun, the affair would be resolved in a violent burst of anger, gunfire and blood.

It was not too many days afterwards that the U.S. Forest Service had seen fit to condemn the old bridge, citing a serious threat to public safety due to a decades-long deterioration of the structure's supports (No mention of the events of that dark night had accompanied the announcement, though I suspected that the attention they'd generated at the time was what had, in fact, led to the discovery of the bridge's dilapidated condition.) Three months after that announcement, the bridge was removed. But though the General Patch no longer existed—the only traces left being dark squares of tortured earth on opposite sides of the river where the concrete abutments had been—, Kelly and I stubbornly continued to refer to the location as "The Bridge," choosing to regard it both as a solemn shrine to a murdered woman, as well as a landmark of our union.

Pulling free of my embrace, Kelly announced "I'm really hungry," and marched off into the kitchen, which is cozily tucked into the northeast corner of the great room behind an angled cooking island, directly opposite the dining table. I smiled. Kelly is never shy about her healthy appetite, something I find gratifying, and in stark contrast to most of the other women I've known. Nevertheless, between an evidently higher-than-normal basal metabolism and her penchant for keeping those long, perpetually tanned legs of hers in constant motion throughout the day, she never seems to have any trouble burning calories. I, on the other hand, have been forced into a religious (word for the day) commitment of at least an hour sweating on every bench and machine in my ground-floor gym to keep the pounds from accumulating—an endeavor, I'm sorry to say, I've not been entirely successful at.

"Want an omelet?" she called out.

"Tempting," I said, and it was, "but I've already had a bowl of cereal, and I need to get upstairs to the computer."

"Suit yourself," she mumbled, already munching a piece of cheese. "What's the subject?"

"Runaway kid."

"The preacher's?"

"Yeah. What'd you think of him?"

She shrugged. "Seemed kind of rude, but, aside from that I didn't get much of a look, so I guess I should try to reserve judgment. I do think he bothered *Satch*, though: she was tugging on her leash like the guy was the county dog catcher."

"Smart girl."

"So who's missing?"

"His son. Sixteen. And a half."

"Typical age for a runaway," she said. "Although these days they call them 'runaway/thrownaway teens.'"

"Yeah?"

"Uh-huh. Most kids don't just run off on their own; they need a reason, and often as not it's because the parents don't want them, are too drugged or drunk to function, or are physically abusing them. You might want to keep that in mind."

"I intend to," I said. A committed career elementary school teacher, Kelly is someone to pay attention to when it comes to discussing kids' issues. "Though," I added, "the reverend doesn't strike me as a drug or alcohol user, and as for the physical abuse part; well, his son looks at least three inches taller and a lot more athletic than he is."

"You're skipping over door number one."

"Because that could be a possibility," I said, thoughtfully. "I didn't detect a whole lot of warmth in the guy when he was talking about his boy...or about his wife, for that matter. In fact I kind of get the sense that this preacher only has room in his heart for the Sunday Social Club—and, of course, his adoring congregation."

"Sunday Social Club?"

"That's what my dad used to call the characters in the Bible."

Kelly smiled. "Ah...the iconoclastic sort."

"I would have to say so. Actually, both he and my mom were pretty spiritual in their own way; they just weren't very high on religious doctrine."

"And that would also tend to explain a lot about this fellow, here," she said, winking at me with mock solemnity.

I laughed, and said, "Guess it would."

"Anyway," she said, "if what you're saying about the reverend is true; if he really doesn't care that much about his kid—then why is he bothering with *this?*" She gestured at the signed check lying on the table. "Why's he hiring you?"

"'Covering all the bases,' was his explanation; said I might be able to plug the holes in the cops' efforts—although 'covering the bases' probably applies more to what he feels he has to do to maintain his public image. Wouldn't be kosher for a prominent Christian minister to be seen as not doing everything he can to find his own son."

"You're mixing your religious references, my sweet."

"Enjoy your omelet," I grumbled, and reluctantly headed up the stairs.

Chapter Four

My computer is located in what qualifies as the real office, on the second floor; the one with a genuine wood work station, swiveling chair, credenza, book cases, file cabinet, wall calendar, staple gun, etc. But with all the furniture and equipment crammed in there the room is way too small to comfortably accommodate guests, so when I have to deal with clients I either entertain them downstairs, or drive to their homes or into town to meet them at some suitable neutral location.

I sat in the cushioned executive chair, pushed the power button on the CPU, and stared out the window at the river as I waited for the computer to boot up. In the clear sunshine the horizon was razor-sharp and dominated by the imposing, symmetrical volcanic cone of Mount Bachelor, twenty miles distant, its dark summit currently snow-free as late summer drifted, lazily, towards fall.

The machine beeped, prompting me for my password and yanking me away from the view. Typing it in, I then went online and Googled "finding runaway teens, Oregon." Not surprisingly, this produced a wealth of resources; 28,600, in fact. Many of these turned out to be sites for private investigative firms, offering, in large, impressive fonts, to do exactly what I'd just been hired to do, and reminding me—not for the first time—that I really needed to find a professional to help me design a web-page for my business.

A large number of the other links led to foundations and organizations concerned with reducing the incidence of runaway child cases, as well as helping to reunite families with their lost offspring. Some of them provided networking facilities, working with shelters to identify the kids who had shown up there, while also functioning as intermediaries for the police, allowing them to match up anxious parents at one end with frightened, wayward kids seeking sanctuary at the other.

I visited a number of these sites and wrote down organization names, along with some of the more salient statistics each of them cited. One site belonged to OMCC––Oregon Missing Children Clearinghouse—created by the state legislature in 1989 and designed to gather leads regarding missing children via use of a hotline and other resources, while providing technical and logistical assistance to authorities, maintaining an online photo bulletin board and offering training and child identification kits to those in need of instruction. Another was the National Center for Missing and Exploited Children, working with the U.S. Department of Justice's Office of Juvenile Justice and Delinquency Prevention to "help investigate cases of missing and sexually exploited children." Yet another was Runaway Teens.org—an arm of The Kidsearch Network, which, among other things, offered a wealth of experience and statistical data on the subject.

The numbers were daunting and depressing: at some point one in seven kids between the ages of 10 and 18 will run away from home; upwards of three million runaway and homeless kids are currently living on the streets in the U.S, seventy-one percent of them facing critical endangerment due to drugs and alcohol, sexual or physical abuse and proximity to violent criminal activity.

And Kelly was right; most runaway kids—sixty-eight percent—are older teens, fifteen to seventeen years old. The explanations for this made sense: the age group tends to be more independent, more resistant to parental authority, and more likely to be chastised by their folks for their social activities. Joshua's disappearance in July also fit with a proportionally larger number of teens leaving during summer months, corresponding to the greater freedom of movement afforded by the school-less days, as well as the more physically comfortable travel conditions made possible by the increased likelihood of pleasant weather.

The Kidsearch Network also offered sobering information regarding cases of abduction, stressing that, because the "vast majority (seventy-four percent) of the abducted children who are murdered are dead within three hours of the abduction, it is critical that the response to the disappearance of a child be both immediate and massive." According to Denove, the County Sheriff response to the Sayles teenager's disappearance *had* been massive—still was, in many ways. But considering that both of Joshua's parents had been unaware of his status for most of that first day, had the response come too late?

These musings led to a host of other questions. Was Joshua Sayles a runaway, or was he abducted? If a runaway, had he been driven from his home by the actions of his parents, or had he been enticed into leaving by someone dangling the prospect of something new and exciting? If abducted; how, by whom, and to what end? Judging from the lack of a ransom note, it wouldn't have been a kidnapping for profit. So, if not for that purpose, what then? A number of ugly possibilities presented themselves based upon what I'd just been reading, but in the absence of any current information pointing in those directions, I decided it was best to push them aside, at least for the moment.

Next, I thought about the money. What did the boy's rapid and systematic draining of his bank account signify? Didn't it mean that kidnapping was off the table, and that this disappearance was in fact the boy's own production?

Yes, it did—but only if he'd indeed been the one standing in front of those ATM cameras. What if it wasn't him, then? What would that mean?

As I pushed my chair back from the desk and stretched my back, wearily, I realized that the myriad questions really boiled down to two:

Where was Joshua Sayles...and was he still alive?

Deciding it was time for a break, I leaned forward and put my hand on the mouse, intending to log off; but before I clicked on the *shutdown* icon a familiar impulse caused me to switch over, instead, to my home page. There, I pulled up my favorite Vegas betting line site from my bookmark list, spent fifteen minutes or so studying the spreads and over/unders for this coming Sunday's football games, then reached for my cell phone and punched in Rudy Pankow's speed-dial number. Though these days it's much easier and faster to make bets online with any number of available sports books, I still prefer, perhaps superstitiously, to continue to place the bulk of my game wagers with a real live bookie.

"Yeah?" As usual, Pankow's tone was gruff, impatient.

"Hey Rudy," I said.

Instantly, the voice lost its edge, and become more animated and friendly. "Hank! Hey, how's it hangin' *Paisan*?" In Rudy's universe, if you happen to stand in his good graces, you are officially a *"Paison"*— no matter whether your ancestors made their crossing from Palermo, Paris, or Podunk.

Wondering, as I often did, if it's a bad sign when your bookie can identify you merely by the sound of your voice, I said: "I have a couple for you."

"Sure thing; whatcha got?"

"Steelers-Redskins still four and a half?"

"Let's see...yep."

"Is Roethlisberger playing?"

"Well, they're calling it a game-time decision; but you know Ben—if he can walk, he's playing."

"I don't know," I said, hesitating; "maybe I should wait a couple of days."

"Yeah, you can," he said, "but if you do, and they firm up that he's playing, you know you'll have to lay at least six and a half."

"Alright, you win," I said. "Give me Pittsburgh."

"How much?"

I hesitated again, then said, "A hundred."

There was a pause, followed by a disapproving throat-clear. "Okay—one *very* thin C-note. What else?"

I selected two other games, this time betting the *under* in each, for fifty dollars apiece. In this sort of bet I always take the *under*—gambling that the combined score of the competing teams will be lower than the officially predicted number. I recognize that doing so plays to the curmudgeon in me. With this sort of subversive wager I get to watch the game, not caring at all who's winning, while rooting loudly for both teams to drop passes, fumble their hand-offs, and shank all of their field-goal attempts.

"And that'll have to do it for this week," I said, hating how apologetic I sounded.

"What?" he exclaimed. "That's it—two hundred? Come on, Hank; action like this I can get outside the fence at the local grade school!"

"Yeah," I said, "but the conversation won't be nearly as stimulating."

He snorted. "For stimulation, I got my wife. From you, I need risk-taking."

"If I win, you'll get more next week. Ciao, Rudy." I clicked off; finished shutting down the computer, then rose from my chair and headed out into the hallway.

Chapter Five

I descended the stairway, my middle-aged body stiff and complaining from hours planted in front of a computer screen, and with only the vaguest notions of a plan regarding the Sayles case beginning to form in my head. To eradicate the stiffness, and to augment my thought processes—or, possibly, to attempt to avoid them—I headed left at the bottom of the stairs, past the fireplace and towards the large room behind it that I'd equipped as a gym. As I did I waved to Kelly, who was busy at her own computer, a laptop, which she'd set up at her usual sunny spot at the dining table. She waved back, smiling brightly, then returned to the lesson plans she was germinating.

I smiled at her unbridled enthusiasm. Last year, when she'd first moved in with me, she'd been unable to apply for an elementary school teaching position, having at that time lacked an Oregon credential, and had therefore been forced to make do with various volunteer jobs at the local elementary school.

In a way, though, the delay had ultimately proved beneficial, allowing her to get to know, and become known by, the other teachers and administrators at the school. This had led to her being in exactly the right spot when a second-grade teaching vacancy opened for this coming fall, which was immediately offered to her, and which she was able to accept, now that her credential had at last come through. Though she'd been relatively content with her life last year, clearly she now was going to be free to do the thing that made her happiest: teaching and inspiring young children. Her delight and anticipation at her new job showed plainly on her face every time I saw her planning for her first day of class.

For my own part I was just as delighted—more, perhaps—since the more securely Kelly became ensconced in her new life, the more firmly, it seemed, the two of us might solidify as a couple.

When it comes to my love life my sentiments have always tended, unfortunately, toward the empty half of the glass. In fact, the best feeling I ever seem to achieve with a woman I'm seeing is precarious optimism, with the vastly greater number of my expectations generally leaning toward impending doom. Prior to Kelly, in recent years I'd had only one genuinely serious involvement, and, trust me, *that* dainty little episode had gone a long way towards reinforcing my negativity, leaving me, if not exactly calcified into confirmed bachelorhood, then at least largely ambivalent towards the concept of a steady romance.

And yet, here I was, not only neck-deep in a live-in relationship, but willing to admit—at least to myself—just how overwhelmingly important to my happiness it was becoming. For me this was one scary revelation, indeed. Having now spent over sixteen months living with Kelly Wilhoit—basking in the warmth of her smile, delighting in her sharp wit, luxuriating in her passionate embrace in the dark—, I was finding it increasingly difficult to imagine life without her. This, coupled with my own damnably constitutional negativity, had given rise to an anxiousness I'd never suffered from before. Fighting my inbred prejudice that everything might—or rather, probably would—eventually come crashing down, I tried to cling to a corresponding, almost desperate hopefulness that this initial golden period we were enjoying might somehow be extended, especially when I saw in Kelly—as I did this morning—signs that she was becoming happier and more secure in her life here.

And, of course, I also did my utmost to keep this ridiculous, unreasoning anxiety entirely to myself.

Entering the gym, I swapped my street clothes for workout sweats and sneakers, which I stored in a metal locker in the spacious bathroom, and then proceeded to the elliptical trainer for a ten minute warm-up. The machine was deliberately angled to take full advantage of a wall-mounted TV, as well as that of a broad view of the river afforded by the fixed picture window next to which it stood. But this time I left the TV off and, after just a cursory glance outside, I allowed my thoughts to wander back to the Sayles case as I mounted the machine.

In my reading about the various runaway organizations, I'd easily recognized that most of them had been set up specifically to work hand in hand with the police departments. I had little doubt that the County Sheriffs had already established contact with all of the relevant agencies (although I intended to ask Denove to verify this against the list I had assembled), and therefore anything I might be able to achieve by petitioning their assistance would probably be rendered superfluous.

What was thus quickly becoming obvious to me was that whatever my contribution, if any, to this effort might be; it was going to be made locally. If Joshua Sayles had left the area; had gone off to Portland, Seattle or San Francisco, or possibly cities in states much further away, then my own chances of finding him were next to nil. If, however, he'd stayed in the region; if he'd sought sanctuary with a friend or an acquaintance within a fifty mile or so radius, then my odds were greatly improved. And as Reverend Sayles had intimated—and Denove had said outright—there were probably some people around here who might open up to me; people from whom the police were far less likely to elicit information. As I worked the arms and pedals of my machine furiously enough to generate a sweat, I mentally considered a list, regrettably short at the moment, of people to interview, along with strategies on how best to coax information from them.

And topping that list was Nadine Sayles.

Chapter Six

As it turned out, I didn't have to wait long to get around to the minister's wife. Shortly after I emerged from the gym, having showered, dumped my sweats in the hamper and re-donned my jeans and work shirt, Kelly approached and handed me the phone, an amused, quizzical look on her face.

"Mr. Cassidy?" said a reedy, female voice. "This is Nadine Sayles."

"Thanks for calling, Ms. Sayles." I said.

"My husband told me to," she said, dully.

Rolling my eyes at Kelly, I said, "You think we could meet somewhere tomorrow evening, maybe grab a bite while we talk?"

"If you say so," was the listless response.

"How about Frank's?"

"Okay."

"You know where it is?"

"I do."

"Say, about five?"

"Fine."

"Okay," I said, "I'll see you then."

Click.

I blew out a long, slow exhale as I put the cordless phone back into its cradle. "Yikes."

Kelly, who'd already swapped words with the woman and then eavesdropped my phone conversation from her seat at the table, laughed and said, "Pretty unresponsive, wasn't she?"

"You might say that."

"Well," she said, "her son *is* missing."

"Yeah," I said, "but she's had two months to adjust. Anyway, what I was hearing, that wasn't the issue."

"So what was it?"

"Extreme reluctance. Sounds like she's not exactly thrilled about having to talk to me."

"Why's that, you think?"

"If I had to guess, I'd say it's because her husband's forcing her to. There might be something going on between them—in fact Denove hinted as much when I talked to him. Who knows; maybe there isn't, and she's just painfully shy. But if there *is* something, then in her eyes my working for her husband makes me a bad guy—hence the resistance. Which means that if I'm going to get her to open up, I'll have to figure a way to convince her that I'm not exactly J.T. Sayles' right-hand man."

"How do you do that?"

"I don't know," I said, shrugging. "Maybe let it slip out that I'm an agnostic…"

Kelly laughed. "Honey, I'm not sure that would work. After all, she *is* a preacher's wife. She's probably just as much a believer as he is."

"That's true," I conceded. "I don't know; I guess I'll just have to do what I always do in these circumstances."

"Wing it?"

I nodded.

"Wing it."

Chapter Seven

Frank's is a restaurant which, if not exactly fancy, is nevertheless at least a couple of notches above a your typical coffee shop; appropriate, considering its location on the west side of Bend, where just about everything—living, shopping, eating—is expected to be a couple of notches above. The restaurant's décor is a combination of rich woods and abstract mountain art; eating there, you can pretty much imagine yourself just a few short paces from the main chair-lift of any major, upscale ski resort in the U.S.

I'd picked the place tonight because, with few windows, the fact that at Five o'clock daylight still had at least a couple of hours left wouldn't impact the interior lighting, which tended, decidedly, towards subdued. Add to that the privacy of the high-backed booths and the restaurant's location on the opposite side of the city from the eastern outskirts where the Reverend's house and church were located, and I felt we had about as reasonable a chance of conducting our talk with a degree of privacy as is possible in a town this size.

I arrived ten minutes early, left my name with the hostess, and selected the booth in the most obscure and remote corner of the dining room; not a difficult feat at this early hour on a Thursday night, when most of the tables were still unoccupied.

Nadine Sayles arrived at precisely five o'clock. After scanning the room, she turned to the hostess, who guided her over to my booth. As she approached, I could see, even in the dim light, that she was surprisingly attractive: thick, shiny auburn hair surrounding a pale face with large, liquid blue eyes, prominent cheekbones and full, red lips; a figure which, while not exactly voluptuous, would nevertheless have still have inspired some rather impure thoughts, had she chosen to wear something a bit more provocative than the modest green sundress she currently had on.

I found myself wondering how someone like this could have hooked up with a drip like J.T. Sayles until I performed a little quick mental math: the woman looked to be no more, and probably quite a bit less than, thirty-five. Given that their son was sixteen...and a half, I calculated that she must have been married well before she had departed her teens; certainly at an age where many people are apt to make the kinds of choices they might not have made had they waited a few years.

In this case, perhaps a choice which she might have long since come to regret?

When she reached the table I stood, introduced myself, and extended my hand, which she ignored, instead sliding, silently, onto the padded booth-bench opposite mine.

"Mr. Cassidy," she then said, coolly.

I gestured towards my glass of cabernet. "What're you drinking?"

"Just a coke, please."

I motioned to the waitress, gave her the order, and received two padded menus, one of which I passed to her. Though she accepted it, she shook her head. "I really don't think I'm going to want anything to eat," she said.

"That's all right," I replied; "let's just hang onto these for now. Maybe you'll feel like having something later."

She nodded, but said nothing.

In fact, neither of us said anything until her drink arrived. After informing the waitress that we were going to need considerably more time to decide, I sent her away, and then turned back to the Reverend's wife. "Now we can talk," I said.

She stirred her coke, aimlessly, with her straw. "I'm not sure there's anything to talk about."

"How about we talk about your son?"

Her eyes rose quickly, met mine and challenged me. "My son? My son is *gone*, Mr. Cassidy." There was considerable anguish in the words, along with an unmistakable note of finality.

"Ms. Sayles," I said, gently, "I've been hired to find him. To have any chance of doing that, I'm going to need all the help, information...and cooperation...that I can get––from everyone, and, especially, from you."

At that, her face seemed to crumble slightly and abandon most of its defiance, while her eyes retreated to her coke. "I...I don't think there's anything I can tell you..."

Can, I thought, *or **will**?*

"I know it's been hard for you," I said, gently.

Her gaze regained its defiance. "You have no idea *how* hard," she said, this time refusing to look away, and making me wonder exactly what she was referring to. I decided to take a chance.

"Is your husband being difficult?"

After taking a swift, cautious glance around the room, she brought her eyes back again to meet mine. "Mr. Cassidy, my husband *is* difficult."

"You think that might be why your son left?"

"Yes," she mumbled, then repeated, a bit more forcefully: *"Yes."* But there was something else in her response—and a distorted, stricken look on her face which suggested self recrimination.

Mentally filing the woman's reaction, I decided to keep the focus on father and son for the time being. "They didn't get along, did they?"

"No," she said; "they didn't. J.T. was always on us...on *Joshua,* I mean, about not being committed one hundred percent to him, and to his church. And it wasn't like Josh wasn't helping; he *was*—all the time, setting up chairs, passing out hymnals, running to the printer to pick up pamphlets, making repairs to the building. I mean, there were times when I thought Josh was sleeping with his tool belt on. But nothing he did was ever enough: J.T. was constantly after him about shirking his duties, about his laziness, especially about his not leading 'a proper life in Christ.'" She leaned in towards me, lowering her voice. "Mr. Cassidy, my son is a good boy; better than most, in fact. And here you have his own father practically accusing him of being some sort of servant of the Devil!"

Nodding sympathetically, I then sipped from my wine glass, slowly, as I considered whether to walk through the door she'd just left open. Finally, I put the glass down and looked at her. "Excuse me for mentioning this," I said, "but just now I couldn't help but notice you saying at first-–accidentally—that J.T. was always 'on us.' Only I'm not exactly convinced that it *was* an accident. Your husband has been hard on you, too, hasn't he?"

Once again staring into her coke, she nodded slightly. "Yes, Mr. Cassidy, he has. I guess we—my son and I—just don't ever seem to measure up to his high standards." She looked up, anxiously. "Are you...are you going to tell him what I've just said to you? I mean, after all, you *are* working for him—"

I shook my head. "Your husband didn't hire me to deal with his marital issues, Ms. Sayles."

Nadine Sayles exhaled slowly. "Thank-you," she said.

It was time for another gamble. "Ms. Sayles," I asked, "I need to know: do you really want me to find your son?"

"Of course I do!" she snapped, tears beginning to well up in her eyes; "How can you ask such a question? He's my...my *boy!* I'm his *mother!*" But then she looked away, and again I found myself thinking that Denove had been right; that she felt she owned at least some part of this situation, too.

Now it was my turn to glance around, self-consciously, observing that, fortunately, no one had yet taken notice of the drama playing out in our booth. The closest party, three tables away, was a middle-aged couple displaying the casual insouciance of regulars, who appeared to be studying their menus in a manner which suggested they already knew what was in them, but continued to peruse them as a way to avoid having to converse with each other. I turned back to Nadine Sayles, who was quietly weeping.

"Ms. Sayles," I said, reaching across the table to touch her hand; "I'm sorry. I didn't mean it to sound quite the way it did. What I was trying to say was: do you really think that it's in your son's best interests to return to your home, life there being what you're telling me it is? Again, I'm sorry."

"It's...no, it's okay," she said, dabbing at her eyes with a paper napkin. "I guess I should have understood. The answer to your question is: I don't know; maybe he *is* better off somewhere else." She looked at me. "The problem is that I have no idea where that 'somewhere' is. What if 'somewhere' means some rat-hole tenement or a cardboard box under a bridge—or maybe even something worse? At least here he had a roof over his head."

"Ms. Sayles—"

Her head down, tears falling silently, she murmured: "Please, Mr. Cassidy, stop calling me that."

"You mean Ms?" I said, confused. "I'm sorry; I just thought it was proper to use the correct—"

"No," she said, taking breaths in sharp, short gasps; "not *that*—Sayles; please don't call me Ms. *Sayles*. I'm Nadine…just Nadine."

Curiouser and curiouser.

"Okay," I said, "no problem. Nadine."

There was a moment of silence, as, with an effort, she began to reassemble herself. Realizing the scene she must have been presenting, she looked around, furtively, flipped a quick glance at me, and then cast her eyes downward. "I'm, I'm sorry about that. It's been kind of a lot of strain."

"Like I said, Nadine, it's not a problem."

She looked up again, this time the plea written plainly on her face. "You really won't tell him? About what I've been saying?"

"Like I said, my job is to find Joshua; nothing more."

"Okay, thank-you" she said, primly, reaching into her purse for a Kleenex, using it to wipe the remaining moisture from her face, then daintily blowing her nose.

"Listen," I said, once she was done; "I don't mean to be indiscreet, but, well, if you're not crazy about your last name, why don't you have it changed?"

She smiled thinly. "You mean you're asking me why I don't divorce my husband. Believe me, that is something

I've been wanting to do for the longest time." Straightening herself, she said: "In fact, after all of this—with Josh, I mean—is over, I plan to do just that. But...well, you see, Mr. Cassidy, I've been married an awfully long time—since I was a girl, really, and J.T, well, he's been a rather overwhelming force in our...in my life. And if you knew what things were like for me back in Idaho before he married me—what J.T. saved me from, I mean—I guess that you could say that my reluctance about leaving him is partly me feeling like I still owe him, and partly, you know, just a case of old habits dying hard."

Her eyes became unfocused as she continued; "That and the same old story about being a woman afraid of having nowhere else to go..." She paused, and then mumbled, almost to herself: "at least until now." Quickly recovering, she added: "Then of course there's his church and all of our—all of *his* plans for the TV ministry," she finished with a shrug.

"Does that really matter to you?"

She managed a small smile. "Well, no," she said, "I guess it doesn't. But like I said, I still feel I owe him something; like maybe just holding off long enough until he can get the ball rolling..."

I noticed that in making that last comment she'd dropped her son's return as the qualifying agent, but said nothing. "Hungry yet?" I asked.

For the first time, her face brightened, suddenly looking five years younger. "You know, Mr. Cassidy, I do think I *could* eat something." She grinned. "I guess you could say confession might be as good for the appetite as it is for the soul."

"Call me Hank. And, unfortunately, in my case," I said, patting my slightly oversized gut, "even *breathing* is good for the appetite."

Nadine Sayles allowed a small laugh to escape her as she reached for the menu.

Chapter Eight

Later that evening Kelly and I were sharing a redwood loveseat on our back deck, sipping wine and enjoying the sunset and each other. Against my lazier tendencies I'd planted a lawn last spring, which stretched fifty feet from the cedar deck at the back of the house to the stone steps leading down to the small boat dock at the river's edge. Mowing and caring for it, along with tending the eight quaking aspens I'd placed strategically about the backyard and the mountain azaleas I'd planted in the shade along the back of the house, added up to a great deal more work than I'd ever planned to devote to backyard maintenance. But sitting here now, with everything in place and thriving, I had to admit it'd been well worth the effort—a little like having my own miniature riverfront park—especially with Kelly here to share it with me.

Satch, having made a few largely symbolic efforts at chasing squirrels and birds around the yard, had settled down on the cool grass just off the deck, an entirely contented, dreamy look on her face as she rested her head on her forepaws.

I'd just finished telling Kelly about the details of my dinner with Nadine Sayles, particularly expressing my surprise at her willingness—eagerness, even—to open up so quickly and frankly to me about the diseased state of her marriage.

"That doesn't surprise me at all," said Kelly. You're really pretty good at getting people to relax and blab about themselves: remember all the juicy stuff I confessed to you on our first date?"

"Yeah," I said, reaching for the hand she wasn't using to hold her wine glass, "but that was because on that particular night my charm was on overdrive."

She laughed, kissed me, and said; "Sweetie, your charm is *always* on overdrive! I just hope that you never take advantage of it with any woman but me."

Knowing that it was pointless to try to explain how farfetched a notion *that* was, I just returned the kiss and then smiled.

"Besides," she said, leaning back, and directing her gaze, idly, to the setting sun, "I think the preacher's wife must've been dying to open up to *somebody*."

"Sure seemed that way to me," I agreed.

"Of course it did," she said. "Think about it: to whom else could she confide? From the way you've described it; with the way her husband exerts such ironclad control over her life, I don't think he'd ever allow her to have any friendships with people he didn't approve of—meaning people who might use what she'd revealed to them to threaten that little empire he's been building."

"So the only 'friends' he lets her have are ones she can never make anything but small-talk with."

"Or worse," she said; "friends who are bound to run to him, lickety-split, with whatever juicy tidbit she might let slip."

"Lickety-split?"

She giggled. "Just a bit of quaint country idiom, my dear. We *are* living out in the country, aren't we?"

There then followed a pause, which caused me to look at Kelly and watch as the amusement slowly drained from her face and became replaced by something darker. "You know, Hank," she said, sighing; "when it comes to talking about this particular kind of sick relationship, I'm one person who's on very familiar ground."

I had to agree. Kelly's ex-husband had been a classic control-freak; physically and mentally abusive, and forcing her into progressively tighter concentric circles, until eventually she'd been practically incapable of taking a breath without his permission. In fact it was only after the doctors had informed them that Kelly was clinically unable to bear children that he'd abruptly walked out on her, thereby releasing her from his domination.

That her new freedom was something that Kelly would eventually come to cherish was tempered, mightily, by the nagging, persistent awareness that she'd not played an active role in creating it. Eventually, this sense of powerlessness had been ameliorated somewhat in the period before we met by months of intense therapy, but I knew that it continued to eat at Kelly that she'd been unable to leave the bastard on her own, and it would always remain an ugly scar, at times lurking, ghost-like, just beneath her smile and good humor, and occasionally, even breaking the surface in the form of a fleeting fit of distracted melancholy when she thought I wasn't looking—which of course I, with my own private collection of insecurities, then immediately took as a sign of my own helplessness.

As if expressing a mutual desire to banish such thoughts, we again impulsively reached for each other, indulging in a prolonged and almost urgently passionate kiss. Then, somewhat self-consciously, we separated, and turned our attention back to the view.

Angling in obliquely from just above the five hundred foot, tree-clad volcanic dome of Bate's Butte, a mile distant, the setting sun caromed its rays off of the slow moving current of the Deschutes River, burnishing its surface to a smooth, coppery sheen in the breezeless conditions. Beyond the golden willows and tall grass of the wetlands bordering the opposite shore the dark, thick pine forest stood sentinel, unmoving and silent. In the rose-tinted sky above us a formation of Canada geese wheeled gracefully, if noisily, moving north to south. I looked at Kelly, then, involuntarily, sighed. Can life possibly get better than this?

...But will it last?

Angry with myself for allowing this traitorous thought to intrude, I sought to stifle it by resuming our conversation:

"So," I said, "the preacher's got his wife under his thumb."

"Yes," she said; "but you say that she's openly talking about divorce."

"She did use the word, yes."

"Because she's got herself a new honey."

I looked at her. "What makes you say that?"

"It's easy," she said; "a woman who's spent the whole of her adult life 'under the thumb,' as you say, of a tyrannical husband; one who's essentially never had a chance at anything else, never even dreamt of other options—this is a person with very little sense of self, and absolutely no confidence in her ability to strike out on her own. Trust me, there's no way a woman like this is ever going to even casually entertain—let alone give voice to—the idea of breaking up her marriage, until she knows she's got some comfortable place to land."

"You mean someone comfortable to land *on.*"

"Exactly."

I thought about Nadine Sayles' thrown-away line about not having anywhere else to go "until now." That comment certainly fit in with what Kelly was suggesting.

An elbow gently prodded my side. "So, Mister Private Investigator, what's your next step in this case?" she asked.

"Joshua's friends, I think." I sighed. "Not that I've got much to work with. His mom gave me what she had—which looks to be next to nothing. A couple of names of male friends from church was all; she had trouble even coming up with those and she wasn't able to give me their phone numbers. And from the way his dad reacted to the same request yesterday morning, I'm not bound to get much of anything from him, either."

"Weak," Kelly said; "very weak. And, no girlfriends? Come on, I've seen the photo: that kid looks like a potential lady killer—a grownup one, too; he could easily pass for a sophomore in college."

"Yeah," I said; "that was my impression, too. So what we have here is either a teenage boy who is severely stunted socially—which is certainly plausible, coming as he does from such a strict religious environment—or else a couple of parents completely in the dark about their son's social life, which is far more likely, I think."

"So what do you do?"

"Well," I said, "first I exhaust whatever names I get from Mom and Dad. My guess is that I won't get a lot from talking to those kids, mainly because they're probably just acceptable characters that Josh put out to his folks as cover, especially to his domineering father. Next I find out who Josh's *real* friends are—and I do *that* by finding out where the most likely suspects hang out after school, and then I go and hang out with them."

Kelly chuckled. "Hank Cassidy; hangin' with the homies. And you think these kids will open up to you because—"

I smiled broadly. "Because my charm is always on overdrive."

"Ah."

We were silent for a moment, then Kelly said: "Sun's down."

"So I notice," I said.

"Cooling off."

"A little."

"Stars won't be out for a while."

"True."

"Come on," she said, standing; "let's go inside. I feel like a little nibble…"

"You do?" I said; "I thought you just had dinner."

"Uh-uh, Sherlock," she said, shaking her head deliciously and peering sideways at me, "that's not exactly what I was getting at."

"It's not…oh."

"Uh-huh."

"I'm right behind you…Satch, come!"

Chapter Nine

Fortunately, Reverend J.T. Sayles had the good taste not to phone me until Kelly and I had finished with the bulk of our sinning. That, however, turned out to be the limit of his manners.

"What did my wife tell you?" he demanded, not bothering to greet me or even identify himself.

"Sadly, not much," I lied, playing it smoothly and wondering if my overdriven charm might extend to suspicious evangelical ministers. "She seems to be as in the dark about this thing as you."

"I see," he replied, then paused, lowering his voice and acquiring an oddly cagey tone as he continued: "but did she have…anything else to say?"

"About what?"

"About…*anything.* You know…"

"No," I said, "I guess I don't."

"Yes, yes," he said, fighting impatience, "anything else—you know, anything *else;* anything about our…after all, you *did* spend almost two hours together."

"Yeah," I said, "I suppose we did. But mostly all we did was eat, and drink wine," I said, then added: "and don't worry: we went Dutch and I'm not going to charge you for my share of the tab."

"Yes, thank-you, whatever," he said, quickly, then pressed on. "Did my wife say anything about our family?"

"Why would she do that?" I asked, innocently. Answering a question with a question; always a favorite.

A pause, then a sigh. "I don't know...I thought perhaps...well, never mind." His telephonic voice reeked of mistrust and frustration. I loved it.

But it wouldn't be wise to gloat. "Do you have that list I asked for?" I said, breaking the spell.

"List?" he asked, nonplussed. "Ah, yes; the list of friends and relatives. Well, I'm afraid that I haven't got a great deal of information for you. We have no relatives living nearby, and we've not had any contact at all with those we left behind years ago in Idaho. Unfortunately, both Nadine and I come from families which have...strayed much too far from the Righteous Path to be tolerated. And frankly I doubt that Joshua would have had reason to correspond with them, either, as we left there when he was practically in diapers. Besides, if he had, I would most certainly have known."

"And as for his friends, well, my son has always been a solitary boy, kind of moody, and not inclined to accumulate many companions. There are, however, two boys I've seen Joshua sitting with at church on Sundays and on Wednesday nights in bible study. Nice boys; good boys—good, devout Christians. Their parents are among my most loyal followers." He gave me the names, which turned out to be the same ones Nadine had provided. In this case, though, he did have the phone numbers, which I wrote down.

Probably realizing how meager the list must've sounded, he added: "I suppose I should have spent more time with the boy, encouraged him to strike up a few more friendships; but, well, with my calling, with my responsibility to my church and all—after all, I've got Sunday sermons to write, classes to teach, couples to counsel, radio broadcasts to prepare for, and...did I tell you about my coming television ministry? Anyway, in my life, there just isn't the space for that kind of selfishness."

No, Reverend, apparently there's only space in your life for an entirely different kind of selfishness...

I almost told him that his wife had already mentioned the TV gig, but decided that, as innocent as that should have sounded, to him it might have constituted some sort of sinister breach of trust, so instead I said, with as much phony enthusiasm as I could muster: "Television, huh? How about that. Good for you."

Must not have mustered very much, because his "Thanks" sounded about as arid and chilly as a windblown belfry on a winter's night.

From there the rest of the conversation meandered aimlessly. It was obvious that I wasn't going to provide the preacher with anything further concerning my visit with his wife, and there also didn't seem to be much that he could add to the information he'd already given me; so, after verbally dancing for a few uncomfortable minutes, we both sought to bring things to a close.

"Oh, one more thing, Reverend," I said, before ringing off.

"Yes?"

"I'm going to probably need, at some point, to speak with some of your regular...uh, patrons; maybe catch up with some of them at the end of one of your Sunday services, if you don't mind."

"Mind? Of course I mind!" he blurted, then recovered. "I mean, is that really necessary? They've already been subjected to far more than they should have, answering police questions and all. And, well, I just don't think that these good people should have to endure even more of it from you if they don't have to."

Meaning: doncha rock dat ole gravy boat...

"Your call, Reverend," I said; "I'm just trying to do a job here."

"I know; I appreciate that, I do," he said. "But, if there were any way to—"

"Tell you what," I said; "I'll be getting the case file from the police tomorrow. If what I see there tells me that they've dealt thoroughly enough with your congregation, then I won't need to bother them."

"I'm sure they have," he said, a bit too eagerly.

"You're probably right," I said. "Good-night, Reverend."

I hung up, then reached over and pinched Kelly's naked left breast, which, along with its right-side partner had floated, distractingly, a few inches above the covers the whole time I'd been on the phone.

"Hey…what was that for?"

"Just needed a reality check."

She laughed, then snuck a strategic, *very* effective hand of her own under the covers. "Well in that case, you just mosey on over here, Pardner, and I'll give you all the reality you can handle…"

"Mosey? Pardner?"

"More quaint country idiom."

"Yeehaw," I murmured.

Chapter Ten

Friday morning, cognizant of the fact that today was the final weekday of summer vacation, I dialed the numbers on my list and arranged to meet with Joshua's two church buddies for lunch at the MacDonald's off of Route 20 on the east side of town.

Right after I hung up I pulled on my leathers, swung a leg over my motorcycle and rode off, my purpose being to stop, on the way there, for a visit to the Reverend Sayles' home and religious compound, which I had yet to see. Riding easily in the mild weather and light traffic, I reached the church complex in just over thirty minutes.

A few blocks east of 27th Street, the place was situated in a district just outside of the eastern border of Bend; away from the mountains, where the pine trees become markedly sparser, gradually giving way to the junipers and scrub-brush more characteristic of the high desert. It appeared to be a mixed-use zone of roughly rural character, with modest, one-story homes on over-sized lots sharing streets with landscape nurseries, ramshackle child day-care centers, and at least a dozen assorted churches.

A couple of the religious institutions I rode past were acutely humble: converted double-wide manufactured homes sprouting like moles from the centers of unkempt, weed-ridden fields, with hand-painted signs crudely advertising their denominational affiliations at the roadside. Others were far more prosperous, with architecture suggesting they'd been crated in, piece by piece, from New England; proud basilicas with expensive red brick construction, white-trimmed windows and majestic, pointed steeples, surrounded by acres of freshly-paved and lined asphalt, with tidy walkways bordered by immaculately-trimmed hedges and tightly-mown lawns.

The Church of the Holy Messenger was not quite as grand as those more classically-executed facilities, although in many ways it might have been considered a more impressive accomplishment. Evidently at one time part of a sprawling farm most of whose surrounding fields had long since been parceled out for development, what still remained was substantial: at least fifteen acres, many of them currently unused, although they were obviously being neatly maintained in preparation for ambitious expansion plans.

Three structures occupied the developed part of the property: closest to the road, the Sayles house; off to the left and abutting an expansive parking lot a small, tidily constructed square schoolhouse with adjoining, chain-link fenced playground; lastly, looming behind both, the imposing, massive horse-barn-to-cathedral conversion.

All three buildings wore fresh coats of brown and gray paint, and were decorated, wherever wall space would permit, with giant, white crosses, professionally painted and outlined with black borders on one side, which imparted to them a three-dimensional appearance. Sitting atop the wooden, chimney-shaped chapel spire, which during a more rustic period had probably supported a weather vane, was yet another cross; this one at least ten feet high and made of what looked to be highly polished copper, shining gloriously in the morning sun. Interestingly, the sprawling parking area fronting the school house was unpaved, and was instead uniformly covered with a fine layer of pea-gravel. Considering that the rest of the complex seemed to reflect the fruits of a healthy church budget, I suspected that the parking lot had been deliberately kept unimproved in order to perpetuate some sort of "we're just plain folks here" atmosphere; conducive to the particular brand of grass-roots, populist evangelism the Reverend was peddling. As if to punctuate that thought, a huge, gray metal glass-enclosed sign at the street entrance to the lot proclaimed, in large moveable letters: "Welcome, Everyone, to Our Heavenly Father's Humble Homestead."

I was glad that there at least existed a smooth, paved driveway leading from the road to the attached garage of the single-story, cinder block ranch house, as I would not have relished attempting to negotiate all of that loose gravel on my entirely street-oriented motorcycle tires. I pulled in, dropped the kickstand and then dismounted, hanging my helmet on the bike's throttle grip.

The garage door was up, revealing a late nineties vintage, dark-brown Ford Explorer, and, next to it, a slightly newer, beige Toyota Camry. On the Explorer, a "Praise the Lord" bumper sticker hugged the space just to the left of the rear license plate. That and the stenciled white crucifix on lower right corner of the Ford's rear window, along with the complete absence of any such symbolic tokens on the Camry, gave me a fairly clear indication of whose wheels were whose. To the left of the garage, a battered and ancient pale-blue Ford F100 pickup truck—circa nineteen seventy-five or so—was parked, unsheltered and apparently fighting a losing battle with the elements.

As I unzipped my jacket, the preacher emerged through the front door out onto the covered porch. He was decked out pretty much as he'd been the day before: nondescript, mud-brown slacks, cheap, loose-fitting off-white dress shirt and decidedly non-designer, unpolished, black lace-up oxfords.

He frowned disapprovingly as he glanced past me to my motorcycle; evidently having at some point come to the conclusion that such racy contraptions must be the unclean instruments of You-Know-Who. But whatever his thoughts were, he kept them to himself, perhaps mindful of what I'd warned him about attempting to comment on my personal life choices.

As I mounted the steps to the porch, the minister made no move to greet me, instead pulling open the door, standing to the side and waving me past. "I really don't see the point of all of this," he grumbled. "The police have already given the boy's room a thorough going-over."

"Oh, I'm sure that's true," I replied; "I just need to see it for myself, get some sense of your son, a feel for his personality, his tastes and habits."

"Sounds like a bunch of New-Age psychobabble to me."

"Just indulge me, please, Reverend," I said, trying—but not entirely succeeding—to keep the annoyance out of my voice. It was really beginning to bug me how unhelpful this guy was turning out to be. Of course, what I didn't tell him was that at least part of my purpose in dropping by included getting a sense of the *entire* home; of the sort of familial atmosphere—or lack of it—which might have led a teenage boy to conclude that a life away from his father's house was preferable to the one he'd been forced to endure within it.

Stepping across the threshold and turning to my right, I immediately found myself gazing upon an unexceptional yet neat living room which occupied the right front quadrant of the rectangular home. Beyond it, through an open archway toward the rear of the house, I could see what appeared to be a compact dining area and adjacent kitchen. To my left, the modest entry branched off into a hallway, which led, I assumed, to the bedrooms.

The living room furniture was decidedly rudimentary. There were three pieces, all of them standard-issue,

American Colonial maple. Two easy chairs flanked a sofa, each upholstered in a synthetic fabric of an uncertain shade of blue. A medium-sized, old-fashioned cathode ray television squatted, dormant, in the corner. Washes of indifferent light leaked out from under the ecru shades of three Holiday Inn-caliber floor lamps. The carpeting was short pile of an aging, faded beige, but unstained and apparently recently vacuumed. No coffee table, no magazine rack, no knickknack cabinet; just the absolute minimum, on the whole articulating what appeared to be an acute lack of social inclination.

If the furniture was bare bones, however, it was more than compensated for by an absolute righteous riot crowding the walls; artwork everywhere I looked loudly proclaiming the ultra-religious sentiments of at least one of the home's inhabitants. Crucifixes galore: some hand-carved and rubbed to a glossy sheen in hard wood; some baroquely wrought from an assortment of metals; even a couple molded in cheap, gaudy plastic, and customized with a fake gilt patina. Interspersed among these were four medium sized, badly executed oils in ornate frames, each of them crying out with graphic, iconic depictions of Christ's agony on his fateful, final day. Taking up the remaining wall space were four modest, wood-framed, needle-point samplers, each reproducing some key piece of text from the Gospels. To a believer, maybe bearing witness to such an outlandish religious display might have been inspiring. To me it was suffocating.

Nadine Sayles was standing in the midst of this array, and she greeted me with a minimal inclination of her head and a tight, humorless smile, but said nothing, either to me or her husband. I noticed that today she was dressed considerably more frumpily than she'd been the previous night at the restaurant: shapeless, dun-colored floor-length frock, no make-up, flats, hair carelessly brushed, hanging loosely. As I stood there, I became instantly aware of a palpable sense of coldness between the two of them—not the normal chilly marital awkwardness which might possibly have followed a recent spat, but rather, a glacial freeze; the kind of stark, emotional void that can only result from lengthy, active neglect.

"Nadine," said the preacher sternly, "show Mr. Cassidy to the boy's room."

As his wife wordlessly led me out of the living room and down the hall towards the bedrooms, I could feel the preacher's beady eyes following us. And like Lot making his celebrated getaway from Sodom, I took scrupulous care not to look back.

The hallway we had now entered bisected the other half of the house. At its far end was a closed door, the other side of which, Nadine told me using a few mumbled words, was the master bedroom. On the right, toward the rear of the house, were two more doors, the first evidently leading to a bathroom, with the second opening into what turned out to be Josh's room. As I approached it, I glanced through the single open doorway on my left, and observed another bedroom, whose decidedly feminine appointments suggested strongly that Mr. and Mrs. Reverend were not currently sharing the same bed. I found myself pondering this arrangement, and speculating as to just how long it had been in force.

Adorning the length of both walls of the hallway were still more cheap-looking religious artifacts, the overall total making me wonder if the Reverend were some sort of inveterate Christian garage sale prowler. Or maybe it was that this seemingly bottomless, bizarre collection of sacred iconography simply represented years of gifts from grateful members of his flock. Whatever; there was no point in further cataloguing this batch, especially since I'd already been more than a little creeped out by the stuff I'd seen in the living room.

I doubted that the cops had ever actually bothered to string crime scene tape across the doorway to Josh's room, but if they had, it was long gone now. We entered it—or, rather, *I* did; Nadine Sayles remained, watching impassively, from the doorway.

I stood for a few minutes in the center of the room, trying to get a feel for the boy who'd spent much of his life here. Failed, utterly; this space felt far more like a seldom-used guest room than a typical teenager's digs. Occupying the rear wall, under a window, was a narrow bed, neatly made up—possibly untouched since the police had seen it—and covered with an inexpensive green cotton bedspread, neatly turned down to expose a single white pillow. Next to the bed sat a simple wooden nightstand supporting a cheap, goose-neck reading lamp. Against the wall directly opposite them was a sturdy, unremarkable maple-veneer, six-drawer dresser, and, next to it, a desk and wooden chair. On top of the desk were a computer, monitor and printer, the models of which looked to be at least several generations short of technology's latest. A single metal folding chair sat in the corner farthest from the doorway. There was no other furniture. If Joshua Sayles had friends, I doubted that any of them had ever kicked back in this sterile environment.

But if anything truly testified to the complete absence of young Joshua Sayles' impact on this room, it was the bare walls. Make that *almost* bare: there was, in fact, one large, ornately-framed print adorning the wall above the dresser, a scene depicting a smiling Jesus, arms spread with palms outward, gliding through an adoring crowd of cherubic children. With his spotless white robe, his glowing, air-brushed face and beard, and his shining, flowing, shoulder-length reddish-golden locks, I couldn't help but conjure an admittedly irreverent mental image of one of those glossy Clairol shampoo ads on the back covers of a woman's fashion magazine. I had little doubt that this particular piece of artwork had in no way been chosen by the boy, but rather, obviously, by his omnipotent, overbearing father. But as to a more characteristic collection of teenage art—the rock posters, the action movie one-sheets, the X-treme sports photos—they were nowhere to be seen, and I suspected that any such heathen tokens would have been expressly forbidden.

Moving to the closet door I pulled it open, and was immediately confronted by what I assumed were the pair of daypacks Denove had mentioned in our phone conversation, suspended from a hook on the door's reverse side. Inside, the closet space was crowded, the single wooden rod spanning it loaded with plastic hangers struggling to keep separate an assortment of standard teen apparel: hoodies, jeans, flannel shirts, tees, and a modest variety of jackets and sweaters. I examined the jackets last, wondering which of them matched the one seen in the ATM videos, and made a mental note to ask my detective friend if I could view them.

There wasn't much else to be gleaned from Josh's closet—aside from a sad acknowledgement that the contents of this four foot by four space seemed to constitute the only real evidence of the boy's existence—so I closed the door, and crossed the room to Joshua's desk.

It was a standard student model: two deep drawers on the left, chair on the right, with a shallow utility drawer directly beneath the computer keyboard. Opening the top left drawer revealed a stack of blank printer paper, a dozen unused file folders, and four empty, unlabeled manila envelopes; while the bottom drawer held only computer manuals and back-up disks. The shallow drawer contained a few ballpoint pens, a box of #2 pencils, two red felt markers and a ruler. That was it. Not a single personal item anywhere. No journal, address book or album; no random, scribbled notes or numbers; no homework. On the desktop no knick-knacks or framed photos—not even a blotter. Like the room it was in, this desk seemed to speak absence— fluently.

So stark, in fact, was this sense of utter non-use, that on impulse I leaned over the desk to check to see if the computer's power cords were actually plugged in. They were, but as I observed this I also noticed the lack of a modem or phone line connection to the machine. And that meant no internet; meant no web-surfing, no Face Book, no Twitter, no You Tube—no email. All of the sorts of electronic intercourse carried on, these days, by youth everywhere—from Madison to Mumbai, London to Leopoldville—had, evidently, not been happening at this desk.

Nor anywhere else, I reflected, considering what Denove had told me about Josh not having had a cell phone.

It was beginning to look like Joshua Sayles had been one extraordinarily isolated teenager.

With a shrug, I headed to the doorway, where Nadine Sayles continued to wait silently. I didn't want to give voice to my overwhelming impression: that this kid had not been having much of a life—or rather, that if he *had* experienced any sort of existence, it must've have been done well away from this room, away from this house—so instead I asked her to show me around the grounds. She nodded, and turned back towards the hall, nothing in her face suggesting that she was in any way attuned to my thoughts.

Not finding the preacher waiting for us when we returned to the living room, Nadine Sayles then guided me to the left; past the small dining area furnished with an austere aluminum-and-Formica dinette set, to the rear door, which opened out to the backyard—or rather, to the open, unfenced space separating the house from the other buildings. You couldn't really call it a yard; it was mostly just compacted earth, heavily carpeted with pine needles and juniper detritus, and populated here and there with neglected yet stubborn non-native flora, no doubt remnants of an earlier time when landscaping here had mattered to a different owner. I also couldn't help but notice the lack of a barbeque grill, or of a picnic table and benches, which might have at least reflected some minimal degree of outdoor family communality.

A hundred feet or so behind and to the left of the house we came to the cube-shaped school building. Nadine explained that the structure was divided into four classrooms, used for bible studies, Christian family-training classes and abstinence-only instruction—as well as for daycare, which the church made available most weekdays and, especially, on Sundays. Taking in the brightly colored plastic swing set, tepee and play slide strategically placed about the segregated area behind the chain-link fencing, I nodded, smiling to myself: your average five-year-old can only take so much old-time religion before he begins to crave a little quality time on the monkey bars.

I had no interest in visiting the classrooms, so we immediately moved on to the chapel. I had to admit, from the outside it really was an impressive affair: at least a hundred feet long and fifty wide, with twenty foot high walls topped by a blue metal gambrel roof, spire and shining cross. Ironically, in opting for the doubtless more economical choice of converting an existing structure rather than building from scratch, the minister had ended up with an edifice of impressive, almost European grandeur, which most likely would not have been achieved had he gone the more conventional architectural route.

Nadine led me to the end of the building, and then up three broad, stained and polished wooden steps, to a landing which fronted a pair of massive, ornately carved oak doors—which constituted the grand entrance to the rear of the sanctuary, and incidentally, the setting I recognized as being the backdrop for the photograph of the reverend and his son. Pulling open the left-side door, I waited for the woman to pass by, then followed her. Once inside, I was immediately confronted by a custom made, slant-top oak pedestal, which supported a leather-bound, richly-embroidered guest book, and was bolted to the floor at the center of an attractive, roomy foyer. To the left and right the walls of the foyer were almost completely lined with sturdy, built-in oak bookcases extending from the hardwood flooring to the nine-foot ceiling, their shelves stuffed with hundreds of prayer books and hymnals.

We walked through that low-ceilinged room, and then passed beneath a wide archway on the opposite wall, where, suddenly, everything opened up, vertically and horizontally. I found myself, mouth agape and blinking, in the bright, awesome expanse of one very impressive assembly hall.

Tall ranks of clear-paned windows had been located, high up, on all four walls, thus encircling the entire building and providing an overwhelming sense of airiness and light. Currently, the rays were slanting, in a most biblical manner, at a steep angle from the east. I had to admit; the effect really was uncanny.

There were no pews; instead, the hall was filled with row upon row of what appeared to be comfortable, high-quality, upholstered folding chairs, which had been meticulously arranged, with breaks between the ranks providing a broad aisle down the center axis of the room, as well as two more narrow ones, each along an outer wall. I figured that this employment of moveable seating, while necessitating that the devotional literature and hymnals would have to be stored elsewhere, allowed them to adapt the building to a wide variety of uses: weddings, receptions, church socials, and the like. Glancing down, I could see that a sizeable portion of the high-quality, commercial-grade carpeting was edge-bound, and could be rolled up and moved aside, likely to expose a dance floor beneath, and further reinforcing the feeling of multi-purpose intent. I then looked back and to my left, and saw through an open doorway a large kitchen, next to the foyer, fully equipped with what appeared to be professional, stainless-steel appliances.

Whatever his eccentricities, J.T. Sayles evidently fully understood the importance of making maximum economic use of his facility.

A familiar booming voice from the opposite end of the hall drew my attention, and I turned to see the preacher, standing on a raised dais behind the pulpit, gesticulating energetically and issuing sharp commands to a two man crew, who were perched atop metal scaffolding and apparently in the process of fine-tuning an extensive array of variously colored stage lights. To the left and right of the Reverend, suspended high above him from the cathedral ceiling (at last, a literal use of the term), were two massive Altec Lansing loudspeakers, angled downward towards the audience. Considering the mighty range and power of the minister's pipes, I thought that the sound system represented by those speakers seemed unnecessary, to say the least. Fire and brimstone, I got that; but bleeding eardrums?

Has to be for the choir—probably needs at least a couple of hundred watts just to compete with the guy....

Interestingly, where Sayles' house had seemed an exercise in bargain basement furnishings and religious tackiness, this massive room positively radiated warmth and good taste. Everything in the hall spoke of refinement and restraint: color choices were muted and soothing, lighting fixtures were attractively indirect, furniture was comfortable and stylish. On the walls, polished, slatted hardwood acoustical panels were expertly angled to diffuse echoes. Even the floor-to-ceiling wooden cross at the back of the pulpit seemed understated. It was clear to me that, if nothing else, J.T. Sayles had gone to great lengths here in order to synthesize a first-class architectural embodiment of the words, "Relax, leave your worldly cares at the door; we'll take it from here."

Seeing us entering the chapel, the minister issued a final instruction to the crew, then stepped off the dais and strode, purposefully, to the rear of the room. Reaching us, he blessed me with a broad smile, while making a sweeping gesture. "Well? So, what do you think of my little chapel?" he asked, his voice loaded with good humor and false modesty, clearly confident of what my answer must be.

I didn't disappoint him. "It's beautiful, Reverend," I said, honestly. "You've really accomplished something here."

"Yes," he agreed, enthusiastically; "praise the Lord, I have, haven't I? But there's still much, much more to do."

"The vacant land, you mean."

"That's right," he said. "When I first saw this place, I knew right off that the Almighty had chosen it for me; that he had great plans for me. Of course, at the time it wasn't at all as you see it now—pretty run-down in fact. Weeds as high as your chest everywhere you looked, buildings too dilapidated and dangerous to even walk through. A lesser man might not have recognized the potential. But I did: as if seized by a holy vision, I walked about this property, praying, imagining and mentally transforming everything I saw."

"The first product of my vision, obviously, was this glorious chapel"—another broad sweep of the arm—"and, soon after that, our little schoolhouse." He paused, dramatically. "But there is far more to my dream than just these two buildings, including the elementary/high school that I plan to construct out there on the remaining acres—a holy place of learning where the children of the righteous will grow and thrive, their precious, malleable young minds safely out of reach of the unclean, heathen public schools, with their evolutionism, their sex education and their endless spewing of Godless literature and blasphemous philosophy!" He paused again, training defiant, expectant eyes upon me.

After just barely choking back a laugh (which I'm guessing would not have been well-received), and mindful that the man was, after all, currently my employer, I composed myself, and managed to conjure a bland smile while offering up a physician's "Um-hmm."

Unfazed by my tepid response, he plowed ahead. "And now that you've seen what the Lord and I have already wrought here, how can you possibly doubt that we will succeed with the rest of our plans?" Here, he gestured towards the lighting crew. "I *have* told you about our coming telecast, have I not?"

"Yes, Reverend," I said patiently. "At least twice, as I recall."

"We're just putting the final touches to the lighting and sound systems, so that they don't cause problems for the television station's technicians."

"When do you air?"

"Less than three weeks; third Sunday from now. A bit of strategic planning, really," he said, offering me what I could only describe as an owlish grin and sounding inordinately pleased with what he must have regarded as a fine display of public relations acumen. "Everyone in Central Oregon, even the stragglers, will have returned from summer vacation by then; and at that point, with deer-hunting season essentially over, I calculate that we should be able to attract the maximum possible audience for our inaugural telecast."

"Very practical; good for you," I mumbled with as much phony enthusiasm as I could muster, and then glanced, conspicuously, at my watch. "Ah, look at the time. I really have to get going—got a meeting."

"With whom?" he asked, sounding annoyed that I was running out on him just as he was getting his rev on.

"As a matter of fact," I said, "it's with those two boys; Josh's friends; the ones you told me about."

"Ah, yes," he said, brusquely, "of course. Well, anyway I *do* have my *own* work to get back to…"

With that he turned his back to us and marched toward the pulpit; as complete and abrupt a dismissal as one could imagine. I turned to Nadine, but she just shrugged, the look on her face clearly reading: *I get this all the time.*

Ms. Sayles and I walked from the building in silence. For my part, I was trying to digest all that I'd just seen and heard. As for her; once or twice I sensed that she was glancing, sideways, at me, wanting to say something, but each time falling mute.

Once we reached my motorcycle, however—and possibly because the house was now interposed between us and the chapel—she turned to me.

"You see what I'm talking about, don't you?" she said, locking my eyes with her own, which were narrowed down to slits.

"I'm not sure that I—"

"That my husband has only one true love in his life; and it's certainly not me, or his missing son."

"You're talking about his love of Jesus."

"Jesus? Now *there's* a laugh," she said, derisively, her girlish voice suddenly turning harsh, gutteral; "J. T. Sayles could care *less* about Jesus! J.T. Sayles, Mr. Cassidy, is completely, exclusively, head over heels in love with J.T. *Sayles!*"

It being, apparently, a morning for noncommittal response, I merely nodded.

"Uh-huh, Mr. Cassidy," she continued; "that's the way it is; and that's the way it's *been* for more years than...well, for more years than any wife should be forced to put up with!" Then she turned, ran up the steps and disappeared into the house.

As I rode away from the compound, I considered what she'd just said. From the entirely pedestrian nature of their living quarters and appointments, as well as the reverend's late-model cars and b-flat clothing, a dispassionate observer might be led to believe that, at least on the surface, J.T. Sayles wasn't exactly a material guy. But the price-no-object, every detail seen to, custom quality of his chapel clearly demonstrated a connoisseur's touch, a fanatic's devotion and argued, strenuously, to the contrary. But couldn't this meticulous—if possibly single-minded—attention to his project simply be taken as an expression of the profound depth of devotion to his calling?

Possibly—but Nadine Sayles obviously thought not, and I was inclined to agree. It was hard to ignore the way the minister had consistently billed himself in at least a co-starring role with God when it came to accepting credit for this establishment. I suspected that the bottom-line truth was that the chapel—in fact the entire concept of the Church of the Holy Messenger, right down to the daycare center, planned el/hi school, and...oh yes, don't forget that TV ministry—constituted more a shining monument to Reverend Sayles' own personal ambitions, than it did to the glory of Jehovah.

I also had to agree with her that constructing this monument of his had apparently completely eclipsed everything else in his life, including his family and, in particular, his son, Joshua.

Joshua—had the preacher even mentioned him today? Yes, he had, I recalled; but only in the context of arguing the pointlessness of my visit.

But, while I found much to agree with in Nadine's scathing indictment of her husband, there appeared to be nearly as much to wonder about *her*. It certainly seemed that, in much the same way J.T. was consumed by ambition, Nadine Sayles seemed equally eaten up with her own private misery and resentment of her husband.

Meaning: there again, no room for the kid.

Was I being unfair? Was her apparent emotional disconnect from the case merely a product of having been ground down by two months of anxiety paired with consistent disappointment? Or was it, possibly, that she had by now managed to convince herself that wherever Joshua had ended up, he was better off?

On the other hand, was I being *too* fair?

"That's the way it's been for more years than any wife should be forced to put up with."

I wondered about that comment. Obviously, Nadine Sayles had spat out those words to impress upon me just how long her suffering had gone on. But I wondered if, perhaps, it could also be used to describe the years-long span of an *entire* dysfunctional family dynamic: rising-star preacher too caught up in self-adoration to bother being husband or father; wife stifled by the combination of a negligent yet overbearing mate and the arrested development which comes from having married way too young; teenage son so used to being reduced to a familial nonentity that running away hardly seems like such a drastic action.

Door number one.

I thought again about the brief glimpse I'd had of that entirely feminine bedroom. Was that also what she'd been referring to? A woman's physical needs going completely unfulfilled for years?

If Kelly's guess was accurate, then Nadine Sayles had finally worked up the gumption to act on those needs.

Unless there'd been others…

I shook my head hard enough to make my helmet rattle. That sort of speculation was none of my business, not to mention that it was an unproductive can of worms probably best left unopened.

At least, by me.

One interesting couple, though.

Down-shifting the Ducati, I sped away.

Chapter Eleven

As was the case with my previous evening's appointment with Nadine Sayles, I arrived deliberately early to Mickey D's. In this instance, of course, there was no hope of conducting business in a private, out of the way booth, so I contented myself with a table by the window, which looked directly out to the space where I'd parked my bike. Holding off on ordering my extra-value feast until the boys showed up, I instead just sat there quietly in a seat facing the entrance; my attention divided between insistent, unpleasant recollections of recent images of the minister, his church complex and his wife, and the far more immediate and certainly more cheerful clamor of the bustling, munching, gabbing crowd around me. Studying the various faces and physiques coming in through the swinging glass doors, I idly speculated on how difficult it was going to be to spot my young subjects.

Not difficult at all, as it happened. Ten minutes after my arrival, a few minutes after twelve o'clock, two teenage boys stepped inside and scanned the room, nervously. Not exactly twins—one being short, skinny, and sandy-haired with a narrow, pale, acne-ridden face; the other, taller, at least thirty pounds overweight with a round, ruddy countenance and a blond, military-style crew cut—in all other respects they could have been cloned: identical khaki slacks and nearly identical short-sleeve, button-collar plaid shirts, shiny black oxfords and horn-rimmed glasses with coke-bottle lenses. Far as I could see, the only items lacking from the package were a couple of plastic pocket protectors.

I waved to them, and they both responded with their own, timid gestures, and then reluctantly approached my table, with expressions suggesting that I was brandishing a

Smith and Wesson instead of a notepad. I decided against standing to greet them; I'm a very large six-two, and these poor kids were nervous enough as it was.

"Hey, Guys," I said, cheerily, and extended a hand. Each responded with a weak, clammy grip, producing a sensation roughly akin to grabbing a couple of uncooked filets of sole. The skinny kid turned out to be Paul Haver, the chubby one, Eliot Wilkins. I gestured to the two swivel seats opposite me and said, "Park yourselves, and I'll go get the grub." I took their identical orders for Big Mac meals—super-sized, of course—and then headed for the counter. Upon reaching it I turned, and noticed them whispering urgently to each other. No doubt discussing their chances of making a clean getaway…

Whatever it was that had passed between them, however, they were still in their seats when I returned with the food (probably something to do with never looking a gift burger in the mouth), and silently nodded their thanks as I passed it out to them.

Not knowing quite how to begin, and wanting to at least start out in territory I thought might be comfortable for the two boys, I smiled at the skinny one and offered: "So Paul, did your folks name you after the apostle?"

To my surprise, the question provoked a smirk, a rolling of the eyes, and a decisive head-shake. "Nah," he said, disgustedly; "when I was born, my parents were into the Beatles, big time."

"Well," I said, trying to be conciliatory, "it could have been worse; at least they didn't name you Ringo."

"Yeah," he said, "although now that we're evangelicals, my mom's not real happy they picked that name."

"What?" I said; "'Paul' isn't biblical enough for her?"

"She thinks it sounds too Catholic." He shrugged. "Anyway, I guess they figure that by now it's too late to change it."

Too Catholic. Not anxious to venture down that potentially thorny path, I instead turned to his friend. "And I suppose your mom was an Elliot Gould fan."

He looked at me blankly. "Who?" Then shook his head. "Oh, you mean that old guy in those 'Ocean's Eleven.' movies. Uh-uh, I got my name because my parents went to New York once and saw 'Cats' on Broadway."

"Ah," I said; "T.S. One L—"

"And one T," he mumbled, his mouth now full of beef, cheese, special sauce and sesame seeds.

"How long have the two of you been going to Reverend Sayles' church?" I asked.

"A couple of years, now," said Eliot, with a decided lack of enthusiasm which matched his friend's expression, and which spoke volumes about the true extent of their commitment to this particular brand of gospel.

"I see." Noticing how quickly both boys were tearing into their meals, I figured I'd better press on. "And you guys hung out there with Josh, right?"

They exchanged a look, and then Eliot displayed a pained, weary gaze which suggested a life consisting of more years than his actual sixteen. "No," he said; "it's…it wasn't really like that."

"It wasn't?" I asked. "But I thought—"

"Well," Paul chimed in, "he let us hang out with him at church and bible study, but we weren't really friends."

"He *let* you…"

Paul matched his buddy's world-weary look. "Yeah," he said; "I guess you could say that. Josh...see, he's one of the cool kids at school, and us...well, we're just not. So us hanging out with him at the church, it's only because he was letting us." Eyes fixed on his half-eaten burger, he shrugged. "And he was probably only doing *that* because having us around would look good to his parents...and most of all, to the Reverend."

I looked at his partner, caught him nodding his agreement.

Paul's last comment certainly came as no surprise, as it more or less validated my previous surmise about Joshua's motives concerning his friendship with these two boys. But the frankness with which it was expressed caused me to look upon them with fresh appreciation. What I heard in their voices and read in their faces spoke eloquently of an ages-long absence of social standing—an arbitrary childhood stigma probably slapped on them as far back as the earliest years of grade school—but also of a degree of quiet resignation and frank, mature acceptance, as well as that measure of dignity and self-respect which derives from having endured hard times. In some ways, I thought, they might actually profit from this adolescent ordeal; might end up better able than their essentially-untested peers to cope with the sorts of slings and arrows apt to confront them in a larger world.

"So then," I said, "who did Josh hang with away from the church?"

Paul answered, this time betraying a slight trace of bitterness: "You mean who were his *real* friends?" He shrugged again. "Who else—all the *other* cools."

"Jocks?"

"Nope," replied Eliot; "Josh wasn't much into sports; didn't really have to be. He was smart, good-looking, funny; wasn't much need for him to leak sweat to get the girls to notice him."

I nodded my understanding, thinking back to my own high school years; to the peculiar accounting system employed by teen-age boys, wherein excelling at sports was valued not so much for the fun or achievement of the thing as it was an asset to be hoarded and then exploited socially. A badge, in the form of an embroidered letter on a thick, uncomfortable wool sweater, which could be artfully employed to open certain doors—namely, the ones leading to the bedrooms of the A-list girls.

"So who are these 'real' friends, then?" I asked.

"Mostly it's the Mirror Pond crowd," said Eliot.

"Mirror Pond."

"Yeah," said Paul; "there's a bunch of 'em that hang out down there, at Drake Park, right by the public parking lot, pretty much every day after school."

"What do they do there?"

"What do they do?" said Eliot. He snorted. "You know; they just...*hang out:* they talk, they smoke, they flirt—sometimes they fight. Mostly they just stand around congratulating each other on how cool they think they are." He smiled ruefully, then added, "And sometimes they pound on kids they think don't belong there."

"Like you, for instance."

He shrugged. "A couple of times."

"Did Josh participate?" I asked.

"In the pounding? Not really," said Paul; "he's not that bad a guy. Besides, he wasn't down there all the time."

"But those are his friends."

"Yeah, I guess."

"Any girlfriends?"

"Yeah," said Eliot, the envy clear in his voice, "a bunch, although he hasn't really had a steady one for a long time."

"Who was the last one?"

"Jennifer Longwell," said Paul, a look of profound longing passing between him and his buddy.

"Good looking girl, huh?" I said.

"Uh, yeah," said Paul, coloring. "But he dumped her almost a year ago, and he hasn't been seeing anyone since."

"No one for almost a year?"

"Well," he said, "six months, anyway."

"Does Jennifer hang out at Mirror Pond?"

"Yeah," said Paul, "she does. Sometimes. But she's not really like the rest of them…not rowdy or pierced or tatted out or anything. She's…well, she's really nice," he said with the sad reverence of one who yearns for something hopelessly unattainable. "I guess that sometimes she just doesn't have anywhere else to go. Besides, I think she hangs out there because she's hoping that maybe Josh'll show up."

"Still has a crush, huh?"

"Big time."

"So why'd he dump her?"

"Dunno," said Eliot. "It's crazy, you know? I mean, Jenny's about the best-looking girl in the school...and really nice, too," he said, not realizing that he was repeating himself. "And smart," he added, then stared out the window. "But...well, I guess sometimes Josh can be...kind of weird."

"Weird? How?"

"Well," Eliot continued, "one time he..." He hesitated, then looked at Paul, who was shaking his head. "Maybe I shouldn't—"

"All right, Guys," I said; "cards on the table. Joshua Sayles is missing, right? And for all we know he might be in some serious trouble. Now, it's my job to find him, and in order to do that, I've got to turn up every piece of information I can; every seemingly unimportant little scrap that might point to why he left, and where he might have gone. And that especially includes any sort of strange behavior he may have exhibited in the last few months before his disappearance. So, if you've got something..."

Eliot looked at me, then down at the remnants of his meal. "I dunno; it's just that it probably doesn't have anything to do with anything."

"Let me be the judge of that," I insisted. "Tell you what: if I think you're right, then it doesn't have to go any farther than here."

Eliot shrugged, then sighed. "All right," he said, "I'll tell you. Like I said, it probably doesn't mean anything but...well, there was this one time when, out of nowhere, Josh went nuts, slammed me up against the back wall of the church and threatened to beat my brains in." His face blanched at the memory, and he began to sweat as he took an impulsive, nervous sip from his coke.

"Why would he do that?"

"Because of something I said."

"What did you say?"

A pause, then a breath. "Just something about his mom. Nothing, really; I was just complimenting his mother, and he went all crazy on me."

"Complimenting her how?"

Using a paper napkin to wipe his brow, he said: "Oh...I just told him that I thought his mom was beautiful"—he looked at me, his eyes pleading—"because she *is*...she's really beautiful. Have you met her?"

"Yes I have," I said, "and you're right; Mrs. Sayles is a very attractive woman. Was there anything about the way you said it that might have—"

"No!" he interrupted. "It wasn't anything like that...I swear! I just said, straight up, 'I think your mom's really beautiful'...nothing dirty, just a compliment. But the way he tore into me you would have thought I'd told him I had the hots for her!"

"How long ago was this?"

"Five, maybe six months ago. Matter of fact, it was right around the time he broke up with Jenny. A couple of days afterward he came up to me right before bible class and apologized; said he'd had a lot on his mind, what with breaking up with his girlfriend and stuff; said he'd been bugged about some other things, too. Anyway, from then on he was a lot nicer to me...to *us*"—he tilted his head towards Paul—"than he'd been before, I guess trying to make up for being so freaky that day. But I forgave him." He smiled, ironically. "I guess it wouldn't have been very Christian, would it—you know, refusing to forgive a guy, and then walking into a bible study class. But one thing for sure, I never mentioned his mom after that."

"Smart," I said.

"Once burned, twice shy, my dad always says."

"Any idea what really set him off?"

"No," he said, "and he never came close to anything like that again. So maybe it was like he said...just something on his mind that day."

"Maybe," I agreed. *Unexpected outburst. Emotionally unstable?* I wrote nothing on my pad, not wanting to signal the boys that it might be important; probably, it wasn't. But if nothing else, the story did serve to add a few more colorful brush strokes to my portrait of this boy I'd never met.

The rest of the lunch didn't produce much else of value, although I attempted to grease the skids with another round of Big Macs. At one point, Paul glanced at my motorcycle jacket, draped over the back of the chair next to me, and then gestured outside, towards my bike. "That yours?"

"Uh-huh."

"Sweet," he said, staring wistfully at it.

"Do you ride?"

He looked at me as if I'd just spoken in tongues.

"Are you kidding?" he said; "with *my* folks? I'm lucky they let me walk across the street."

The two smirked at each other; an obvious acknowledgement of having had to endure similarly restrictive lives at the hands of overprotective parents.

This thought reminded me of the modem-less computer I'd just examined. "By the way," I said; "do either of you happen to know Josh's email address?" Then, just in case the cops had gotten their information wrong, I added: "or his cell phone number?"

They both shook their heads. "Don't think he had either one," said Paul. "Anyway that's what he told us; said his father wouldn't allow it."

"Pretty weird, huh?" said Eliot, with a fairly triumphant look which said that, at least in these two areas, they were more socially hip than Josh Sayles.

"Yeah," I agreed; "that *is* pretty weird."

As we ended our meal, I thanked them and shook their hands, saying, "So you guys are seniors this fall, right?"

They both nodded.

"Got plans for college?"

"Well," said Paul, "nothing's for sure yet, but I'm hoping to get into NYU, and Eliot has Penn State at the top of his list."

"Impressive," I said; "got the grades for it?"

Their faces said: *You've got to be kidding...*

"Sorry," I said, "of course you do. NYU and Penn State; I'd say that's considerably more of a deal than crossing the street."

They exchanged a conspiratorial look, and then grinned at me. "Isn't it, though?" said Paul.

"Sounds like you're looking forward to it."

Paul glanced again at my Ducati.

"Can't wait," he said. Eliot, standing beside him, nodded his enthusiastic agreement. A couple of misfits with a host of reasons for going as far away to college as possible.

"I hear you," I said.

Chapter Twelve

Frank Whalen faxed me the Joshua Sayles case file Saturday morning, but for one reason or another I didn't get around to reading it until that evening, after dinner. At last settling into my upstairs office chair, I picked up the report and scanned through it once, quickly, then went back and read it, a second time, far more slowly. When I was done, I leaned back, discouraged. Frankly there wasn't much in there for me to grab onto. I glanced at my still-virgin legal pad lying next to the report, and sighed.

It wasn't that the cops hadn't been thorough; they had: exhaustive forensics of the kid's room, endless interviews and follow-ups with every possible witness or lead they could conjure, blanket appeals made through all of the local media. And, as I'd expected, they'd gone well beyond my own admittedly limited efforts in terms of contacting public and private agencies and organizations; adding considerably, with their far greater resources, to the list of groups I'd pulled down from the internet. In addition, they'd contacted all of the relevant governmental institutions not available to me, including—as Denove had mentioned—the FBI's National Crime Information Center.

The problem, though, was a simple one: after two months all of these efforts had turned up nothing. In fact, I could sense the unwritten bottom line in the space at the end of the report: Josh Sayles was gone, and despite all their efforts they weren't a single step closer to understanding why he'd left, where he might be—or, in fact, whether he was still breathing—than they'd been the day the case first broke.

There *was,* I realized, one item of note in the folder; but like the report's unspoken conclusion it was notable not for what was there, but, rather, what *wasn't.* Although, like me, the police had questioned Josh's ersatz church buddies, Paul Haver and Eliot Wilkins, the answers they'd gotten from the two had basically amounted to zilch. Reading that entry, I could easily imagine their pale, nervous faces, numerous shrugs, throat-clearings and averted eyes; hear Paul and Eliot's barely audible "yes sirs" and "no sirs," as they provided only the bare minimum in responding to the inquiries. Yes Sir, we were sort-of friends—bible studies and all—but, no Sir, we really didn't know much about him. Not one word hinting who Josh's *real* friends might be, and certainly nothing about ex-girlfriends. Just a couple of brief paragraphs of adolescent don't-want-to-get-involved; all dutifully typed up, inserted into the file and then instantly forgotten.

Which made that a venue where my questions had so far yielded more fruit than had the cops; and *that* left me in possession of a possible source of information of which the police were currently unaware: the collection of "cools" from Josh's school who were in the habit of haunting the same tree-shaded corner of Drake Park every day after class. I hoped that this habit of theirs was going to hold for the semester's first day, because it was my intention to be there, waiting for them, this coming Monday afternoon. I did feel fairly confident that they would show up, though: having established their own particular stomping grounds and traditions, most kids tend to cling to them just as rigorously as adults do to their favorite neighborhood watering holes, country clubs and bowling leagues.

So should I let Denove and Whalen in on my plans?

Absolutely; no really good reason not to. It wasn't as if my mentioning these kids would immediately result in the police flooding the park with uniforms. Cops aren't stupid; they know that sometimes their best play is to hang back. My guess was that the two detectives would wait at least until I'd had a chance to talk to Josh's friends, and then act on whatever information I was able to pass along to them.

The other reason to inform them was the simpler, more obvious one: it just might help with the case.

All too often a private investigator will choose to hold pertinent information back from the cops, either to maintain some sort of perceived professional advantage, or maybe just out of sheer orneriness; a response, most PI's argue, to constant, antagonistic treatment at the hands of the police. Of course the cops will tell you that it's the other way around; that their attitudes towards them are justified, having been conditioned by years of questionable, and, often, illegal, PI behavior. My suspicion, of course, is that there is probably ample evidence to support both positions.

For my part, I generally do my best to stay out of the debate. Maybe it has to do with the fact that my best friend of nearly three decades is a homicide cop in Los Angeles, or that I've already spent a substantial chunk of my spare time, since moving to Bend, in Detective Sal Denove's back yard, sampling Oregon microbrews and grilling steaks. Or perhaps it's just that I haven't played the game long enough to run afoul of some of the more PI-baiting, asshole-types on the force. Whatever the reason, so far I had chosen to operate according to the possibly quaint notion that cops and private investigators should be able to swap intelligence without prejudice. Besides, I told myself, looking at things on a purely practical level, shouldn't it just make good business sense to cultivate the people most likely to have the dope you're always looking for?

And as a matter of fact, after staring blankly at the top page of the case file for a few minutes, I decided that what was called for at this point was a little actual face time with my law enforcement connection. I looked at my watch, decided it wasn't too late, picked up the phone and dialed

Denove at home, asking him when he answered if we could meet for lunch the next day to discuss the Josh Sayles case. Happily, he agreed to the proposition, and upped the ante considerably by suggesting that lead detective Frank Whalen join us. We then settled on a restaurant in the Old Mill District and clicked off; whereupon I then picked up the police file and read it through a third, and final, time. Unfortunately, third-time's-the-charm failed to pay off, so I dropped the thing on my desk, picked up my photo of the missing boy and his dad, and stared at it, trying to will talismanic powers from the glossy image.

*Where **are** you, Josh?*

Chapter Thirteen

"Mirror Pond, huh?" Frank Whalen's eyes crinkled from behind a fork-load of arugula, oil and vinegar dripping from it onto his plate.

"Yeah, that's what they told me."

Denove, Whalen, and I were sharing a table at Lucella's, an Italian bistro with a rear patio overlooking the Deschutes River. The restaurant was one of several in the Old Mill District; the former site of Bend's largest lumber mill, whose abandoned, dilapidated buildings and grounds had been cleverly transformed into a fresh collection of trendy eateries, clothing stores, art galleries and movie theaters while at the same time managing to retain an architectural connection to the industrial past.

Though I found this café a tad incongruous as the setting for a round of serious cop-talk, with a rather antiseptic, un-cozy modern-minimalist décor uncomfortably reminiscent of hundreds of *tres chic* restaurants I'd left behind in L.A, the two detectives were obviously enthusiastically familiar with the place and its cuisine, each of them having ordered his pasta dish without bothering to resort to a menu, while confidently recommending several other possible selections to me.

As the other two continued to dig into their salads, I glanced outside and noticed that all of the tables out on the back deck were empty, their umbrellas lowered under dark, threatening clouds, and inhospitable, chilly air. Summer had been stubborn, managing to hold its own well into the last days of September; but now, it appeared, it was finally surrendering to the inevitable falling temperatures and unsettled weather patterns of the fall. With a resigned sigh, I turned back to my companions.

Frank Whalen is clearly "Jeff" to Sal Denove's "Mutt." Where Denove is tall, thin to the point of gauntness, cave-dweller pale and reticent, Whalen is a walking, fast-talking fire-plug: short—five-nine, if you're being charitable—with the sort of tank-like heaviness of anatomy that derives from density rather than flab (my guess is that if you tossed the man into the river he'd sink straight to the bottom.) Added to this mix is a genial collection of broad, florid facial features, tree-trunk neck, thick, unkempt curly brown hair, and mild, hazel-tinged eyes which, more often than not, sparkle with amusement. And, where Denove's sparse sentences are inflected with what could be best described as a "media accent"—meaning no accent at all—Whalen's far more animated, colorful utterances are markedly flavored with southern cadence and intonation.

Two things I'd found out almost immediately about the stocky detective: as the catcher on the department softball team, he is almost impregnable—often, painfully so—in any close play at the plate; and, with a glass of India Pale Ale in his hand, he is a constantly amiable, unfailingly entertaining bar companion.

Today, however, I could see that the rigors and constant disappointments of the Sayles case had been sorely challenging Whalen's characteristic ebullience (though not, considering the determined manner in which he attacked the food, his appetite), causing him to look away at times, distracted, in the midst of our conversation. And when I got around to asking him whether they'd come up with any solid leads in the Sayles case, the detective's normal sunny demeanor turned positively gloomy.

"Leads?" he muttered. "Yeah, we got us some leads; a whole shitload of mutha-lovin' leads—friggin' desks lookin' like they made outta Post-its! A dozen new ones a day, it seems like; but most of 'em ain't worth the time it takes to write 'em up, none of 'em ever come to squat, and some of 'em...well, some of 'em are so colossally ass-brained that I can't hardly believe the jokers got the nards to call 'em in."

He paused just long enough to take a healthy sip of Chianti. "Hell," he continued, "this one gen-u-wine genius contacts us—very excited, mind you—says he was down in Los Lunas, New Mexico on a sales trip; swears up and down he seen Josh working behind the counter at a Blake's Lot-A-Burger. Even give us the alias the boy's s'posedly usin'. So we run it down. Turns out that the kid he's talkin' about is three inches *shorter* than Josh, with natural *red* hair and glasses; two years older, still livin' with his folks and ain't never been nowhere outside of the state in his life! I mean, what in *tarnation* is this guy stuffin' in his pipe?"

"Green chilies?" I offered, helpfully.

He looked at me.

"New Mexico," I said, by way of explanation.

"Yeah, whatever," he mumbled. "And, compared to the rest of the tips we got, this one looked to've had at least some kinda half-assed chance of bein' plausible. So, as y'all can see, Cassidy, what we got us here after eight long, hard weeks of po-leece dumpster divin' is a whole lotta *squa-doosh*..."

I nodded my sympathy, while masking my amusement at Whalen's use of the Italian term—obviously inherited from Denove—which sounded particularly incongruous when pronounced with a molasses-thick southern drawl.

"Anyway," he went on, "with time slippin' by the way it is, our chances of ever closin' this thing is gettin' 'bout as thin as a vegan in a slaughterhouse. Fact is: assumin' he's alive, if this kid really don't wanna be found—we ain't gonna find him." He looked at me. "Y'all got any idea how many kids split their homes and never come back?"

I nodded, remembering some of the on-line statistics I'd read.

He sighed, studying his empty fork. "Don't matter, though; until the horn sounds, we still gotta…or rather, *I* still gotta work it." Pointed the utensil at me. "So lookee here, Cassidy: if y'all got your hooks in anything worthwhile—anything at all—please bless me with it, so's that my poor wife can actually look forward to her ole man's company at supper for a change."

I looked at Denove, who merely shrugged. Habitually taciturn, he was more than willing to let his partner carry the bulk of the conversation.

Thus prompted, I then told them about my meeting with Paul Haver and Eliot Wilkins; about their informing me that Josh had been using them mainly as religious "beards;" how his real friends were the slightly unsavory crowd that used Drake Park and Mirror Pond as their daily meeting place.

"Yeah," said Whalen. "Well, now, that ain't no big surprise. Kid had to've had more friends than we knew about. But the parents were completely clueless, and I guess your two little buddies ain't been so keen on openin' up to the cops. Mirror Pond; yeah, I know 'em. We all do. Hard to miss, hangin' out there all the time the way they do. They ain't such a bad lot, really, as juvenile delinquents go. Just a bunch of over-stimulated teen-agers, bored out of their ever lovin' minds and waitin' for their high school string to run out so's they can move on to OU or Oregon State, or COCC or whatever other fine institution of higher learnin' their mommas and daddies got halfa mind to send 'em to."

"Ever interact with any of them?"

"You mean in a professional capacity?" he said. "Yeah, sure—but not there; ain't our jurisdiction. We deal with 'em elsewhere: like during the summer, when we catch 'em engagin' in the usual mindless adolescent bullshit on the river north or south of town; or maybe when we walk in on a couple'a boys'n girls doin' the ole grope 'n slurp behind the bitterbrush out there in the forest. But down at the park whatever mischief they choose to get themselves into belongs to Bend Police."

"I do know that the city boys bust one or two of that crew from time to time," he continued, after a pause; "most times for reefer. By and large, though, they leave 'em alone, figurin' that as long as the kids ain't doin' nothin' genuinely dangerous, or harassin' the civilians or shop owners, or threatenin' the ducks and geese in the Pond, they got much more important matters to spend their time on."

Our conversation was suspended for a time as the entrees arrived at our table, and we busily set about tasting the dishes, and then customizing them with the provided Italian table condiments and parmesan cheese. I had to admit, the *penne arrabbiata* they'd recommended turned out to be quite good—loaded with fresh garlic, and with a nice chili kick to it.

"So," said Denove, once we'd settled down, "I assume you've got plans to talk to these kids."

"Yeah."

"When?" asked Whalen.

"Monday," I said. "After the first day of school, assuming they show up." I looked from Denove, to Whalen, and then back. "Now that I've told you about it, you guys thinking of cutting in on my action?"

Whalen shook his head. "Nope," he said. He slipped a forkful of fettuccini into his mouth and chewed thoughtfully. "Y'all go right ahead. Five-O always seems to bring out the clam in your average teen."

"Yeah, they're all yours, Cassidy," said Denove. "We've got no problem taking a back seat, so long as you come back to us with whatever nuggets they drop on you."

"Of course," I said.

"Well, well," interrupted a loud, gravelly voice to our left; "if it isn't Central Oregon's brightest and finest..."

We turned, and beheld the vast, rotund figure of Aubrey McKenna approaching us from the front of the restaurant. Resplendent in a purple velour jogging suit and immaculate white running shoes (for Aubrey entirely inappropriate, since it's likely that the only jogging he ever does is while making urgent, middle of the night dashes to the head to drain an overactive bladder), he ambled up to our table, a saucy, jack-o-lantern smile dominating a face that gave one the impression that, as it had grown more corpulent over the years, it must also have lost definition in equal measure: small grey eyes, wide nostrils, thick lips and cheekbones, all struggling to surface above an ocean of florid, spider web-veined flesh. Adding to this dermal extravagance was a vast, unkempt riot of silver/blonde hair, worn long in back to the collar; and fleshy earlobes, each of which sported a gaudy diamond stud. His arms, because of his girth incapable of hanging straight down, seemed too short for his body, and ended in stubby, fat, gold-ringed fingers with nails professionally manicured and polished.

Despite this garish display—which had forks all over the restaurant pausing halfway between plates and mouths––I was aware of my own instinctive twinge of jealousy, and immediately chastised myself for being so damnably susceptible. Unfortunately, though, that's how you tend to react when you're still relatively new to a business, and the top guy in your profession makes an unexpected appearance.

And McKenna was certainly the top dog, at least in Central Oregon. Where I'd been fortunate in making enough money in commercial real estate to build my dream home here, Aubrey had achieved roughly the same result using the actual proceeds of a successful investigative business. I envied that: envied his warehouse full of sophisticated electronic gear, envied his efficient front office staff, envied his stable of skilled, energetic operatives; even envied his elaborate, full-sized Yellow Pages ad, which dwarfed mine and looked as if it had been hatched on Madison Avenue. That this waddling dirigible of a man was hopelessly diabetic and probably destined to drop dead of a heart-slammer before he was sixty should have been at least for me some small consolation; but…well I suppose that professional insecurity has an insidious way of subverting one's sense of proportion.

But though this physically overwhelming person's entrances were generally taken by most people as gross intrusions, and the sentences he seemed most often to manufacture were perceived as cringe worthy, at least on some level I couldn't quite bring myself to think entirely ill of him, particularly since he'd once seen fit to offer me a position with his firm back when the ink on my permit was still wet. I'd turned him down at the time, having had neither the inclination nor the economic need to go to work for someone else. And though overall I didn't regret my decision, the financial reversals I'd experienced in the past year did force some fugitive thoughts into the back of my mind, causing me to wonder, from time to time, if the man's offer might still remain open. And, aside from that, there was always that persistent itch to get a little hands-on time with some of the equipment in his back room.

But where I myself held no stronger negative feelings other than slight repugnance—and, oh yes, the envy—towards the ponderous, flamboyant PI, it was clear that my lunch mates' opinion of him veered, decidedly, towards outright animosity. Both cops acknowledged his appearance at our table with frowns and reluctant grunts, and then, looking like inmates in a prison mess hall, immediately and single-mindedly devoted themselves to hunching over and devouring their pasta.

From what Denove had told me, I could certainly understand this lack of enthusiasm. Mckenna had hardly been one to court favor with the authorities, seeming instead to derive a perverse satisfaction from getting under their skin; often showing up, inappropriately, at various crime scenes, just outside the tape but well within range of the TV cameras and microphones, where he ostentatiously presented himself as an "expert" outside observer to the media, offering unsolicited opinions, while at the same time always managing to point out that his firm had consistently compiled a better solve rate than had the cops.

The situation at our table quickly became uncomfortable, as McKenna stood there, futilely yet pugnaciously awaiting an invitation to join us—a period during which, unfortunately, the three of us became increasingly aware that the garlic aroma from our dishes was losing out to the cloying excess of the large man's cologne. Finally, though, he exhaled dramatically and nodded, as if only just then realizing the advanced state of his unpopularity, and flashed another broad, completely supercilious smile.

"Guess I must be intruding," he said. "Probably deep into some serious brainstorming, right?"

After a quick glance at my companions, which confirmed my suspicion that the responsibility for conversing with the gentleman had fallen entirely upon my shoulders, I turned to him, trying to avoid an impolite tone, yet knowing that, when taken with the looks on my companions' faces, whatever I said was more or less going to sound rude:

"You could say that," I said.

"How's it going, anyway?"

"It's going."

"Must be," he said, then sighed; "Sayles case, right? Shee-it! Nice, big greasy public affair like that. Really can't do much better, when you think about it. One lucky sonofabitch, you are, Cassidy. No way to lose, way I see it. Kid gone for good, turns up dead or the cops find him shivering his scrawny ass off in some skid row flophouse...no sweat: at worst, you put in the time, so you still got yourself a stack of juicy invoices to turn over to the daddy. But now, Cassidy, if by some lucky chance you should happen to stumble over the goods yourself—well then, badda bing, badda boom; your ugly puss is front-page and from there on I got me some serious competition."

"Sounds a little like professional jealousy, doesn't it, Aubrey?" I said.

"Might be; so what if it is?"

I shrugged. "Well, I'm sure you had your shot at it."

"I did?" he asked, looking honestly surprised. "Exactly when did *that* happen?"

Now it was my turn to be surprised. "Well, I just assumed..." I said, and then stopped. "Wait...the reverend didn't contact you?"

"Hell no," he said; "you think I would've turned that kind of a gig down? My friend, I don't turn *anything* down; not with the nut I gotta come up with every month…"

"I just figured that with your rep and that big, fancy operation of yours, you'd have been the first one he'd have turned to."

"Yeah," he snorted, "that was my thought, too."

I smiled. So gracious. But now the fat man had my interest. "What about all the other guys?" I asked.

"What other guys…oh you mean the other PIs in town?" He shook his head, in apparent wonder. "Yeah, I talked to them, too; most of 'em, anyway. Not one got tapped by Holy Joe before he hooked you up. Far as I know, you're the only dick the preacher even *called*." His eyes became slightly unfocused. "Doesn't make much sense, does it?"

"Thanks a lot."

"Aw, come on, Cassidy, you know what I mean…"

Of course I did. And because of it, now I was confused. I looked at Denove and Whalen, but both remained steadfastly unwilling to contribute. I then turned back to McKenna, and was rewarded with a shrug.

"Sure beats the fuck out of me," he said. "Anyway, it's been a ball, but I gotta beat feet to my table before my waitress sends out a search party. Sayonara."

I watched him walk away, then turned to my companions. "Any of that make sense to you? Sayles called me *first?*"

"Who knows," said Whalen, "maybe the guy thought you were the religious type."

"Did either of you recommend me?"

They looked at each other, then both said "nope" simultaneously, in a way that gave me to understand that such a notion was patently absurd. Which, of course it was; the last thing the cops want to do in the midst of a case is to suggest that they can't get by without outside assistance.

Whalen shrugged. "Dunno," he said, "maybe it was because of that deal last year at the General Patch bridge; you *did* get about a week's worth of ink on that one—"

"Well, first of all," I protested, "I wasn't even a private investigator back then. And second, if you'd read any of those articles, about all you would have gotten from them was that I managed to get myself shot up that night, while Denove here rode in with the cavalry and saved my ass."

Denove grinned, then shook his head, indulgently. "But, after all, *you* were the one who ran the killer to ground. All I did was back your play."

"That's mighty generous, Sal," I said, nodding to him; "but even if that were true, you wouldn't have learned it from anything the reporters wrote."

"Well," said Whalen, "it was just a thought, anyway."

We then turned our full attention back to the food. But as I chewed, the question continued to tug at me:

Why had Sayles come to me first?

Chapter Fourteen

Monday morning, after having seen my very-excited girlfriend off to her first day of class, I treated myself to a leisurely breakfast, then committed to an intense hour in the gym; after which I showered and made preparations for my trip into town.

On the eastern slope of the Cascades lightning storms usually strike early in the afternoon. Today was no different, and by the time I backed my Toyota 4Runner from the garage, I'd already been treated to an hour's worth of nature's percussive entertainment from inside the house, and was now grimacing as a shower of pea-sized hail assaulted the waxed finish of my car. Satchmo, an absolute coward when it comes to thunder, had dived, shaking, under the bed at the first distant drum roll, and had refused to come out, even when I announced last call before I left. I felt somewhat guilty, leaving without having given her any sort of afternoon breather, but she'd just have to hang on until Kelly got home from school.

Driving the twenty miles to downtown Bend, I was concerned that the severe weather might possibly interfere with the Mirror Pond crowd's afternoon plans; but, as I passed the red-cinder dome of Lava Butte and descended towards the city limits, I could see that my fears had been groundless. Given the distance between my home and town, and the fact that Bend sits some six hundred feet lower than my spot on the river, it's not at all unusual to experience completely different weather conditions at the two locations. As a matter of fact, several times during the past winter I'd left home in a driving snowstorm, only to arrive in town drenched in sunlight and rolling on bone-dry asphalt. Happily, today was another example of this contrast: outside of a distant suggestion of dirty-white clouds hugging the line of peaks to the west, the city's quaint civic center as I approached it was basking under a perfect, chamber of commerce fall sky.

Before I headed for the park I stopped off at the bank and deposited J.T. Sayles' retainer check. Should have done that when I'd driven in last Thursday to have dinner with the Reverend's wife, but, I'd neglected to, mainly out of long established practice. It's a quirk of mine—I suppose, at least thirty percent superstition—; the idea that if you immediately run to the bank when somebody writes you a check, you're as much as admitting that you really need the dough.

But four days was the pretty much the limit for that quirk, because fact was I *did* need the money. Besides which, making the substantial Monday afternoon deposit would also have the affect of easing a sour stomach caused by yesterday's football results (lost the Steelers game, mostly because of four disastrous Roethlisberger interceptions, while splitting the two over/under bets, thanks to an entirely superfluous forty-seven yard field goal, kicked in the last two minutes of a blow-out—bottom line: down a hundred.)

My spirits at least partially mollified by the cash infusion, I then cruised into downtown and arrived at the public lot adjacent to the park about two-thirty. I found an advantageous space on the perimeter of the blacktop which faced the park at approximately the spot where I'd been told the kids were going to congregate, and eased the 4Runner into it. Since it was still at least forty-five minutes before I figured the gang would show up, I decided to take advantage of the interval by walking a block or so over to the Goodies on Wall Street for an ice cream. I then returned to the car, trying to tell myself that a double-scoop of chocolate-chip on a sugar cone was somehow a healthier choice than a box of frosted doughnuts, while promising my conscience at least another hour of workout when I got home.

Climbing back into the driver's seat, I turned the key to *accessory,* and then inserted a "Miles Smiles" CD into the player, wondering, as I did so, if it might be better that, instead of Miles Davis, I was playing something like 50 Cent or Ludacris with the windows down and the decibels up to burnish my street cred. Unfortunately, whether it would or not the fact was that I currently didn't have anything approaching that sort of music in my glove compartment (nor at my home, for that matter.) Besides, I really didn't think an old geezer of forty-nine would be able to sell that sort of an act to the kids anyway.

As I sat there, wondering if they were, in fact, going to show up, I ran over an assortment of possible opening lines, rejected them all, and finally decided to just wait for the kids and see what happened to pop into my head when I approached them. Having thus disposed of that decision I relaxed, enjoying the view of the Pond and the accompanying sounds of Miles, Wayne Shorter, Herbie Hancock, Ron Carter and Tony Williams, while trying to make my ice cream cone last as long as possible without dripping any of it onto the leather upholstery.

Drake Park is a favorite location of mine. I come here frequently; often with Kelly and Satch—more often with just Satch, who, aside from delighting in tormenting the ducks and geese into noisy protest, also loves to wade into the water from the compact, sandy beach at the park's south end. Seldom do I find myself solo here; but when I do, I always make it a point to quietly occupy a bench for at least a few minutes, to soak up the peace and view and temporarily slow myself down from whatever I happen to have going at the time.

The public lot where my car was currently planted is adjacent to the highest ground in the park, which immediately slopes away, losing about twenty feet or so in elevation as it marches towards the edge of Mirror Pond, which is actually just a wide spot in the Deschutes River, created near the beginning of the last century when a small hydro-electric dam was constructed at what was at the time the north end of town.

As city parks go, Drake is a fairly modest swath of greenery—perhaps a hundred yards at its widest and a half mile long—which boarders the eastern side of Mirror Pond in the oldest section of Bend—an officially designated historic district of picturesque, beautifully maintained craftsman-styled homes. The park is a collection of winding, paved paths, wrought iron benches and stone picnic tables, with a concrete bandstand at its midpoint, and a rustic wooden footbridge spanning the river over to another, smaller park on the western shore. All of these elements are connected by broad, neatly manicured lawns and hedges, and generously interspersed with healthy ponderosa pines and ancient oaks, many of which I imagine must have been there long before the city was founded.

On the quiet waters of the pond armadas of ducks and Canada geese placidly cruise, fearlessly accosting people who stroll along the paths at the river's edge, in hopes of receiving tossed favors. Two graceful white swans, just as eager as the others for the breadcrumbs, also participate in the petitioning; but they seem, somehow, to be able to accomplish their begging with some greater degree of dignity.

With the ice cream all too quickly consumed, I felt uncomfortably conspicuous, sitting in my car with nothing to do but stare at passersby, so I got out of the car and made one more trip to Wall Street; this time to patronize a sidewalk hot dog vendor. Thus it was that I was returning, chomping on a Polish sausage with onions and deli mustard in a steamed bun while mentally adding even more time to my workout schedule, when the first of the cools' cars lurched noisily into the parking lot.

It wasn't much of a strain on my sleuthing instincts to make them. The first vehicle to drive up was a bright, purple-metallic Mitsubishi sports coupe; perhaps ten years old, with dark tinted windows, fiberglass ground-effects skirts, chin and trunk spoiler, and custom chrome wheels. From its twin tailpipes was belching the species of obnoxious, loud, buzzy exhaust note familiar to anyone who'd sat through a "Fast and Furious" movie, and accompanying this racket was a thudding, muddy mélange of sub-woofer powered drums and bass oozing from the car's interior in spite of the rolled-up windows. I noticed that in numerous places the tinting on the rear hatch window was cracked and flaking, and also that quite a few of the custom plastic attachments were scratched and chipped, and guessed that this driver was neither the original owner, nor the instigator of the car's customization.

Close on the rear bumper of the Mitsubishi was a slightly more subdued yet similarly dated and equipped lime-green Honda Civic, also broadcasting obnoxious exhaust noise and ponderous, low frequency music. It dutifully pulled in next to the lead car, and then idled a few minutes as its inhabitants waited, no doubt savoring the final, pulsating strains of whatever rap ballad was serenading them, before they killed the motor.

Last in line was an entirely un-customized, late-model white Ford Focus with a single occupant, which passed my car so quietly that I almost didn't notice it until it joined the others. In fact, so clearly unlike the first two was this car in its lack of noise and garish automotive accoutrements that my first thought was that its arrival had just been coincidental, until it indicated its inclusion in the wagon train by disdaining a number of more convenient open spots in order to occupy the space next to the Honda.

As soon as the tunes in the first two cars ended, the engines shut down, and an absurd number of kids began to tumble out, looking a lot like clowns exiting miniature cars at the circus: five from the first, five from the second, and only the one from the third. Leaning, casually, against my own car, I watched as they assembled and then marched off to what was apparently—both figuratively and literally—their turf: an area of green, just off the parking lot and to my left, in the shadow of a giant oak.

As they arrayed themselves at the base of the tree, it quickly became easy to identify the alpha male of the group: the driver of the Mitsubishi. Tall, lanky, swaggering—he immediately selected what must have been for him his customary, preferred location, slouching, Brando-like, with his back against the gnarled bark of the ancient oak. He then proceeded to preside over the group's activities with an expression which managed to combine theatrical paternalism with exaggerated nonchalance.

Although the rest of the kids were attired similarly, and affected much the same sort of arrogant carelessness as did this fellow, he nevertheless stood out from them, as much for his stature, extravagant attitude and extreme choice of clothes, as for the fact that he obviously looked at least two years older than any of the others.

His clothing reeked of ghetto chic: black hi-top basketball sneakers with laces left untied; black socks; black gangsta cargo shorts suspended precariously low on his hips and extending down to his calves; long, un-tucked white t-shirt, brazenly leaking out from under a black, sleeveless sweatshirt which failed to reach his waist.

Several prominent, colorful oriental-looking tattoos snaked around both of his arms, and from each of his earlobes hung a small, silver hoop. Up top his hair was dark, long and stringy, and spilled out from under an elaborately patterned black and white knit African *kufi* cap. His face was clean-shaven—aside from a rather meager soul patch, a below-the-lip effort whose sparseness argued strongly that attempts at more ambitious facial hair would probably have proven embarrassing. And, after using his naked eyes to inventory the group for a few minutes, he then hid them behind a pair of black Oakley sunglasses, which, though now obscuring the upper part of his face, somehow seemed only to accentuate the perpetual smirk that remained in view upon his lips.

The overall effect of the ensemble was evidently intended to project some species of who-gives-a-fuck slovenliness. But to me the obvious care and coordination with which the individual pieces had been chosen seemed to smack more of prissy self-absorption. It wasn't too much of a stretch to imagine that this was a guy in the habit of striking magazine cover poses in front of his mirror.

My other guess—hardly inspired—was that the kid was no high-schooler, but rather someone who'd graduated—or, more likely, simply left—the institution some years previous. And as his flashy yet decaying car seemed to suggest, this was also a guy playing out a string; destined eventually to lose his lofty social standing and influence as his minions matured and abandoned him for more productive pursuits.

But at least for now this self-satisfied *jamoke* was a celebrity, and so the rest of the kids—with one notable exception—were gathering dutifully around him; seemingly in random, careless knots, but nevertheless always with some form of orientation towards his position at the tree, which manifestly bespoke the deference accorded him. I realized that this circumstance was going to both simplify and complicate my task: simplify it, because, in order to gain information, I had only to curry favor with the one guy; complicate it, because if I didn't succeed with him, I wouldn't be likely to establish anything with any of the others.

As I debated how to go about approaching the group; and, more specifically, their head honcho, my attention was drawn to the one person who did not seem to fit the group profile. The last to arrive in her nondescript, compact Ford, the girl who had emerged was neither clad in the self-consciously sloppy uniform of the rest of the kids, nor seemingly possessed of any tendency to indicate respect towards anyone, particularly the tall, brash character dominating the scene. Instead, she evidently chose to hold herself aloof, standing at least five feet from the outer rim of the group, apparently watching and listening to all that was going on, but, at least so far, not actually engaging with any of them herself.

I studied her: she was of medium height and slender, with long blonde hair which had been braided into a single tail hanging midway down her back. Her clothes were basic, loose: jeans, work shirt, hiking boots; and there was no evidence of makeup. Strong yet graceful hands, with unpolished nails, cut short. But though she'd obviously done nothing to enhance it, her beauty was undeniable: Nordic facial features, with flawless, golden skin, pale blue eyes, dark eyebrows and full, red lips. And, as she watched the group from her self-appointed position of isolation, I could see in her eyes and turned-down smile a degree of wisdom and self-possession, along with a rather apparent etching of sadness. Her sober expression seemed to suggest that this was a teenage girl who had been forced to endure an unpleasant, premature baptism into adulthood.

Could this be Jennifer Longwell?

Knowing a bit of Jennifer's history with Josh Sayles, I was tempted to approach the girl first; but I sensed that, on some level, it would not be in keeping with the group's social protocol; and besides, if this were, in fact, Jenny Longwell, then a stranger confronting her too abruptly might have the effect of scaring her off—so instead I eased from my car and, then, threading my way, slalom-style, through the stubbornly un-parting crowd, approached the cocky, gangly leader of the pack.

And immediately found that my lengthy inner debate about conjuring an opening line had been unnecessary.

"Yo," he announced loudly, as I walked up to him; "you the dude lookin' for J. Mayka." A statement.

"J...who?" I asked.

"J. Mayk—Josh Sayles," he said, with some impatience. "You be lookin' for Josh." Again, not a question.

"What is that; some sort of rap name?" I asked.

He sniffed. "Name I gave him."

"My, my; how amazingly creative of you," I said. "My name is Hank Cassidy. And yours would be—"

"It be F-O-E-space-E-V-A-H," Each letter was pronounced with exaggerated slowness, as if he were patiently tutoring a weak student. When he was finished, he then grandly summarized:

"Foe. Evah."

Though his eyes were hidden behind dark lenses, I could feel the amusement and dare in them.

Easily resisting the impulse to rise to the guy's obvious bait by asking for a real name, I instead inquired, my voice noncommittal, "So, how did you know I was looking for Josh Sayles?"

My question produced a smug, triumphant smile. "Yo," he said; "saw you flappin' gums with the two McGeeks at McDuck's. Braced them two after you rode off. Nice bike, by the way."

"Thanks," I said, sighing inwardly. How about that; hadn't even noticed that I was being checked out that day by some kid barely out of his teens. The old senses must've dulled more than I had thought...

"So," he said, "you be havin' any luck, Mr. Pee Eye Man?"

"Just got started," I said.

He smirked. "Which mean you ain't gettin' *nowhere*, right? And that's why you be all up in here, talkin' to the Foe." He looked around arrogantly as he uttered this, and was rewarded with hoots and titters from the others.

Realizing it was probably a gross social indiscretion to trade verbal jabs with the guy, yet sufficiently irritated not to care, I shot back: "You? You. Frankly, up until five minutes ago I didn't even know there *was* a 'you.' Fact is, Big Time, I'm *still* not sure; you seem more like some sort of cardboard cutout than anything breathing."

Though he continued to lean against the oak, the man/boy stiffened, and some of the blood drained from his face. I stole a glance at the group and noticed several startled expressions, particularly among the males; I also noticed, surreptitiously, that the lonely girl on the periphery had cracked a smile. Thinking that ultimately she might be my real target audience, I raised my voice a notch. "I came here because I heard that this was where Josh Sayles hung out regularly, that he had friends here, friends who might be willing to help me find him. I'm beginning to have my doubts…"

There was some shuffling of feet, and a few whispers and murmurs. Behind the sunglasses, I could feel the heat of Mr. Evah's glare. "Yo, big man," he said, acidly, "You say you come here askin' for our help—meanin' *mah* help––but, how'm Ah s'pose to help if you be dissin' me like that, Yo?"

"Whoa…so touchy," I said, raising my hands in surrender. "All right; please allow me to retract the dis. Now, would you be interested in helping me or what?"

"What kinda help?" he asked, his voice flat.

"Nothing too complicated," I said. "I'm just looking for a little information, that's all. By you answering a few of my questions; by maybe helping me to get to know about Josh's habits and attitudes a little better, I might be able to figure out why he left, or maybe even where he might've gone."

"That's it. Just a few questions."

"That's it."

"And you think that's what happened, huh; dude just rabbited," he said, smiling crookedly.

I mirrored the smile, and shook my head. "I don't think *anything,* yet. How about you? Do you have any ideas about what might have happened to him?"

"Me?" he said, his tone becoming, if possible, even cockier, even more urban. "Yeah, Foe gots all kinda ideas, you know. But mostly Foe think some muthafucka bust a cap in the dude's sorry ass, know what Ah'm sayin'?"

Stealing another glance at the girl, I noticed that her pretty face had contorted painfully at this careless reference to the possibility of Josh Sayles' demise. *Jenny Longwell for sure.* Keeping my voice studiously casual, I said, "And what makes you say that?"

"What makes me say that?" he said; "'cause dude wouldn'a just split on his own like you be s'pposin'."

"He wouldn't?"

"Naw," he said, this time deliberately casting his eyes and his voice in Jenny's direction. "Dude was ghetto, Yo; just didn't have the stones to play somethin' that epic, know what Ah'm sayin'?" he said, his voice rich with contempt.

So *that's* how the terrain lay. My boy "Foe" here saw Josh Sayles as a rival for Jenny Longwell's affections. Which meant it wasn't probable he'd consider it in his best interest to help me find him. And with this character calling the shots, it also didn't appear likely that I'd get anything from the rest of the crowd, either; at least, not while they were standing within range of his influence. Realizing that my little fishing expedition was quickly morphing into a salvage job, I shifted gears:

"Did you happen to notice anything unusual about Josh's behavior during the last few weeks before he disappeared?"

"Unusual," said Foe, derisively; "Dude was *always* unusual, know what Ah'm sayin'? But—yeah, if you be lookin' for somethin' new about his behavior, okay, Foe tell you somethin' new: last few weeks, dude was angry— an' Ah mean an-*gray,* Yo." He looked around, addressing the group. "Fo real?" he called out, and was rewarded with multiple gestures of assent from the crew members.

"Angry. About what?"

"Name it; 'bout school, 'bout his parents, 'bout life…'bout every fuckin' little thing. Muthafucka be *trippin,*' Yo."

"How about his friends; did he act angry towards any of you?"

He caught my look. Nodded, knowingly. "By 'any,' you mean *me, specific,* doncha, Cuz?" He shook his head, grinning crookedly. "Naw...dude wouldn't *dare* get all up in *mah* grill, know what Ah'm sayin'?" Looking out over his disciples, he raised his voice. "Woulda been *tres* foolish for dude to tangle with the *Foe.*"

There were more general noises and gestures of agreement coming from the group at this comment, and I could tell from their reactions that, whether or not they actually believed the cocky leader's assertion to be true, they nevertheless felt it wise to continue to cast their lot with him. This also meant that whatever measure of favor Josh Sayles might have once enjoyed among these kids, it had apparently been largely dissipated in the last few weeks before his vanishing act.

Which naturally gave rise to the thought: *Could any of these kids have had something to do with the disappearance? Our man, Foe Evah, perhaps?*

And, as if somehow replying to my unspoken question, Foe Evah grinned at me and said: "Word up, Yo."

I was really getting tired of this guy's performance—an extremely weak, Central Oregon cartoon impression of the South Bronx. And if that weren't annoying enough, the kid kept insisting on referring to himself in the third person, a peculiar affectation I've always found particularly grating. Barely controlling an impulse to grab this character, drag his protesting carcass down the hill and toss him, carefully-constructed gangsta ensemble and all, into the muddiest part of the pond, I cast another look out to the solitary girl on the perimeter. Her expression seemed to be one of undisguised disgust at what she'd been hearing, which suggested to me that, despite my failure to get anywhere with the obnoxious chieftain and his tribe, my words weren't completely going to waste.

A loud snort brought my attention back around to the group's leader.

"Shit, dude," exclaimed Foe Evah, his inner-city inflections becoming if possible even more exaggerated as he checked his watch with a theatrical flourish; "it's been righteous and all; but it be gettin' kinda late; no mo time for questions, Yo. We gotta go; don't wanna be overdue for the Fo-Twenty, know what Ah'm sayin'?"

There were multiple snickers from the crowd as he uttered this, along with several smug juvenile expressions typical of those moments when youngsters think that they're putting one over on the old fart. I just shook my head and smiled. "4:20" had been code for marijuana since the seventies, and yet for some reason each successive generation had appropriated it, and then immediately insisted on believing that it had somehow originated with them, therefore institutionalizing the assumption that anyone older than they couldn't possibly catch on to what was being hinted at.

But it also meant that our interview was at an end. Knowing the futility of trying to get anything further from this crowd, I opted for a strategic withdrawal—no point in pushing things—on the off-chance that some opportunity to question any of the other kids individually should happen to present itself at a later date. Pulling several business cards from my shirt pocket, I handed them to the group's leader. "Here," I said, as diplomatically as possible; "if you don't mind, please pass these around. If anything occurs to you or anyone else here, anything that might help me find Josh, feel free to give me a call."

"Yeah," grinned Foe, sardonically; "no doubt."

Meaning: no chance.

"Thanks," I said, drily.

"No big thang, Yo," he responded, flashing a double-handed gang sign.

"Word," I said, doing my best to imitate the gesture, and then turning back towards my car, after making sure to cast one last significant look in Jenny Longwell's direction. As I walked, I began to consider how to make contact with the girl, wondering if she was listed, or if Eliot or Paul might have her number. I was tempted to divert towards her, but, again, I felt that an action that blatant might be counter-productive, so I dismissed the impulse and kept going, not stopping until I reached my car.

I slid into the driver's seat, then paused before inserting the key into the ignition, and stared at the Mirror Pond Crowd, and, in particular, at their badass commander-in-chief. As if sensing my look, he turned and stared back at me, then waved, a broad, sarcastic smile etched on his face. I nodded my acknowledgement; whereupon he raised his other hand, which was clutching the business cards I'd given him; then spread his fingers, allowing the cards to flutter, confetti-like, to the grass.

At that, the entire group of kids dutifully broke into laughter, as they turned, simultaneously, to look at me. So these were the "cools." My vote was that Eliot and Paul had grossly overstated the group's social relevance. To me this ragged assemblage appeared to be more like a collection of outcasts than anything resembling a popular high school clique. Of course, to two boys whose present status in that world seemed to be painfully nonexistent, belonging to *any* group probably would have constituted something desirable, and therefore worthy of envy.

That said, what was Josh Sayles doing with this crowd? Somehow the notion didn't seem to track with what I'd heard about him so far; and certainly an image of him as scruffy teen rebel didn't exactly square with the glossy photo of the well-groomed and conservatively-dressed young man currently taking up space in my glove compartment. Of course, that the photo itself might represent a false portrait hardly seemed farfetched; kids routinely strike counterfeit poses in order to placate demanding, overbearing parents. Yet after spending a few minutes with this crew and, in particular, their outlandish leader, it seemed just as hard to imagine that Josh had whole-heartedly thrown in with *them*. So, which was it: constitutionally obedient son indulging an occasional walk on the wild side? Or sullen teenage malcontent, forced, under his minister-father's relentlessly judgmental glare, to maintain a silent, obedient, and entirely bogus persona at home?

Then I pictured the boy's barren bedroom; a room so oddly vacant, so devoid of personal touches and habits, that it seemed to represent more an absence spanning a lifetime than a mere couple of months, and I began to think that the truth might be neither. Adding to that stark image the thought of a computer deliberately disconnected from the outside world, and I began to imagine Josh Sayles as a species of hyper-introvert; someone able, at least nominally, to function around peers and family, but mostly a kid far more comfortable with a life conducted primarily within the safe, tightly-defined architecture of his own head.

As I considered this possibility—fully realizing that without having actually met the kid what I was mainly doing here was indulging in gratuitous, and likely, entirely bullshit psycho-speculation—I glanced again at the group, and, especially, at the girl I was pretty sure was Jennifer

Longwell. If anybody was going to have a real handle on Josh Sayles, it would be a girlfriend—even an *ex*-girlfriend six months removed. Once again I considered jumping out of the car and catching up with her before she left; but as I deliberated I saw Foe Evah slide away from his tree and ease toward the girl, himself.

As he neared her, he flashed a broad, shark-like grin and spoke, his words inaudible to me behind the closed windows of my car. Considering the confidence he was exuding, his comments must have been loaded with irrepressible charm. Unfortunately, they were also falling on unreceptive ears, because without a word the girl spun on her heels and strode back to her car, the disdain on her face clear enough to be read even from where I was sitting. With the abrupt shutting of her car door her would-be suitor was suddenly left alone; looking foolish, awkward, and, obviously, badly in need of some industrial-strength face-saving. This he attempted to achieve by casting a malevolent look at the girl's compact car as she fired it up, and then turning back to his gang while laughing loudly and tossing off something careless, obnoxious and probably exceptionally misogynistic—given the way the males in the group hooted, while the females blanched and swapped furtive, pained looks.

Watching the girl roll out of the parking lot in her Focus, I turned my own key in the ignition, yet paused once more as the engine caught, frustration at having achieved so little with the group preventing me from throwing the transmission into reverse. Frankly, my inclination at that moment was to stick around; to wait for these kids to pile back into their jalopies and then follow them, concentrating on, of course, the driver of the purple Mitsubishi. Foe Evah's frank display of animosity towards Joshua Sayles had certainly earned for him at least a few more hours of my time and attention. Besides, if nothing else, tailing this clown would serve to indulge my own curiosity about what might be lurking behind the guy's garish costume and cheap theatrics.

But at least for today, that was not to be. Frankly, it's kind of hard shadowing people when you've just been speaking to them less than five minutes before. And it's particularly difficult following a car while driving the vehicle your targets have just seen you climbing into. Apart from that, the essential fact is that your basic SUV is generally a piss-poor tailing device. The tail was certainly worth doing; but what I needed to accomplish it properly were a change of wheels, different clothing, and a much less conspicuous starting position. For that, I'd have to wait until tomorrow.

Chapter Fifteen

I arrived home at six o'clock, having first made a quick detour to the Bulletin's headquarters, on the way back from the park, to pick up archival copies of all of the newspaper articles about the Sayles case.

Kelly was out on our back deck, grilling steaks and humming something jazzy, upbeat and entirely unrecognizable (beautiful, intelligent, witty, sexy—but she can't sing a note.) The afternoon storm having cleared out of the area, we were left with a mostly cloudless, pleasantly warm evening, the atmosphere redolent with the butterscotch aroma of ponderosa bark after a recent rainfall, the river cruising placidly by with no wind to cause so much as a ripple on its surface.

I moved in, kissed her, and in return received a smooch and robust hug which lasted a bit longer than usual; which, along with the humming, spoke of enthusiasm and high spirits, of which I was at the moment the sole and extremely fortunate beneficiary.

"Good first day?" I asked.

"*Great* first day," she corrected, her eyes sparkling.

"Tell me."

"Ah, those kids!" she enthused. "I'd almost forgotten how much fun it is to have a roomful of second graders hanging on your every word."

"Angels, every one, of course."

"Well, not exactly," she laughed. "It didn't take long to spot a couple of miscreants who should prove to be a bit of a challenge this year; and, as usual, a good third of my day was more crowd control than teaching. But I never once had to resort to tear-gas, so all in all I'd say that the launch was a rousing success."

We spent the rest of the early evening enjoying our dinner (Kelly's primarily an indifferent chef, but she's accomplished enough with a grill and a T-bone), while swapping stories about her first day on the job with those of my meet-and-greet with the Mirror Pond Social Club.

"Foe Evah," she said. "Now *that* is one hell of a moniker."

"What an act," I said, grimacing; "reminded me of that guy—Britney Spears' ex…K-Fed? I don't quite get it; this compulsion to go around doing bad Busta Rhymes impressions in the middle of Central Oregon."

Kelly smiled, shook her head, condescendingly, at me, then squeezed her nose while doing an exaggerated impression of a Catskills comic: *"What is the madda with kids these days?"*

"I don't sound like that," I protested.

"You might as well," she said. "Come on, now, Cassidy, that's just what the kids do, no matter where they're living: they emulate their heroes. At the moment, those heroes happen to be rappers. So what?" She pointed a finger at me. "Could be worse, you know. Hmm, let's see…bell-bottoms with wide belts; white patent leather boots and obnoxious paisley shirts with huge lapels; shakin' one's skinny booty to 'Kung Fu Fighting' and 'Disco Duck.' Or have I got the wrong decade?"

"No," I admitted; "That's about right—although I never owned any white boots. And I hated 'Disco Duck.'"

"Alright; so how about the rest?"

I felt my shoulders shrugging, reflexively. "Wasn't pretty—white boy's afro; I looked like a giant neon Q-Tip. Anyway, what's wrong with 'Kung Fu Fighting'?"

"I rest my case."

Sitting in my office later that night, I did my best to banish those embarrassing aural and visual images while I threw myself into the small stack of newspaper articles about the Sayles case that I'd brought home with me.

Unfortunately, there wasn't much in them.

The first article was a rather perfunctory announcement of Josh's disappearance, with the dry details—mother, father, father's ministry—and little else.

The next, dated two days later, was far more expansive, and included in-depth descriptions of Josh, his school activities, and his life at home—with a heavy emphasis on his participation in his father's church. There were a number of quotes from Josh's classmates, all complimentary, yet consistently spoken as if from an emotional distance, with none expressing anything approaching real friendship. And there was no mention at all of Jennifer Longwell—or, for that matter, of any other girlfriend, past or present. I suspected that whatever inquiry the reporter might have made into Josh's adolescent love life, the results had been consciously scotched—possibly out of deference to Reverend J.T. Sayles.

By far most of the quotes contained in the article had come from the minister and his wife. Hers were emotional, distressed, and entirely understandable; they were consistent in tone with what I'd seen and heard when I'd spoken with her. The Reverend's, on the other hand, were not, in light of my experience with him, quite as easy to swallow.

The preacher's comments to the paper had consisted largely of loud, religiously-flavored expressions of parental, and strikingly selfish, martyrdom ("Only another father can imagine the depth of my suffering"), coupled with eloquent, heart-felt proclamations about his deep, abiding love for his son. Added to this was his effusive, unqualified admiration for the superior efforts of the local authorities. And, throughout, the whole discourse was laced with fervent prayers to The Heavenly Father for "my beloved son's return."

Had I read this article without having met the minister, I suppose I might not have noticed anything untoward about this—just one extremely religious man struggling to cope with the loss of his offspring. But in light of the marginal consideration he'd shown for "the boy" on that first day at my house, reinforced as it was by Nadine Sayles' biting comments at the restaurant about her husband's lack of regard for his son—not to mention his clearly unsupportive attitude towards my own efforts while I was paying a visit to his compound—the quotes I was now reading seemed patently contrived and dripping with insincerity. In fact, it was amusing to note how much the tenor of his comments reminded me of Hollywood-style public relations; of the sort of fetid, manufactured bathos which had constantly wafted up at me from articles in the L.A. Times entertainment section.

The rest of the pieces about the disappearance were essentially follow-ups, steadily diminishing in length while increasing in interval, which spoke mainly of the frustration on the part of the police at a lack of progress in the case, and which contained only a minimum number of "We're still hoping for the best" pronouncements from the father, while nothing further from the mother.

In the end, I tossed the stack of papers aside, dissatisfied. No information to be gleaned, aside from a reinforcement of some of my previous impressions.

I leaned back. What did I have, so far?

Not much.

Grabbing a pen and sliding my legal pad over, I started scribbling, anyway.

One teenage boy, missing since ten a.m., first Tuesday in July, two months ago. No warning of his impending departure, other than some probably characteristic moodiness in his behavior; but afterward a discovery of the kid having drained his bank account—possible indication of premeditation—if the withdrawer was actually him. No sign of him since; no ransom note, no phone calls, no confirmed sighting, nothing. No evidence to suggest abduction; yet, other than the bank withdrawals, nothing to argue that he'd left on his own.

The parents: celebrity preacher father, consumed by his own massive religious ambitions, and apparently displaying far less concern for his son's well-being than he does for his own public image; the mother, similarly eaten up and distracted by her own private marital miseries, although the expressions of emotion regarding her boy's disappearance coming from her do appear to sound a far more genuine note than the father's. No indication of what the boy's relationship with the mother may have been, but plenty to believe that for some time he hasn't gotten along with the father, including the mom's description of the preacher's constant browbeating of the son, the stiff postures of the two in the photograph, and the caustic comments about the teenager coming from the father's own mouth.

I paused, then added: *But how, exactly, does any of this stuff figure in the disappearance?*

Reading this last sentence, I frowned, then stubbornly continued writing.

Both inside and outside of the family home, the teenager appears not to have had much of a life. Surprisingly few friendships: a fairly surface, mostly bogus relationship with two nerdy church kids, and what now appears to have been an equally superficial, and lately soured, association with a decidedly fringe element from his high school. Here again, one or two questions perhaps come to mind; but, overall, not much to grab onto, in terms of a connection to the case.

Some general indications of a change in behavior in the months leading to his disappearance, ranging from moodiness to outright displays of anger.

One possible adversary, so far: the redoubtable "Foe Evah;" definitely worth exploring further, though if Josh left voluntarily, this would hardly be a candidate for having aided and abetted...

One ex-girlfriend.

Here, again, I paused. As of now, it was much too soon for me to be able to jot down what Jenny Longwell's contribution to this case might be. If I was lucky, she might shed a little light on a few of the things I'd listed above. If I was really lucky, speaking with her would give rise to a few more questions; hopefully propel me in some new direction, perhaps towards more fertile territory than the arid wastelands I'd thus far visited. And aside from this, there was the hope that the girl's own, personal insights into the character of her ex-boyfriend could help me to understand him better, to at least partially resolve the fuzzy image of the boy I was currently dealing with;

perhaps explain why he might have left, where he might have gone.

"If this kid really don't wanna be found...we ain't gonna find him."

True enough, I thought, sighing. For all I knew, Joshua Sayles could be sitting at this very moment at some palm-shaded, beachside bar in Cancun, happily sipping *Cuba Libres* and making time with the local *chiquitas*.

Or he could be dead.

Which, in either case, would mean that all of the above speculation—and my efforts arising from them—were destined to come to nothing.

A question crept, mocking and unbidden, into my head: how long does a private dick remain on a missing-persons case before sheer lack of results and prospects force him to give it up?

Long after I'd ceased to bill the client for my time, I suspected.

"Knock it off, Cassidy," I muttered, sourly, and stared out the window, my eyes seeking the river, whose barely-visible water was flowing blackly under a moonless sky.

It was a question born of an annoying, professional insecurity I'd been subject to since taking out my PI license. I even had a name for it: "empty deck syndrome"––the unreasoning fear that, long before getting anywhere near the resolution of a case, I'd find that I had completely run out of ideas, of strategies, of options—in short, of cards to play. That this sort of situation had never actually arisen so far in any of my assignments didn't seem to matter: whatever I was working at, I always seemed to be dogged by the feeling that, where my far more experienced competitors would no doubt possess bottomless reserves of clever PI techniques and ingenious stratagems, eventually I myself was destined to run short, eventually finding myself attempting to deal from an empty deck.

Knock it off, I again intoned, this time, silently; *it's way too early for this kind of thinking.* And it certainly was—less than a week, in fact. There were still plenty of cards in the deck—like, for example, the prospect of an eventual meeting with Jennifer Longwell; or, more immediately, tomorrow afternoon's surveillance on Foe Evah and his minions.

Deciding that an overworked brain was responsible for my so readily heading down an unproductive blind alley, I pushed my chair resolutely back from the desk and got up. The thing to do right now was to temporarily forget about the case and spend the rest of the evening bothering my girlfriend and hugging my dog.

Or maybe vice-versa.

I headed for the stairs, hugely grateful for life's pleasant distractions.

Chapter Sixteen

Tuesday afternoon found me slouched in the driver's seat of Kelly's black Honda Accord, munching chocolate doughnuts (which aside from their obvious charms had the added benefit of making me feel like a real cop) and pretending to scan the paper while keeping tabs on the Mirror Pond gang, half a block away from the shaded spot on the side street where I'd inconspicuously parked.

Kelly and I had swapped cars this morning, and I smiled at the echo of her parting admonition:

"No high-speed chases, dammit!"

As if such an action scenario were plausible. For one thing, Kelly's car is at least two cylinders and a hundred horsepower short of anything approaching high speed. For another, once you've been spotted and your shadow turns into a pursuit, there's really not much point in continuing.

Aside from my newspaper and the box of doughnuts, I had brought along my Parks 7x50 astronomical binoculars, but for now they remained tucked away in a black leather case on the passenger seat; frankly, at the moment there wasn't much to be learned by using them that couldn't be seen with the naked eye. Essentially, all I was doing right now was waiting for the kids to head for their cars so that I could follow them. The binoculars would be for later tonight, after sundown—hopefully, once I'd tracked the gang's big cheese to his ultimate destination. Besides, I suspect that there can hardly be a more attention-grabbing occupation than sitting in a car in broad daylight with your hands and eyes glued to a pair of binoculars.

Though from where I sat the gathering looked to be of roughly the same size and composition as yesterday, I could see that Jennifer Longwell was not among them, nor was her car anywhere to be found in the parking lot. I was amused to note how easy it was to deduce this: even from where I was sitting, had she been there Jenny would have stood out in that bunch like an oboe in a jug band.

Anyway, the girl's absence was hardly surprising. I really couldn't see her dropping in daily to hang with a group with which she clearly had so little in common. She probably only appeared there just frequently enough to maintain contact with them, against the possibility that they might have heard news of Josh Sayles. Reflecting on this sporadic attendance, I felt fortunate that I'd been there on a day when she'd actually shown up. Now that she'd had a chance to see and hear me, hopefully when I did make the move to contact her she'd a bit more receptive than if the call had come out of the blue.

The kids had rolled in around three-thirty, so I'd had ample time to observe them in action, this time without the disruption to their routine that my presence had caused the previous afternoon. Frankly, though, there wasn't a whole lot to observe. Eliot Wilkins was right: the Mirror Pond Crowd didn't really do much. Idling, aimlessly, with elaborate, exaggerated boredom etched on their faces; cracking jokes and laughing far too boisterously at the punch-lines; puffing on cigarettes in the awkward, self-conscious manner of beginners; males playing grab-ass with females, with females boldly reciprocating in almost equal measure; pairs of boys squaring off in mock combat, assuming video-game karate fighting poses, and then exchanging pulled punches, poorly-executed side-kicks, and, mostly, clumsy shoves.

I also couldn't help but notice that, however any of the other kids chose to occupy themselves, Foe Evah seemed to feel no need to participate—aside, perhaps, from the standing around and looking bored part, which he accomplished the entire time without budging from his station, the base of the ancient oak tree. And, as was the case yesterday, whatever activity was occurring around him, it was always conducted with some deferential orientation, as if everything were being performed, at least in part, for his entertainment. In response to all of this, the tall gangsta leader (who, by the way, was today dressed so similarly to the way he'd been the day before that I wondered if his closet contained anything that *wasn't* black or white) seemed to feel that the sum total of his responsibilities was to acknowledge the regard being shown him with an occasional condescending nod, brief word or indulgent half-smile.

It only took a few minutes for me to appraise the entirety of this burlesque, after which I quickly wearied of the show and turned my attention back to my newspaper and doughnuts, only raising my eyes, from time to time, to make sure that the group had not yet begun to make their move to the parking lot.

At five-thirty, Just as I was working my way through the articles in the Bulletin for the third time and lamenting the meager size of a small-town Tuesday edition, the Mirror Pond garden party finally broke up. Led by their swaggering patriarch, they boisterously trooped back to their two vehicles, clumsily crammed themselves into the seats, and then fired up the engines; revving them, noisily and unnecessarily, before they began to back the cars out of their spaces.

Relieved at finally having something to do, I turned the ignition on Kelly's car, then idled quietly as I waited for the two cars to complete their left turns onto the street before I pulled away from the curb.

Chapter Seventeen

It wasn't exactly a struggle to follow them. Aside from the very convenient fact that both of the cars I was tailing were done up like Las Vegas floozies, the environment in which we were performing our dance suited my purposes extremely well. Bend traffic is ideal for a proper tail: not so busy that you risk getting stuck while your subject, a couple of blocks ahead, makes an unexpected left into the hills and loses you; nor so sparse that there's a likelihood of your being spotted as you mirror every move he makes. In addition, the streets of the city are generally laid out in a regular pattern, with numerous stop signs and well-enforced, conservative speed limits, so that if you do happen to lose sight of your quarry, it's fairly easy to re-acquire him in short order.

We quickly settled into an easy rhythm, as the procession threaded its way up Franklin Avenue from downtown toward the east side of Bend. I stayed almost a block back, it being a ridiculously simple matter to stay in visual contact with not just one, but two such gaudy vehicles. After five minutes or so, they turned off of Franklin and began to wander, seemingly without much object, along the side streets and thoroughfares on the east side of town, leading me to theorize that the group had by now commenced a rolling version of a "4:20," their rides converted into cloudy, thudding marijuana dens as they meandered through the various neighborhoods.

At last, however, after almost an hour of lazy, random turns and occasional side-by-side stops to exchange banter or paraphernalia, the two cars pulled over near Juniper Park, whereupon, with flashing lights and the characteristically nasal bleating of Japanese car horns, they split up—the Honda turned left onto Ninth Street and headed north, while the Mitsubishi hung a right, and then cruised south, past the high school football stadium. My main object of interest in today's exercise being, of course, Foe Evah, I committed to the lavender Mitsubishi, taking care to lengthen my following distance in order to compensate for the diminished cover the sparser traffic on this artery afforded me.

My quarry stayed on Ninth only a few blocks to Wilson Avenue, where he then made a right, crossed the railroad tracks, and then quickly turned left into a neighborhood consisting entirely of modest yet tidy single-story dwellings. I hung well back, as the streets around there were nearly deserted and there was much more risk of Kelly's Accord, common model though it was, becoming too conspicuous.

It was in this subdivision that my driver began to shed his passengers. Three times the purple car pulled to the curb and the right-side door swung open, disgorging a giggling rider, along with a prodigious volume of tell-tale, dirty-white smoke. At the last stop two kids exited, leaving Foe Evah as the sole occupant of his car. I noticed that each of these stops had occurred at a street corner instead of in front of a house, and guessed that none of the kids wanted to be seen emerging from this particular guy's car by their parents; which therefore added another, rather predictable layer to my profile of their leader. This was obviously a person of some fairly widespread local notoriety, which probably served a two-fold function: that of making him *persona non grata* around the folks, while substantially enhancing his bad-dude street cred to their teenage offspring.

As I waited for the distance between us to increase so that I could safely pull away from the curb, I wondered about this kid's facade: Was all of his ostentatious badness just an illusion—a tacky, mock-urban persona as insubstantial and easy to shed as those black and white clothes he was flaunting? Or might there be more to it—something more fundamental, where the threatening rhetoric and attitude might actually be matched with dark deeds?

In short: was this *bad* dude bad enough to have had a hand in Josh Sayles' disappearance?

Chapter Eighteen

By the time we reached our next stop, it was almost seven. A quarter mile ahead of me the purple hot rod braked suddenly and then dived right from 27th Street into the parking lot of an A.M. P.M, and pulled abruptly into a space in front of the store. Fortunately, there happened to be a small collection of closed and deserted shops catty-corner from the mini mart, and I was far enough back to be able to execute a quick left turn into the lot behind it without seeming precipitous; then to slide into a narrow, deeply shaded alley between two of the buildings, which served to provide me with an unobstructed yet sheltered view across the street.

As I watched, the kid unfolded himself from the car and strode purposefully to the glass front doors of the building, pushing them open, and disappearing inside, where he remained a surprisingly long time before re-emerging, carrying a naked bottle of what looked to be a cheap brand of red wine. He then casually hopped up onto the left front fender of his car, unscrewed the cap, and took a long swig, then wiped his mouth lazily with the sleeve of his black hoody. Swinging both of his legs onto the fender, he then employed the windshield of his car as a backrest as he lit a cigarette and proceeded to alternate drags and quaffs.

I was puzzling over his extended time spent inside the store—had to have been almost twenty minutes—and his excessively casual behavior in the parking lot, when the door opened and a man appeared, waving an envelope. He was heavy set, balding, and looked at least ten years older than the kid reclining on the car, wearing black sneakers, gray slacks, and a white shirt with a plastic name tag pinned to the pocket (through the binoculars it looked like

"Stan.") Wedging the door wide open—no doubt to allow him to hear if the phone inside should ring—he then approached Foe Evah, and handed him the envelope, in exchange for a cigarette, which he then immediately ignited, drawing the smoke deeply with the relieved expression of an addict too long deprived.

Friend?

Drug connection?

Continuing to use the binoculars, I watched as the younger man opened the envelope and removed a light green check, which he then studied after removing the attached pay stub.

Boss.

So this was where Central Oregon's preeminent hip-hop personality financed his wardrobe.

But though the older man was probably the kid's superior, he certainly could not have been the owner: no proprietor would ever have allowed one of his employees to loiter like that in front of his establishment; blatantly stretched out on his car, smoking cigarettes and swilling cheap wine like a skid-row dilettante. Most likely, the older fellow was either a co-worker or, at best, an extremely lenient store manager—perhaps the very man who'd gotten the kid the job in the first place.

As if to punctuate that thought, both of them simultaneously broke off their conversation and waved as a Bend Police patrol car slowed to stop for a red light at the intersection, while the kid stashed his wine bottle, in one quick, smooth movement, out of sight behind his right leg. The two patrolmen in the car returned the greeting, and then drove off, whereupon the waves from the two in the parking lot instantly turned into up-thrust middle fingers. They laughed, conspiratorially, and then the older man, having carelessly tossed his still-smoking butt to the asphalt, walked back inside the store, pulling the glass door after him.

Having procured his paycheck, I fully expected that the kid would immediately jump back into his car and drive off, but instead he continued to remain perched on the hood, drinking and chain-smoking, while occasionally casting dark glances at his watch, and then staring, unfocused, at the deepening night sky, seemingly oblivious to the other customers as they came and went. After a while, I began to recognize this as procrastination—the behavior of someone extremely reluctant to head for home. This reluctance was borne out, finally, and long after dark had fallen, in the painfully slow way he finally slid off of the hood, opened the car door, and, with a shrug and a vague gesture towards his cohort, slid into the Mitsubishi and turned the ignition.

Chapter Nineteen

I had to wait a bit before I followed the Mitsubishi back out onto 27th Street, and I was careful to do it from the parking lot behind the shops, in order to screen my movements from the kid's buddy in the mini mart. But soon I was back in the hunt, positioned two cars back, following easily and feeling a bit more secure than I had earlier. Shadowing is a hell of a lot easier to do after dark, when the only features of your vehicle discernable in a rear-view mirror are essentially the same two headlights that everyone else has. Therefore, until you and your prey end up on a deserted road, at night you can follow much more closely, with a gap of perhaps as few as one or two cars, without fear of being noticed.

We continued in this manner for a half mile or so; at which point the purple car turned right onto Reed Market Road, heading west until it once again crossed over the north-south railroad tracks. It rolled on another two blocks, and then made another right onto a side street. Deliberately slowing down, I waited at the corner before completing my turn, in order to put sufficient distance between us to keep my headlights from attracting his attention. By the time I'd accomplished it, in fact, his red tail lights were only dimly perceptible, and I had to speed up a bit to maintain contact.

We were now driving through a section of town which might, some years ago, have been primarily residential, but which had long since surrendered to the transformative, homogenizing effects of light industry. Everywhere along the street non-descript, medium-sized warehouses jostled each other, separated, here and there, by narrow driveways; with virtually nothing architecturally to differentiate them, other than modest business signs, which seemed to betoken, primarily, their involvement in various aspects of the building trade: custom windows, custom garage openers, custom screen doors, etc.

I was wondering why the kid had driven into this area when, without signaling, he turned right onto another street. By the time I reached the corner, I noticed that it was guarded by a yellow "no outlet" sign, and immediately pulled over. With my subject thus cornered, there was no need to follow him in my car—in fact it'd be way too noticeable. Time, instead, to hoof it. Reaching over, I opened the glove compartment and retrieved and pocketed my compact flashlight, then grabbed the binocular case and exited the car.

Hugging the shadows, I turned the right corner and scanned the avenue. It was less than a block long and abruptly terminated in a steep, gravel bank, atop which looked to be a railroad siding occupied by a line of vacant flat-cars. Up the right side of the dead-end street marched a line of warehouses, each dimly lit over its front entrance by a single yellow security lamp. The left side was similar in makeup, but with one notable exception.

Though most of the trees on this street had evidently been removed to make room for buildings, about halfway up on the left there remained a cluster of tall pines; dark, twisted, ghostly shapes, silhouetted against the night sky and signaling a gap in the otherwise uninterrupted row of businesses. Also, in sharp contrast to the rest of the street's gloom, a lurid wash of white light was illuminating the area beneath the trees, though its source was blocked from view by the gray bulk of an adjacent warehouse.

Keeping to the right side, and taking full advantage of a number of handy shrubs and deep shadows, I slowly worked my way towards a point even with the lighted area. I had dressed appropriately for the occasion: navy blue sweat pants; dark gray, long-sleeved Henley; black Bend

Elks baseball cap, with the bill turned backwards. Not exactly up to cat-burglar specs, but close enough, if I kept myself out of the light.

Arriving opposite the illuminated area, I then ducked behind a ragged hedge in front of a custom bathroom-design shop and knelt, pulling the binoculars from the case and finding a gap in the bush just large enough to permit a magnified view of the scene across the way.

The light, I could now see, was streaming from three rectangular, industrial work-lamps, strung high above in the pine trees, which exposed, beneath them, the sole residence on this lane: a shabby, unadorned, double-wide manufactured home, set back thirty feet from the street, its length perpendicular to the road along the right edge of the dusty lot. Three wooden stairs led up the left flank of the house to a small porch with flimsy metal railings, which apparently constituted the structure's sole entrance.

The Mitsubishi had been parked just off the street, on the opposite side of the lot from the house, squeezing into a yard already crowded with at least a half dozen other vehicles. Of these, only three looked like they had any actual shot at mobility: a battered Chevy pickup, a rusty yet relatively intact Ford Taurus, and a five or six year-old Toyota Camry. The rest of the heaps, up on blocks, were in such advanced states of disrepair that they looked to qualify for little more than last rites.

After completing the inventory, my attention was then drawn back to the Taurus, currently with its hood propped up—and to two figures; one bent over the exposed engine, the other, erect, and constantly shifting his stance, restlessly. Training my glass on them, I recognized the erect, edgy one as Foe Evah, his stature and cocky attitude now seemingly diminished by his proximity to the other man, whose features remained hidden. I could hear sporadic conversation between the two, but from this distance, it sounded mostly like mumbling—with an occasional angry *"damn right," "shit,"* and *"this fucking cocksucker"* poking above an otherwise indistinguishable mix.

Memo to self: stop procrastinating and fork out the dough for that shotgun microphone you've been looking at online...

Finally, the other man straightened up, wiped his sweaty face with what appeared to be a greasy shop rag, then slid a tall-boy beer can off of the car's fender and took a healthy pull from it. When he was finished, he belched loudly, and, still gripping the can, staggered slightly, turning and leaning his butt against the front bumper, which now allowed me to get a good look at his face:

It was Foe Evah's face—or rather, Foe Evah's face twenty-five years down an extremely bad road.

Dear old Dad.

The unintelligible mumbling continued, and now I could see that it was coming mostly, in brooding, beer-soaked bursts, from the father; while the son, his own uncertain legs riding out a squall of recently imbibed wine, stayed mostly silent.

Finally—and possibly in response to some muttered comment from the kid—the older man's voice raised enough for my ears to pick out an entire sentence:

"Getcher fuckin' lazy ass outta my sight! Fuckin' dickweed loser—goddam waste of sperm..."

Looking thoroughly deflated, the kid turned, and slouched toward the porch steps. He must've then tossed some sort of nasty parting shot over his shoulder, though, because his father suddenly straightened up and hurled the can of beer at him—with amazing accuracy, too, considering his apparent state of inebriation—striking the boy solidly on the back of the head, and sending him reeling until he smacked, noisily, against the side of the mobile home. From the trajectory of the toss, as well as the effect of the impact, I judged that the can must have been at least half full; which would give it roughly the mass of a good-sized rock. Taking in the action from my hiding place, I couldn't help but wonder how many times a week this sort of Tobacco-Road theater had been playing out. I could now certainly understand Foe Evah's earlier reluctance to head for home. No surprise, either, the boy's assumption of an alternative identity. You couldn't really blame the kid for wanting to abandon whatever name his abusive old man had saddled him with.

At that moment the door of the house opened, and a small, dark figure appeared, pausing in the doorway with only one foot extended out onto the porch. Because the figure was backlit I wasn't able to make out much beyond long hair and a feminine shape, but I guessed that it must be the boy's mother. She seemed to say something to him, because he shook his head, and then, after casting one final, baleful look back at his father, climbed the steps and disappeared around the woman into the house. The door continued to remain ajar, though, and I sensed that she had fixed her husband with some form of withering glare, in response to which he merely shrugged; then turned back to the car and, after bending down to retrieve a fresh beer from what was probably an ice chest, resumed clattering about the engine compartment. His wife stood there silently for another ten seconds, and then silently withdrew, closing the door behind her.

I continued to squat there for at least another hour, watching as the man wrestled noisily with the car's engine, while consuming heroic measures of cheap beer and alternating belches with operatically shouted oaths. At the end of that period he slammed the hood, tossed his tools carelessly into a portable metal box, arched his back with a groan and then walked unsteadily up onto the porch and snapped an outside wall switch, which doused the work lights and plunged the yard into sullen darkness. This gloom was broken, only briefly, by a dim, bluish television glow as he opened the door, and then, with one last curse and a slam, the darkness was restored for good, the various cars and wrecks lying about the yard having now been transformed into somber, indistinct shapes.

It was time to move. With the wind picking up the air had become noticeably chillier, and my middle-aged joints had long since begun to beat the Anvil Chorus from having been held too long in a crouching position. Moreover, there really wasn't much point in continuing to spend my time staring at a blank house and dark yard. If the kid did choose to sneak out later, he'd have to drive past my car, where, with my hands already on the steering wheel, I'd be ideally positioned to resume the tail. So, still taking care to move slowly and work the dark areas, I made my way back to the Honda.

Having gained the far more comfortable accommodations of driver seat, I slumped, gratefully, munching the by-now pathetically stale remains of my last doughnut and digesting what I'd just witnessed up the dead-end street. Tonight's exercise had certainly added substantially to my understanding of the origins of Foe Evah's outlandish name and behavior. From what I had seen of the father, the psychology of the kid's predicament looked to be roughly equal parts nature/nurture. Bad genes, miserable environment—two massive strikes against; and in this rigged game my guess is that you don't get three. I sat there, in the silence and darkness of my girlfriend's car, aware of feeling at least some small measure of sympathy for the losing hand the boy had been dealt.

Unfortunately, though, I wasn't at all convinced that this additional knowledge did anything to advance my *own* particular cause. Despite my now knowing that Foe Evah was leading an especially rotten home life, there was nothing in this understanding to necessarily suggest a connection to Josh Sayles' disappearance, other than to reinforce my sense that any revelation of foul play concerning Josh would automatically bolt this kid to the top of the suspect list. That said, the likelihood was that all I'd been doing tonight was spinning my—or rather, Kelly's—wheels.

But despite this general feeling of time and effort wasted, I decided to let things play out a while longer, just in case the kid did decide to slip out on some clandestine, nocturnal mission. To fill the interval, I used my cell phone to access a friendly internet poker site, where I spent the next several hours playing low-stakes Texas Hold'em—increasing my account balance, to my delight, by a grand total of eighty-seven dollars. By two o'clock, however, even the thrill of filling a gut-shot straight could no longer sustain my enthusiasm, and, so, with a sour stomach and protesting rear end convincing me that my quarry wasn't going anywhere, I yawned loudly, started Kelly's car and headed for home.

It was nearly three a.m. by the time I eased slowly into our bed, trying hard not to disturb either my girlfriend, who had her face buried into her pillow (amazing how she can sleep this way without suffocating herself), or my dog, who, having staked out the prime spot next to Kelly, barely acknowledged my presence with a raised head, and then re-settled with a low grunt and a lengthy sigh.

As I tugged at the covers, Kelly stirred slightly. "That you?" came her sleepy, pillow-muffled voice.

"Uh, no. It's Emanuel Raveli."

"That's nice," she mumbled, and immediately resumed her snoring.

Chapter Twenty

I awoke to the chirping of the nightstand phone.

Struggling to lift a soggy head feeling roughly twice its normal weight, I squinted at the clock; saw that it was just after ten a.m. Kelly was long gone, but Satch was still here—sitting upright on the bed, head cocked to one side and staring at me as if I were some sort of fascinating, alien life-form. Making an ugly face at my dog, I reached for the handset, clearing the gravel from my throat before I lifted it, and preparing to pretend, as we all seem, neurotically, to do in such circumstances, that whoever was calling had not, in fact, yanked me out of unconsciousness.

"Mr. Cassidy?" The voice was feminine, yet deep-throated, husky; decidedly mature—to my finely-tuned ears a woman at least thirty-five years of age.

Thinking that the voice might represent a possible new client, I sat up in bed, and threw as much energetic charm as I could muster into my "Yes?"

"My name is Jennifer Longwell. I was at the park the other day."

So much for finely-tuned ears.

"Mr. Cassidy?" she repeated.

Fighting off the surprise and my still-groggy condition, I finally managed to respond. "Right," I said; "Hi." Rubbing my eyes, I said; "How did you get my number?"

"From your business card," she said. "I went back after they all left; picked one up from the grass. He threw them away, you know."

"Yes, I know; I saw that," I said, recalling the contemptuous look Foe Evah had given me as he deliberately let my cards slip from his fingers. Now it looked like my offering them to him hadn't been a wasted effort, after all.

"Before we go on," I said; "I need you to tell me something…"

"Yes?"

"What is that guy's real name?"

"Oh him," she said, and laughed—a rich, full-throated, entirely grown-up laugh. "It's Weldon—Weldon Potter."

I whistled. "No wonder he changed it."

"He's a jerk," she said, dismissively. "They're *all* jerks…but he's definitely the biggest one."

"So why do you hang out with them?"

"I don't know," she said, and paused; "I guess…well, maybe…maybe I'm just hoping to hear something; or maybe I'm just hoping that—" She paused again, and I could imagine her shrugging at the other end.

"That he'll show up," I said, completing the thought; "Josh."

"Yes," she said, her voice now sounding somewhat younger.

"I noticed you weren't at the park yesterday," I said.

"I don't go very often," she replied; "in fact, I usually try to show up when Weldon's not around."

"Oh? He doesn't always hang out with the group?"

"Sometimes he has to work."

"At the A.M. P.M. on 27th."

"I wouldn't know," she said.

"He hits on you, doesn't he?"

"Yes, he does."

"And you turn him down."

I loathe him."

I smiled. "That's apparent."

There was a moment of silence. I broke it.

"So, are you going to help me, Jennifer?"

"Help you…" she echoed. "Yes, of course…if I can. That's why I called."

"Thanks," I said.

"But not right now; break's almost over, and I have to get to class. Can we talk; meet somewhere—tomorrow, maybe?"

"No problem. So where: do you have a favorite restaurant or something?" As I said it, I noticed with some distaste that with me it always seems to be restaurants.

Her voice turned decisive. "No, I'd rather not. I think something like that might not…you know, look right."

I nodded, impressed with the girl's sense of propriety. These days there are all sorts of negative connotations attached to an older man being seen dining out with a teenage girl who isn't his daughter. "Okay. Where, then?" I asked.

"I know a place," she responded, quickly enough that I realized she'd already given the matter some thought. "And it's ideal. You know the High Desert Museum?"

"Yes, of course I do."

"That's the place," she said. "There are a number of seating areas outside along the pathways where we can talk with some privacy and quiet." She spoke with a calm maturity and self-assuredness. I couldn't help but think that this was one exceptional—not to mention beautiful—girl.

So why on earth had Josh broken up with her?

"Great," I said, "the museum it is. What time?"

She paused a moment. "About four o'clock? I've got a couple of things to do after school, but they shouldn't take long. Four'll give me plenty of time to get there, even if the traffic's bad."

I had to smile at that. Your average Bend resident has absolutely no concept of what heavy traffic is really like, constantly ascribing the term "traffic jam" to situations I wouldn't even classify as minor inconveniences. In fact, it's been my observation that the busiest street in this town, at the worst time of the day, is hardly a match for *any* street in Los Angeles, at *any* time, day or night.

"Four o'clock, then," I said. "Just outside the entrance?"

"I'll be there," she said. "Gotta go. And…thanks, Mr. Cassidy."

"No," I said; "thank-*you.*"

Chapter Twenty-One

Thursday afternoon, I rode the Ducati into town early, and was therefore able to accomplish several errands—loading my saddlebags to the max with non-perishables—and still have time to roll up the hill to the museum parking lot well ahead of my appointment with Jennifer Longwell.

The High Desert Museum is an attractive, expansive facility, tucked away amid the tall pines of the forest, four miles south of Bend and a half mile or so east of Highway 97. Part historical and cultural institution, part nature center, the museum is divided between indoor and outdoor venues. The indoor section is comprised of several halls and galleries, which feature Native American lifestyle exhibits, dioramas and photos depicting the region's history. There is also a well-executed walk-through replica of a frontier town, a live display of desert flora and fauna, as well as a regionally-flavored library, reception/lecture hall, gift shop and café.

By far the greater portion of the facility, however, is maintained outdoors. Bucolic winding paths thread their way through a mature, pristine ponderosa forest, across gurgling streams, around silent pools, up gentle rises and down into shallow glens. These intertwining trails connect various venues, such as the House of Prey, with its live, feathered raptors; an authentic, working frontier sawmill; mustang corral, wildlife observation area and river otter exhibit.

Since I had some time to kill, I walked past the deer sculptures standing in the garden at the museum's entrance, passed through the doors and turnstile while flashing my membership card at the receptionist, then quickly strode through the building's lobby and exited by the side door which led to the outside area.

In the late afternoon, clouds were rolling in, though, considering their pristine, fluffy whiteness, not quite yet threatening anything serious. Nevertheless, they had succeeded in dropping the afternoon's temperature sufficiently to make me glad that I was wearing my cold weather gear.

Without any sense of destination, I slowed my pace and meandered along the paths, enjoying the peaceful atmosphere. I've been in numerous museums around the world, large and small; some overflowing with rare and ancient relics, some crowded with old masters, some merely existing as solemn tributes to major historical events. But as I see it the High Desert Museum is unique among them in that its chief attraction exists not so much in its collections of historical and cultural artifacts, as it does in the picturesque setting. If, In fact, you were to lose the main buildings and do away with all of the cultural exhibits—thus rendering it something other than a museum—I would still be content to continue to walk the park-like grounds, which seem to me especially well-suited for deep contemplation.

Eventually tiring of mere aimless wandering, I directed my steps along the path down the hill toward the otter exhibit, ducking at the end down the ramp into the below-ground observation area. There I concentrated on attempting to attract the attention of the critters as they frolicked in and out of the water behind the glass barrier. Typically independent, they reacted to my gestures by scorning me, diving into the pool, swimming to the back and then disappearing into their rock caves. I waited a few minutes for them to reappear, finally gave up, and left. I checked my watch, and saw that I now had just enough time to make it back to the entrance to meet Jennifer, so I headed up the hill.

My timing was good: I was just pushing through the glass front doors when the girl appeared, stepping up to the sidewalk from the asphalt of the parking lot and waving, tentatively, as she spotted me. She was dressed pretty much as she'd been Monday: this time brown jeans instead of blue, tan sweater instead of long-sleeved shirt, and was carrying what appeared to be an inexpensive, entirely utilitarian cloth purse with a shoulder strap. Her long blond hair, as before, was modestly woven into a single braid. I smiled, returned the wave, and waited for her at the door. As I ushered her through the gates, I noticed that she too produced a museum membership card. Gesturing towards the café, I asked her if she was hungry, but she shook her head, saying that a drink from the vending machine would suffice. I bought her one, as well as a coke for me, and we headed outside.

"You come here a lot?" I asked, and blanched. Oh man; that sounded way too much like a pickup line. *Of course she comes here a lot; she has a card, idiot!* Flustered, I wondered how you go about engaging in small talk with a teenage girl—thinking that, at least for the moment, the generational gap was feeling more like a chasm.

"Yes, I do," she answered, apparently sensing neither the clichéd quality of my question, nor my discomfort; "It's one of my favorite places. More often than not I come here, and I don't even visit any of the exhibits. I just kind of walk around for an hour or so, enjoying the atmosphere––especially on days like today, when there aren't too many people around. Or sometimes all I do is find a bench and sit. It's so beautiful, so peaceful, you know?"

I agreed, then asked, "Any particular place you'd like to sit?"

"Yes," she said, readily, and pointed across the pond to the hill on the opposite side. Over there was a small, semi-circular overlook carved into the slope, equipped with benches and accessible over a footbridge via the path we were on. I nodded, and we walked, silently, to the spot, and took our places on a bench.

"Ever come here with Josh?" I said.

Her eyes grew wistful. "Yes. We always called it 'our place'—right here, in fact," she said, indicating the seats we were occupying. "You might say it was our little refuge...our holy *sanctuary,* so to speak," she added, with some asperity. I sensed that this deliberate, sarcastic choice of words was aimed at Josh's father.

"How long have you known him?"

"Feels like forever," she said, her eyes again losing focus. "It was elementary school—I think it might even have been back in the first grade. Even way back then Josh stood out from the other kids; taller, smarter...so cute, so solemn."

I smiled. *"Way back then."* It's always a little strange to hear teenagers reminisce about the "old days." But when you're sixteen, ten years amounts to more than half your life, so I guess in a way the phrase does carry about it a certain legitimacy.

"Anyway," she continued, "we were just close friends for the longest; wasn't even until about two years ago that we actually started...dating."

"Good way to do it," I agreed; "that way you really get to know each other before you take the plunge." *God, that sounded pathetically patronizing.* I looked at her, but her face remained neutral, still lost in other times. She was silent for a minute or so. Then she turned on the bench and confronted me.

"You think he's dead, don't you," she said, the frank words and the deliberate, sober sound of her challenge catching me somewhat off-guard.

After a second I recovered, and shook my head. "Jennifer," I said, "at this point I don't know what to believe. Anyway, so far I really don't have enough information to form any sort of opinion. Besides which, if I did think...well, *that*...then there really wouldn't be much point in my continuing to look for him, would there?"

She nodded, but it was clear that she wasn't buying my logic; probably inferring more from my hesitation than my words.

"Is that what *you* think?" I asked, feeling it probably best to fall in with her matter-of-fact method of approaching the subject.

She looked away, towards the pond; then glanced at me, sideways, and nodded. "Yes it is. I think he's dead," she said, simply. Her eyes remained dry.

"Why do you think that?"

Now her stoicism began, slightly, to falter. "Because," she said, her voice pitching up, for the first time genuinely matching her years, "he never even *called* me. I mean, I know that we're not...you know, *together*, right now; but we were still supposed to be friends—the *best* of friends. He would never have just run off like that, not without first contacting me, or at least getting in touch with me later, when he got to wherever he was going." Two fingers massaged her right temple. "He would've known that I'd be worried..."

It made sense, if they'd truly had the relationship she was describing. I reflected: that now made it three people who suspected various flavors of foul play, though each for entirely different and purely personal reasons. The preacher, because he couldn't accept the idea of his son defying him so willfully by leaving on his own; Foe Evah (oh *come on,* now—Weldon Potter!), because such a violent scenario dovetailed so nicely with his ultra-urban, ultra hard-boiled view of the world, as well as it did with his obvious desire that his chief rival should no longer be drawing breath. And now there was Jennifer Longwell, whose reasons for supposing that her ex-boyfriend had met with ultimate violence seemed to me the most practical, logical and convincing. Only the police seemed to feel otherwise, and their grounds for thinking so were probably just as self-serving. If the kid turned up alive, then their efforts would be deemed successful. But if he were dead, public opinion would likely find a way to lay at least part of the blame at their feet.

"Look," I said, putting a hand on her shoulder. "Let's not be thinking that way. Maybe Josh *did* leave on his own, is safe somewhere, and he's got some good reason for not contacting you—just yet."

Though doubt still clouded her face, she looked up at me. "Do you think that's what it might be?" she asked, a small tremor of hope creeping into her voice.

"*Might* be," I cautioned. "No promises, mind you, but let's at least for now operate under that assumption. Now, in order for me to guess at where he might have gone, I first need to understand *why* he would have wanted to leave; his state of mind at the time. I've asked his parents and his other friends, and none of them seem to have any good answers for me. When it comes down to it, I think you might be the only one who knows him well enough to answer that question."

I could see by the pleased look on her face that I'd said the right thing.

"Yes," she said, "I'm sure that I knew...that I *know* Josh better than anyone. Even his parents," she added, with some bitterness. "*Especially* his parents."

"Good," I said. "Now, the first thing I'm looking for is any sudden change of behavior, of mood. A couple of people—even your friend, Weldon (she smiled at that)—told me that he *had* changed; that he'd become angry and combative. Was that true?"

"Yes," she said, sadly; "he had changed."

"Can you trace it back; maybe identify the time when that change may have occurred?"

She nodded without speaking, and I knew exactly where her thoughts had traveled.

"Listen, Jennifer," I said, gently, then paused. "Which do you prefer; 'Jennifer,' or 'Jenny'?"

She shrugged. "Jenny's fine."

"Okay," I said. "Anyway, Jenny, I know this isn't going to be easy, but I've got to know: You and Josh were boyfriend and girlfriend for what, a year and a half?"

"Yes," she said, her eyes fixed on the bench, seeing nothing. "We were."

"And then it ended, right?"

Still avoiding my face, she said: "Yes, it did. It ended."

"Who ended it?" I knew the answer, but I thought it best to at least give her an out.

She didn't take it.

"Josh did," she said, simply.

"But why? Had you been fighting?"

Looking directly at me, she said: "No, no...it was nothing like that; nothing like that at all. We were getting along fine the whole time, right up until the day he...broke it off."

"You were."

"Uh-huh," she said. Then her face reddened, and she averted her eyes. "In fact, we'd kind of gotten to the point where we were talking about..." She waved a hand, helplessly. "We were..." she paused again, lowered her voice. "We were both still virgins, and...well, you know..."

"I understand," I said. "The two of you were thinking about taking a big step."

At that moment an elderly couple strolled by, temporarily suspending our conversation, and causing us, reflexively, to simultaneously behave as though the entire focus of our interest was in the sights and sounds around us. Self-consciously, I was glad, as the people passed, of the couple of feet of space which currently separated Jenny and me on the bench. We continued our silence until, after casting a brief glance our way, the couple pushed on, and headed up the hill towards the sawmill exhibit.

"Yes," she said, as soon as they were far enough away.

"Yes, what?"

"We were about to take a big step—*that* big step."

"But you never did."

"That's right," she said, with regret, "we never did. Josh broke up with me before it... before we did it." Her face darkened at the memory. "It was maybe six or seven months ago. He came to me, said he'd given it some thought, felt it might be wrong at this point for us to push things 'over the line,' as he put it. Meaning the sex, of course. Then he suggested that maybe we should cool the whole thing for a while." She paused, her face now on the verge of crumbling. "It hit me like a ton of bricks. I couldn't accept it, so I asked him if we could still be friends—hoping that maybe this was just some mood...some sort of thing he was going through; that he'd get past it and then we could get back together after a few days or maybe even weeks. He said sure, we'd always be friends. But, then, after that..." She shrugged.

"Do you have any idea why he broke up with you?"

"No," she said, anguish suffusing her face; "I don't. At all." She looked off, across the pond, at distant, unpleasant memories. "That's just it: to this day I have no idea why he broke up with me. I tried to get him to talk, too many times; but he just wouldn't open up. But, you know, that's the thing with Josh: he's always been kind of inward—kind of mysterious." She smiled, wanly. "In a way, maybe that's one of the reasons I was attracted to him. But it also meant that when he broke it off, I was left without a clue. I think about that all the time; trying to figure out what I might have done, or said, or"— She looked at me—"I guess that's what you do, isn't it?"

"Yes," I said; "that's exactly what you do: without any sort of good explanation, you instinctively take the blame to yourself, and then you wrack your brain for whatever it was that you were guilty of, hoping that if you can find it and then correct it, they'll come back and it'll all be the way it used to be. The problem is, though, the reason you can't come up with anything, is simply because you didn't *do* anything. You weren't the one to blame, and in a way that's the worst, because that means there's nothing you can do to fix it."

The look on her face told me that I'd hit the mark; it read equal parts surprise, gratitude, and resignation. "I guess you've been there," she said.

"Me? Yeah, of course I've been there. At my age, I've been dumped lots of times." I chuckled. "Although in most of those cases the reasons weren't exactly a mystery: my exes always seemed to be more than willing to tell me exactly where I'd blown it."

Smiling shyly, she said, "And were they right?"

I grimaced. "More often than not, I'm afraid. Although that's something strictly between you and me: not a word to my girlfriend, *please*."

"I promise," she said, with a small laugh.

"So," I said, "after you guys broke up, did you continue to be friends?"

"Yes, we did," she said, her smile disappearing. "But it wasn't easy—at least, not for me. See, from then on, whenever we were together, Josh seemed to be doing his best never to slip up in front of me; always kept his comments short—friendly, but kind of distant. And polite...always so freaking polite." She shuddered. "You know, I think that might have been the worst thing about it; when someone you've been so close to, so comfortable with, suddenly starts to treat you so politely..."

I nodded, startled at hearing a teenager give voice to a sentiment I'd always considered exclusive to adults. As much to myself as to her, I said: "Yes; they think that by treating you that way they're showing you some consideration, but all *you* feel they're doing is insulting your intelligence."

"Exactly," she said, studying my face. "I'm really glad I decided to speak with you today."

"I'm glad, too, Jenny. Anyway, I guess with all that 'politeness' you never had a chance to find out what was bothering him before he disap—"

"No," she said, interrupting me. "Actually, I did...not about us, I mean. But Josh *did* come to me—once, towards the end; and that's really why I wanted to talk to you." She hesitated. "But now that we're down to it, I'm not sure that it's right for me to—"

"Jenny, look," I said: "right now, I think that you and I might be the only two people capable of finding out what really happened to Josh. But in order for that to happen, you can't shut down on me now; you've got to tell me everything—and I mean *everything*—that you know."

There was a long pause, and I became aware of the harsh sounds of the blue jays in the distance, the breath of the freshening breeze as it filtered through the trees, and the forlorn croaking of a solitary chorus frog, perched on a rock at the edge of the pond below us. Then the girl sighed.

"Okay," she said, "I'll tell you. One day, maybe two weeks before he dis...before he went away, Josh came to me, really upset."

"About what?" I prodded, gently.

"He said he'd caught his mom cheating."

"He did? How'd he find out?"

"He said that she'd begun to act strange around him, and that made him suspicious; so one day he took the family truck and followed her." She looked at me, then added, significantly: "To a motel. The Bluebird, in La Pine. You know it? You do."

"Yes, I do; and he saw her there with someone?"

"Yes." She shivered. "God, he was so miserable."

"Did he get a good look at the man she was with?"

"The man she *met* there, you mean. Yes, he did. Said he was a short guy, but tough-looking; some kind of low-life cowboy type—pointy boots, crummy old sweat-stained ten-gallon hat and all. Drove up in his own pickup; Josh said it was a real rust bucket. In fact, he was pretty sure that his mom was the one who paid for the room, because the guy sat in his truck while she went into the motel office."

"And he was sure of what they were doing there?"

"Yes," she said, frowning; "he was sure. He waited across the road from the motel, behind some bushes, until they came out of the room a couple of hours later. Saw them kissing and hugging; said they were all over each other. He even told me his mom was still buttoning up her blouse when she came through the door." She shook her head. "I felt so bad for him. He was *crying;* I'd never seen Josh cry before…"

"And you say this happened two weeks before he disappeared."

"Yes."

"Sounds like a pretty good reason for wanting to run away," I said.

"Yes," she said, "I thought so too, at the time—at least, when he first disappeared. But then he never got in touch with me and after a while…" She gestured, helplessly.

"Did he consider telling his father about what he'd seen?"

"The *Reverend,*" she snorted, making the word sound like an epithet; "I *doubt* that. Anyway, he sure never mentioned it to me. The truth is, Mr. Cassidy, Josh really didn't have much use for his dad. I don't think he would've cared one way or the other if his father found out about what his mom was doing. Besides, he'd told me a long time ago that his parents hadn't shared a bedroom practically since he was born. Said he really doubted they'd even had sex since then, either. In fact,"— she lowered her voice, though there were no longer any people within fifty yards of us—"he once told me that he thought his father might be…you know…gay…"

Gay, I thought. Certainly plausible. Wouldn't be the first case of a holy man practicing what he was preaching against.

"Really," I said, carefully noncommittal. "Had Josh ever seen anything to make him think that?"

"No," she said quickly; "nothing like that. It was just…well, when your father and mother never sleep together, I guess it kind of makes you wonder."

"Sounds like the sort of thing that might not go over too well with the Reverend's congregation, doesn't it?"

"Yes," she said, "I guess so. If it's true. But, as I said, Josh never actually saw anything; it was just a feeling he'd had. Maybe he was wrong; maybe his father is just not interested in…maybe he's—"

"Asexual?"

"Yes," she said, "that's the word. Asexual. But it sure as anything looks like his mom isn't, doesn't it?" She gazed at the ground. "Though I guess you really can't blame her, all things considered."

It was getting harder and harder for me to accept that I was having this kind of conversation with a youngster. Jenny Longwell was one girl matured miles beyond callow youth. And I also couldn't help but notice that not once during the entire conversation had she resorted to the standard juvenile practice of inserting the word "like" into every sentence. I remembered that the same had held true the other day for Paul Haver and Eliot Wilkins; but in their case I had credited it—perhaps unfairly—to their forced internment in the dweeb's bubble, where, with little peer interaction, there was a lot less chance of their picking up the usual verbal idiosyncrasies of the other teenagers. With Jenny, however, I sensed that this avoidance of lazy verbal expression was something she had consciously worked on. And, from the apparent ease with which she seemed to form her sentences, she had succeeded.

"No," I agreed, "if what you say about his parents' relationship is true, then I suppose you can't blame the Reverend's wife for stepping out from time to time. But it certainly appears that Josh did."

"Yes," she said, thoughtfully, "he sure did. But I guess it's one thing to…to sit around and speculate about what might be going on between your parents, and another thing entirely, watching your own mother coming out of a crummy motel room with some loser…" She looked at me.

"Yeah," I agreed. "Pretty nasty dose of reality."

Averting her eyes again, she said, "You know, actually, when he told me about it, I kind of hoped that maybe the shock might cause him to—"

"Get back together with you."

She blushed, then nodded, eyes downcast. "Yes. Pretty selfish thought, huh?" She looked out at the pond, shook her head, sadly. "Doesn't matter though, because two weeks later Joshua was gone, and…and…"

The tears had begun to flow freely, now. Like a lawyer with a distraught witness on the stand I felt that, though I still had several more questions to ask, we had gone about as far as we could today. As I watched her sobbing, I wanted to draw the girl to me, hug the tears away; but I was acutely aware of the interpretations such an image might invite, so I confined myself to reaching out and rubbing her shoulder. She initially tensed at the touch, then relaxed, and eventually the tears subsided and she looked at me.

"I'm sorry to have to put you through this, Jenny," I said.

"No," she said, sniffing and reaching into the cloth purse for a Kleenex, "it's okay; really. I wanted to talk to you, and I'm glad I did. I think you're right: we're the only two who might have a chance to solve this thing, and I'd hate to have to spend the rest of my life wondering if there'd been things I could have done to help, but hadn't. So, if anything I've told you today helps you to find him"—her gaze shifted back to the pond—"one way or the other…then it'll have been the right thing to do. And if there's anything else you want to ask—"

"I'm sure there will be, Jenny," I said; "but, for now I think that's about all I've got." A lie, we both knew, but an appropriate one at this point.

Despite all of her brave talk, the girl's expression clearly showed relief. "Okay," she said, then again reached into her purse. "Here's my cell number," she said, pulling out a piece of paper with the number already written on it, and handing it to me.

"Thanks, Jenny," I said, folding, and then slipping the paper into my jacket pocket. "By the way, did Josh have a cell phone?"

Her headshake was emphatic. "No, he didn't; never wanted one. I guess you could say he was kind of odd that way: used to say that he hated the idea of always being reachable." She hunched her shoulders. "Though sometimes I think the real reason he was saying it was to cover his embarrassment that his father wouldn't let him have one."

"So, no cell phone, no texting, no email?"

She smiled. "No. Once in a while, if he absolutely had to make a call, he'd just borrow mine. But he never had his own, and he never had an email address—in fact, I don't think his computer was even connected to the internet."

That, I knew, was true enough. And what Jenny was telling me was more or less a confirmation of what I'd already seen and heard. But coming from the person who'd probably known Josh Sayles best it also argued forcefully against his having indulged in any sort of electronic communication on the sly. And, that, in turn, appeared to eliminate any possibility of using that avenue as a way to track him down.

My disappointment must have shown on my face, because Jenny looked at me, and then smiled, and said: "I guess that sounds like a pretty strange attitude for today's typical teenager, doesn't it?"

"Yes, it sure does," I agreed. "But, you know, if in fact that's really how Josh felt about things, in a way it might explain why he'd want to run off to some place where nobody could reach him."

"Yeah right," she said, sadly; "*nobody*. Including *me…*"

"Yeah, I know," I said; "whatever his reasons might have been, it wasn't fair to leave you in the dark like this. But like I was saying before, maybe he just needs some time to get settled in before he contacts you."

"I hope so," she said, without conviction. Her shoulders then slumped, and I knew it was past time to wrap things up.

"All right, Jenny" I said, rising, and attempting to inject some cheer into my words; "let's you and I keep a positive thought, okay? I've got your number. If I think of anything else I need to ask, I'll call you."

"Good, thank-you," she said. She stood, dabbed at her eyes with the Kleenex, then leveled them at me. "And, even if you don't...I mean, even if...well, no matter what, you'll call me, anyway?"

I knew what she was getting at. "Yes, Jenny, I will...one way or the other."

"Thank-you."

I smiled.

"You're a heck of a girl, Jenny."

Beneath drying eyes, she smiled back.

"Yes," she said, "I know."

Chapter Twenty-Two

I headed home, and, noticing that the clouds had darkened considerably, rode a bit more aggressively than normal to head off a possible storm, arriving at the house just short of six o'clock. Pulling into the garage, I parked my bike as close to the wall, and as far from Kelly's car, as possible. Fortunately Kelly is the cautious sort and so far there'd been no paint exchanges between driver's door and bike. Still, it paid to be careful.

I hung up my helmet on the wall rack, retrieved the goods from the saddlebags and then headed for the door which led from the garage, past the washing machine and dryer in the utility area, into the great room. At this hour I fully expected to find Kelly planted in front of her laptop in the dining area, wrestling with her lesson plans, while waiting impatiently for dinner preparations to begin (for the most part, by mutual agreement proprietary duties in the kitchen had been relegated to me.)

But, aside from Satchmo enthusiastically greeting me before I'd made it through the doorway, the house was silent: no mellow, dissonant strains of jazz wafting towards me from the media center speakers on the far side of the great room; no determined tapping coming from Kelly's keypad on the dining table; no distant call-outs of "It's about time!" reaching my ears from anywhere, downstairs or up.

"Kelly?"

After a quick glance out into the backyard, I made a sweep of the ground floor, then climbed the stairs, and looked into the master bedroom, the guest room, and my office. I'd noticed, since we'd gotten together, how much larger my house always seemed when she wasn't there;

today, the place felt positively cavernous. I returned downstairs and, on an impulse, walked over to her laptop.

The machine was humming. On the screen schools of colorful cartoon fish swam in lazy, somnambulant circles, the screen-saver indicating that Kelly had been away from the computer at least ten minutes. I jogged the touchpad and the fish disappeared, revealing the expected view of her school work.

I stepped into the backyard, and made a thorough scan, looking along the banks far up-river and then down, thinking that she might possibly have been drawn outside by some rare wildlife sighting, or just a need to stretch her legs a bit. No luck. I then checked both sides of the house, as well as the front, again without result.

So where was she? Visiting a neighbor? Possible, although unlikely; frankly, Kelly and I had not done much in the last year to multiply friendships in our small community, and the few friends we did have in the area were currently out of town. Beyond that, it is more or less an unspoken rule that around here neighbors don't just drop in on each other, a custom which suits us, with our passion for privacy, just fine. Besides, of the two of us, Kelly is by far the least apt to impose upon an unfamiliar neighbor.

Had she just slipped out for an impromptu walk?

Without Satch?

No, I realized, glancing down at the dog, who was sitting by one leg of the table and watching me intently. That sort of notion didn't make any sense at all—seemed, in fact, tantamount to a gross dereliction of duty. In this household, you never passed up an opportunity to let Satchmo burn as much energy as possible out on the forest trail, thereby making more probable the luxury of a full night's sleep without the intrusion of an early-morning, canine alarm clock.

And yet Kelly wasn't here, and there was her still-running computer, the screen reflecting a ghostly image off of the window behind it.

It was the computer which bothered me more than anything else.

I freely admit that I'm an inveterate order freak; in fact I often credit this need to create order out of chaos as one of the driving forces behind whatever modest success I've achieved so far as an investigator.

Next to Kelly, though, I'm a piker. In addition to easily matching my mania for order, Kelly Wilhoit is a woman beset by a virtual legion of neatness demons (always amusing to watch her stubbornly battling the June pine pollen for control of the house windows; endlessly dusting the furniture, shelves, and audio equipment; trailing after Satch, shaking her head at what has just been transferred from outdoors to in while wielding her mop like a samurai—as well as being consumed by a Midwesterner's preoccupation with practicality and frugality, which has her obsessively running around shutting off unnecessary lights and noisily tsk-tsking my carelessness.

And when it comes to her computer, Kelly is particularly fastidious about not wasting energy, never even allowing the thing to sit idle long enough for the screen-saver to make an appearance. This severe electronic discipline has come to infect my own workstation habits, causing me to feel uncomfortably guilty about taking a bathroom break without having at least taken the minimum step of putting the monitor into "stand-by" mode.

And that's why, standing there, staring at the blatancy of her laptop screen image, every alarm in my head began to heat up.

Something had interrupted Kelly as she'd sat pouring over her school work; something which had evidently agitated her so much that she'd dropped what she was doing and run out of the house, in the process forsaking a virtual lifetime of hard-core habits.

My stomach churning much more than I cared to admit, I walked over to where the most likely source of this upset was to be found sitting on a stand against the wall, and lifted the cordless telephone handset from its cradle. The screen immediately lit up, and I could see that several items had yet to be erased from the caller ID log. Pressing the menu button, I scrolled down. Most of the numbers were innocent enough and spread out over the last two or three days, the next to last call being, in fact, from my own cell phone, some time earlier, when I'd checked in to ask if there was anything she needed in town while I was running errands.

But the final call on the list didn't seem quite so innocent. With a time stamp indicating that it had been received just over an hour ago, the item read: "out of area," meaning long distance with the number blocked.

Certainly there could have been any number of innocuous explanations for this call: solicitation; out-of-town friends checking in; prospective private-investigation clients—maybe even a wrong number.

But it couldn't have been a client, because Kelly would've jotted something down, and the note pad next to the phone was blank. Nor, by the same reasoning, would it have been one of my out of state buddies. And as I stood there, my growing paranoia convinced me that this entry referred neither to a phone solicitation, nor to one of

Kelly's friends or a wrong number. It was this long distance call, I felt sure, which had chased Kelly from our home.

And from that anxious assumption, it was a mental excursion of perhaps a second and a half to settle upon the likely owner of the blocked-out phone number:

Kelly's rat-fuck of an ex-husband, Jack Melcher.

That he knew how to reach her was no mystery: they'd had a couple of contacts, in the last year, about resolving various paperwork issues left over from the divorce. Even in those instances, both having been brief and purely routine, Kelly had come away distracted and blue, and had not managed to shake herself loose from her funk until several hours had passed. At those times I'd taken care not to press her, as it seemed obvious that what she'd needed most was simply to be left alone.

But if it were, in fact, true that this caller ID entry *did* represent a conversation between Kelly and Jack, the mere fact of Kelly's current absence, along her uncharacteristic abandonment of her computer, told me that something far more serious had taken place on that phone than a mere sorting out of legal documents.

Fighting a feeling of helplessness, and irritated that Kelly had left Satchmo overdue for an afternoon walk, I pulled the leash from the wrought iron wall hook and set out from the house with the dog. At the end of the driveway, I deliberately turned right, towards the highway and the trailhead which led towards the river path, and which, I judged, was the most likely direction Kelly would have chosen.

Once on the trail and moving away from the highway, I unhooked Satch's leash, and watched as she sprinted down the path ahead of me. I followed her, barely conscious of the threatening afternoon weather, the interplay of light and shadow along the path, or the brief glimpses of miniature life scurrying in and out of the dense undergrowth around me as I walked; my mind was far too overheated with a range of possible unpleasant scenarios concerning Kelly and her ex-husband. As I reached the place where the path curved southward to align itself with the river, I could hear my dog happily splashing in the shallows. Satchmo's not much of a swimmer, but she's crazy about water.

I tried to calm myself; tried to tell myself that I was overreacting, and that I would find that Kelly had merely OD'ed on schoolwork and had gone for a stroll, this one time having committed the careless but eminently forgivable act of having left her computer on. Nothing deeper; nothing more serious than that.

Tried, but failed. As Satch noisily rejoined me on the trail, I was once again reminded that Kelly had overlooked more than just her laptop—she would never have so cavalierly left our dog in the house. Maybe it was purely my own neurotic anxiety, but I *knew* something was wrong, and I *knew* that it had to do with Kelly's ex.

Ten minutes later, Satch found her.

She was seated on a log at the base of a low bluff, staring disconsolately at the silent water as it flowed past her. As the dog sprang down the bluff towards her, Kelly looked up, and, even from this distance, I could see that she'd been crying. Wiping her dark eyes self-consciously, she turned away from me, towards the river, and her shoulders hunched, as if fighting a sudden, imaginary chilling breeze.

I made my way down to her, and then sat on the log, a respectful three feet away, and stared, as she did, at the dark current, noting the occasional fugitive circlet blooming on the surface of the water as sparse raindrops began to fall. Satch, with unerring instinct, kept her distance, and contented herself with continuing to wade in the shallow water, pausing now and then to glance at Kelly, as if to assure her that she was available if needed.

It was several minutes before she spoke. "Hi," she said, tonelessly, without looking at me.

"Hi."

"Sorry."

I glanced at her. "For what?"

She shrugged. "I dunno. For...this." She waved a hand, vaguely, at her tear-streaked face.

"Want to talk?"

"No...yes...I don't know." Again she shrugged, and fresh tears appeared, threading down both sides of her nose towards her lips. I moved closer, and put a tentative arm around her; felt how knotted and tense her muscles were.

"I'm sorry I took off without letting you know where I was going," she said.

"It's alright, Honey," I said, stroking her back. "I was just a little concerned, you know?"

She leaned into me, her head finding my shoulder. "I'm so confused."

"What is it?"

"He...he called."

"Jack."

She nodded.

I inhaled, not knowing whether I wanted to hear the rest of this. But you can't hold your breath indefinitely. "What is it?" I asked, as the air escaped my lungs.

"He's sick," she said.

"Sick?"

"Very sick; he's got cancer—pancreatic cancer." She looked away. "He says that...he says that he needs me."

I sighed. I felt as if the log I was sitting on had just been uprooted and dropped onto my chest.

"So, are you going?" I managed.

"Me? No," she said, quickly; "I mean...well, I don't know—"

"Kelly. Do you still love him?" It was a question I loathed to ask; one whose answer I feared, even more, to hear.

This time, though, Kelly looked right at me; searched my face, my eyes, raised her hand and stroked my cheek. "No, Hank," she said, with a small, tired smile; "of course I don't love him." Patting her chest, she added, "I've only got room for one man in here, and that's *you,* my sweet."

I felt the log partially lift from my lungs, then said: "That's reassuring. But you *are* thinking of going down there, aren't you?"

Dropping her hand, she nodded. "Yes," she said; "I guess I am."

"But why? And what about your job?"

"Don't worry," she answered, this time firmly; "I'm not going to throw everything away because of him. If I go, it won't be until next week-end, and I won't stay any longer than Sunday."

"And after that?"

"After that," she repeated, slowly, chewing on the words. "I don't know; maybe I'll have to spend a few week-ends there. Not many. I don't know..." Her voice trailed off. "He was my husband..."

"Yes he was," I said, trying to control my temper; "he was your husband and he *beat* you."

"Yes," she said, "he beat me, he humiliated me and then he dumped me. But now the man's sick, he may be dying and he's got no one else to turn to."

"You don't owe him a thing, Kelly."

"I *know* I don't," she insisted. "With all he's done to me, I know that the bastard deserves to spend his last hours in a cold, dark room with no one at his side. But I don't know that I have it in me to let him go out that way. I don't love him anymore, but there's still at least *some* kind of connection—"

"Yeah there is," I said, as gently as possible. "There's still a connection because you weren't the one to sever it."

That produced another tired smile. "Hank Cassidy: always so good at getting right down to it. Yes, I suppose that's the largest part—and because of it there still remains a remnant of me; a small piece of a young, insecure girl who once allowed herself to be dominated by the wrong man."

"And you're going to give in to that remnant now?"

"No," she said, slowly, her eyes turning inward; "not exactly. Maybe what I need to do is to go down there; to give him some of the support he needs...but also to face him—face myself—so that I can once and for all deal with this thing that's bothered me for so long. Deal with it and put an end to it for good, and then walk away from him on my own terms. Maybe that's what I need..."

Noble words, but delivered with a marked lack of conviction.

I took in one more, large breath, then let it out slowly. "Okay. Obviously I'm not going to attempt to stand in your way; if you really think you need to do this, then that's how it's got to be. But, look, you've still got a week. Don't make any decisions right now; give yourself a chance to think about it before you commit. After that, whatever you decide to do, you know I'll support you." Also noble words; I only hoped that my own lack of certainty hadn't been nearly as obvious as hers.

"Thanks, Sweetheart. I really needed to hear that," she said, pulling me to her and kissing me full on the lips, with just enough warmth and pressure to roll most of that log from my chest. Then she jumped to her feet and slapped her forehead. "You know what?" she said, "I think I left my computer on! Son of a bitch!"

Despite everything, I had to laugh.

Chapter Twenty-Three

Friday morning, having risen uncharacteristically early, I surprised Kelly by volunteering to take care of the morning dog-walking duties, and then headed out towards the forest with Satch.

Once we'd gained the trail, I released my dog, then pulled out my cell phone and called my long-time friend, Cyrus Brooks, in Los Angeles.

It was seven o'clock, and, as I expected, I found Cy already at his cubicle, downtown at the new LAPD building. The veteran homicide detective sounded harried as usual as he barked "Brooks" into my ear.

"Hey, Cy," I said.

"Well now," he said, amusement quickly supplanting his standard, hassled-cop phone persona; "if it ain't m'brutha from anutha mutha."

"Come on," I groaned; "that is *so* last week."

"Last *century,* actually," he corrected; "but appropriate, just the same."

True enough. Our comradeship, originally forged, decades ago, in our close collaboration working for the government, has progressed, over the years, to the point where these days we tend to behave more as siblings than mere close friends. As Cyrus is so fond of alliterating, "Aside from the fact that I am bald, black and brilliant, and you are mangy, milky and mediocre—we might as well be twins."

"What could possibly have rolled your sorry ass out of bed so early?" he asked.

"The fact that I didn't sleep last night," I said, wearily.

"Uh-oh—problem," he said, his voice immediately losing the phony street inflection and signaling that I had his full attention.

"Yes," I said, "a problem and I need your help."

"Of course you do. What's up?"

I told him about Kelly's situation. I didn't have to provide background: Cyrus had, through me, developed a close kinship with my lady, and was already well aware of the unhappy particulars of her previous marriage.

It didn't take long for him to guess my line of reasoning. "You think the guy's scamming her about the illness."

"Yeah, I do. This asshole's a consummate manipulator, Cy. And of all the possible ruses he could cook up, some sort of bogus fatal illness would probably be the surest way to get Kelly to respond."

"And you want me to look into it."

"I figured you might have some way of getting at the man's medical records."

Pause. I waited; conversations with Cyrus Brooks, a classic word measurer, invariably contain long pauses.

Finally, he exhaled, and then said, "You *have* heard of doctor-patient confidentiality, have you not?"

"Of course I have. I was thinking there might be other options—"

This time Cyrus' silence was even lengthier, and I could tell that now the wheels had begun to turn. In making the transition from covert government operations to the frankly far more lawfully restrictive world of police detective work, Cy had deliberately continued to maintain his connections to the *sub rosa* world of information-gathering. Not surprisingly, this precaution had turned out to be immensely profitable to his new career. Though he'd been careful not to overuse these resources, and even more careful not to advertise that fact when he had, I knew that at least a portion of his enviable solve rate at the department had been made possible by data gleaned from some rather interesting—not to mention slightly extralegal—sources.

"Yeah," he said, at last, "I think I might have an idea or two."

"For instance?"

"Well, as I see it, the easiest, most direct route would be through his medical insurance," he said. "If this guy has advanced—what'd you say—pancreatic cancer? Then he's got to have compiled one genuinely obese file for himself: batteries of blood and urine tests, sophisticated scans, a medicine cabinet full of arcane prescriptions, perhaps a procedure or two; not to mention multiple office visits with internists, oncologists, maybe even psychologists—all unimaginably expensive, and all billable to his insurance company. So, like the man says, we 'follow the money.' Got some idea of his health coverage?"

"No, but he's a labor lawyer in a high-powered firm—not quite a full partner, but close; I'm sure they've got him on a heavy-duty group policy." I gave Cy the firm's name and location. "So, you can do this?"

He smirked. "What a question…"

I laughed. "Thanks, Cy."

Pause. "Cassidy?"

"Yeah?"

"What will you do when we find out this cancer thing is a crock?"

"I don't know," I admitted. "I'm pretty sure Kelly would pitch a fit if she found out I was meddling."

"No doubt," said Cy.

"The problem is that she's always obsessed over how completely powerless she was in that marriage and about how she'd not even had a role in ending it. Yesterday she was talking about how part of her motive for going to see him this time—if she does decide to go—is to be able to feel like she's finally taking some proactive steps of her own, and in that way, achieving a little closure."

"'Closure,'" Brooks repeated, caustically; "not high on my list of favorite pop-psychology terms."

"Yeah, no doubt overused in your line of work," I said, thinking about the families of the homicide victims he'd had to deal with.

"Overused. Misused. A-bused," he chanted.

"But," I argued, "exactly how is hopping on a plane just because her ex-husband snaps his fingers and cries 'sick' proactive?"

"She thinks it is."

It was my turn to pause

"Come on, now, Hank," Cy said; "obviously your lady's got some unfinished business to deal with. Whatever you may think of it, if *she* thinks that doing this will somehow settle things in her mind—"

"Yeah," I said, fighting impatience, "I know, I *know*—but I can't just stand by and do *nothing,* Cy," I said. "If this guy *is* scamming Kelly, then there's no telling what he might do to her once she gets down there and sniffs out the truth. Remember, this is an unrepentant wife-beater we're talking about."

"I know," he said. "Would you like me to go have a little preliminary sit down with him?"

"That's tempting," I said, "but let's hold off for the moment; besides, it might be something I'll want to do, myself."

"Believe me, it'd be my pleasure."

"I get *that*," I said. "It would be mine, too. Anyway, first things first; let's make sure that his illness really is counterfeit."

"And if it isn't?"

I hesitated, but only for a second. "Then, the bastard will die, and we won't have to bother with him anymore."

"That's *cold,* Breh."

"He doesn't deserve any better."

"True enough."

"Can you get right on it?"

Another long pause. Then another sigh. Finally he spoke: "Yeah. You know, it's kind of a nice morning down here—not too hot yet, a little less smog than normal. I think maybe I'll take a little break; go out for a constitutional around Pershing Square, grab some coffee from a street vendor, make a few discrete cell phone calls while I'm at it. With any luck I should have some info for you later today—tomorrow at the outside."

"You're the best, man."

"Goes without saying," he said, and hung up.

Chapter Twenty-Four

In fact, Cyrus did get back to me that afternoon. With Kelly at school in a staff meeting, I had the house to myself, but, out of long-established habit, Cy had disdained the land-line and called my cell.

"So, what's the word?" I asked.

"The word is *'factitious disorder.'*"

"That's two words."

"That's very petty, Cassidy—besides, you're deliberately ignoring the impressiveness of my erudition."

"All right, Mr. Erudite; so I'm impressed. What does it mean?"

"Means bullshit illness."

Voila.

"No claims filed with his health insurance?"

"No," he said; "actually there *were* some claims, but they were mostly of the usual middle age maintenance variety." He then went on to list a number of routine check-ups and screenings from the last twenty-four months, along with the ubiquitous—at least among those in our age group—colonoscopy; which caused me, involuntarily, to pucker, as I was reminded that my own was due to be scheduled for early next year.

"And that was it?"

His response, surprisingly, was a hearty laugh. "Well," he said, "Not exactly; there were also a couple of exploratory claims, both within the last four months."

"Exploratory claims?"

"Yeah," he said; "what you do when you're contemplating something but you're not sure you'll be covered for it. In this joker's case it seems to have been a prudent move; both claims were refused."

"What kind of claims?"

"Two separate procedures: one called 'lower lid blepharoplasty,' the other, 'follicular unit transplantation.'"

"Once again, please; only this time let's pretend that I'm not a medical expert."

Big sigh. "Philistine. Okay: the first is surgery for removing bags under the eyes; the second is your basic hair transplant."

"Cosmetic surgery."

"Yep." Cy smirked. "Looks like the bloom is decidedly off our boy's rose."

"Yeah," I said, thoughtfully; "and that would explain why he'd be calling Kelly. The prick's crashing into middle-age; stuff all over his body is starting to sag, droop and wrinkle—all of which tends to be rather off-putting to those sweet young twenty-somethings whose knickers he's been invading—"

"Which," Cy chimed in, "leads to rigorous physical self-appraisal, followed by consultations with a parade of ridiculously upscale Beverly Hills plasticians."

"*Plasticians,*" I said; "is that a word?"

"Probably not."

"Should be. Anyway I wouldn't be surprised if his surgical wish list goes well beyond the couple of items you've noted—those were probably just the first two he checked with his insurance company. But after having both of them turned down flat, he realizes that, whatever he's got in mind, he's going to have to table everything while he spends extra weeks juggling the books and scrounging spare change from his couch cushions so that he can foot all that silicone, himself. And that also means that, until he can get this makeover done, he's going to be out of the local swinging dick competition. But, since his bloated ego and uncontrolled libido don't allow for that kind of down time, he figures, 'what the hell; I'll just fall back on the old standby.'"

"Right; the ex-wife," said Cy. "And the douche bag thinks he can still yank her strings, because—"

"Because she wasn't the one to walk out; *he* was," I said. "Remember, Cy, according to Kelly there's no bottom to the depths of this man's self-worship. He's probably convinced that his ex-wife's just as hung up on him as ever. But, just in case those feelings *might* have faded a tad, the piece of shit concocts a scheme to draw her down to him, counting on his charm and the old, familiar household dynamic, once she gets there, to seal the deal."

"Pancreatic cancer," said Cy, disgustedly. "'I'm dying, Baby—got to have someone to comfort me as I get ready to face the Great Beyond.' By the by, that is one hell of a disease selection if you're out to garner some big-time sympathy. I looked it up: thirty-seven thousand cases of pancreatic cancer in this country last year, thirty-four thousand of them fatal."

It was a good thing my cell phone had a metal case; it was all I could do to keep from crushing it in my hand.

"Anything else?" I asked, hearing the tightness in my voice.

"Yeah," he said, "as a matter of fact, there is. As we all know, bullshit artists tend to spread the fertilizer more or less uniformly in all directions, not just at home. And that thought, of course, stimulates the imagination. So I decided to also do a little digging into this guy's professional life. Ever check him out?"

"No," I said; "I was hoping I'd never have to."

"You should have; makes for some pretty lively reading. Jack Melcher, labor lawyer extraordinaire. Firm of Abernathy, Selmick, and Chase. High powered outfit, specializing in mergers, probate, taxes—rich people stuff—and, of course, labor law, naturally, from the *corporate* side of the ledger. Swank offices occupying the entire third floor of a choice building on Beverly Drive, just south of Wilshire; stratospheric hourly rates."

"First, most obvious thing for me to do was to see if the partnership had ever been tied to anything notorious, so I made a friendly call to one of my more accessible and chatty deputy D.A. buddies, and in the course of the conversation happened to casually toss out the firm's name. Bingo—my friend's verbiage instantly turns scatological. Seems that this firm has been far too closely associated with a couple of corporate clients on the hook for possible RICO violations. Want to guess in what area these clients were transgressing?"

"Labor relations."

"How about that. As it happens, these fairly large companies were being seriously targeted for organizing by a couple of union locals, naturally, at great risk to their bottom lines. After some protracted and contentious maneuvering, they both miraculously managed to head the organizers off and remain union-free, but only, apparently, after resorting to some pretty drastic, coercive, and—according to the file—allegedly illegal tactics. My D.A. friend came close to indicting in both cases, but struck out when critical evidence of the use of blackmail and other dark arts suddenly dematerialized."

"Somebody on the union side got paid off."

"Possibly," he said. "But the way he was talking, it sounded more likely that they'd been leaned on in some particularly heavy-handed fashion."

"And Jack Melcher was acting as labor counsel."

"In both instances. In fact," he said, "reading between the lines, one gets the distinct impression that our man Melcher was the guy with the heavy hands. Considering how similar the charges would have been had each case progressed to trial, and noting that the only point of intersection between the two companies appears to have been their choice of legal counsel, one needn't jump more than half a foot to get to the proper conclusion about Mr. Labor Lawyer's penchant for unsavory techniques."

"'Unsavory techniques,'" I repeated, approvingly; "Nicely put. Kind of makes you wonder how frequently he resorts to them."

"A specialty, perhaps? Modus operandi whispered among prospective clientele? That would certainly be my guess: a reputation for a willingness to go the extra, *extremely* crooked mile—a sure-fire way to get an edge on the competition."

I was silent for a moment. What Cyrus had told me just now suggested some interesting possibilities.

"Hey."

"What?" I said, still working through my thoughts.

"You're sounding pensive, Cassidy," said Cy. "With you that's never good."

"Just trying to put one or two things together."

"Like what?"

"Too soon, Cyrus," I said; "much too soon; I'm just starting to work it out. Get back to you later."

"Call me before you do anything stupid," he warned.

"I will. Give my best to your wife."

He snorted, and his voice recaptured the street inflection. "Sorry, Breh; with Toni, only *my* best will do."

Chapter Twenty-Five

After spending an hour or so ruminating over the ramifications of my conversation with Cyrus Brooks, I picked up the phone and called my big-shot industrialist friend, Sam Arguaio, who lives in the San Francisco Bay area—specifically Mill Valley, a picturesque, upscale community located in Marin County, a few miles north of the Golden Gate Bridge.

Back in the early nineties Sam had had the good fortune—and good judgment—to dive, headlong, into snowboard manufacturing, at a time when the nascent sport was poised to explode upon the world's ski slopes. Within a few short years, Sam's company, Arguaio Board Works, was riding the crest (pun intended) of a snowboarding boom, with Sammy's factory working around the clock to fill orders. Since then his success had continued almost unabated, despite the onslaught of tough competition, the dampening effects of several economic downturns, and the upheaval of a couple of severe industry shakeouts. Today ABW enjoys a position as one of the giants in the field—as I myself have noted many times while skiing at Mount Bachelor, in the dominating number of snowboards emblazoned with the ABW logo.

"Hank! Ah, my good friend!" Sam's voice crackled in my earpiece with his characteristic exuberance—causing me to hold the phone an inch or so away from my ear. "Great to hear your voice!"

"How are you, Sammy?"

"Never better!" was the enthusiastic reply. I smiled; clouds seldom gather over Sam Arguaio's head.

"The wife, kids?"

"I'm the luckiest of men."

We exchanged a few additional pleasantries, and then I got to the point.

"Sam," I said, "I'm in need of a rather large favor."

"Anything, my friend," he said; "you know that."

I do. Several years ago, I'd performed a service of some consequence for Sam; as a result, he'd pronounced himself forever in my debt—an oath to be taken seriously, coming, as it did, from someone for whom fierce loyalty among friends is sacrosanct.

"You haven't heard what it is yet, Sam," I warned. "It's kind of devious."

"Just name it."

"Thanks, Sammy," I said. "Your factory is still a non-union house?"

"Yes, it is," he said; "why?"

I told him.

Chapter Twenty-Six

The weekend: for most people, a much-desired forty-eight hour liberty; respite from five days of workplace drudgery. TGIF. Time for play. Recharge the old D-Cells, indulge in the frivolous, perfect that golf swing, take an extra drink—or three. Hell, kick back and do absolutely nothing.

But in my present, restless state, this particular coming weekend held no attraction at all. I now had two issues simmering on the burners, and it looked like there wasn't much I could do about either one of them until the following week; that made Saturday and Sunday seem more like frustrating barriers than pleasant prospects.

Of course, the main reason I was not exactly sanguine about the approaching weekend was that at the moment Kelly was treating me like a stranger.

Obviously wrestling with the decision whether or not to bend to her ex-husband's entreaties and fly to Los Angeles, Kelly had deliberately and single mindedly channeled her anxiety into yet another manic round of lesson plan re-editing at her dining table work station. I would have laughed at this, considering that she was already a week into the semester, and, come on, we're talking about second grade here—how much more fine-tuning could your lesson plans possibly need? But, fully understanding the compulsion that was really motivating this activity, I was careful not to comment.

Besides, I was just as knotted up, in my own way, with Kelly's situation. While, on one hand, I prayed that she'd opt not to fly down there; on the other, I knew that it was far more likely that she would go, and therefore I found myself preoccupied with my own preparations for Monday.

Fortunately, to Kelly my obvious distraction could have easily been written off to simple concern for her predicament, so there was no need for me to attempt to disguise it. Nevertheless our interactions Friday night and Saturday were awkward: Kelly treating me with self-conscious politeness whenever an encounter was unavoidable; me doing my level best to keep those encounters to a minimum.

It was the politeness that bothered me more than anything else. Jenny Longwell was right: anger, scorn, jealousy—even in the best of relationships you expect these things to surface from time to time. But, *politeness?* That's the kind of treatment you reserve for people you'd just as soon not have to deal with. From Kelly, I was finding it intolerable, and eventually I began to search for some pretext for leaving the house.

Sunday morning, after an all too quiet breakfast which had found both of us with our noses buried, silently and deliberately, in the paper, I jumped up from the table, scrubbed the frying pan, rinsed out the coffee pot, placed the dishes in the dishwasher, and then grabbed my jacket.

Kelly looked up from her half-finished Sunday *sudoku*.

"You're leaving?"

"Yeah."

"Where're you going?"

"To work."

"But…where?" she repeated.

I shrugged. "It's Sunday. I am going to church."

For the first time in a couple of days, her face showed interest. "Church—you mean the *Reverend's* church?"

I nodded.

"But," she said, "I thought he told you not to show up there; that he didn't want you bothering his congregation."

"And I won't," I said. "I'm just going there to observe."

"He won't like it."

I smiled. "He can kiss my furry little pagan behind."

That brought a laugh and at least a partial thaw in the room. I started to move toward the door.

"Hank?"

I turned, and saw that, from the look on Kelly face, she understood my real motive for getting out of the house. Her right hand fiddling idly with her coffee mug, she said: "I'm sorry, Baby."

"For what?"

Her eyes fell, unfocused to the table. "For being such lousy company."

I wanted to say either "Yeah, you have been, haven't you;" or "Don't worry; I completely understand." Instead, I just said, "It's okay."

She raised her eyes to mine, held them. Smiled. Then stretched her arms out, and did a pretty fair Mae West: "How about a little kiss, Sailor?"

I walked over to her, ran my fingers through her hair, and then bent over, my lips seeking, and then finding, hers. As always, they were impossibly soft, sweet—intoxicating, but I deliberately kept the encounter short, and then began to back away. Kelly reached up and, grabbing the back of my head, pulled my face back down to her. "More," she pleaded, panting, and opened her mouth to mine. I yielded, and we fell into a long, awkward embrace; me standing, her seated. Her tongue tasted, faintly, of coffee and bacon, and I was tempted to call off my Sunday go-to-meeting.

Then we pulled apart, and gazed, fondly—hungrily, at each other. "You want me to stay?" I asked.

"No," she said, with an indulgent smile; "you go. Have some fun; make the preacher squirm. Just don't be home too late, okay?"

Chapter Twenty-Seven

The parking lot at the Church of the Holy Messenger was packed. Despite a lack of lines on the gravel, the cars were arranged in surprisingly neat rows, leading me to conclude that they must have been employing a lot attendant, by now absent, to direct traffic.

I drove in, and selected one of the few remaining open spaces at the back of the lot, nearest to the road; then got out and made my way, slowly, through the ranks of cars, towards the church complex, making a casual demographic survey of them as I walked. There were only a few luxury vehicles in sight, though I did notice several rather pricey 4X4 diesel pick-ups, complete with four-door crew cabs and fat, chromed dual rear wheels. Mostly, though, the parking lot's automotive lineup looked to be basic working-class: a large cross-section of late-model economy coupes and sedans, augmented with almost equal numbers of utilitarian trucks, vans and SUV's.

Passing the innermost row of cars, I headed for the chapel. Loud music—some gospel number I was unfamiliar with—was billowing from the high windows of the building, all of which had evidently been cranked open to take advantage of the mild weather. I was surprised to hear what sounded like a large, entirely professional instrumental ensemble—at least an octet—accompanying the congregation's singing.

Competing with these sounds were the more immediate shrieks and yelps of a virtual army of single-digit youngsters frantically playing in the fenced schoolyard just ahead of me. As I passed it, I saw that the playground was standing-room-only—or, more accurately, standing, swinging, squatting, digging, sliding and rolling. This noisy, manic activity was being supervised in a frankly lackluster manner by a pair of girls barely into their teens. As I skirted the chain-link fence, I waved to the nearest of these yard monitors—a skinny, sandy-haired maiden with a pinched, exasperated expression seemingly permanently etched onto her avian face. "Hi," I said.

"Hey," was her sullen reply.

I gestured towards the chapel.

"How long have they been at it?"

She rolled her eyes. "Like, forever," she said, mournfully. "Like almost an hour, anyway…"

My guess was that it was just this sort of lack of enthusiasm for religious pomp and circumstance which had probably earned for her a stretch in daycare Siberia—a sentence obviously issued at least some time prior to today, considering the decidedly non-church, scruffy quality of her jeans, sneakers and t-shirt.

"It could be worse, you know," I offered, diplomatically.

Waving her arms frantically at two five-year-olds who'd begun to wrestle in the dirt, she shouted, "Hey, come on, damn it…knock it off!" She then turned, presented me with a you-have-got-to-be-kidding-me look, and muttered, "Yeah? How?"

I pointed, again, at the church. "You could be stuck in *there*."

The brittle look immediately softened a bit, and a giggle escaped her. "You sure got that right." Sticking a finger in her mouth, she volunteered a particularly colorful gagging sound. "It's, like, just shoot me, *puh-leeeze! Sooo boring*…"

"Then count your blessings," I said.

"Yeah, guess I should," she said, then cast a disgusted look back at her noisy charges. "But," she muttered, acidly, "whatever, I'm, like, *never* gonna have kids! I *swear* I'm not!"

With a wave and a last, sympathetic nod, I left the frazzled girl to her responsibilities and moved on towards the open double doors of the chapel. I was hardly concerned at having learned that I'd already missed out on most of the service: it wasn't my intention to take in the show—just the patrons.

The music—that same old gospel tune, droning and repetitious—continued to play as I entered the foyer. Inside, I could now hear more clearly hundreds of voices raised in song—all of them exuberant, all, apparently, imbued with copious quantities of Holy Spirit. Unfortunately, too many of the most heavily imbued (read, *loudest*) were also heavily tone-deaf—which caused me to wince as their dissonance clashed with the ensemble and other, less sonically-challenged voices in the room.

At this late stage in the proceedings there was no longer anyone in the reception area to greet me, so I slid past the guest book on the pedestal without bothering to sign in (not having any particular desire to end up on the church mailing list), and stepped up to the archway entrance to the massive chapel, looking down the rows of bobbing heads, while fully expecting to see a large band playing at the opposite end of the hall, with their instruments spread out the full width of the stage.

But, aside from Reverend J.T. Sayles, standing several feet behind the pulpit with a couple of young attendants flanking him, the platform was vacant. Looking across at the throbbing, booming Lansing speakers suspended above the crowd, I now comprehended their function: the song's instrumentals were canned—probably the pre-packaged product of some sort of religious-themed "Music Minus One" series. Knowing that it would have looked tacky for Sayles to be controlling the tracks himself, I guessed that there must be a sound engineer working a board somewhere—possibly in a balcony directly above me. And if that were the case, he was bound to have a pretty decent overview of the entire crowd. Glancing to my right, I spotted an unmarked door breaking the continuity of the floor-to-ceiling shelving which lined the wall, and made for it.

Sure enough, the door opened to a steep, narrow stairwell, leading, to the left, up to the very balcony area that I'd theorized. I quickly climbed the steps, and found myself on a broad, open, carpeted area, which extended the entire width of the chapel, and was fronted by a low wooden railing overlooking the interior. Most of this space was bare, aside from a few stacked boxes and small pieces of furniture tucked against the back wall; but in the middle and directly behind the railing was a long table with a compact Yamaha mixing console—the fairly modest sort of audio equipment you might find at a nightclub or minor league concert venue—sitting atop it.

In a chair behind the sound board sat a thin young man with short, spiky red hair and a pasty face, wearing a dark suit with narrow lapels and sleeves at least two sizes too short. He was hunched over the console, both hands delicately manipulating the sliding volume-control faders, his face a study in concentration. He looked up, startled, as I emerged from the stairwell, his expression quickly turning negative as he marked my stranger status. But, tied up as he was with the music tracks, he was unable to do little more than cast a series of disapproving frowns in my direction.

In response, I smiled back at him, reassuringly, and put a finger to my lips, signaling that I fully understood the house rules and intended to abide by them, and then stepped to the railing, discreetly hugging the right-hand wall near the stairs, and looking out upon the congregation below.

Scanning the crowd, I now realized that I had absolutely no idea what I was looking for, aside from some vague notion that maybe something might pop up to grab my attention, and perhaps justify the miles I'd just put on my odometer.

As I watched, I saw that most of the women in the crowd were similarly attired: ankle-length dresses, floral or plaid patterns, everything conservatively buttoned to the throat. Next to them, a surprising number of their husbands were fully decked out in suits, although at least an equal percentage were dressed far more casually, though neatly. I also counted quite a few cowboy hats riding on laps, perched directly beneath fancy western shirts with string ties—many of them secured with what looked like religious-icon bolos. There were a good number of children in the crowd, the kids seeming to mirror the clothing preferences of the adults they were with—although from their strained expressions and the way they fidgeted in their seats most of them looked a great deal less comfortable than their elders.

At this point the throng was laboring its way through yet another refrain of the marathon devotional, which by now had become positively Dylanesque in its number of verses. Fortunately, though, by the end of this stanza they ran out of lyrics, and so, with a final, retardant flourish the music drew itself to an exhausted close, with everybody then settling back into their seats as Reverend Sayles made his way to the pulpit.

The minister, clad in what appeared to be the same somber black suit as the one in my photograph, waited patiently until the metallic creaking of the chairs died away, his dark eyes sweeping the room from side to side, with a huge, paternal smile animating only the lower half of his face. Finally, he spoke, his massive voice swelling, filling the vast space from wall to wall, corner to corner, floor to lofty ceiling.

"My beloved children," he thundered, then paused, dramatically, before resuming. *"Sunday next! On Sunday next, you will all bear witness to our Heavenly Father's latest **miracle!** On that day, you will see our beautiful holy message take flight...on the wings of the **electronic medium**—that is to say, on **television**—spreading the **Word,** out beyond the hallowed walls of this blessed church...and right on into the waiting homes and ears and hearts of **thousands** of our neighbors!"*

This pronouncement was greeted with a hearty, widespread chorus of "amen's."

He leaned forward, and his baritone voice deepened even further, now verging on *basso profundo:*

*"Yet that, my brethren, will only be the **beginning!** Before long, with your prayers—and, of course, with your generous assistance—the voice of your humble shepherd will spread **far** and **wide:** soaring over **majestic,** snow-capped peaks and beyond **barren deserts;** gliding, gracefully, across golden fields of corn and wheat and above **mighty rivers,** where it will then descend into humble hamlets, medium-sized towns and giant, sprawling cities in states hundreds...yes, **thousands** of miles away from this very pulpit—from the west coast to the east coast, from the Canadian border to the Gulf of Mexico. But it will not end there, O my children! No! Ultimately, with **irresistible** righteousness and **majesty** of **purpose**...you will see your Reverend's voice journeying even further; even beyond the **Lord's** mighty **oceans** themselves, into **countries** with*

*foreign names on distant **continents,** where live **millions** upon **millions** of benighted souls, **desperately** in need of the **power** of our special...perfect... message; **the** message, **our** message; a message of **salvation** for **all...man...kind!***"

Even more "amen's," along with a fair number of "hallelujah's."

*"Yes, that's right, my children: millions of needy souls...each desperately hungering for spiritual sustenance, will finally come to hear...and to be comforted, and to be transformed...yes...to be **saved...**by the supreme **wonder**...the **power**...the **glory**...the **majesty**...of our...**holy...perfect...message!**"*

At this, the response became positively thunderous— almost raucous—with several enthusiastic patrons in the audience actually leaping to their feet and applauding. The preacher drank deep this adoring demonstration, displaying a broad, generous, and—in my estimation—smugly satisfied smile, and then, having no doubt decided that he had extracted the maximum benefit from the outburst, slowly raised both hands, palms down, in an indulgent, calming, and entirely paternalistic manner.

Once the room had settled down again, the Reverend then dialed the vocal intensity back a notch or two and switched gears, smoothly transitioning into the central theme of his sermon, which this morning appeared to be one's complete submission and commitment to Christ and, not incidentally, to this particular church. With the minister employing phrases like *"giving a hundred and ten percent,"* and *"sublimating the wants of the self for the needs of the many,"* the speech began to remind me, oddly, of those grainy old film clips of Knute Rockne exhorting his football team in the Notre Dame locker room at halftime. Eventually, though, it became obvious to me that what the "ten" of the "hundred and ten percent" was referring to, was support, in the form of some serious cash contributions; that this sermon was essentially an exhortation to his loyal and generous "flock" to pony up big time for the Reverend's bold, ambitious, and, not incidentally, financially demanding new crusade.

Indeed, as the preacher got further into the meat of his oration, these references gradually became less subtle, the appeals for dough more strident, more direct; the result being that, as his rant veered more and more toward infomercial territory, my own interest in it rapidly flagged. Fortunately, I found that by concentrating my attention on various individual members of the audience below, I was miraculously able to push the minister's voice, loud though it was, into the background.

Inspecting the crowd, two things quickly became obvious: the first was how completely spellbound these people were, many of them actually staring at their minister with mouths hanging agape; the second was that, because of precisely this nearly total uniformity of response, it was fairly easy to spot those few people in the audience who had remained stubbornly un-transported by the Reverend's oratory. I was amused to note that two of those who stood out were my young friends, Eliot and Paul—on the left side of the room, two-thirds of the way back—sitting next to their parents and probably doing their utmost to appear attentive, yet by their stony expressions and restless, swiveling heads clearly indicating a passionate, mutual desire to be anywhere else but here.

But it was one other disgruntled listener who eventually attracted, and then monopolized, my attention. Almost directly below me, in the next to last row, I saw a knee impatiently bobbing, while stubby fingers, the nails of which had apparently resisted all efforts at removing the grime, drummed a fitful rhythm against the other leg, interrupted, twice, by a restraining hand and disapproving glance from his spouse, seated next to him.

At first, I was not able to make anything of the man's features, other than his thick head of black hair, broad shoulders and clothing—which seemed among all of the outfits in the room to be the most carelessly chosen and least suitable for the occasion: faded jeans, open-collared work shirt, industrial work boots. But then his head slowly craned upward and began moving from side to side, seemingly to resolve a crick in the neck, at which point his face was brought, plainly, into view, with a supremely bored expression imprinted upon it:

Foe Evah's—or rather, *Weldon Potter's*—father.

Just barely able to prevent what would have been an audible and extraordinarily inappropriate "What the fuck?" from escaping my lips, I stared; first at the man fidgeting down there, then at his wife, who continued to flash scolding eyes at him. Since I'd not gotten a good look at her last Tuesday, the only feature I was able to recognize from that night was her shoulder-length hair. Now, I could see more: an extremely plain, unadorned and care-worn countenance, with skin yellowed from an acute shortage of time spent outdoors; un-manicured hands coarsened, apparently, from long years of manual labor; drab, colorless clothing, looking crudely hand-made and seemingly designed more for maximum coverage than for style. And, unlike her antsy husband, the woman was clearly hanging on the Reverend's every syllable—that is, when she wasn't fretting over the embarrassing impression her partner's restless behavior was making on those seated around them.

Fascinated, I shifted my gaze back to the man. It was obvious that the husband was one supremely unhappy fellow. It was hardly a stretch to surmise that he was here only because his wife had dragged him. I wondered if this was a first visit; and, if not, exactly how many other Sunday services he'd been forced to endure. Judging from the advanced state of his unconcealed impatience, it couldn't have been many.

Weldon Potter's parents, showing up at the Sayles church.

Foe Evah's parents.

Joshua Sayles' father's church.

As I stood there, I tried to make some sense of what I was seeing. Weldon Potter, Josh Sayles: from all I'd heard, not friends—in fact, more likely, implacable foes. Certainly socially unconnected, one would think, outside of their common membership in the scruffy park group. And yet, here…

If nothing else, it did constitute one *hell* of a coincidence.

But was that really all it was? Coincidence? Or, rather, might there be something more to be understood—some connection in all of this to Josh's disappearance?

I continued to watch the couple for another five minutes, then decided there was little else to be gleaned from the image; so, after having made a few more perfunctory, unfruitful scans of the rest of the room, I decided to quit my post, so that I could be outside when the thing broke up. If possible, I hoped that there might be an opportunity to waylay Eliot or Paul, to see if either of the boys might have some insights into what I'd just witnessed. With a parting nod to the young man at the console, I headed back down the stairs, just as Reverend Sayles finished his sermon with one last entreaty to his audience to *"open your **hearts**…your **purses**…your **wallets**,"* and then moved on to the benediction. By the time I was through the front doors and out into the sunshine, he'd finished with his final prayer and a rousing celebratory chorale had begun to vibrate the building.

Chapter Twenty-Eight

Once outside, I took up a strategic position, leaning, casually, against a tree halfway between the school house and the chapel; strategic, because it provided me with an unobstructed view of the church steps—where by now Reverend Sayles had appeared and was bidding adieu to his people—, and also because it would force the congregation members to pass me on their way to the parking lot.

The movement of the crowd as they left the building was sluggish, as a significant number of them paused to chat with the minister and each other before they broke up and headed for their cars. Among them I soon spotted the Potters, idling just off to the left of the landing: the wife, waiting patiently for a chance to get in a few words with the reverend; her husband, doing a slow boil, kicking at the ground and looking like he was only moments away from grabbing the woman by the arm and yanking her out of there.

Fortunately before anything like that could happen Paul and Eliot emerged through the doors. Though both their parents tarried along with so many others near the preacher, the boys immediately split off and wandered, idly, towards the parking lot. Then they saw me, and, like refugees spotting a long-lost relative, their faces immediately brightened, and they practically sprinted, smiling and waving, to where I was standing. They were again dressed similarly, although not identically: both sported gray pants, white shirt, black shoes; but where Eliot wore a blue jacket and blue tie, Paul had opted for black and black.

"Hey guys," I said, shaking their hands when they reached me (this time, I noticed that their grips felt dryer, more robust; much more like actual hands than they had when I'd first met them.) "I've been waiting for you two; spotted you during the service, thought I'd snag you when you came out."

They both looked pleased and flattered at this. Paul said, "Where were you? I didn't even know you were here."

"I was upstairs."

"Really...upstairs, in back?" said Eliot, with some surprise. "I thought that area was off limits. Did you get permission from Reverend Sayles?"

"No," I said, "but I figured that what he didn't know wouldn't hurt him."

Again the boys grinned; this time evidently relishing a shared bit of subversion. "How'd you like the service?" asked Paul.

I shrugged. "Missed most of it; caught the sermon, though."

"The *come-on*, you mean," said Eliot, shaking his head.

"The Reverend's quite the pitch-man, isn't he?" I said.

"Yeah," said Eliot, with distaste; "The congregation swallows it, too; hook, line and sinker."

"How come you guys don't?"

It was their turn to shrug. "I dunno," said Paul. "When you've been...well, outsiders...as long as we have, you kind of get into the habit of not exactly accepting things you hear at face value, you know?"

I was really getting to like these boys. "I'd say that's a mighty healthy way of doing business."

"Thanks," said Paul, blushing.

"Got a question."

They both said, "Yeah?" simultaneously.

Turning, so as to face the crowd at the front of the church, I nodded without pointing: "See the two people over there, by the minister? Husband and wife; wife's got long, brown hair; man not very well dressed?"

They both followed my look. "Oh," said Eliot; "you mean Weldon Potter's mom and dad."

"Exactly. What's their story?"

"Well," Eliot replied; "I don't really know much about them. His mom's been a member of the church a long time—longer than we have, actually. I've only seen his dad here maybe for the last four or five weeks."

"What about Weldon? He ever come to church?"

They both looked at me like my I.Q. had just cratered.

"Weldon Potter?" exclaimed Paul. "Here? Are you kidding? Foe Evah—the Deacon of Depravity?"

I laughed. "Is that what you call him?"

They both nodded, grinning. "Yeah," said Paul; "but not to his face. And please don't tell him; we've already had more than we need from that guy."

"The pounding, you mean."

They exchanged distressed looks. "Right," said Paul.

"Don't worry; I won't tell." For a moment I considered asking them about the conversation they'd had with Foe Evah at MacDonald's the previous week, but decided that there was little to be gained from it, aside from needlessly making two insecure boys feel guilty about having been so easily coerced into divulging information about me. Instead I nodded again in the direction of the couple. "Kind of looks like his dad's out of place here, too, don't you think?"

"I'm not sure he has much choice," said Eliot.

"What do you mean?"

Lowering his voice, he said, "I heard he got into some trouble."

"What? Trouble with the law?"

"Yeah," he said; "although I don't know exactly what kind. Only that he probably has to show up here whether he wants to or not."

"I'd say it's pretty clear he doesn't want to."

"Maybe even more than us," said Paul.

"But just barely," added Eliot, grinning.

I laughed, and clapped both of them on the shoulder. "Count the months, boys; just a few more, and you'll be busy flouting social conventions on the east coast."

"It can't come soon enough," said Paul, fiercely.

"Any idea what that guy's first name is?"

"Mr. Potter?" said Paul, then looked at his partner, questioningly.

"I think it's Wade," said Eliot.

"Ah," I said; "Wade. Weldon; both *W's*. I'll bet Grandpa's name is Wilbur. See you later, fellas."

I left to the accompaniment of their laughter, and headed for my car, feeling the energizing effects of fresh information. It might turn out to be nothing, but, at least for now, my view of this case had widened somewhat.

Chapter Twenty-Nine

When I got home, I called Denove, intending to ask him about the exact nature of Wade Potter's "trouble" with the law. Unfortunately, I got his voice mail, which, considering that the workaholic detective was almost always reachable on his cell phone, meant that he must have had something really special going with his wife that night, and didn't want to be disturbed. I smiled. *Laissez les bon temps rouler,* my friend. I left a message, saying, no problem; I'd get back to him later.

The pleasant residue of this morning's warming between Kelly and me had not entirely dissipated, and so our dinner was upbeat—at least at first. Kelly plied me with questions about my day in church, and laughed at most of my impressions. I began to have hopeful thoughts about possibilities for the rest of the evening.

Unfortunately, as the meal continued, Kelly grew more distracted, and started to poke at her food, while responding to my attempts at keeping the banter cheerful with increasingly fitful replies and, at best, weak smiles. Eventually, our conversation died away altogether, supplanted by an uneasy silence, with Kelly intermittently glancing up at me, as if trying to summon the courage to speak.

I waited.

"Hank," she said at last, putting her fork down; "I've decided to go."

"You have." It was hardly unexpected. But I still felt a void in my gut despite the food I'd just consumed.

"I've got to."

"Okay."

She looked at me, pleadingly. "I...I hope you'll understand."

I returned the look, smiled; reached for her hand. "I'm trying, Babe."

"It's okay," she said; "*really*...it *will* be okay."

"I hope so," I said; but I was thinking: *Gotta get upstairs, print out my boarding pass for my flight to L.A. tomorrow.*

We cleared the table together, washed and dried the pots and pans; put the dishes in the washer. Then Kelly turned to me, looking up, shyly.

"Still love me?"

I hugged her, burying my face in her neck, inhaling her always-fresh scent. "What a question. Of course I love you."

And that's why I'll be dropping the hammer on your ex-husband tomorrow.

Later that night, we were at our respective work stations: Kelly, downstairs on the dining room table; me, up in my office.

I'd quickly finished with my trip prep, mainly because I didn't want Kelly to walk in on me and discover what I was planning to do. Then I turned my thoughts back to the case; opened my file and began to write.

I now had a few possible leads. First there was Jenny Longwell's revelation about Nadine Sayles carrying on a sleazy motel room rodeo with her cowboy lover. Which reminded me: digging through the newspaper articles in my file, I was able to locate fairly high-quality medium close-up of Nadine Sayles, and scan it into my computer. After cropping and enhancing it as much as possible in Photoshop, I then printed the picture out onto high quality photo paper; nodding when I pulled it from the printer—it wasn't perfect, but she was certainly easily recognizable. Satisfied with my work, I laid it on the desk blotter, and turned my attention to the other two leads:

Weldon Potter—AKA Foe Evah—and his father, Wade. Weldon, who flamboyantly projects a fabricated gangsta persona while also loudly proclaiming his lack of regard for Josh Sayles. And now Wade Potter, extremely reluctant visitor to the Church of the Holy Messenger; by my own nocturnal, binocular witness a man easily prone to combining alcohol with violence—and, if my two young contacts are accurate, someone who has made at least one guest appearance on a police blotter.

Then I leaned back, dissatisfied. Fact was, despite what I'd learned today about Weldon Potter's wayward father, despite what I'd observed in his or his son's behavior, despite what Jenny had told me last week about Nadine Sayles' sexual proclivities; odds still remained likely that none of this would have anything to do with Josh Sayles' disappearance. No matter how I tried to distill some meaning to all of this, tried to manufacture dots and draw lines to connect them, my efforts never seemed to get past idle speculation. I realized that if Potters senior and junior were involved somehow with the missing teen, it would only be if something nasty had happened to him. And as far as Josh's mom's dalliances were concerned, that wouldn't necessarily come to anything, either, unless I could establish that it had been the prime reason for him running away on his own.

The real problem with all of this was that, for all of my efforts to identify potential bad actors in this play, for all of my rambling conjecture regarding their possible involvement, what I was in fact doing right now was looking at this case through the wrong end of the telescope, drumming up suspects for a crime which had yet to be identified—if, in fact, any crime had been committed at all. Without knowing first what exactly had happened to Josh Sayles, it would be difficult, if not impossible, to know whether anything I'd picked up so far bore any actual relevance.

And, I admitted, wearily, when it came to any progress in determining the one critical piece of information that mattered—the actual dope on Josh Sayles' current status—I was essentially no further along than I'd been that first morning when J.T. Sayles had dropped the retainer check on my table.

Sitting at my desk, I ran yet another in a series of frustrated hands through my hair.

C'mon, Josh; give me a hint...anything....

I was sure that Denove would smile at this scene; at how, without my ever having met him, my growing obsession with the missing Joshua Sayles had assumed an almost physical manifestation. In fact, though his photo was at the moment tucked away in my glove compartment, a residual image of the young man's face continued, stubbornly, to hang in my thoughts, a lot like those floaters swimming across the insides of my eyelids when I shut them. I'd heard Cyrus Brooks describing this phenomenon often enough. "That's the thing about a missing persons case," he'd said: "the biggest presence in the room is always the one who's not there."

As I chewed over the echo of that comment, I heard the rumble of multiple feet ascending the stairs, two human, four canine. The human ones paused as they reached the landing.

"Hank? You coming to bed?"

"Be right there, Hon."

Closing the file, I yawned, stretched, and got up from my office chair. As I shut the lights and made my way slowly down the hall to our bedroom, I told myself that I should count my blessings. After all, despite being stymied about Josh's present whereabouts and condition, at least now there were a few things I could focus on, tasks I could perform, including a visit with the Bluebird Motel's manager to chat about Nadine Sayles' indiscretions, and my call to Denove or Whalen to get some background on whatever legal hot water Wade Potter had gotten himself into.

A few more cards in the deck.

But just before reaching the open bedroom doorway, I paused, realizing that I wouldn't be getting to either of these options until Tuesday. Sam Arguaio had reached me on my cell phone earlier, confirming that tomorrow I had a 1:30 lunch date with Jack Melcher at the Carillon Hotel in Los Angeles.

Ducking my head into the bedroom, I saw Kelly lying on her side in the subtle glow of her bedside reading lamp. Clad only in a tee shirt, she had pulled the covers partly to the side, exposing the entire length her long, shapely left leg. Between that enticing view and the unmistakable expression on her face I realized that, at least for tonight, an attempt was being made to put other concerns aside. I waved and said: "Just a second, Babe; I forgot to turn off my computer. I'll be right back."

I heard her voice at my back as I retraced my steps to my office: "That's a good boy—but hurry, Sweetie; I'm getting' kind of...*anxious,* if you know what I mean—"

That brought a smile. It was a line from "Beetlejuice," one of our favorite movies. One heck of a woman: with all she had going on, she'd obviously decided to do her best to behave as though nothing were wrong. That is, for the next hour or so, anyway.

Least I could do was reciprocate.

My walk turned into a trot.

That night we made love with an intensity bordering on desperation. And when we were done, we clung, sweating, to each other, as if by doing so we might somehow ward off evil thoughts of a man whose name we'd spent the last two days avoiding. But in the occasional, fugitive shades that I saw crossing Kelly's face, along with my own fleeting yet stubbornly persistent feelings, it was obvious that we'd not been entirely successful.

The biggest presence in the room is always the one who's not there.

True for other things besides missing persons cases.

Chapter Thirty

Monday dawned, bright, crisp, clear and restless. Kelly had evidently risen well ahead of me and already walked Satchmo: the shower was running and steam was wafting into the bedroom through the partially-closed bathroom door. Staggering out of bed, I threw on my sweats and lumbered downstairs, using the entryway bathroom and the spare toothbrush I had stashed there—a standard fall-back position whenever Kelly was monopolizing the master bath—and then hustled into the kitchen when I was done to prepare breakfast.

With an aim toward sustaining some of the momentum from last night's romantic interlude, I hurried to prepare a couple of my signature bacon-mushroom-cheddar omelets (secret ingredient: tarragon) to have them ready by the time Kelly was dressed. Almost made it, too; I was just tossing the last of the ingredients into the pan when her shoes noisily hit the ground floor.

But though when she reached the kitchen she hugged me from behind as I loaded the eggs onto the plates, and murmured her thanks while planting a kiss on my neck, the smooch felt perfunctory, the thanks arid. And, once we'd settled down into our chairs, Kelly toyed, listlessly, with her eggs.

"Kelly," I said, observing this unusual lack of appetite, "are you sure you want to go through with this?"

Last chance for me to unplug my own plans, was my admittedly selfish thought.

Before responding, she stared out the window. In the distance, the bright morning sunlight was beginning to lose momentum, and clouds were building, piling on top of each other over the western mountains like an angry mob at the palace gates. This time of year that meant yet another round of thunderstorms. When she turned back, she avoided my gaze, looking down, distracted, at the still substantial remains on her plate. "I *have* to go, Hank." She looked at her watch. "As a matter of fact, I really *do* have to go."—she grinned; a weak attempt at humor—"You know how I am about showing up late for work."

"Kelly…"

Standing, she grabbed her briefcase, and walked to the door leading to the garage. As she opened it, she turned, and stood there, looking at me, smiling wanly. She was dressed simply, in a plain, buttoned up white blouse, ankle-length brown suede skirt, and laced dress boots. And at that moment she was so beautiful it hurt to look.

"It's going to be alright, Hank," she said; "really, it is."

I didn't believe her. I knew too much; Jack was going to play her, and if she saw through his game and confronted him, he was going to hurt her.

And I couldn't let that happen.

I waited until I heard her car exiting out onto the road, then rose, and headed for the stairs.

Chapter Thirty-One

The Carillon was less than a mile from Los Angeles International Airport. I could have taken a cab from LAX, but I needed a car as a prop, and so I'd arranged to have a rental waiting for me when I arrived. The result was that twenty minutes after my plane landed I was cruising east past the Century Boulevard entrance to the hotel in a taupe Toyota sedan with an "Avis" sticker on the rear bumper.

Architecturally looking like a transplant from Miami's South Beach, the Carillon Hotel was a twenty story parfait, primarily salmon-colored, with floors alternating in white and teal. The building squatted just far enough back from the street to allow for a grand, overhanging entrance, from under which an army of valets was busily shepherding vehicles down a ramp to the left of the circular driveway. Having no interest in that service today, I continued past the building, made a left, and drove to the self-service parking structure in back.

Yanking a ticket from the automated gate, I entered, and, ignoring several open spots on the crowded street-level floor, cruised up the ramps, not stopping until I arrived at the least populated area, one level below the far too conspicuous roof. After making a careful circuit, and determining which sections were covered by surveillance cameras, I located a remote space in a dim, back corner of the building which was un-televised, and eased the car into it.

I exited the rental car, and, after taking one last look around to verify that I hadn't missed a video cam, then made the lengthy trek to the elevators at the front of the structure, observing with some satisfaction how inadequately the fluorescents lit the low-ceilinged expanse.

Two minutes later, I was standing on the broad, caramel-colored marble floor of the Carillon Hotel's cavernous lobby, staring at the stylish copper sign posted on the wall next to the entrance to the Pearl Restaurant.

Entering the bistro's cozy, fern-enhanced foyer, I announced myself at the front desk, and was immediately conducted through the crowded, dark space by a smiling host dressed in an immaculate cream-colored linen suit to a roomy booth at the back wall of the room. The décor inside was very much in keeping with the Caribbean theme of the hotel: bleached wood tables surrounded by rattan chairs; booths of thick, tufted leather dyed in some subtle shade of mauve; lush ferns in over-sized pots; metal-framed prints of enticing tropical vistas, each subtly lit by micro spot lamps.

When we arrived at the table, a dark figure slid out from the booth, and I then found myself shaking the hand of a man who'd once broken my girlfriend's arm. I couldn't help but imagine as I grasped it how easy—not to mention satisfying—it would feel to repay that act right now…with interest.

Chapter Thirty-Two

"Jack Melcher," he said, smiling genially.

"Marcus Miller," I responded. Needing an alias, I'd taken the name of a favorite jazz bass player. Not *the* favorite; frankly I didn't think that the guy would have bought me as Jaco Pastorius.

I had to admit, he was a good-looking man; the kind of good-looking that tends to make the rest of us average Joes uncomfortable. Taller, by an inch, than me. Thinning yet immaculately-groomed dark hair, with just the right smattering of gray at the temples. Dark, Roman-chiseled face, clean shaven, with expressive brown eyes under thick eyebrows. Trim, agile body which suggested not so much athleticism as it did rigid adherence to an expensive health club regimen. All tastefully swaddled in a navy Hugo Boss blazer, white shirt with blue pin-stripes, matching tie and gray gabardine slacks. Gold Rolex Submariner on a slender wrist. Artist's hands: long fingers, nails professionally trimmed and polished. Day-glo smile; perfect teeth. Italian loafers, complete with tassels.

I hate tassels.

While taking this inventory, I did in fact notice the bags under his eyes which, according to Cy, had driven the man to seek professional remedies. To me, though, they hardly looked worthy of concern; in fact, compared to those modest pouches of his, my own looked like a full set of Samsonite.

We completed the greeting ritual by exchanging business cards, and I saw, with some annoyance—considering the trouble I'd gone through to have mine printed—that he'd slipped it into his inside coat pocket without so much as a glance.

We took our respective places at opposite ends of the scalloped booth, facing each other like air-hockey opponents. Melcher's demeanor was affable, confident. Parked atop a cocktail napkin on the table in front of him was an over-sized, nearly-empty goblet of red wine. As he settled in, Melcher picked it up, drained the remains, then raised it as a signal.

A cocktail waitress quickly materialized, took my order of a Chevis on the rocks, another glass of red for him, and then melted away into the darkness.

"Sorry I was late," I said. "I probably should have taken an earlier flight—didn't realize how long it would take for me to get out of the terminal."

"Not a problem," Melcher responded, though with a look that said it *was;* that any experienced businessman would have known better. "Anyway, it just gave me a few extra moments to enjoy the wine. In my life even fifteen minutes of free time can be precious."

"Busy guy, huh?"

"I am that."

"Good for you, considering what the economy is doing these days."

"Oh," he said, airily, "actually the current economic climate works very much to our advantage. Between upside-down mortgages, rising credit-card rates and health insurance costs, your average worker is desperate to find some way to squeeze more income, or, at least, benefits, from his boss. As a result we're seeing a steady up-tick in attempts to unionize businesses." He leaned back, bringing the tips of his fingers together. "Bottom is that I've got all the work I can handle."

"Guess that means we're lucky to be getting some of your time," I said, careful to keep the sarcasm out of my voice.

"Oh, it does, and you are," he said smugly, flashing a predatory smile which immediately called to mind at least a half dozen attorney/shark jokes.

Our drinks arrived, and I took a modest sip. I'm not much of a drinker, and though I do enjoy an occasional single-malt, I'm most likely apt to nurse a Scotch until long after the rocks have melted.

The same, I saw, could not be said for my lunch partner. Melcher immediately grabbed his fresh glass, tilted it towards me and said "Cheers," and then proceeded to down a decidedly un-oenophilic volume in one prolonged gulp. I didn't recall Kelly ever having mentioned alcohol as an issue in their marriage, wondered if this behavior might be something new; decided that I really didn't care, so long as his love for the grape helped to loosen his tongue.

"Melcher leaned back, eyeing me. "Before we get started, I have a couple of questions."

"Yes?" I said, my face and voice blank, though I was pretty sure what was coming.

"Sam Arguaio told me that your title is Vice President in Charge of Labor Relations. And yet, we weren't able to find your name anywhere in the company's literature."

"Yeah," I said, feigning embarrassment; "that's because until recently I wasn't listed as a full-time company employee."

"You're weren't…," Melcher said slowly, twin notes of confusion and suspicion creeping into his voice.

"See," I said, "Sam's been using me as an independent contractor for tax purposes." I shrugged. "*My* tax purposes, actually. Personnel consultant. The job's no big deal: collect workers' W-2 forms, make sure they fill out their I-9's—you know, citizenship verification? Of course you do; labor lawyer. Anyway, that's about all there is to it, except for maybe passing out an occasional pink-slip, and keeping track of vacation days, sick leave and such."

"For a while it was pretty easy sledding," I continued, "until one day, when this group of workers caught up with me in the lunch room and told me that they'd decided to organize. I tried to head them off, talk them out of it. But...well, frankly I just don't think I've got the chops for anything this...this—"

—"Complicated?" the lawyer offered, indulgently. "That *does* seem evident, doesn't it?" He flicked a nail against his glass. "Which brings me to my other question: What are *you* doing here?"

After allowing a slight, uncertain pause, I took a sip of my drink and then spoke. "Oh, you mean me instead of Sam." I shrugged. "'Last Chance Saloon,' I guess you could call it. Or maybe in a way it's some kind of punishment. But frankly, Mr. Melcher, I think the real reason I'm here is because Sam's a little...ahem, uncomfortable with the idea of meeting with you himself—you know, what with your reputation and all. Don't get me wrong; he knows he's got to hire you. Fact is, without your help we're screwed. It's just that, I guess you could say that with whatever you hinted to him over the phone, he's not crazy about getting his hands dirty, know what I mean?"

Melcher grunted; obviously he'd heard variations on this theme before. But he was clearly annoyed that the boss's timid attitude had resulted in his being forced to meet with a flunky.

"Anyway," I said, "here I am. And that's also why the fancy executive title—temporary, I expect." I frowned. "Suppose with me that's just Sam's idea of a joke."

"Got yourself in a tight spot, haven't you?" he asked, his smile a model of false compassion.

I hung my head. "You could say that," I said, making my voice small.

"All right then," he said, authoritatively, "no worries; we'll just have to call in the A-team."

I looked up, gratefully. "I sure appreciate that, Jack."

"Oh," he said, archly, "it's going to take quite a bit more than your appreciation." Then he sighed. "Am I correct in assuming that you have no power to sign contracts?"

I nodded.

"Okay," he said, dismissively; "whatever." He patted a leather portfolio on the seat next to him. "We'll send these back with you. Get them signed and faxed back to us, so we can get started right away. You can messenger the originals down to our office the next day."

"Will do."

"Now, I won't bother you with numbers"—he smiled faintly—"you'd probably burst an artery if you saw our hourly rate. But just so you know, the meter *did* start running the moment I left the office today. And as to our sizeable retainer, I have already discussed that with your boss, and I'll expect to see that included with the signed documents."

"No problem. Anyway, it's not my money," I tossed out carelessly, appending to the comment the requisite foolish grin.

"That's right," he laughed; "it isn't, is it? Good, glad we're done with that; I always find discussion of the financial arrangements rather distasteful."

The look on his face said that *that* was a lie.

"Now, let's talk about what you *can* do," he said. "To get started, I'll need a complete employee roster, with all of the people leading the organizing effort highlighted, along with their expanded profiles. I'll also need to know which union local they plan to become affiliated with." Fixing me with a flinty look, he said, "Did you happen to bring any of that with you?"

"Yes, I did," I said, brightly. "It's out in my car. But…well, I'm not sure how complete the profiles are, and I'll have to get back to you about the dope on the local."

"Don't worry about it," he said, dismissively. "We'll deal with it. For now, the list of employees will have to do."

"You want me to go get it now?" That was taking a chance, but I wanted to stay consistent with my character: anxious, obsequious.

"No, don't bother," he said, waving me off impatiently and signaling to the waiter; "no reason to interrupt our meal—you and I can walk out to your car when we're done."

Perfect.

"So, what's the plan?" I asked.

"The first thing we'll do is to file papers delaying the organizing vote. I won't bore you with the particulars; all just a bunch of legal maneuvering, nothing you need to understand…"

*Meaning: nothing you **can** understand.*

"Anyway, that's just a sideshow. The main act begins when we work the list."

"The list…"

We paused, as the waiter arrived to take our orders. In the dim light I grabbed the decorative electric candle from the center of the table, tilting it, awkwardly, in order to read the menu. Jack smirked, and pulled a credit card flashlight from his coat pocket. "Use this—although I'd just skip it and order the bouillabaisse; it's the best thing here." He emptied his glass, watched as it was removed and nodded impatiently at the offer of another to go with the meal. "But, don't wait for the food," he told the waiter: "bring it right away."

Bouillabaisse sounded fine to me, so we ordered identically. Turning back to Melcher, I could see, despite the darkness, that his eyes were becoming glassy.

Was he on his first or second when I got here?

"We were discussing the list," he resumed, as soon as the waiter had gone. "We go over it, circle the ringleaders, identify the cohorts, and then sic our investigative team on them, keeping most of our focus on the one or two leaders; because without them, the whole thing won't hang together. Now, unless these guys are saints—and, believe me, I've yet to meet one—our boys will have no trouble finding sufficient incriminating info to make them see the error of their ways."

"You're talking…blackmail," I said, deliberately sounding as if I were afraid to voice the thought.

"I dislike that word," he said, casually. "I much prefer to call it: 'persuasion with prejudice.'" He laughed at this bit of cleverness.

"Are you *that* certain you'll be able to find something on them?"

He looked at me, shaking his head. "Marcus, you worry much too much," he said, leaning back and smiling like some bizarrely corrupt Buddha. "Human nature stinks. Fact is, the only sure way to make it from cradle to grave without stepping in your own shit is to die in the crib. Everybody's got at least one or two skeletons buried somewhere. Whether it's illegal, unethical, or just plain embarrassing, there's always going to be something worth finding."

"But," I insisted, "what if you don't find anything? Or, say, what if you do, but it still doesn't scare these people enough?"

He'd obviously expected this question, and now he leaned forward; his glassy eyes lit up like coal mine lanterns, his handsome face distorted by a crooked smile.

"Well, then, Mr. Miller," he murmured, "that's when the real fun begins…"

"I don't get you."

"That's when we get to play hardball."

"Hardball…," I repeated, not wanting to telegraph that I already knew where he was going.

He shot me an impatient look. "Oh, come on, now, Mr. Miller."

"Oh," I said. "I see. Hardball."

Gotta love this guy; such an enthusiastic, unrepentant scumbag…

"That's right, my friend; *hardball*," he said, inhibitions apparently completely washed away by at least two very large glasses of wine. "See, I've got a tight little phone directory of—let's call them 'special associates'—tucked into a *very* private corner of my desk. From time to time, whenever one of our adversaries has proven to be…particularly intractable, I turn to these gentlemen. It's always a last resort, mind you; ninety percent of the time it's not even necessary to move beyond the, um, *prejudiced* persuasion. But for those moments when it *is*, it's always a good thing to have a few lads handy with scar tissue on their knuckles. And, trust me; these guys are talented—very results-oriented, if you get my drift…"

He paused, his eyes glinting, unpleasantly. "When it comes to pain, a little goes a long way. You'd be amazed at what breaking a finger or two on a dominant hand will do to a man's stubborn streak."

It was my turn to lean back. I'm sure surprise was written plainly on my face; although, from Melcher's smug reaction, I knew he was misreading it.

Was it wine or bravado—or both—that was loosening this idiot's tongue beyond all expectation?

"Sounds like you really got a handle on things, Jack," I said, thinking exactly the opposite and savoring the irony; "gotta say we've definitely found ourselves the right attorney."

"You have," he said, complacently; "trust me, you have. I doubt you'd find another firm within three thousand miles with our kinds of resources—*and* the stones to employ them."

I bowed my head with respect.

"So don't worry," Melcher said, with another kindly, crooked smile; "from here on, your troubles are over. And, who knows? You might even get to keep that fancy job title."

"If I do," I said, "I'll owe you big time, Jack."

"That you will. Tell you what, though," he said, after taking another healthy sip, "just make sure your boss signs all the papers, and pays our fees in a timely manner, and we'll call it square. Oh, and maybe you might want to drop a couple of your best boards on me."

"Oh?" I said. "You a snowboarder?"

"Of course I am," he said, casually; "pretty good at it, too, if I say so myself."

That led to a spirited winter-sports discussion, which continued as our food arrived. The bouillabaisse—*ciappino,* actually—turned out to be excellent: well-spiced and loaded with seafood in a thick broth. Beyond that, my enjoyment of the food was enhanced by the satisfaction of having had this guy spill so much dirt on himself, and with so little prodding.

There still remained one item: the matter of Jack Melcher's phony illness. It was obvious, as I watched him alternately gorging on *ciappino* and slurping wine that he was hardly sweating out a death sentence. But I still desired, perhaps superstitiously, to hear something of the man's robust health coming directly from his own mouth.

"Hey," I said, between spoonfuls, "you should think about coming up for our Winterfest this year."

"Yeah?" he mumbled, his mouth full. "What's that?"

"It's our annual season-opening celebration; early December, at Heavenly Valley."

This comment, for a change, had some truth to it. Every year since I'd known Sam, he'd been inviting me to his company's shindig at South Lake Tahoe. Everything—

transportation, room at Harrah's, meals, lift tickets—on the house. I'd never taken him up on it, my general aversion to crowds having somehow always managed to overcome the temptation to partake of the slopes, the festivities, and, especially, the gaming tables. But this year, I mused, maybe I'd mention it to Kelly.

"Sounds interesting," said Melcher, breaking into my thoughts and forcing me back into my performance.

"Oh, it is," I said, enthusiastically; "new models to demo, one-on-ones with the pros, great music, plenty of food and drink, casino action, parties in our suite upstairs…"

I now had his full attention. "That *does* sound interesting."

"And it's all comped: rooms, food, lift passes, plane tickets for you and your date—"

"My date?" he said, shaking his head. "Listen, my friend: when it comes to the kind of bash you're describing I have one very hard and fast rule."

"What's that?"

Flashing a feral grin, he said: "Never take a sandwich to a banquet."

"Huh? Oh, yeah," I said, smiling thinly, not quite able, through clenched teeth, to echo his laughter. "Sounds like words to live by."

"Damn straight. With all the loose talent at those things? It'd cramp my style."

"So," I said, "I take it you're not married."

Displaying a naked ring finger, he said: "Life's much too short, Marcus. Funny you should mention it, though: as it happens, this week-end I'm having a little reunion with my ex."

"You are," I said, hearing my voice turn to gravel.

"Yeah," he said; "but just for this week-end." He again grinned unattractively. "At least so far."

"Really." I didn't dare attempt to squeeze out more than one or two words at a time.

"Uh-huh," He said. "Just filling in a little down time, if you know what I mean…"

Again flashing that predatory smirk, causing my blood temperature to inch even higher. At that moment I could have dived over the table at him. Instead I concentrated, zen-like, on the programmed, electric flickering of the fake candle. "Nice that you and your…ex…can still get along," I managed. "I've been through it myself, and it's for damned sure *we* won't be getting together any time soon."

"For us that's no problem, because I dumped *her*," he said, smugly. "Other way around, that would have been it. But it wasn't, and that works to my advantage. Of course, she was pissed—wouldn't talk to me for months. But, fact is, she never really got over me. So now, when I get the old itch—"

"You call her," I said, tightly.

"Yep; long distance, as it happens—at the moment she's shacking up with some loser in Oregon. Anyway, I call, give her a dose of 'I need you,' and come Friday night, she'll be walking through my door."

"Wow," I said, dryly, "as simple as that…"

"Well," he said, laughing, "not quite. But it's all *you* need to know."

"But couldn't that sort of thing get kind of…complicated?"

"Nah," he said, dismissively. "When I'm done, I cut her loose. Ciao, Baby, thanks for the ride. Besides, she's well worth the expense of a plane ticket and a couple of meals. You should see this lady; she is one helluva piece of ass."

"Really," I said; "so how come you dumped her?"

"She's getting old," he shrugged. "Pushing forty. You know how it is; still great-looking, but for how long? I'm not exactly the 'til death do us part' type; can't stand the thought of waking up next to a prune. Besides, girls in their twenties tend to be a whole lot easier to—"

"Yeah, right," I said; then stuffed another spoonful into my mouth, wanting to finish the meal as quickly as my utensils allowed. At this point I'd heard more than enough.

I looked at my watch, then said, "We'd better finish up; got a flight to catch, and I need to turn in the rental."

"Why didn't you grab a taxi?" he asked.

"I hate them," I lied; "One time in Portland my cab driver smashed us into a parked UPS truck. What a mess; I was lucky to walk away from it with all my parts still attached."

I signaled the waiter for the check. When he arrived, I reached for it, noticing that Melcher didn't make a move. But when I pulled out my money clip, peeled some bills and inserted them into the padded binder, he raised an eyebrow.

"Cash?" he said.

"Told you; Sam's nervous. He doesn't want there to be any kind of record. I paid cash for everything." Another lie: In fact, I *had* used my card for everything else.

The reason for not pulling out the plastic here, of course, was that the name *Hank Cassidy* was embossed upon it.

"Oh come on," he said, rolling his eyes, "how paranoid can you get?"

I just shrugged.

Chapter Thirty-Three

Melcher was happily, tipsily gabby as we walked from the hotel to the parking structure. What he was saying I had no idea, because I wasn't listening. Halfway across the garage, however, as he saw where my car was parked, his chattiness abruptly fell away.

"Why'd you park all the way back there?" he asked.

"Oh," I said, "just a foible, I guess. Hate having to explain why the rental's got a dent, so I always park it as far away as I can. Tell you the truth; I also do it with my own car. Pretty neurotic, huh?"

"Uh-huh," he grunted, and was mostly silent for the rest of the walk.

When we reached my car, I slowed just enough to let Melcher pass me. Then I spoke:

"You know, Jack; for a guy dying of cancer, you sure look healthy to me…"

At these words, surprise, then a wary, if hazy, look of caution spread across his face.

"Huh?"

I shrugged, and squared my stance as I faced him.

"Hey, what the fuck *is* this?" he demanded, attempting, yet not quite achieving an imperious tone as he cast anxious glances over my shoulder, towards the distant elevators.

"Well, I guess the first thing I should tell you is that my name's not really Marcus Miller."

"Who the fuck *are* you?" He asked, his face now a roadmap of confusion.

"Oh, come on now, Jack," I replied, pleasantly; "who am I?"

He hesitated. Hesitated some more. Then his eyes narrowed. "Hank Cassidy," he said.

"There you go. The loser your ex-wife is shacking up with."

"Look," he said, indignantly; "if you think that you're going to—"

"No, don't," I said, holding up a hand, and enjoying the instinctive flinch it produced; "don't bother. You've already talked plenty; now you get to listen."

"But, I—"

I slapped him.

Hard.

A slap can be quite the handy device; a real attention getter—not to mention much faster at sobering a foggy subject than a half dozen cups of strong black coffee. In this case it was particularly effective: Melcher did stagger a bit, but then he quickly righted himself, and stood silently, rubbing his cheek and glaring at me resentfully, like a chastised child.

"What do you want?" he muttered.

"Not that much, really. But before we get into that, you need to know how things stand."

He was silent.

"First, you might want to recall the way you ran your yap over the fish stew. Talk about being hoisted by your own *petard;* land sakes, Jack, that is *some* kind of careless for a lawyer."

"Hearsay," he insisted, trying to somehow resurrect his confidence, his still-tender jaw jutting, pugnaciously; "nothing but hearsay—my word against yours."

"Actually," I said, producing a slim, very stylish digital recorder from my inside coat pocket; "more like *your* word against yours." I hit rewind, ran it back, then pressed forward and played just enough to prove that I had, in fact, recorded our entire conversation. "Nice fidelity, don't you think? Man, the stuff you can buy right off the shelf these days…"

Melcher gaped, as I slipped the machine back into my coat pocket.

"That's right, Counselor; the hidden recorder—oldest trick in the book."

He opened his mouth as if to speak, then closed it.

"Face it, Jack," I said; "this time you've stepped in your *own* shit. Big time."

The squealing of tires interrupted us. Lack of accompanying engine noise suggested that it was coming from a lower level, but by now it didn't really matter: from the way his eyes kept straying to my jacket, I knew that Melcher wasn't going anywhere. Besides, anyone driving by at the moment would've just assumed us to be a couple of businessmen, deep in conversation.

"Now," I said, "about Kelly: You have succeeded in conning her into coming down here. But if you think she's looking forward to it, then you've also conned yourself, because she's been making herself sick just thinking about having to breathe the same air as you."

"But it really doesn't matter any more, because we both know that you're not sick. In fact, aside from what I'd call a neurotic preoccupation with cosmetic surgery, I'd say that you are one healthy son of a bitch."

Melcher's eyes widened. "What? How did you—"

"As it happens, Jack, I've got some pretty sharp resources of my own. Thanks to them I now have a fairly comprehensive knowledge of your medical record—from last year's colonoscopy, to your latest check-up. And, guess what—not a single test or treatment anywhere for pancreatic cancer."

The misery on the man's face was so acute that I almost felt sorry for him. Worst thing that can happen to a control freak; having every scheme suddenly laid naked, rendered impotent. Melcher stared at the concrete, his eyes unwilling or unable to meet mine.

"Now," I said, "my resources could have stopped with your medical records; but being thorough, they also dug into your professional life, and, wouldn't you know, they found enough material there to suggest that you're just as miserable an attorney as you were a husband. Word on the street is that there isn't a D.A. in town who wouldn't give his left nut to have a shot at you. Of course, until now they've not been quite able to pull it off—but, with this?"——Again I produced the recorder—"Kind of a new ballgame, don't you think?"

Seemingly against his will, Melcher's eyes rose, and he stared at the device with painful fascination, as if I'd just torn a vital organ from his body and held it, dripping, in front of him.

"You'll never make it stick, Cassidy," he hissed; "you can't…this is bullshit. This is entrapment—"

"Entrapment? No, not exactly, since I'm a civilian. And, you're right; it's also probably not admissible evidence. But when I turn it over, I'm guessing there're gonna be all sorts of official types crawling up your ass. Stones that got left unturned before will surely get flipped this time. At the very least, you'll be disbarred, disowned by your firm, dumped by friends. And the girls? Hell, Jack, my guess is after all of this is over you won't be able to get a date with an eight-dollar hooker. Of course, with what's more likely to come of this, it won't matter. Handsome guy like you, I imagine you'll be the belle of the ball up there at Corcoran..."

"It won't happen," he managed, in a strangled voice; "they'll never accept it."

"Maybe," I said; "maybe they won't. Maybe the district attorney will tell me to take a hike. Maybe you *won't* go to prison and become Bubba's bitch. *Maybe...*"

"What do you want?" he said, eyes still glued to my machine.

"First, you call Kelly. Tell her you're cured, tell her you lied, tell her you've got a new twenty-something with rock-hard titties—I really don't care. What matters is that the trip is off. Whatever she says, you don't need her anymore. And, after that, you never contact her again."

"What else?"

"What else is you lose the file on Arguaio. There was no union issue; Sam was just doing me a favor, setting up this appointment and providing me with cover. But as far as you and your firm are concerned, ABW doesn't exist."

"What am I supposed to tell them back at the office?" he asked, truculently. "This lunch was on the books; we spent time on research! What am I supposed to say about that?"

"That's your problem, Jack. You fix it. You've been there long enough; I'm sure you have the pull to make it all go away. Just do it."

He nodded, then nodded at the digital recorder. "And in return you'll hand that over?"

"No," I said, patiently, "in return I won't turn it over to the *authorities*. The machine stays with me—insurance, let's say, against your ever having a change of heart."

"I see," he said, his face hardening. "And if I refuse? I *am* a lawyer, you know—a fucking good one; I think I know better than you how far you'll get with an unverifiable voice recording."

"Besides," he continued, his eyes glinting despite the dim light, "if you're thinking of using that thing against me you might want to remember that I *do* have my...*friends*."

I shook my head. I wasn't asking for much. Kelly meant nothing to him; leaving her alone would hardly be a sacrifice. And as for his firm's abortive relationship with ABW; wiping the slate clean would barely cause a ripple at the office.

But obviously Jack was a man who couldn't stand to lose, no matter how minor the stakes.

"Ah," I said, with a smile that caused Melcher's smugness to falter; "Your *friends;* scar tissue, knuckles, yadda yadda. You really want to go there? For this? My guess is that those horses belong to someone else's stable. You can't possibly be employing them full-time."

Despite an effort to conceal it, Melcher's face told me that I was spot on.

"Now," I said; "if that's true, then the proprietors of that stable aren't going to be too pleased to hear that you've been wagging your tongue like a Skid Row snitch. They don't like that, Jack; wise guys tend to be allergic to the light. My guess is that they might want to take you off the board, themselves."

Then I allowed my smile to disappear, my voice to go flat.

"No matter, though, because if you cross me, I will kill you long before they get a chance."

Startled, Melcher looked at me; searched my face for some sign of bluff, found none.

"All right," he mumbled, examining his tassled loafers.

"You win."

Chapter Thirty-Four

I should have felt pretty good on the flight back to Bend.

After all, in one, brief afternoon, I'd utterly demolished a foe and eliminated a physical threat to Kelly—with very little actual violence and not a single drop of spilled blood.

I felt lousy.

It didn't help that the plane was even more crowded than it had been on the trip down, and that my window seat was providing me with a severe challenge to be able to fit my legs into the tiny space allotted them without rubbing up against those of my neighbor. I was left squirming, contorting; and silently, impatiently intoning the mantra: *just a two hour flight...just two hours...*

But physical discomfort wasn't really the issue; the problem was what to do about Kelly.

Should I tell her what I'd done? Or should I hold off, and wait to first see if Melcher contacted her to call the trip off? And if I was going to do that, what story should I give her when she asked me how my day had gone? I'd already deceived her by neglecting to mention my plans; could I push the omission into commission and lie outright?

How would Kelly react when she found out?

Man, this plane was cramped.

Chapter Thirty-Five

As it turned out, it was a waste of time chewing over what to say to my girlfriend.

And what told me this was Kelly's computer case.

More an elaborate satchel than mere laptop carrier, it had been my extravagant gift to Kelly in celebration of her new teaching position. She loved the thing: distressed, hand-tooled saddle leather, a plethora of pockets and slots, a myriad of buckles and straps. Kelly joked that in it she could tote the computer, her lesson plans for an entire year, and half of the smaller kids in her class. But the only times I ever actually saw the case fully loaded and fastened were when she was either leaving for work, or had just come home. At all other times, her laptop and a good portion of her paperwork were to be seen strewn out over at least a corner of the dining room table—even while we were eating. I suppose that some alternate location would have to be found if we were ever to have company for dinner; but, as with our habitual isolationism that circumstance had not yet arisen, the laptop on the table was as expected a sight as the table itself.

And yet today, as I walked into the great room after having been warmly greeted by Satchmo, I saw that the table was bare, and, sitting next to it on the floor, Kelly's case was both packed full and securely strapped close.

My unease growing, I turned, to find Kelly sitting on one of the over-stuffed leather chairs flanking the empty stone fireplace on the far wall, her eyes fixed upon me as I moved into the room, her face a mask. I realized now that my options had shrunk to one:

"He called," I said.

"He called," she responded, tonelessly.

"He was lying to you," I said, adding, unnecessarily: "about his illness."

"So what?" she snapped. "You think I didn't suspect it? That I was that stupid?"

"No, Honey, of course not," I said, feeling pretty much that anything I attempted to say, at the moment, was going to be wrong, but pushing ahead anyway. "But, it's just that, I was afraid…afraid that he might—"

"Beat me up," she said, growing hotter. "Will you look at that—I've got my own private Galahad. Well, Sir Knight, were you that certain I'd be unable to handle things myself? Do you really think so little of me?"

I couldn't answer. Fact was, I really *didn't* think Kelly capable of handling a man who'd dominated her so completely and violently. But to voice that sentiment now was to somehow suggest that I had no faith in her at all, and that, of course, was far from the truth.

But that's how it would have sounded, and so I remained silent—which was probably just as bad. Looking towards the window, I saw Satch sitting in front of the glass, watching the two of us attentively, alternately, like a tennis spectator. Ordinarily, upon greeting me she would've immediately returned to the opposite side of the great room and assumed a place on the sofa, near as possible to Kelly; but today, with that unerring situational sense, she kept a respectful distance.

"You know, Hank," Kelly said, "two seconds after I saw Jack, I would've known he was faking. Two seconds after that I would've been telling him what a colossal dickhead he was; and ten minutes after *that,* I would have been on my way back to the airport. Case *closed.*"

"If he let you go," I said.

"You mean, if he didn't break my nose or my arm, or strangle me, right?" she barked. "But you weren't about to let *that* happen, were you, hero? You were just going to pre-empt the whole thing; fly down there like some glorious avenging angel, put the fear of Cassidy in my ex-husband's head, and then fly back in magnificent triumph, huh?"

"Kelly, I was worried...I just wanted to help," I said, hating how pathetic I was sounding.

The heat in her voice dropping slightly, she said: "So, how did you find out he was faking?"

"We did a little research."

"*We?* Who besides you?"

"Cy," I admitted. Lying would have only made it worse. "He accessed Jack's insurance records, found no charges for cancer treatment, or even for preliminary testing and diagnosis."

Kelly was quiet, weighing what I'd just told her.

"And that wasn't all he found," I added.

"Oh?" In spite of herself, she was curious.

I then went on to explain Cy's exploration into Melcher's shady legal dealings. "Were you aware that your husband was a crook?" I asked when I'd finished.

"Me?" she said, "Well, nothing concrete, but I always suspected that something was off. Jack liked to brag about his tactics; always used words like 'muscle,' 'strong-arm,' and 'intimidation.' With all the tough-guy talk, he sounded more like a *consigliere* than a labor attorney. I often thought that if the mob ever approached him with a direct offer, he'd probably jump at the chance."

"No doubt," I said.

Now we were both silent: Kelly, obviously digesting the fresh information; I, relishing a moment of mutual opinion which had at least temporarily stemmed the wave of anger.

Unfortunately, the respite was short-lived.

"So, what'd you do," she asked, sarcastically; "knock him around a little, threaten to give him a taste of his own medicine?"

Nothing like that; just one little attention-getting slap was all.

"No," I said, trying to sound reasonable. "What I did was threaten to expose him." I went on to explain how I'd taken advantage of Melcher's wine-loosened tongue, gotten him to reveal some damning details into my hidden recorder, then used his own words to blackmail him. What I *didn't* mention, of course, was my bottom-line threat to kill him. But after all, I had no real intention of following through with that one; the fact that he happened to believe it was just one of those convenient things.

"Quite a little sting operation," she said, without a trace of admiration.

"It worked," I said.

"So, why didn't you tell me?"

"What?"

Kelly turned full upon me. "Why didn't you run it by me *before* you hopped the plane?"

It was an obvious question. And yet, I realized, in all my calculations I'd never actually given it much thought. Now that she'd asked, it seemed unbelievably foolish that I hadn't.

"I don't know," I said, not daring to avert my eyes, "I guess I just thought you'd—"

"What?" she said, her anger freshening. "Tell you not to go through with it? And what if I had? This is *my* life we're talking about, isn't it? Don't you think I deserve a little consideration? Couldn't you have come to me, shown me what you'd learned about Jack's fake illness and sleazy business practices? Who knows…maybe I would have hit the roof right there; called him and told him to fuck off—and that would have been that, wouldn't it?"

"Hank, you really don't understand, do you?" she continued. "The worst thing, the most awful thing about my marriage, wasn't that Jack verbally abused me, or that he cheated, or even that he knocked me around; it was that, in every major decision of our life together, I never got to have a vote. He made all of those decisions with absolutely no concern for, or even a willingness to listen to, my opinions. I was a non-person in that house; just a blank Stepford wife—there to look pretty for him and his friends, cook and clean, and to service him whenever he felt the urge."

"And that little dictatorship of his held all the way through to the final act—to our breakup. Jack simply walked away, ended it, and I was left to wonder how much of what had gone wrong had been my fault; how much my own lack of self-worth had contributed to the disdain he had shown me. It also left me wondering if I'd ever be able to be an equal partner in any future relationship."

Kelly rose from the chair, moved to her briefcase, and stood over it. "And now here *you* are, taking this masterful, decisive action in a major event in *my* life, without so much as a word about it to me." Her voice softened. "I don't know, Hank; maybe that's just the way you are. You're a man of action: you analyze the situation, make a firm choice, and then act without hesitation—probably always successfully. It works for you; I get it. But, far as I'm concerned, it's my marriage all over again. I can't excuse it, Hank, I *can't;* because if I do, it's as much as admitting that I'm really not capable of running my own life." She bent over, picked up the case, and faced me, sighing. "And that's why I've got to leave."

I watched helplessly as she made her way to the door to the garage. "But…where will you go?" I asked, hearing the choked quality of my voice.

"I'm going to a friend of mine's place, another teacher," she said, coldly; "someone whose name you don't need to know, because I don't want you to try to contact me."

"But, Kelly," I said, "is that really it? All the time we've had; all the good feelings, the happiness…this one thing happens and it's over? Are you really prepared to say that?"

She paused at the door, and I could see that she was just barely keeping herself together. "I…I don't know, Hank," she said, her voice breaking; "I need time to think. I don't know…"

"Kelly, I am so sorry."

She smiled sadly. "I know you are, Honey."

"I wish you'd stay here, let us talk this out."

"Yes," she said, "I'm sure you do. But, today…well, today you don't get to have a vote."

And with that she was gone.

Chapter Thirty-Six

I rose early Tuesday morning, suffering from a massive hangover headache caused, not so much by alcohol consumption—although there'd been plenty of that—as by acute fatigue and despair.

Monday evening had been a miserable blur. Though I'd gone up to my office and attempted to get back into the Sayles case, I wasn't able to concentrate, and, after an hour or so of staring uselessly at my notes, I'd given up and headed downstairs, pausing, at the bottom, to consider whether to commit to a sweaty session in the gym, or a couple of hours of vegetation in front of the TV. In the end, both seemed too much like work, so I'd retreated to the liquor cabinet, pulling out a bottle of Johnnie Walker Black, filling a tall glass with ice from the fridge, and then moving to the dining table, where I spent a hazy and indeterminate period drinking and gazing out the window at the impenetrable blackness of a starless, unforgiving night.

When, belatedly, I realized that eighty-proof was only exacerbating the problem, I left the glass and bottle on the table and staggered back up the stairs, this time trying to find sanctuary in the master bedroom, where I flopped, fully-clothed, onto the bed. I then spent another fitful couple of hours, alternating between woefully short stretches of sleep, each rudely terminating in spasmodic jolts of painful awareness; and far more extended periods of insomnia, spent staring at the dark, blank ceiling and begging my brain to for heaven sakes *please* shut down.

By three a.m., I'd had enough of both, and so, out of desperation, I wandered back to my office, where I booted up my computer, went online and spent the rest of the night hunched over, mindlessly playing craps, until I finally passed out in my chair sometime before sunrise. It was there that I awoke, a few minutes after eight, to the sound of my dog whining, her snout planted firmly on my knee, eyes staring up at me, expectantly. Glancing at the screen, I saw that while I slept I'd timed out from my seat at the online craps table; but that, apparently, I'd stayed awake long enough prior to that to actually *win* money—over four hundred dollars, in fact. I shook my head. With absolutely no memory of anything I could just as easily have lost a couple thousand. Nevertheless, as I slowly pulled myself out of my chair, with my leaden mind I was numb to any sense of good fortune, or, even, relief at possible financial disaster averted.

Skipping a shower, I trudged slowly downstairs, picked up the leash and robotically followed Satch out the front door, trying—and failing—to ignore the nagging thought that I was now about to perform a task which had only yesterday had fallen to Kelly. And, as we made our way along the familiar path to the river, my raw, susceptible emotions turned every angle of the path, every bush and tree into reminders of moments we'd shared. By the time we'd made it back to the house, I was faced with the inevitable conclusion that if I allowed my day to continue in this manner I would be surrounded, haunted by a legion of stark symbols of Kelly's absence, and along with it, my stupidity.

I needed to shake things up.

After hanging up Satch's leash and then putting down a bowl of her food, I finally obliged myself to down a quick breakfast, then ran upstairs to the bathroom, showered, gave my hair a quick once-over; then dressed and headed back to the ground floor, and thence, to the garage.

I needed to get busy with work. It was the last thing I felt like doing at the moment; my stomach was permanently sour, my body heavy with fatigue, mind dull and lifeless. But I knew that throwing myself into something more closely resembling work was far a far better choice than the alternative: a full day of worry, regret and self-flagellation, followed by another equally wretched, empty, sleep-deprived night.

Kelly was right; this *is* the way I'm wired. If you were being extremely charitable, you might call me *decisive.* If not; the more appropriate descriptions would likely be *impulsive*, *stubborn*—and, if you were being brutally frank; *pig-headed.* I know that, in certain areas, this attitude has worked to my advantage—years ago in my government work; more recently in the steel-cage arena of commercial real estate.

But, where it concerns the other part of my life; the part that might involve and affect someone close to me, it's a particularly crummy way to behave. This is because when I calculate and reach those decisions, my tendency is to do so with such tunnel vision that I seldom leave room for outside opinion. As my long-ago partner, Cyrus Brooks had well understood this: in order to assert his own priorities, he'd literally had to shoulder his way into those calculations. We'd had quite a number of arguments about it, a few times almost coming to blows (which, considering Cy's enormous size and skill, likely would not have ended well for me), before I finally came to understand that I was going to have to concede to him an equal share in our decision-making.

I also know that this attitude probably has its genesis in a single day. A Friday, in fact, just over a week before my first day of college. A blustery, biting, merciless, early-autumn day. I can still see the riot of freshly-fallen brown and gold leaves blanketing the front yard as I open the door to a matched pair of tall, sallow, uniformed policemen. I can sense their reluctance; see their shifting feet, their averted eyes as I wait for one of them to speak. Finally the cop on the left takes the plunge, first verifying that I am, in fact, the person they have been sent here to see; then informing me, in flat, institutional tones, of the catastrophic, multi-auto smash-up on the D.C. Beltway which has just stolen both of my parents from me.

I remember that, at that moment, I sank to the floor, unable to speak—unable, even, to cry; and yet, inside my head I could hear screaming; a caterwauling so intense that, in my fever, I half-imagined that the neighbors must've been clapping their hands over their ears. I'm not sure how long it took for the banshee's wailing to fade away: days, weeks—maybe even months; but when it finally did, the emptiness which replaced it was almost worse, because within it I was forced to grapple with the fact that from then on I would be completely alone (I did have two relatives: a slightly dotty aunt on my mother's side—useless from the standpoint of any meaningful contact; and my father's older brother, whom I'd never met, and who lived a monastic existence in the western woods of Maine.)

But, over time, we adjust to our situations, no matter how trying, no matter how crushingly unfair—simply because we have no other choice. The circumstance which had been so violently thrust upon me that fall day eventually became tolerable, then familiar—ultimately, comfortable. Fortunately, I was old enough at the time to avoid the nightmare of being shuffled from one foster home to another, while sufficiently young and resilient to be able to adapt to my new life without becoming consumed and paralyzed by the injustice of it. In time I learned and become accustomed to making all of the major decisions of my life without the benefit of anyone close to consult with.

Helping me with this was the fact that my parents had left behind the proceeds of a fairly generous life insurance policy, along with the deed to our two-story Georgetown brownstone, which, fortunately, was free and clear—the mortgage having been retired several years before. With the cash from the policy, along with earnings from a succession of part-time jobs, I'd been able to maintain my home as I studied my way to a bachelor's, and then a master's degree in international relations at the university, which was walking distance from my front door. And when I was done, when Uncle Sam's recruiter subsequently approached me with the offer of a new, exotic career, I then immediately sold the family home, shoved most of the proceeds into government notes, and resolutely walked away, having by now molded a mental process which had begun as reflexive self-preservation, into something solid and sturdy.

Eventually, this peculiar, iron-clad decision-making process of mine had worked its way so deeply into my bones, that it had become automatic, almost unconscious. It had served me well, personally and professionally over the years, so long as I never allowed anyone deeply enough into my life to be affected by it. I'd had any number of romantic entanglements over the years; but none important enough to ever cause me to seriously address this stubborn, selfish aspect of my personality.

Until now. With the shocking sound of a door slamming I was forced to realize that my actions had resulted in driving Kelly from my home—possibly, from my life. Ironically, I also realized that in being so instinctively resolute in cutting her out of my decision to scare off her ex-husband, I now found myself in a position where any consideration of our possible future together would be entirely beyond my control. Kelly would decide, on her own—or, at least, entirely without any input from me—whether or not she wanted to come back. And, until she made that decision, there was nothing I could do about it.

Faced with this, therefore, I knew that the only course of action left open to me at the moment—aside from staying home and continuing to flog myself—was to turn my attention away from my personal problems, and dive back into my work.

And, most immediately, that meant climbing into my car and driving fifteen miles south to La Pine; to the Bluebird Motel.

Chapter Thirty-Seven

The Bluebird is located in the heart of the business strip of La Pine, a small Oregon city only incorporated a few years back. In classic small-town American tradition, Highway 97 doubles as the main drag, bisecting the city north-south for approximately a mile, its extent dotted on either side with home-style eateries, modest strip-malls, auto parts and appliance stores, and unpretentious real estate offices. I'd not spent much time there, though I had attended a couple of football games at La Pine High School, and had stopped two or three times, while passing through, at a local stand for burgers and fries.

The motel itself, one of the older establishments in the town, was drab, rundown; far more of the *Bates* about it than *Ramada:* an L-shaped, shabby collection of connected bungalows partially surrounding a lumpy, cracked parking lot haphazardly marked with weathered, barely visible lines. The architecture style—if such it could be called— seemed to be early sixties roadhouse, with wood walls covered in peeling, faded paint whose original color may or may not have once passed for mahogany, and a covered gallery, which fronted the entire length of the building and robbed every room of the possibility of direct sunlight.

Looking up as I pulled into the parking lot driveway, I noticed a cheap plastic sign positioned just beneath the motel's name on the tall, metal pole, advertising "Free Cable" and "Kitchenette Units," while also offering "Bargain Rates—Daily, Weekly, Monthly." In the city, I reflected, such a dive would also be flashing hourly prices--but since the working girls of La Pine were likely plying their trade up the road at the local truck stop or back in the woods out of their own trailers, the pay-for-play business would hardly be hopping at this joint—therefore the nearly empty lot and the well-lit "vacancy" sign. I wondered what a monthly charge might run to, looked at two extremely dilapidated sedans parked in front of units at the far end of the building and guessed that these belonged to long-term tenants. For them, instead of *Bluebird,* the place more appropriately should have been named *End of the Line.*

While absorbing all of this, I glanced across the street and noticed a thick hedge fronting a grocery store parking lot—which immediately conjured an image of Joshua Sayles, hidden behind it in his father's pickup; crouching in the driver's seat with his stomach churning as he waits for his mother to emerge from the seedy motel room with her cowboy lover. One could easily imagine his feelings: dismay that his suspicions about his mom's actions have been confirmed, combined with disgust at her choice of companion and revulsion at the amazingly sleazy location of their rendezvous.

The motel office occupied the front half of the bungalow at the end closest to the highway, and was distinguished by a dingy, streaked, plate glass window, along with a small neon *manager* sign which was suspended above the door next to it.

I parked in the space directly in front of the office, got out of my car, and entered, pushing open the slightly warped, creaky wood and glass door. Inside, I found myself in a cramped reception area rank with the odor of mildewed, threadbare carpet and ancient cigarette smoke. At the far end to my right stood a battered table carelessly strewn with faded tourist pamphlets and local maps, next to which was a dusty rotating metal display stand, partially and haphazardly stocked with an assortment of "Welcome to Oregon" and "Greetings from La Pine" postcards. Directly in front of me, parallel with the window, was the reception counter, currently unmanned, and adorned solely with the requisite front desk bell and well-worn, three-ring registration book. Behind the counter was a cluttered metal desk with an ancient black rotary telephone; above it, a blank, water-stained wall, the only apparent attempt to decorate it being an "Ace Hardware" calendar, hung on a nail, with the wrong month displayed.

To the right of the desk was an open doorway, out of which was blaring the tinny, distorted, and extraordinarily loud television strains of one of those "World's Stupidest Criminals" or "Worst Drivers," or "Craziest Pedestrians," or some such. I stepped to the counter, and, wondering if it was going to be piercing enough to cut through a hundred or so decibels of overly dramatic canned music, editorially-augmented tire screeches and shrill voiceovers, hammered away at the bell.

Somewhat to my surprise, my efforts were rewarded. Almost immediately, the volume on the unseen TV dropped away, and a surly, gravelly male voice barked out: "With you in a second, alright?" I then waited patiently, listening to a medley of clothes-rustling, zipper-pulling and knocking of thick rubber heels against wood as the guy took his sweet time putting himself together. At last, he appeared in the doorway, rubbing a stubbly chin and squinting at me, myopically, before he scuffled in and took up a position behind the counter.

I have occasionally heard tales from people in Bend about how La Pine had been originally settled by fugitives on the run from the Law, who'd found in the almost impenetrable forests of the region a convenient refuge. I've never taken any of these comments seriously, sensing that the stories tend to smack, mainly, of unkind urban legend, most likely arising out of the condescension many Bend residents appear to display for their "poor relations" twenty-five miles to the south. But if in fact there is any truth to those claims, then the guy presently standing on the opposite side of the counter from me could well have been one of the founding fathers.

Aged anywhere from forty-five to sixty, he was tall, pale, and kind of spindly; but with a body of ropey, sinewy construction that suggested scrappy strength, and alert, darting eyes that hinted at a kind of rudimentary, animal-like intelligence. He had a wide, shiny forehead, which reached all the way to the middle of his scalp, for which he apparently chose to compensate by wearing what remained of his gray-black hair long, allowing it to pour, in thin, greasy rivulets onto his bony shoulders. His cheekbones were high and prominent, and his hawk-nose looked to have been broken several times, with no evidence of any medical attention ever having been paid to it. Though there was no beard, my guess was that the man was adhering to a strict, every-fourth-day shaving regimen—that fourth day being, apparently, tomorrow.

His baggy, well-worn jeans were held up by a wide, seriously-weathered black leather belt secured with a massive Smith and Wesson crossed-pistols buckle; his upper body was covered by a once black but long since faded-to-gray Harley-Davidson T-shirt; and his feet traveled in black, beat-up, square-toed motorcycle boots with chains girding them. These metal links were matched by a heavier biker key chain, decorated with tiny silver skulls, which draped from a belt loop and disappeared into his right jeans pocket. His skinny, exposed arms were extensively adorned with crude, monochromatic prison tattoos, many of which proudly advertised his Aryan Brotherhood affiliation, and his dirty fingernails suggested that his main transportation was a late-model, high-maintenance Hog—a panhead, perhaps, maybe even a knucklehead—which was probably at this very moment leaning on its kickstand over a substantial oil spot in the alley behind his room.

He gave me a silent once-over, evidently noting that while my clothes were hardly fancy, they were still freshly washed and pressed, and fit me well; then glanced over my shoulder, and took in both the newness and cleanliness of my 4-Runner parked out front. From these observations he must have deduced that there was little chance of my being a potential customer, because he made no move to slide the registration book towards me.

"What can I do you for, Hoss?" he asked, pleasantly, flashing an inmate's servile grin and revealing a mouth filled with more gaps than teeth—which, along with his gaunt stature, blatantly proclaimed a long and passionate association with crystal meth.

"Just a little information," I responded.

"Yeah?" he said, his eyes narrowing as he ran a greasy hand through his greasy hair. "You ain't no cop, man."

It wasn't a question, but it demanded an answer. "You're right," I said, "I'm not the police."

He nodded, satisfied. It was an old and widely-understood dance: once you got the guy to announce that he wasn't a cop, he was then supposedly legally proscribed from subsequently pulling his badge. Prostitutes had long used the technique as an opening line whenever their suspicions were aroused about a prospective john, and the practice had eventually spread to all areas where undercover cops were likely to operate.

"So," he said, once again displaying a mostly toothless—though this time somewhat craftier—grin, "what *are* you; hired dick or somethin'?"

"You nailed it, pardner," I said. "I'm a private investigator—name's Hank Cassidy." I did not extend a hand, since I suspected he would have ignored the gesture, which would then have resulted in unnecessary awkwardness. Besides, I'd just bathed...

"Jackson," he responded, dully.

"First name or last name?"

"Just Jackson."

"Okay."

"I ain't gotta talk to you, brother." As he said this, his right hand slid out of sight behind the counter, making me wonder whether there was a tire iron, a switchblade, or possibly even a pistol or sawed-off shotgun stashed under there.

"That's true," I said, reaching extravagantly (albeit *very* slowly) for my wallet; "you don't, Jackson. But then again if you don't, you're gonna be out some beer money."

"Yeah?" he said, his voice showing interest, but still sounding a note of caution. "And how much beer might that be?"

"Depends on what brand you're partial to. At any rate, I'd say at least a good couple of cases..."

From the way his eyes widened at this estimate, I suspected that I probably could have gotten all I wanted with a couple of six-packs.

"So, whaddaya wanna know, Hoss?" he said, now sounding considerably more friendly and cooperative.

I pulled Nadine Sayles' picture from my jacket pocket. But before showing it to him, I said:

"You're pretty much the Man around here, right?"

Even from across the counter his harsh laugh smelled strongly of stale beer, tobacco and acute lack of Listerine.

"The *Man*," he snorted; "Yeah, guess you could put it that way," he said, taking a step back and then hocking up and discharging a mouthful of something unspeakable into the corner to the right. "See, my brother, he owns the place." He grinned, sourly, then muttered: "Baby-fuckin'-brother—the successful one'a the family." "Which kinda makes me the black sheep...case you're wonderin'. Anyway, he gimme this job. Mighty big of him, ain't it? Yeah...mighty generous."—another editorial loogie lofted, gracefully, into the same corner—"Shit wages, work my fuckin' ass off...long hours; day'n night—practically nobody else around the dump to spell me." He jerked a thumb towards the open doorway. "'Course, he *is* kind enough to let me crash in the fuckin' broom closet back there." He shrugged, then said, "Yeah; the fuckin' Man, that's what I am—fuckin' *slave,* more like..."

I nodded, keeping my face neutral. Evidently Jackson was a man starved for sympathetic ears. I also couldn't help but be amused by his definition of "successful,"—considering the bare-bones maintenance condition of this flea-bag Ritz, along with its nearly-empty parking lot. Anyway, my guess about the true state of things was that Jackson had a revolving door association with various regional penal institutions, and therefore his current employment status had far less to do with family loyalty than it did a lack of alternative prospects.

"How long have you been here?" I asked.

"Ev'ry since I got outta the joint, back in Feb-yuary." He grinned. "Yeah, I know you made me for a con right off. Kinda hard to disguise it walkin' 'round with all this fuckin' brickyard art." He defiantly held out both heavily tatted arms for my perusal.

"So," I said, pushing on, "you'd be the one most likely to check people in and out over the last few months..."

Again, a grin. "Just *in,* Hoss, just in; don't nobody never bother to check out; they pays up front when they come in, splits the next morning, leave the fuckin' keys in the room—if the assholes even remember to do *that* much."

Satisfied that I had the right guy, and, further, that I'd established something of a rapport with him, I said, "Okay," and showed him the picture. "Recognize her?"

I could see that he, in fact, did, right away. But for purely dramatic purposes, he took his time, scratching at his grizzled chin and sideburns thoughtfully, before finally nodding:

"Yeah, guess I seen her."

"How often?"

He shrugged. "Lotsa times." Then he grinned, archly. "Lady has been *busy,* if you know what I mean."

"You happen to see who she was being busy with?"

He started to answer, then stopped, and fixed a sly stare on me. "You serious about the cash, brother?"

I pulled a twenty from my wallet and dropped it onto the counter, where it was greedily snatched up as soon as it hit the grime-stained Formica. I then deliberately kept the wallet in my right hand where he could see it.

"Who was the guy?" I said.

"Well now," he said, now smiling cheerfully while continuing to cast furtive, hopeful glimpses at my billfold; "most of the times it was Darryl; Darryl Turnick."

"*Most* of the times," I repeated, working hard to keep the surprise out of my voice. "You mean there were others?"

"Yeah, Boss," he said; "that's 'zactly what I mean. Toldja the quiff was busy, didn't I? I guess you could say that ole Darryl's only been her latest an' greatest; though I think this 'ticular ho-down's been goin' on for some time, now. But before him there was at least two others that I knowed about."

I considered pursuing this, then decided, at least for the moment, to keep it simple. "So how long *has* she been seeing Darryl?"

More chin-scratching, more greedy looks at the wallet. "Oh...let's say 'bout two months or so, give or take." He again displayed his meager collection of teeth. "Might say they was our best customers, 'side from the monthlies. Yeah...been back there in that room bumpin' uglies just 'bout ever' week." He smirked. "Pretty noisy about it too––if you know what I mean..."

This last comment conjured up an unpleasant, grinning image of Jackson, ears cocked, making numerous unnecessary excursions past their motel room door. I immediately banished the thought and moved on:

"You know this guy Turnick?"

"I guess I do..." Another significant pause; another covetous glance at my wallet as he rubbed at a "1%" tattoo on the right side of his neck. Time to prime the pump. Out came another twenty, which disappeared just as fast as its brother into his greasy pants pocket. "Yeah," he said, "Darryl's a dude hangs out at George's, down there on Taylor. Know where that is?"

I said I had a pretty fair idea. "When's the best time to catch him there?"

He laughed. "Darryl? Most anytime, Hoss; dude practically lives there. Probably shootin' pool right now, matter of fact."

"Great," I said. "What about the other two?"

"Who?"

"The earlier ones; the guys you saw the lady with before she took up with Darryl; you know them too?"

"Not really," he said, regretfully, obviously making the connection between the quality of his information and my supply of twenties. "Never got muchuva good look at 'em. Mos' likely 'nother couple'a shit-kickers, just like Darryl. Looks like that sort might be to the lady's taste; slummin,' know what I mean? Musta been others, too…but I ain't never seen'em. Come down to it, ain't 'zackly my job to keep tabs on who's doin' what to who." He cackled again––a dry rattle which degenerated into a hacking cough, which in turn was curtailed with another gorge-rising wad splatting onto the floor.

"Anyway I tole you the lady been busy, ain't I?" he said, wiping his lips with the back of a bare hand. "Prob'ly gets her all the long dong she can handle, you know." He tapped the photo. "Can see for yourself, she's a helluva good-lookin' piece of poon." He rubbed his chin, thoughtfully. "Been a long time since I had me anything *that* USDA choice…"

Mighty long time, I thought, reflecting that the man's current advanced state of decay probably dictated a rather unattractive starting point. *Like never…*

"I did, though, once," he insisted, as if responding to my thought—"when I was a lot younger. She was also good lookin' like this one: big firm titties, tight round ass, long blonde hair, horny as all get out—you know the drill. She sure rode me; know what I mean, Hoss man? She rode me *real* good…like a fuckin' rodeo queen!"

He chuckled wistfully at a pleasant, private excursion down Memory Lane. I smiled mechanically in response, and was extremely grateful for not being able to share those images with him.

After briefly considering the fresh insight into Nadine Sayles' earlier sexual excursions, I decided that for now there wasn't much of interest in them, other than to force some adjustments as to my previous opinion of the woman as a wife who'd reluctantly and only recently abandoned her marriage vows. Now it looked like she'd gone off that farm a tad earlier than I'd supposed—quite a bit more often, too.

But for the time being it was only Nadine's current frolic with Darryl Turnick that seemed relevant to me, because, if Jenny Longwell's account was accurate, then Josh Sayles had not been aware of the others. Supporting that thought was Jackson's estimate that this present dalliance had spanned at least the last two months, which would have therefore neatly coincided with Joshua's sudden change of attitude, as well as his subsequent disappearance. With that in mind, my obvious next move was to head over to George's and see if I could catch Darryl Turnick between bank shots.

I thanked my new friend Jackson for the info, and punctuated my thanks by transferring an extra ten dollar bill into his custody.

"Anytime, Hoss," he said, by now completely enthusiastic; "anytime at all. Just fall by whenever you need anything, ya hear? Anything at all; I got all kinda connections…"

I climbed back into the Toyota and turned the key; but, as I prepared to take the transmission out of park a sudden, unbidden image of Kelly's face floated before me, yanking me rudely from my thoughts like a bandage torn away too soon from a still-tender wound. My stomach churning with emotional pain rendered physical, I had to resist an irrational urge to forget my plans and point the car homeward, against the possibility that she might have had a change of heart and come back to me; irrational of course because, change of heart or no, at this hour Kelly would have only been halfway through her day at school, and was probably at this very moment standing in front of twenty-three restless second graders.

Musing that I would have given anything at that moment to be sitting in one of those undersized desk-chairs along with them, I instead forced the vision from my head, and pulled the car out of the lot, turning to the left onto Highway 97.

Thirty-Eight

It took me less than five minutes to make it to Taylor Street and then find George's Bar (the actual full name of the place was "George's Orgy," though for obvious reasons I suspected that most people preferred to employ the abbreviated version.) Taylor was a short, narrow, crudely paved road which ran north-south, parallel to and a few blocks to the east of route 97. It was a sparsely developed street, the properties along it alternating between vacant, weed-choked half-acre plots, and forlorn, entry-level businesses, most of them of the lawnmower and power tool repair shop variety. In fact this back road looked to be a sort of default address for proprietors who were desperate for self-employment, yet unable to afford the higher monthly cost of the far more visible locations out on the main drag. Their shops thus well hidden from the awareness of most of the town's walking and driving traffic, my guess was that whatever humble commerce they'd managed to drum up had probably been the result, mainly, of word-of-mouth.

Squatting in the midst of this motley entrepreneurial collection was the tavern, which was housed in an ungainly, single-story rectangular building with a pitched roof, set well back on a dirt lot on the east side of the street. Constructed entirely of gray corrugated metal, the structure was bordered by a shabby auto repair joint on the left side, and an, empty, trash-strewn parcel to the right. The notion that the building must have originally been meant for some other purpose—machine shop, storage, tractor parts supply—was further reinforced by an almost total absence of exterior décor. In fact, the only things indicating the current nature of the business were the small, plastic "George's Orgy" sign, hanging, perpendicular to the building, over the door, and two neon beer displays—one

"Budweiser," the other, "Amstel"—crouching in each of the tiny square windows on either side of the entrance.

There were four vehicles parked in front: one, an extremely late-model Ford LTD with a torn landau roof and a body finished mostly in primer-gray; the other three, ancient Chevy or Dodge pickup trucks, their colors long since weather-beaten into similar, indeterminate hues—any one of which looked sufficiently shabby to have qualified for Jennifer Longwell's description of Darryl's "rust bucket." Since it was probable that the employees' cars would have been parked in back of the building, I surmised that all of these vehicles must belong to the clientele. Regulars, too, considering the mid-day hour.

Locating my own car just far enough away from the others so that any sudden drunken departure might not be as apt to result in my Toyota becoming collateral damage, I sat for a moment, gazing, idly, at the entrance. I reached for the door handle, paused, then flipped open the center console and pulled out my cell phone, telling myself as I did that it was merely good business practice to call the house and check my messages.

Yeah, right.

Turned out that there was a single communication, from Denove; the typically terse message from the detective ordering me to "call in when you get this." Nothing else. Nothing from Kelly. Disappointed, while silently cursing for having set myself up for it, I snapped the phone shut and tossed it back into the console. For a moment, I considered retrieving it and punching in Denove's number, then decided that whatever it was could wait, and climbed out of the car. A moment later I was walking, my hiking boots crunching noisily on uneven gravel as I approached the blank, industrial metal door of George's tavern. After casting one more look around the parking lot, I grasped the door handle, pulled it, and walked in.

Since a saloon is not a place I generally visit during the day, the thick darkness and musty odor of the interior seemed particularly incongruous and uninviting in contrast to the bright, clean sunlight and air outside; it took my sensibilities almost as long as my eyes to adjust to the difference.

Across the room to the left of me, an ancient jukebox was belching scratchy country music; something appropriately twangy, with lots of pedal-steel and fiddle and very few chord changes, and with a nasal male voice whining something about "broken hearts, broken dreams." Not exactly a big fan of the genre, I did my best to ignore it as I waited for the dim shapes in the room to resolve themselves.

Running almost the length of the wall to the right, directly opposite the jukebox, was the bar: rough-hewn, utilitarian and unattractive; long enough to accommodate eight padded, free-standing wooden stools, and wide enough to keep drunken patrons from reaching across and abusing the bartender. The wall behind the bar was mirrored with smoked glass, and supported two long, metal shelves, upon which rested a fair collection of blended Scotches, bourbons, and various other whiskies, but no liqueurs. My guess was that, in this bar, ordering a "mixed drink" probably meant Jack Daniels with a beer back.

The broad, open floor between the bar and jukebox was surfaced with smooth, unpainted concrete generously sprinkled with wood shavings, and was populated with seven or eight knife-scarred, round wooden tables, each surrounded by four mismatched, uncomfortable-looking wood chairs.

Across the room, just to the right of the jukebox, was a small bandstand, crudely covered with a patchwork of ancient carpet remnants. At the back of this platform sat a forlorn, mismatched drum set, its cymbal stands partially covered by a dingy sheet. Flanking the drums against the wall were two ratty guitar speaker cabinets minus their amplifier heads (a standard musician theft-prevention technique), while along the front edge of the stage were three empty mike stands, with tall, narrow P.A. speakers occupying each corner. There was also a relatively small, vacant section of flooring directly in front of the platform, doubtless to accommodate a small number of well-lubricated customers who just couldn't sit still when the boys really got to crankin' it up.

Beyond the bandstand and dance floor and occupying the back quarter of the establishment were two undersized, coin-operated pool tables, lit marginally better than the rest of the building by a couple of hooded industrial lamps, which were suspended directly over each playing surface by lengthy cables from beams under the naked, corrugated ceiling.

Looking just beyond the tables, I could see the back wall of the building, which was essentially featureless, aside from a rear exit and doors leading to storage and separate "guys" and "gals" bathrooms, thus confirming the lack of a kitchen in the place. One more glance at the bar revealed a popcorn machine, hot dog carousel and bun warmer sitting on the lower of the two shelves behind it— which, evidently, constituted the only food options available. Clearly this was a business for hard-core drinking and not much else.

All of the tables out on the floor were vacant, but four consecutive stools at the bar were occupied; all by rough-looking men similarly clad in weathered jeans, cowboy boots and plaid flannel shirts. Two of them were hatless, sporting full, unkempt heads of hair, while the other two hid theirs under baseball caps. A beer bottle sat in front of each of them—no glass—and every man clung to his with both hands as if to prevent it from running off. Beyond them stood the bartender—tall, nondescript; dressed in much the same manner as his patrons, aside from the addition of a dirty white apron. Arms folded, he waited passively for the inevitable next round of beer orders, while no doubt silently counting down the minutes.

Of the four customers at the bar, the two who were bare-headed remained hunched over as I passed, ignoring me as they stared disconsolately at their reflections in the mirror. The other two, however, turned, slowly, simultaneously; minutely tracking my progress and resembling, uncannily, a couple of animatronic robots on a Disneyland ride. As they did so, they pulled their bottles around with them, while their unblinking stares followed me like those trick eyes in a carny funhouse picture.

Even in the gloom I could read on their faces unrestrained curiosity, heavily seasoned with suspicion and the sort of unreasoning, threatening malevolence which was likely triggered by any stranger passing, uninvited, through their field of view. There was very little conversation going on, and it wasn't difficult to see that there must have been some sort of sullen, alcohol-enhanced storm building there for some time. I hoped that my position as the sole outsider in this joint wouldn't result in my being the catalyst for the tempest actually breaking—more to my purpose, my wish was that Darryl Turnick wouldn't turn out to be one of these hard cases.

With this in mind, I turned my attention to the pool tables. One stood vacant, but the other was being used. Two men, both clad in roughly the same denim-leather-flannel coordination as the quartet at the bar, were deep into a game. While one man occupied a tall, wood-backed swivel stool, holding his cue stick in his left hand, and a brown beer bottle in the right, the other circled the table smoothly, brandishing his stick like a rifle, and stalking his next ball as if it were unsuspecting prey. There was purpose and confidence in his movements, and from the slouched posture and bored expression of his seated friend, my guess was that his opponent was in the early stages of what was destined to be a long run of successful shots. It was just speculation, but I sensed that the hustler was Turnick.

I walked slowly towards him as he continued to consider his options. Finally he made his decision, and then, after first planting his almost-full beer bottle out of the way on the edge of the table, he leaned over, a picture of concentration, and delicately executed a perfect bank of the five-ball into the corner pocket.

"Nice one," I said, as I emerged from the shadows into the pale wash of light from the overhead lamp.

"Thanks," he muttered without bothering to look at me, instead devoting his full attention to lining up the next victim.

"Darryl Turnick?"

This caused him to turn and squint at me, straightening up as he did so, while shifting his right hand onto the narrow end of the cue stick, transforming it, potentially, into a traditional barroom weapon.

"Who's askin'?"

I returned the stare without immediately answering. He was short; actually more or less a match in stature to Reverend Sayles, though beyond that any resemblance clearly ended. His light brown hair was full, wavy and long, and held back from falling into his face by a sweat-stained, dirty white Stetson. Though his plaid shirt hung loosely in most places, it strained against his gut—apparent evidence of heavy beer consumption. His face was rugged, deeply-furrowed and sun burnt; it spoke eloquently that at least some substantial portion of his life was being spent outdoors. Actually, with his full mustache and bushy eyebrows, the man looked remarkably like a pint-sized, poor man's version of Tom Selleck—more specifically, the Tom Selleck of those old Marlboro magazine advertisements. His hands were rough, heavily calloused and stubby, and his boot heels showed a distinct uneven outside wear indicative of a typical cowpoke's bow-legged stride.

"My name is Hank Cassidy," I said.

He shrugged. "That don't mean nothin' to me."

"I'm a private investigator. I've been hired by J.T. Sayles to locate his son."

"So?"

"I was hoping you might be able to help."

He snorted. "Don't see how."

I almost laughed; what with the hat, the gait, and the three-words-or-less responses, the guy could have come straight out of Central Casting.

"Can we talk?"

"What about?"

"Nadine Sayles."

"Who?"

I sighed. "Oh, come on now, Darryl."

"Okay," he said, after a moment, "let's go grab us a table." Leaning the cue stick against a nearby metal support post, he picked up his bottle, and then gestured towards the remaining pool balls. "Roady, don't fuck with this…"

We walked over to the first table on the other side of the small dance floor, which I noticed, as we crossed it, was actually slightly raised parquet.

We selected our seats at the table: me, with my back to the bar; him, facing it—and for a few seconds continued to size each other up. Finally, he spoke.

"Want a brew?"

"No thanks."

He shrugged, took a healthy pull on his beer, then belched. "Suit yerseff." His voice had a decided southern cast to it—sounded like Texas—and I wondered if he'd made his way north from there, or else, as a native Oregonian, had simply picked up the cowboy's drawl riding the range.

We continued to swap stares, and then, tiring of it, I decided to come to the point. "How long have you been seeing Nadine?"

"You mean, how long I been *porkin'* the lady," he responded, lazily, accompanying his comment with a grunt that might have been a laugh. "Not that it's any of your business, but it's been a while."

An incurable romantic…

"Did you know that Josh had found out?"

"The kid?" he said with distaste. "Yeah, I knew. Not too surprised, neither; that boy was tied to his mamma like the doc ain't never cut the cord. Bound to happen. And accordin' to her, he weren't too pleased about it."—Belched, casually—"Naw, not too pleased at all."

"Did you talk to him?"

"Me? Nope. Not my kid, not my look-out."

"Not a very long-term perspective," I observed.

"Long-term…" he repeated, thoughtfully, rolling the words around in his mouth. "Whaddaya—oh, you mean long term with *her*?" He spat onto the sawdust-strewn floor. "Naw; what me and Nadine got here ain't nuthin' permanent. Just yer basic county fair thrill ride—somethin' for shits'n grins, you know?" He laughed, gutturally. "Besides, I kinda don't think the wife would approve…"

Ah. I nodded. *The wife.* That would certainly explain the need for a motel room. But that also definitely ran counter to Nadine's expectations, expressed at the restaurant that night when she'd hinted broadly to me about having a fallback position when she finally chose to pull the plug on her marriage.

"So," I said, "you're saying you've got no plans to turn your deal with Nadine into something full time."

"Ain't you listening, mister?" he said, squinting at me as if I'd just asked him to dance. "What did I just say? I'm *married,* for fuck sakes! You think I'd ditch my wife? Nossir…don't think so."

Noble—the devoted husband.

"I'll grant you," he continued, after taking another lengthy pull at the bottle, "my old lady's fat and she's butt ugly; snores like an old hound dog—mean as a snake, too. But she's a passable good cook, and what's more important, she gets her that hefty disability check ever' month—what with her comin' up with the arthuritis after all them years on the line up at Boeing; 'nuff to keep Yours Truly in quarters"—he gestured towards the pool table—"and brewskis. And what with the cost of living down here bein' so much less than it were in that Seattle shithole we bailed out of, I ain't even gotta break a sweat more'n once in a blue moon. All in all, I'd say that steady check more'n makes up for the rest…that is, long's I got me some options whenever the ole' *feelin'* come over me." He took another swig and then wiped his mouth, contentedly.

"Options like Nadine."

"Yeah," he said, agreeably, "like Nadine. Now Nadine," he continued, his Marlboro Man face contorting into an acutely unattractive leer: "she's whatcha might call the opposite kinda female type as my wife: very easy on the eyes, sweet-smellin' and clean, dresses real nice, very eager to please—a fuckin' freak in the saddle, if you wanna know the truth. But, without that limp-dick Holy Joe husband of hers to front the bills, she ain't nuthin' more'n a zero with tits: no income, no prospects, no future; 'cause when it come down to it she ain't got no skills to speak of."

The ugly grin broadened. "Well, *almost* no skills."

So much for the laconic cowboy bit.

"So," he went on, "if I was to split with my old lady so's I could take up with this other one, I'd hafta go back to workin' full-time, mos' likely at some fucked-up paint store job, takin' orders from some piece of shit, pasty-faced, college candy-ass son of an owner. No more easy days for ole Darryl: hangin' out down here at George's, knockin' back suds and shootin' eight-ball or rotation; no more afternoon dee-lites with the honeys over at the Bluebird, neither. Far as I'm concerned, mister, no single piece of ass is worth *that* much hassle. Besides, why pay for the cow if you're already gettin' the milk for free?"

Laughter caused me to turn and look toward the bar, where all four of the men seated there had swiveled on their stools and were now facing us, an extremely entertained audience to Darryl's rant. From their knowing, approving faces I could see that they'd heard some variation of that last joke multiple times before; which also explained why Turnick's voice had been several notches louder than necessary for the close geography of our so-called private conversation.

"My, that's one mighty sharp wit you've got there, Darryl," I said, dryly.

"What's that?" He eyed me, narrowly.

"Nothing."

He shoved his chair back noisily.

"We're done here."

I agreed with him.

We parted company, silently: him, shuffling back to his pool game; me, having to make my way across the room to the front door. Unfortunately that also meant running another half-gauntlet past the bar, which I attempted to accomplish as smoothly and quickly as possible without attracting the undo attention of any of the four birds perched on their stools. Which of course meant that I didn't succeed.

"Hey," one of them called out.

I ignored him.

"I'm talkin' to you, Sunny Jim." The voice was hoarse, the words slightly slurred.

His friends smirked.

I kept walking.

"Hey, faggot…you deaf or somethin'?"

Not much point in responding to that one.

There was a loud, tortured sound of a wooden stool scraping against rough concrete, and a large, lumbering figure barreled by and then interposed itself squarely between me and the front door.

"You think you're leavin' doncha?" he sneered. He'd been one of the two who'd rotated their stools when I had first entered the bar.

"You must be psychic," I said.

"You ain't goin' nowhere 'till I *say* you can."

I sized him up. Tall, beefy: fairly muscular, though much of the muscle had apparently run to fat, possessing an even more substantial beer-belly than old Darryl. Exceptionally ugly, bloated, red-veined face, with small, porcine eyes and a moth-eaten van dyke. Caterpillar cap tilted up on a greasy forehead. Semi-permanent sneer composed of pale, thin lips and crooked, nicotine-stained teeth. Gravelly, three-pack-a-day voice.

Clutching a half-empty bottle of Bud by the neck, hand pointed downward, he stood there threateningly, his cowboy boots spread wide, yet swayed noticeably—enough to advertise that the beer bottle in his hand had been far from his first.

"You serve your country?" he challenged.

"Every day," I replied.

He stared at me, puzzled.

"What the fuck's *that* mean?"

I said nothing.

He patted his chest; "Me. I served. Damned Marines. Fuckin' Desert Storm. Killed me a dozen towel heads. Hoo-rah."

I doubted that, but said, "Good for you."

"You ain't served, you ain't killed the enemy, you ain't no man."

I was surprised to feel some heat in response to this nonsense, but I fought it back and answered with deliberate mildness: "Kind of a narrow interpretation of the word, don't you think?"

This caused some more confusion, as he apparently didn't quite understand my comment.

"You a fuckin' faggot?" he said; evidently his fall-back when he didn't know what else to say.

But this was really getting tiresome. "*Faggot*," I repeated; "you've already tried to bait me with that one, friend—a couple of times, now—and obviously it's getting you nowhere. So, look, why don't we just drop this thing right here; you get yourself back to your beer and your buddies, and I'll get on down the road, okay? I really do have to go." As I said this, I listened carefully for the sound of other bar stools scraping against the floor behind me. Fortunately, so far all I had heard was muttering and sporadic laughter, which meant that, at least for the moment, my sole problem continued to remain the one standing in front of me.

"I don't like people comin' in here an' botherin' my brothers," he proclaimed, far too loudly.

"Yeah," I offered, reasonably, "I wouldn't either; but since your brother Darryl and I are finished with our business, and there really wasn't any harm done, I'll just leave now, and, trust me, you won't ever have to worry about me showing up here again."

His grin turned, if possible, even more ugly. "Oh, you ain't gettin' outta here 'fore I fuck you up a little bit, faggot—"

Then he raised his fists.

Now I'm not sure whether, with a little more patience—
—and perhaps a little less sarcasm—I might have managed to talk my way out of this barroom scrap. But at the moment my patience was running somewhat shorter than usual. Maybe it was my frustration with the Sayles case, or perhaps my foul mood at having watched my girlfriend walk out on me last night. Or maybe it was just that today I'd dealt with one degenerate too many.

My sainted sensei always used to say: "Never allow yourself to strike out in anger."

Didn't say anything about irritation, though.

And this guy *really* irritated me.

Besides, my sainted sensei also used to say: "There is nothing chivalrous in allowing your opponent to strike the first blow."

So I struck.

The whole thing lasted less than fifteen seconds. I began with a well-aimed and executed flying crescent kick to the side of his head, which, to his credit, staggered the man but didn't drop him (it did cause him to let go of the bottle, though, which miraculously didn't break, but instead bounced twice loudly against the floor and then rolled off, spilling its contents, into the darkness.) I then immediately followed the kick with a short, thunderous right-left combination to that massive beer gut, which caused him to double over, and also, unfortunately, forced his last two or three beers and whatever he'd had for lunch (looked like hot dogs—heavy on the mustard and relish) to spew out, in a colorful fan, onto the wood shavings. I considered finishing up with one last punch, a solid right uppercut to the jaw which would have straightened him up and then toppled him over backwards. But I could see that it was unnecessary, as this particular beefy antagonist was now officially *hors d' combat*. Besides, I had no great desire to wade into all that vomit.

Having dispatched him, I now quickly turned to face the bar, just in case any of his companions decided to jump into the fracas, but saw that they hadn't budged. Instead they hung from their barstools, gaping, with identical, profoundly stupid expressions on their faces. No doubt they'd seen—and participated in—more than their share of saloon dust-ups over the years. But your typical bar fight being, invariably, a prolonged, noisy, sloppy affair, I don't think these guys were quite prepared for the sort of combat speed and efficiency they'd just witnessed. So, despite the unintelligent looks, I thought that their continuing to remain rooted to their posts displayed a fair amount of good judgment. I smiled at them, cordially. Waved.

"I think your friend is going to need a little help over here," I said. To the bartender, I added: "and you might also want to bring a wet mop and a bucket."

I then turned around and walked past my opponent—who was still bent over, gagging, with some really unattractive stuff hanging in ropes from his mouth and nose—and pushed through the door; walking, squinting and breathing deeply, into the blessed sunshine and even more blessed atmosphere.

Chapter Thirty-Nine

I pulled into my garage at home feeling unproductive, dissatisfied and ill-tempered.

I'd definitely been off my game. My interview with Darryl Turnick had been a complete bust, providing me with little information other than to support the conclusion that Nadine Sayles was spectacularly bad in her choice of prospective life-partners. There had been at least a dozen other questions that I could have posed to him—*should* have posed to him—but I'd just seemed to run out of steam, given up at the precise moment when I should have pressed on. Ah well; maybe I'd catch up with him in a day or so for a second go-round.

But definitely somewhere else besides the charming ambience of "George's Orgy."

Satch was particularly welcoming as I walked in, perhaps sensing my need at that moment for a little extra-friendly attention; placing a paw on each of my shoulders, she stared into my eyes, thoughtfully, and then proceeded to douse my face with kisses.

"Well, at least *you* still love me."

As a reward for this welcome display, I immediately hustled the two of us out the front door, treating my dog—and myself—to a much longer trek than usual through the forest.

It was a full hour and a half before we returned. After hanging up Satch's leash, I headed for the phone, remembering, belatedly, my obligation to return Denove's call. But when I glanced at the caller ID screen, I saw that he'd phoned me again, this time just over forty minutes ago. And that was unusual, because Denove was hardly the type to push the elevator call button once it was already lit.

So, without bothering to play back his latest message, I immediately dialed his number.

"Where *were* you?" he barked, testily, without bothering to say hello.

"Wasting time," I responded. "What's up?"

"They found him."

"Josh?"

"Josh."

"Alive?"

There was a pause, followed by a long exhale.

"No."

"Where?" I asked, as weariness washed over me.

Chapter Forty

With the history of Central Oregon having been closely tied to the fortunes of the timber industry, the forests around here have naturally reflected its impact. Beginning over a hundred years ago, vast numbers of giant ponderosa pines were harvested to feed the many lumber mills which had sprung up in the region. Back then, there had been no policy of replacing the fallen trees with ponderosa saplings, and therefore the land was left barren, to be eventually taken over by thick stands of faster growing, less desirable lodgepole pines, which, springing up like weeds, tended to crowd out any small ponderosas which had remained. As the years passed, the entire character of the forest changed; from an almost park-like setting of widely-spaced, massive and healthy ponderosas, to crowded stands of spindly lodgepoles, many of them unhealthy and ill-equipped to fight off disease, infestation, and, above all, wildfire.

Adding to the deterioration was the misguided policy, now discredited, of protecting the forest from fire by preventing it entirely. Foresters now understand that in many cases fire can perform a beneficial, cleansing function, ridding the woods of weak and unhealthy trees, while retarding the spread of the kinds of resin-rich undergrowth that can stoke far more serious and destructive "crown" fires.

With this new awareness of the dynamics of forest health and the emphasis on modifying fire behavior rather than preventing it outright, experts, working with the US Forest Service and the Bureau of Land Management, had come up with a remedy. Slowly, acre by acre, foresters had instituted "thinning projects;" cutting down weak, unhealthy and crowded lodgepoles, removing blown-down trees, cropping undergrowth, and creating enough space between the remaining trees to allow for better growth, particularly among ponderosas.

It's a slow, arduous process, particularly given the tens of millions of acres of forest badly in need of attention, and the shortage of funds and manpower necessary to do the work. As a result the planners had been forced to prioritize, choosing to work first on those areas which were closest to populated areas, and, therefore, the most immediate threat.

One such tract selected for thinning was a one hundred fifty acre section, five miles north of Sunriver and ten miles south of Bend. First, larger trees which were considered commercially viable were felled and trucked out. Next, machine operators, employing small tractors fitted with steel masticators, moved in, taking down smaller trees and crunching them into more manageable pieces. Once they were done, they were followed by a team of hand-thinners, who then removed the limbs from the remaining, standing trees, six feet up from the ground.

Finally, a team of at-risk teenagers was bussed in from a nearby correctional facility to complete the clean-up work. These kids were part of a special program, designed to replace long hours of youth-jail tedium with gainful, if laborious, employment, for which they were paid a small yet welcome wage. It was a win-win situation; for the kids who had volunteered for the work it was welcome diversion outside the walls; for the Forest Service, it was an opportunity to get badly needed work done at a far more reasonable rate than if they'd been forced to bring in private contractors.

The kids' job was simple: gather all of the woody debris left behind by the machines and logging trucks, and divide it into sizeable, widely-spaced piles. These piles would then be left there to dry out for a year, after which they would be eliminated the following fall in a series of controlled burns.

It was on Monday, while these kids were working, that Joshua Sayles' body had been found. One of the boys, dragging large branches to be dumped onto a nearby pile, had shrieked and staggered back when he lifted a fallen tree limb and found himself staring at the exposed, grinning face of a dirt-encrusted skull. The Forest Service official in charge of the project had then immediately shut down all work and phoned the county sheriffs, who'd then quickly shown up and transformed the interrupted work site into a crime scene.

* * * * *

"Not very deep," I said.

"That's why they call it a *shallow* grave, Cassidy."

It was Wednesday morning, and Denove and I were standing at the edge of the crumbling, empty depression which had constituted, until two days ago, the repository for Joshua Sayles' remains.

"No," I said, irritated by the detective's sarcasm; "I mean it's *really* shallow; hardly looks deep enough to hold a body."

"The guess is that when the machine operators moved through here," said Denove, "they must've scraped off just enough topsoil to expose him."

About us, within the broad, taped-off perimeter of the thinned tract of forest, county cops were busy scouring the grounds: some walking, hunched over, notebooks in hand; some of them, crawling on hands and knees, latex-gloved fingers delicately moving aside twigs and pine needles. All faces were encrusted with sweat, grime, fatigue and aggravation. They'd been at it for going on three days now without much to show for their efforts—not surprising, considering the disastrous condition of the site: dozens of tractor-treads churning up much of the forest floor; hundreds of worker boot-prints of all sizes and sole patterns, crossing and re-crossing each other and rendering any possible coherent reading virtually impossible; scattered pine tree detritus strewn everywhere. Seemingly, not a single square foot of naked, undisturbed soil in sight. In addition, ten or twelve widely-spaced piles of woody debris, gathered by the youthful work crew, were sitting in various locations about the property, blatantly advertising the annoying possibility that any of them might be resting directly atop vital evidence.

"Nevertheless," I said, stubbornly pursuing my thought, "it does seem like an awfully hasty burial job."

The detective agreed, but said, "Probably didn't see any real need to dig deeper. Killer or killers had no way of knowing that the area was slated for thinning, so they must've thought that, with no hiking trails nearby, the denseness of the standing forest there, along with all the blow-down and the heavy undergrowth, they'd found the ideal place commit murder and then stash the vic."

"Still looks like amateur hour to me…"

"Oh, it *does,* does it?" grumbled Denove. "Is that your considered, *expert* opinion, Citizen?" Then, before I could reply, he shrugged and said, "But, yeah, you're probably right; whoever did it was most likely new to this kind of business."

"How were you able to make the identification so quickly?"

"Well," he said, "to begin with, the body was fully clothed, with his wallet and driver's license still in his pants pocket. Add to that that the clothes matched what his mother had described him as wearing on the day he left, and there really wasn't much doubt. And then last night everything became official when the family dentist matched the skull's dental work with the boy's records."

"Mighty expeditious of him."

"Such a big word. But, yes, it was fast work," he said. "Small town, Cassidy; no problem getting a dentist to go down to the morgue to assist with an ID. Besides, he told us he's had some past forensic experience, and was happy to help."

"So the killer left the boy's wallet on him," I said; "even for an amateur that's pretty careless."

"Yeah," he responded; "but, like I said, he was probably confident that the body would never be found."

"Smells like an element of panic, too—hastily dug grave, neglecting to remove ID—not exactly thinking things through."

"Uh-huh," said Denove; "and that would also argue for a single killer. You're much more likely to be thorough when you've got minds working together."

"Makes sense. Where's Whalen?"

"With the boy's parents."

"How'd they take it?"

"From what he told me, Ms. Sayles took it hard when we first contacted them for permission to access the dental records. Needed heavy sedation right away. Which meant that by the time the ident became official she was too out of it to react at all. At any rate we've got a social worker staying at the house full time with her."

"How about the minister?"

He snorted. "He seemed properly shocked, of course; theatrically so, according to Frank. But then he immediately announced to everyone that he needed to be alone and marched off to his chapel."

"Didn't stick around to comfort his wife?"

"Whalen told me he ignored her completely."

"What a guy."

"Amen, Brother."

I mulled J.T. Sayles' callousness towards his wife for a few seconds, then changed the subject.

"Any idea how long ago the murder went down?"

"Well," he said, "they're still working on it. The dry decomposition's pretty complete; very little meat left on the bones. For that the boy would have had to have been killed soon after he disappeared, if not immediately—which, if I had to lay odds, seems most likely."

"Cause of death?"

"Nothing official yet, but there *are* two rather conspicuous bullet entry holes in the back of the skull, and some scoring mid-spine, indicating another shot to the back."

"All three from behind; didn't see it coming."

"True," he agreed. "I'm guessing that the first one put him down, and the last two finished the job."

"Find any shell casings?"

"Yeah: one—a forty-five."

"Just one?"

"Yeah," he said, sourly; "just one. And we were lucky to find that one, given all this hacking, piling, stomping and just plain mucking around. Hell, you could throw a gilt frame around this site and title it: 'Portrait of a Contaminated Crime Scene'."

I gestured towards the road, where two compact tractors were parked outside the tape near my car and the white SUV's of the Deschutes County Sheriffs. "At least they got those things out of the way," I noted.

"Yeah," he said, sourly, "but who knows how much evidence was ground into the dirt while they were moving them?" He pointed at one of the piles. "And we still need to take these down, to see what's under them." Shook his head. "What a mess…"

My eye was drawn, again, to the crude, packed-earth lumber road fronting the property. In addition to the vehicles, there was a small group of onlookers—all of them teenagers—standing just outside of the tape; milling, and alternating comments among themselves with furtive glances in our direction. Despite the fact that there was really nothing to see—the bones having long since been carted off by the coroner—they persisted, obviously fascinated with the idea of inhaling the heady atmosphere of homicide. Scanning them, I thought I recognized a couple of kids from the Mirror Pond gang. I also noticed that their leader, Weldon Potter, was conspicuously absent––not surprising, considering the unwanted police attention he might have attracted had he shown up.

Turning back to Denove, I said: "How about slugs? Find any?"

"Again, just one."— He pointed to a spot three feet from the hole in the ground—"We found it here; and the shell casing was back there"—he waved, vaguely, behind us—"ten feet away. Skull was empty, and both eye orbits showed exit damage."

"But the shell and slug make it pretty clear that he was killed here."

"Looks like," he said. "Shot the kid, dug a quick hole next to the body, rolled it in."

"But without the other slugs and casings—"

He nodded. "No way to know whether it was three shots from one gun, or one shot from three."

"How about four guns and one of them missed—"

"Not funny."

"Sorry. But we're leaning towards a lone shooter anyway, right?"

"*We* are, huh?" His sour look told me to change the subject.

A thought occurred. "How much money was in his wallet?"

"Seventeen dollars in the wallet; forty-five cents in his pants pocket."

"So what happened to all the money he'd withdrawn?"

Denove sighed. "Just one of many questions—"

"And his debit card?"

"Also missing."

"But," I said, puzzled, "with almost all of his money already drained from his account, what would be the point of taking his ATM card?"

"No idea. Maybe the killer didn't know the account was empty. Maybe the card was never in his wallet. Maybe—"

"Maybe what?"

He exhaled. "Maybe we're just wasting time speculating here, Cassidy."

"Okay," I said, fully appreciating that Denove's head was already crowded with what-ifs, whys, and why-nots. "Any suspects?"

"Yeah," he said, sarcastically; "about eighty-one thousand of them. The kid was killed here, so it's probably someone who lives in the Bend area."

"Daunting," I said. "But I take it no *specific* suspects, so far."

"We prefer to call them 'persons of interest.' But no; no one specific as of yet. How about you; any contributions from the peanut gallery?"

"Actually, I might have," I responded, slowly. "Do you have to stick around?"

He looked at the others. "No, they're all doing what they're supposed to be doing; not much need for me to nursemaid. Why?"

"Because I haven't had breakfast, and I always think better on a full stomach."

"All right," he said; "hang on, while I pass the baton."

Chapter Forty-One

Breakfast meant Café Sintra, located just inside the main entrance to Sunriver. I ordered *linguica*—Portuguese sausage mixed with scrambled eggs, onions and mushrooms—and grabbed a self-service cup of French-roast coffee. Denove contented himself with herbal tea and a small plate of assorted pastries. I was surprised at how hungry I was, not to mention how much better it felt to be doing something other than obsessing about Kelly. Nevertheless, while I ate and talked, thoughts of her continued to stubbornly intrude, forcing me to will myself not to lose track of where I was, what I was doing.

"So," said Denove, delicately munching a muffin; "what do you have?"

I told him about my meeting with Jenny Longwell; about how she'd revealed to me Josh's discovery of his mother's infidelity. I started to move into the particulars of that affair, but Denove stopped me.

"Girlfriend, huh? You say she admits that he broke up with *her,* and that six months later she's still upset about it."

"So?"

"So?" he said, "so what you have here is the textbook definition of a 'woman scorned.'"

"You mean, Jenny Longwell as *suspect?"* I said, feeling slightly embarrassed that the idea had never occurred to me. "But, that one doesn't track at all," I argued, as much to myself as to Denove; "not with the way she opened up to me last week. Besides, I didn't detect anything like anger or resentment; and, if she had killed him, I doubt that she would have gone out of her way to draw attention to herself by contacting me."

"Nevertheless—"

"Yeah, right; nevertheless at this point you're not eliminating anyone."

"Right. So, what else?"

Next, I described what I'd learned about Nadine Sayles' horizontal two-step with cowboy Darryl Turnick; about how the length of their episode had pretty much fit the time-frame of Joshua's disappearance; about how Josh had found out about them and thrown a fit; about how her son might have become an intolerable nuisance to a suitor who appeared to me to be no stranger to the idea of violence.

"Interesting," said Denove. "Might be a serious candidate…"

I paused, then sighed. "No, actually I don't think he is, either. From the conversation I had with Turnick yesterday, my impression is that he doesn't consider Nadine much more than a convenient roll in the hay. If the kid was really annoying him, rather than dealing with it he'd most likely just dump her and move on to the next contestant."

"Maybe," he allowed. "But, again, it sounds like something worth looking into. Maybe this saddle tramp's the sort of low-life who thinks it's just as easy to off the kid as it is to dump his momma. Who knows—maybe she's just too good in the sack to throw away. Besides," he said, shaking a half-eaten scone at me, "this is not helping much—you coming up with possibilities and then yanking them away before I even get a chance to consider them."

"Suspectus interruptus."

"Exactly."

"Sorry."

"So," he said, "do you actually have any *serious* candidates?"

"Yeah; as a matter of fact, I do."

I then went on to tell him about Weldon Potter—alias "Foe Evah;" about his obvious animosity towards Josh Sayles, who might have at the very least represented an obstacle to his complete domination of the Mirror Pond crowd. Not to mention his status as a rival for Jenny Longwell's affections—though it seemed apparent, from Jenny's comments, that this last notion was entirely a figment of Potter's overheated imagination.

Next, I described my tailing of the group the following evening. After touching only briefly on a description of their rolling pot party, I skipped to the end, telling how I'd followed the group's leader to his home and then watched as his drunken father nailed him on the back of the head with a beer can. Finally, I related how, to my surprise, the elder Potter had subsequently shown up as an extremely reluctant participant in last Sunday's services at the Sayles church, and how Paul and Eliot had informed me, afterward, about what they'd heard of the old man having recently run afoul of the law.

"Well, now," said Denove; "that's more like it; maybe you've got something there. Certainly seems like too much of a coincidence, doesn't it? I'll give you this much, Cassidy; you *have* been one busy little shamus."

"So you'll look into the guy's record—"

"His first name is Wade?" said the detective. "Yeah; right away. My guess is that we're talking about a drug rap. From your description of the house with all those derelict cars, you've got the classic front yard decor of a crystal meth dealer. Every so often, they get clients desperate for a taste but out of dough, so they offer to turn over their junk-heaps as payment. Dealer takes them in, figuring that he can then fix the cars up and then sell them for several times what the baggie would have cost in cash. But of course he's a tweaker, too, so he never gets around to doing the work, and therefore eventually ends up with a yard full of rusting scrap metal."

"I watched him working on one of those cars that night," I said. "Maybe that and the fact that he's going to church these days are signs that the guy's trying to get on the straight and narrow."

"Having a hard time of it, too; considering your description of his drunken shit-fit with his son and his surly attitude at the church."

"Old habits dying hard."

"Indeed. At any rate, both father and son definitely qualify as persons of interest. Thanks, Cassidy."

"No problem," I said. "Are the press involved, yet?"

"Naturally," he said; "they were onto it by Monday night. Don't exactly know how they caught wind of it so soon, but they did. Wasn't the Forest Service guys; we never identified the body in front of them. My guess is that it was a contact at the hospital, or else a cop with a mouth––hate to admit *that* one, but it's more than possible. At any rate there's been a crowd of news types staked out in front of the Reverend's compound since noon, yesterday. You didn't see the front page in this morning's Bulletin? Was on last night's local TV news, too. We done, here? I have to get going…"

Chapter Forty-Two

I drove home, bolstered somewhat by the food, as well as by having provided Denove with some useful information he'd not previously had. But the boost was only temporary, and by the time I pulled into the garage, fatigue and discouragement once again caught up with me. Shutting off the engine, I sat there, listening to the ticking of cooling metal and wondering what to do next.

Josh Sayles was dead. That put, for all intents and purposes, a period to my work. And there was a substantial degree of irony in it, too, because, though in the course of my labors I'd uncovered a wealth of juicy details—ambitious, pompous father with little real feeling for his absent son; unfaithful wife with a penchant for low-life bedmates; cartoonish, arrested-development rival whose own father's connection to the church cried out for some sort of explanation—none of this knowledge had actually gotten me closer to my objective: locating the missing boy. He'd been found, all right; but for that honor the fates had nominated some anonymous, random teenage day-laborer.

As I stared at the back wall of the garage, the pointlessness of the whole thing washed over me, and I began to see the last two weeks as an abject failure. I smiled, grimly, as I recalled Aubrey McKenna's comment: *"You still got yourself a stack of juicy invoices..."* At the moment, though, given the way I was feeling, I wasn't even sure I was going to bother sending them in.

I then turned and gazed, emptily, at that vacant space beside my car, and then looked at the door to the house, and recognized that the real reason I was bottoming out was because Kelly would not be found on the other side of it.

Well, at least I have my dog.

And it was that thought which finally got my ass out of the car.

True to form, Satch greeted me excitedly as I came through the door, which brought a tired smile and lifted my spirits momentarily. Then, against my better judgment, I migrated over to the phone machine and felt my mood flagging again as I saw that the only new message on it was yesterday's additional call from Denove that I'd already known about. I erased it without playing it back, then wandered restlessly around the house for a time without alighting anywhere, stepped outside into the backyard, strolled to the river's edge and gazed, without seeing, at the water, gave up and reentered the house, fed up with my miserable frame of mind, but without any sense of how to alleviate it.

Just then, the phone rang. Reminding myself that it was still the middle of the day; that it couldn't be her, I nevertheless crossed the room much too quickly and snatched the receiver from the cradle—

And found myself confronted by the relentlessly overlarge voice of J.T. Sayles, made only slightly thinner by the electronics of the telephone.

"I suppose you've heard the news," he said, brusquely.

"Yes, I have," I said, wondering whether I'd be able to summon anything to sound remotely like sympathy. "Reverend, I'm so sorry; I—"

"Under the circumstances," he interrupted, "your services are no longer required. Please send me your final invoice."

And hung up.

Great, I thought, sourly, as I replaced the receiver in its cradle; *now it's official: I have nothing going for me.*

There then followed more empty minutes of aimless floor-pacing, which ended with me standing in the middle of the great room, eyes unfocused. Then I noticed Satch, sitting a few feet away, staring at me intently.

"How about a walk, girl?"

She cocked her head, questioningly. A dog's internal clock is a finely-tuned instrument, and so for a moment the offer of a walk at least four hours earlier than normal confused her, but when I headed for the door she recovered quickly enough, and, never one to refuse a bonus excursion, bounded after me.

It was almost three-thirty when we re-entered the house and the phone was ringing again. This time I forced myself to walk more deliberately to the side-table, and to check the caller I.D. before I pressed the talk button:

Denove's cell phone number.

"You were right," he said; "Wade Potter *has* had a couple of scrapes with the justice system. I was right, too; both were drug related."

"Interesting."

"Yes," he said; "interesting; unfortunately, however, not very productive—at least for our purposes. It seems that the guy's most recent stretch was a nickel for distributing, which eventually got knocked down to twenty-two months. He was released just about five weeks ago."

"Five weeks—puts him in the joint when Josh Sayles disappeared."

"'Fraid so."

I was disappointed, but said, "I guess that explains why these days he's working on cars and going to church."

"Yep," he said; "being a good boy, keeping the parole officer off his back."

"Can a parole board force a con to go to church?"

"Of course not," said Denove. "That one's probably on his wife, but it certainly couldn't hurt relations with his P.O."

"Yeah. So I guess that convenient little prison sentence lets the dad off the hook. What's his son's story?"

"Oh," he laughed, "you mean 'Foe Evah?'"

"I was trying not to use that name."

"Hard to say it with a straight face, isn't it? Anyway; ahem, *Weldon Potter,* has had a couple of brushes with the law, himself: specifically, picked up twice for possession of cannabis. But both times were underage busts, and both were flushed through the system and dismissed. Since then he's been clean—or at least, I should say, more careful."

"Not *too,* though," I responded, reminding him about the clouds of smoke I'd seen pouring from inside his car. "Was his alibi as good as Papa's?"

"I doubt it—hard to top anything as ironclad as a jail cell—but anyway we haven't had a chance to speak with him yet; we're still tracking him down. Whalen dropped by the house, but no one was home. I suppose if nothing else we can always wait an hour or so, and then hope that today's one of his park days. Frankly, though, we'd rather not; much better to pull him aside in a somewhat less conspicuous way than right out there in front of his posse."

"You might want to try the A.M. P.M. on 27th. I think he works there."

"You do? Well, well; aren't *you* a veritable font of information…" He mumbled "A.M. P.M" to himself, and I could picture him scribbling on his notepad. "Many thanks."

"Don't mention it."

"Talk to the Reverend, yet?" he said.

"Yeah."

"And?"

"He fired me."

"Hardly surprising."

"Yeah. Hardly. Your boys find anything else out at the crime scene?"

There was a small snort of amusement as he marked my deliberate change of subject. "No, not really," he said; "not even after we expanded the search area to include some of the adjacent, un-thinned parcels. Our thought was that maybe the perp might have tossed the murder weapon out there somewhere, but so far all we've found is a shrine that some of Josh's friends must've put up."

"A shrine?"

"Yeah," he said; "you know, the kind of thing you always see along the side of the road whenever somebody's gotten killed in a wreck? Flowers, crosses, notes and poetry?"

"Yeah," I said, "I've seen them." In fact, I'd seen plenty: in this area it seems to be a strong tradition that just about every fatal road accident should be commemorated with some sort of impromptu, flowery testament. Of course, with my paranoid mind, every time I pass one I immediately imagine that the dedicatee was a squashed motorcyclist.

"Where was it?" I asked.

"On that piece of land directly across the logging road from the crime scene; at least fifty feet in, tucked behind a tree. Odd choice of location for that kind of thing, though. You'd have expected them to erect it right there on the road—or out on the highway, even—where people would have a better chance of seeing it. I don't know; guess they didn't want to get in the way of the cops, and just picked the first open spot they could find that was outside of the tape. You saw them all hanging out there, didn't you?"

"Yeah, I did. You talk to them?"

"Of course; but you know how it is with kids and cops: nobody knows 'nuthin.' We took names, though, and we'll be getting back to each one of them sooner or later. You have anything else for me?"

"No, nothing that I can think of."

"Okay," he said. "In that case I'd better get back to work. Talk to you later, Cassidy. And thanks again for the information."

Chapter Forty-Three

I hung up, thought about what we'd just covered, realized that there wasn't much to think about. Looked at the clock: almost four—time to eat, I guess.

Going into the kitchen, I considered cooking something from scratch for dinner but couldn't summon enough enthusiasm, then swung open the refrigerator door and stood there, staring blankly at the contents of the freezer for what could have been five minutes before I finally surrendered, pulled out a frozen Trader Joe's dinner and shoved it into the microwave. When the oven beeped, I mechanically removed it and took it to the table, where I sat, fork in hand, wondering if I could even muster the minimal appetite to eat what would normally have been considered a mere appetizer.

Staring blankly at a plastic tub of nuked chicken gorgonzola and measuring the state of my wretched existence.

When I'd first moved here, I thought I'd pretty much had it nailed. To be sure, there'd been a certain lack of focus, of definition; but that was surely to be expected for a man who'd retired so early in life and wasn't quite centered on what he wanted to do next. In all other respects, though, it was an enviable life by anyone's measure. I had my perfect dream house, with all of the right amenities and luxuries; my perfect setting on the river; my perfect canine companion. No worries, no responsibilities.

Then Kelly had come along, and suddenly my world had become better, more complete, by orders of magnitude. Thanks to her, I'd found that missing focus. More than that, though; it seemed that in her presence everything else in my life seemed enhanced beyond expectation: shapes and colors, sounds—even smells—all were more vivid, more *intense.*

But now she was gone, and unfortunately I was condemned to learn that life is not a zero-sum game. In Kelly's absence my world was not merely reverting back to its previous state—it was shrinking well beyond it. At this moment nothing seemed right at all. My beautiful log home, custom-built to my exacting specifications, now seemed exactly fifty percent too large. Even the garage, with its ample room for two cars plus toys, now mocked me with way too much available space. Worst of all was my king-sized bed: once a comfortable place to stretch out, now it seemed more like massive mattress overindulgence; its vastness only serving to remind me of who wasn't going to be lying beside me in the dark.

My life, once full of pleasant possibilities and promise, now felt empty. Sights and sounds seemed drab and lifeless. Hunger was gone. Interest was minimal. And the worst of it was that for the foreseeable future there wasn't a damned thing I could do to change it.

Do, I thought, bitterly; it was my *doing* which had landed me in this miserable situation.

She hadn't so much as called once.

Maybe she never would.

After I'd tossed my half-eaten meal into the trash, I wandered over to the sofa, turned on the TV, and proceeded to scroll through the satellite's program guide three times, without finding anything of interest. Three hundred channels, nothing to watch. Wednesday night—had to be the worst TV night of the week. Shutting the thing off, I tossed the remote onto the coffee table. For a moment I considered going upstairs for another couple of mindless hours in the online casinos, then decided that even that prospect held no allure. At a loss for ideas, but desperate for *something* diverting, I got up, and fled into the gym, thinking that maybe a couple of hours of sweat might exhaust me enough to sleep through the night.

Actually, it took almost three: an hour on the elliptical trainer; three full circuits of free weight exercises; still more time working out with the speed bag; finally, twelve championship rounds of nonstop kicking and punching with the heavy bag, on which I took out my frustrations violently—far more violence, in fact, than I'd demonstrated while dispatching that beer-soaked idiot in the bar yesterday. By the time I was finished with the workout, I could barely lift my arms.

After staggering into the shower and standing under a hard rain of scalding hot water for fifteen minutes, I toweled off, slipped into some clean sweats and returned to the great room. The thought of trying to sleep in my half-empty bed upstairs, as tired as I was, was for the moment still way too depressing, so I turned on the TV, pulled a DVD from the cabinet and inserted it in the player, then lay down on the sofa. Satch, after verifying that I was indeed going to occupy the entire couch, jumped up on an adjacent easy chair, circled twice, and then settled in with a grunt.

The movie was "People Will Talk," an old Cary Grant flick with a ton of intelligent, clever dialogue, and very little action. It was a favorite of mine—I'd seen it at least a dozen times—but tonight I had no interest in actually watching it. Tonight the movie's sole purpose would be to serve as background noise. I hit play, adjusted the volume so that it was loud enough to drown out my thoughts while not being loud enough to keep me awake. Then, as the opening credits rolled, I set the TV's sleep timer for an hour.

Thankfully, I'm pretty sure I didn't make it past the first scene.

Chapter Forty-Four

Thursday morning, after an extended, early walk with my dog, I returned home, brewed some coffee, buttered a toasted bagel, dug out yesterday's Bulletin and then adjourned to the table.

As Denove had told me, the discovery of Josh's body had made the front page. Actual details were fairly sparse––certainly far less than what I had already gotten from the detective—but there was the mention of the victim's clothing and wallet having been found at the site, which had made identifying the remains such a simple task. Nothing was revealed about cause of death, as "a full coroner's investigation has not yet been completed;" although the likelihood that "foul play is evident" was conceded by detective in charge, Frank Whalen.

Reading further, I realized that the article was mostly a rehash of information from pieces written months earlier, when the boy's disappearance had still been fresh, though it did include a few new quotes by schoolmates, all of whom, it appeared, had hardly known him. There were no quotes at all from Paul and Elliot, certainly nothing from anyone in the Mirror Pond crowd, as well as no comments from Jenny Longwell. I thought about her, wondered whether I should call. The article ended by saying that Nadine Sayles had been too distraught to speak to reporters, and that the Reverend had also begged off, needing to "consult with the Lord in order to make sense of this terrible tragedy."

I frowned as I read that last comment: from what I had observed in all of our conversations, and considering Sayles' emotionless tone on the phone yesterday while he was firing me, it was difficult for me to accept him as the tragic victim. Cynically, my sense about the Reverend J.T.

Sayles was that losing his son probably meant less to him than if he had lost a pet.

I finished the article, then tossed the paper aside and stared out the window. It had been chilly out there on the trail this morning—a damp bite that actually hinted at the possibility of snow. Now the sky looked, if anything, even darker, more threatening. A perfect time to stay indoors; and with no compelling need to leave the house...

I poured myself another cup, and then called Denove.

"Mind if I go back out to the crime scene?" I asked.

"What for?"

"Dunno. Something to do."

"What; your girlfriend kick you out or something?"

A joke—but much too uncomfortably close to home, so I hesitated, then said, as casually as possible: "Or something."

Sal Denove and I are friends, but we've not been friends long enough to get into serious discussions about our private lives. He'd at least gotten to the point with me, though, where he could tell when he was treading on sensitive ground.

"All right," he said.

"Thanks, Sal. Any news?"

"Well," he said, "we've got the coroner's report. According to the pattern of rib damage from the first bullet, the path it took would have sent it right through the heart, so there's a very good likelihood that it was, in fact, the kill shot; and with that in mind, you might have thought that one more to the head at close range would have been sufficient, with a third noisy shot being unnecessary risk-taking. But the wounds also indicate that the final two head shots came from medium distance, which might suggest that this guy was spooked at the idea of getting closer to his victim until he was sure he was dead."

"So again, an amateur; and most likely, a single shooter."

"It's increasingly looking that way."

"Well," I said, "guess I'd better get moving; looks like the weather's about to take a nasty turn."

"Okay," said Denove.

"Talk to you later."

"Cassidy—"

"Yeah?"

"Tread lightly out there; we're still working the scene."

"Well, you know *me*..."

"Yes, I do," he said, his voice flat; "that's why I'm saying 'tread lightly.'"

Chapter Forty-Five

Fifteen minutes later I was turning off from route 97 onto the dirt logging road which led to the crime scene. From the highway, it was less than a mile; due west in a straight line, and over a roadbed heavily compacted from recent logging truck use. As I drove, I made sure to keep a light foot on the accelerator and scan carefully ahead, acutely conscious of what a loose, razor-sharp chunk of dislodged volcanic rock could do to a tire or an undercarriage. Above me, the skies continued to shake a collective fist, but as yet my windshield remained clear. Nevertheless, the road was shrouded deeply in gloom, forcing me to turn on my headlights, and the woods as I rolled past appeared a great deal less welcoming than they'd looked yesterday under bright sunshine.

As expected, I soon spotted two Deschutes County Sheriffs SUV's parked on the right shoulder in front of the five acre parcel surrounded by yellow crime scene tape. Across the road, I saw that additional tape had been strung, indicating the expansion of the site Denove had mentioned yesterday.

Parking behind the vehicles, I got out, and, not exactly knowing what I was going to do, walked around the cars and approached the tape, waving at a small group of cops huddled, about twenty feet off, still working the recently-thinned section in which Josh's body had been found. They broke off their conversation just long enough to wave back, and then resumed talking and consulting their notebooks. Since apparently no one thought it necessary to approach and ask what I was doing there, I assumed that they had already been forewarned of my impending visit. My eyes straining against the murk, I scanned the tract, and noticed that all of the woody piles on the property had, in fact, been dismantled; but, since Denove hadn't mentioned having found anything new, my guess was that it had been a wasted effort.

With no real plan, and mindful of my promise to "tread lightly," I decided to skip the immediate crime scene—which I'd already visited, anyway—and instead direct my steps to the shrine Denove had described, which, he'd told me, was to be found somewhere in the parcel across the road.

It wasn't that I expected to find anything of importance there; I didn't. In fact, I wasn't sure why I was here at all, aside from a vague need to feel that I was doing *something,* and, while I was doing it, to incidentally chew up as many empty hours as possible.

This other piece of land, yet to receive any thinning treatment, was a mess: a rat's nest of unhealthy-looking pines, heavy bitterbrush and thick, green currant bushes. At first glance, it looked almost impassable. But as I walked up and down along the road in front of the parcel, I noticed a fairly sizeable opening in the bushes, which led to a primitive kind of path—most likely a game trail—which disappeared, in the feeble light, into the thick undergrowth beyond. Stepping beneath the tape, I followed this path, my attention divided between the ground, strewn with treacherous downed saplings and exposed roots, and the trees overhead, which menaced my forehead with low-hanging branches.

Fifty or sixty feet in, my concentration was arrested by a flash of color as I passed one of the thicker tree trunks standing next to the narrow trail. I turned to look at it, and saw that I had in fact found the shrine.

It wasn't much: a medium-sized crucifix, nailed to the tree a couple of feet above the ground, flanked on either side by what looked to be home-made flower arrangements, which were themselves connected by a wide, silver-white sash composed of a satin ribbon material. The sash had lettering on it, evidently done with a black felt marker, which was difficult to read in the insubstantial light. I squatted, wishing I'd thought to bring my flashlight along. But as I drew closer, the inscription became more distinct, and I was able to see that it had been carefully executed with almost calligraphic precision:

"JOSHUA SAYLES: A GOOD FRIEND, A GOOD PERSON; MAY THE LORD BE WITH YOU ALWAYS."

I smiled as I read this, then stood, and continued to regard the shrine. Not a difficult task to narrow the authorship field on this one. I couldn't see any of the Mirror Pond crowd going to such lengths—particularly considering the way the message was lettered in such a careful and artistic manner. Nor did the words on the sash reflect anything I would expect from ex-girlfriend Jenny Longwell. The Reverend? Possibly, although I couldn't see him choosing those particular words; and with his penchant for PR, I also couldn't imagine him placing the thing in such an odd, out of the way, unnoticeable location. Nadine Sayles? From what Whalen had reported about her state of mind, I doubted that she would have been physically or emotionally capable of leaving the house, let alone coming anywhere near this place.

No; as a matter of fact I thought the words on the sash were a dead giveaway: swap "Force" for "Lord," and you had Star Wars; which, when added to the painstaking, immaculate script, meant that the sentiment could only have come from a collaboration of Josh's two nerdy, erstwhile church buddies, Eliot and Paul.

As for the selection of this peculiarly out of the way spot for their tribute; that still didn't make a whole lot of sense. Why had they chosen to erect their little tribute here—where nobody could see it from the road; where no one, in fact, without the police having widened their search area, would have been likely to find it at all?

I checked my watch: a little after ten. Jenny had called me from school right about this time last week. Snack time.

I pulled my cell phone and my wallet, fished out my card with the kids' cell numbers, and punched up Eliot's. After only one ring, the boy answered; asking, with some impatience: "What *is* it, Mother?"—which, frankly, spoke volumes about the state of his social life. I then proceeded to both surprise and relieve the kid by turning out not to be his mom; then further pleased him by offering to front him and his buddy yet another burger meal this very evening at Red Robin's in the Old Mill District; to which he responded by mumbling a few words off-mike—evidently to the ever-present Paul, because he then returned to enthusiastically accept the proposal on behalf of both of them.

After tucking my phone back into my pocket, I continued to stand there for several minutes, staring in the darkness at Josh's memorial, and puzzling over its odd location. Then, with a combination of rain and snow beginning to spit from the sky, I gave up, and hiked back out of the woods to my car. For a moment I considered joining the cops for a brief word or two, then decided that it would be a waste of everybody's time, climbed into my Toyota, made a dusty u-turn and pulled away. Glancing at the dashboard clock, I saw, with some small satisfaction, that I'd managed to kill off another couple of hours. I now had enough time left to get back to Satch for an early walk, and then home for an afternoon workout, followed by a leisurely shower and a change of clothes before I made the drive back into town for my dinner with the boys.

Chapter Forty-Six

Several hours later, Satch and I had completed our tour of the river trail and were returning from the highway onto Widewater Road, with our house coming into view. I was wondering if there was really anything useful to be expected from tonight's dinner with Paul and Eliot. Not much, frankly. But superstitiously, I thought that these two had been the ones to give me the information about Josh which had really gotten me started, so...well, why not. Besides, if nothing else I'd be able to satisfy my curiosity about their reasons for locating the little memorial to Josh in such a peculiar, secluded spot. And, of course, there was that ever-present necessity of doing my best to keep my schedule filled and my mind occupied.

When we got to the front door, I expected the usual resistance on the leash from Satchmo, who was always reluctant to officially end a walk by crossing the threshold. But when I pushed the door open, she yelped, and, pulling the leash free from my hand, bolted into the great room, disappearing around the corner.

"Satch!" I said; "What the—"

Then I heard another sound: musical, delighted laughter.

Kelly's laughter.

"Ooh, yes...my goodness, I've missed you too, Sweetheart...yes, yes, that's such a good dog..."

My heart pounding, I walked into the room, and saw Kelly, seated in her favorite spot on the sofa, trading hugs and kisses with my dog, whose tail was wagging furiously. She looked at me and smiled.

"Well," she said; "I'm relieved to see that at least *someone* missed me…"

"Now *that's* an understatement," I said. "And it's short by one."

"I know," she said, confidently, locking her eyes with mine.

"So," I asked, timidly, "does this mean that—"

"I'm back? Yes, it does. Hank…what is that…are those tears?"

"Allergies," I said, sheepishly.

"Right," she said; "allergies—in October. Come on over here."

I joined the two of them, and competed with Satch for embraces and kisses. When we pulled away, I asked: "So, what made you change your mind?"

"Well," she said, "I couldn't just abandon my baby"— nodding at Satch, whom she was now scratching behind the ears.

"Anything else?"

"Yes," she said, rolling her eyes, theatrically; "my new roommate snored like a locomotive."

"Kelly…"

"All right; yeah, there's another reason. I was mad at you, yes…I had every right to be—and no, Mister Man, you're not exactly off the hook just yet; I'm still pissed— but after some soul-searching I began to realize that I was also angry with myself."

"You were?" I asked, puzzled. "Why?"

"Because," she said, "as mad at you as I was when I found out what you'd done, I know now that I was also relieved; relieved that I was freed from having to deal with Jack, relieved that I wouldn't have to face my fears—relieved that you had gotten in there and done the dirty work for me."

"But I should have told you what I was planning."

"Yes," she said, her beautiful dark eyes flashing. "That's absolutely right. You *should* have, but you didn't, and so I blew up in justifiable, righteous indignation, and you felt, properly, like shit—right? Right. And so now it's over, and we can move on."

"Whew," I exhaled, stroking her hair, "I sure hope so."

"And there was one other thing," she said; "maybe a small thing, but I think it's important: if this whole episode had resulted in our breaking it off forever, it would have meant that Jack had won after all; that one way or another he still wielded some power over my life. I can't let that happen. Whether you and I make it or not has to depend entirely upon what happens between us, and not upon the influence of my late, extremely unlamented son-of-a-bitch ex-husband."

"Sounds to me," I said, "like you've been doing a whole lot of decision-making for yourself."

"Yes," she replied, looking pleased, "I have, haven't I?"

We shared a warm, significant moment of silence.

"And how have *you* been?" she asked.

"Me?" I said. "What do you think? Longest three days of my life."

"Good," she said; "you deserved it."

"I did."

She stroked my face. "Tell the truth, they were pretty damned long for me, too."

"I love you, Kelly."

"Of course you do."

We stared at each other.

"I love you, too," she said, matter-of-factly; "now, what do we do about dinner?"

"Oh shit, Honey," I said, and explained about my date with Paul and Eliot.

"Wow," she said, laughing; "you *must* have been desperate—dinner date with a couple of teenage boys."

"I'll be home as soon as I can," I promised.

"That's good," she said, squeezing me playfully, "because I've been feeling terribly deprived, lately, if you know what I mean…"

"Yeah, I think I get the point." I looked at my watch. "I've got to shower, but I do happen to have time for a long one. Feel like joining me?"

"Now *there's* an idea."

There's no sex like make-up sex.

Needless to say, when I drove back into Bend that evening it was with a dramatically improved outlook on life.

Chapter Forty-Seven

"Yeah, that was us."

Paul and Eliot were seated across from me, in a booth at Red Robin's. Each had already made substantial inroads into his bacon-mushroom-cheese monstrosity and fries. Compared to them, I was being downright dainty with my basic, no-frills burger. When I had pointed out that with my choice of restaurants this evening we'd moved decidedly upscale from MacDonald's, Eliot had merely shrugged, and said, with a sense of perspective only a teenager can understand: "I suppose so…though I sort of think of these two places as just being different, you know? Not one better than the other or anything—just different."

I had nodded at this, and then posed the question about Josh's memorial which had provoked the above reply.

"Pretty nice work on that sash," I told them.

"That was Paul's work," said Eliot, quickly. "Calligraphy, you know? He's really good at that stuff."

"Just a hobby, really," said Paul, then added, self-consciously: "you know, like guitar-playing and model building?"

"Yeah," I said, feeling no particular need to step on his analogies; "exactly like that. Did you use stencils?"

"No," said Eliot, who was evidently acting as his friend's agent; "he does everything free-hand."

"Impressive."

Paul grinned, silently, a slight flush suffusing his face.

"One thing I still don't get, though," I said, "is why you guys decided to place it where you did. Let's face it: not a lot of people are ever going to see it."

"Wasn't our choice," mumbled Eliot, his plump cheeks stuffed with ketchup-laden steak fries.

"It wasn't?"

"Uh-uh," said Paul. "We really wanted to put it right out there on the side of the road, near where they found Josh's…where they found him. But when we got there, there was all that crime scene tape, and there were cops—um, police officers—all over the place, and other kids and all, and well, we didn't want to get in the way, so we looked for someplace else."

I nodded. For these two boys, doing their damnedest to stay out of other people's way must have been a constant endeavor.

"Yeah," said Eliot; "so we looked across the road, and saw this opening in the bushes. And there was this trail, and so we followed it—"

"And that's how we found that somebody had already picked out a spot for the shrine," said Paul.

"They had? In what way?"

"The cross," said Paul; "that wasn't ours. We found it there, already nailed to the tree. So we figured what the heck, the site has already been chosen, and so we just added our own stuff to it."

"You're right, though," said Eliot, his chewing slowing, thoughtfully; "it really *is* kind of an odd place for somebody's memorial—almost like whoever put it there didn't really want it to be found."

That thought had already occurred to me. As I nodded my agreement, I knew that I was going to be revisiting the shrine, first thing tomorrow morning.

"They've got bottomless fries here, fellas; should I order more?"

The response was a simultaneous, enthusiastic affirmative.

Chapter Forty-Eight

The next day I arrived at the crime scene somewhat later than I had planned, having spent the bulk of the morning catching Kelly up on the details of the case. After smugly pointing out to me that she'd been proven correct in her assumption that Nadine Sayles had found herself a lover, she expressed particular interest in my description of Cowboy Darryl, and she was also intrigued with the motel manager's revelations about the two other men he'd seen the woman "gettin' busy" with.

"Mmm," she said; "sounds like your classic bad-boy syndrome. It strikes me that if this girl hadn't married the minister, she might have spent the rest of her life in Idaho, bouncing around from one saddle-bum to another."

"Yeah," I agreed; "she'd actually mentioned something along those lines to me that first night I met her; about how J.T. Sayles had 'rescued' her from a pretty crappy life. I'd thought at the time that she was talking about problems with her parents, but maybe it was just that as a teenager she'd already developed a pattern of hooking up with some of the scruffier ranch-hand types back there. And now it seems like, once her marriage started hitting the skids, she just began reverting back to type."

About an hour afterward I was wheeling the Toyota over to a stop on the side of the dirt road next to the crime scene. This time, though, there were no County Sheriffs' vehicles to park behind. Nor, though the yellow tape was still up, were there any cops to be seen wandering the property. I wasn't surprised; by now they'd have surrendered to the thought that whatever evidence might remain out there was probably buried too deeply under the bulldozed dirt and debris for them to find.

Leaving my car, I crossed to the other side of the road, ducked under a low lying branch into the opening in the undergrowth, and followed the trail. Soon I was back, staring with fresh, far more critical eyes, at Josh Sayles' memorial.

I now realized two things: aside from the flowers and sash that Paul and Eliot had placed here, the only other component of the shrine was the crucifix itself, which, in fact, had been screwed, not nailed, into the trunk of the tree.

The other thing, the thing that made my pulse quicken; that made me squat and peer much more closely, while being careful not to extend a hand to it, was that this particular brand of cross looked very, very familiar:

Eighteen inches long. Tacky, cheap, gaudy; wood core with a plastic overlay—the whole thing rubbed with a fake patina of antique gilt.

A crucifix which looked to be the close relative of at least a dozen others I'd just recently seen.

Screwed into the tree. Probably used a cordless power drill, one stored in a tool box lashed to the bed of that old pickup; tool box sharing space with a brand-new shovel recently christened with the earth of a fresh, shallow grave—along with all those other materials listed on the receipt from the hardware store.

After a few minutes absorbing images and emotions generated by the cross, I stood up, reached into my pocket for my cell phone and then dialed Denove.

"Your boys done with the Sayles crime scene?" I asked him.

"For now," he replied, curtly. "Frank pulled them off. Why?"

"I think you'd better get them back out here."

"What's up?"

"Not positive," I said, "but tell them to bring their gear; especially the fingerprint kit. If you're lucky, you may have your killer."

"Who is it?"

"I'd rather not say just yet."

"Why not?"

"Because if I'm wrong—"

"You'll look foolish."

"That's being kind."

"And if you're right?"

I let out a slow breath. "Sal, if I'm right, you'll have set a new bar for *'now I've seen everything.'*"

"I'll bring Whalen."

"I'll be here."

Chapter Forty-Nine

Saturday morning, about ten o'clock, having seriously abused several state and local speed laws driving to town from my home, I pulled into a space in the Deschutes County Sheriffs headquarters lot, jumped from my car and hustled into the building's reception area, where I asked for and received directions to Frank Whalen's cubicle. Upon reaching it, I found the stocky detective sitting behind his desk, consuming coffee and jelly donuts, and consulting, in hushed tones, with Sal Denove.

Whalen had been uncharacteristically enigmatic when he'd called just after breakfast and ordered me to "get your ass down here." Though I'd done my best to pry more information out of him on the phone, all he would relinquish was a gruff, "I think it's just better if y'all are present for this;" leaving me entirely unsatisfied, not to mention apprehensive about the results of the forensic testing that my call to Denove had provoked.

But now that I was here, the message on Whalen's face was clear.

"I was right," I said.

Frank nodded. "Son of a bitch murdered his own son."

"No shit," I said.

"No shit," echoed Whalen, doing absolutely nothing to disguise his satisfaction. "We got us a match," he said, grandly; "whole lotta matches, in fact—latents all over the thing, most of 'em first-rate, and every last one of 'em belonging to the Right Reverend J.T. Sayles."

Smiling like a southern-fried Cheshire cat, he leaned back; putting what seemed to me was a dangerously severe strain on his ratty yet well-padded office chair.

Denove nodded pleasantly to me from his seat at one end of the lead detective's desk. Looking around, I located a stiff metal-and plastic chair in a nearby unoccupied cubicle, pulled it over to the opposite end from Sal and planted myself in it, uncomfortably. With the news I'd just heard, though, at the moment a minor insult to my *gluteus maximus* was something easily tolerated.

"You know," Frank said as I settled in, "our boy really made hisself two humongous mistakes. 'Course the most obvious one is that the asshole left his fingerprints all over the thing"—he paused, and grimaced—"S'pose that ain't hardly a proper way to refer to a crucifix…"

"But that wasn't his worst mistake," Denove said.

"Not by a long shot," he agreed. "By nailin', or, rather, by screwin' that—ahem, *religious token*—to the tree, our boy gave us a dandy way to figure a time frame. After comparin' the bark that was sealed behind the cross to that of the exposed wood around it, our lab techs were able to come up with a pretty fair estimate of the length of time the thing'd been up there."

"Two months," I said.

"*Approximately* two months," he corrected; "impossible to be more accurate than that. But anyway safe to say that it's pretty damn close. Whatever, the important thing is that the evidence we got from that tree bark clearly shows that the cross was pinned to it long before Josh's body was found. Now if the guy'd just *leaned* the crucifix against the tree rather than mountin' it, there wouldn'a been any bark comparison, and we probably woulda had us a much harder time fixin' on a chronological reference point."

"And without that," added Denove, "a fingerprint match would probably have been meaningless; he could have claimed that he'd put the cross out there right after we'd told him about Josh's body having been found."

"But," I insisted, "even without different sections of tree bark to compare, wouldn't you still have had a way to establish a timeframe—by examining the changes over time to the surface of the cross itself?"

"Maybe," Whalen said, doubtfully. "Naturally the lab boys are working that angle right now—far as I'm concerned, at this point there ain't no such thing as too much evidence. But in this dry climate? I dunno; it's probably gonna be a whole lot more difficult to get any kinda accurate reading of time passage just usin' what we found on the face of that cross, than it was with the stuff we found behind it."

"Fact is," he said, "this whole shindig went down in July, long after the pine pollen dispersed, and right through the driest, deadest part of the year. So, any idea of a timeframe woulda been entirely dependant on dust or debris accumulation; and in a particularly dense environment like that one, with the cross mounted only a couple'a feet offa the ground and well sheltered from any wind, the dust buildup woulda been minimal and probably hard to quantify. All you gotta do is look at the pristine condition of the fingerprints we found on it to know that precious little got added over that time period. Besides, without knowin' what kind of environment the thing'd been sittin' in *before* it got moved there, how y'all gonna determine a starting point?"

I raised my hands in surrender. "Okay. So I guess what you're trying to say is we got lucky."

Denove smiled. "Extremely. Not for publication, Cassidy, but luck happens to be one of our most widely employed tools for solving the more difficult whodunits. Luck, that is, which might more appropriately be defined as stupidity and carelessness on the part of the perpetrator. In this case, we were lucky that the guy was stupid enough to nail the cross to the tree with his fingerprints still on it, just as we were lucky he was careless enough not to bother policing his spent cartridges.'"

"Luck," I said; "quite an admission, coming from a professional, Denove."

He shrugged. "Keeps us humble."

"How about that shell casing?" I asked. "Any prints on it?"

"Nothing usable," Denove said, shaking his head; "by the time we found it, the thing had probably been stepped on by at least a half a dozen boots."

"So," I argued, "will it even matter that you found it? Do you really think there's a chance he'll still have the gun on him?"

"Maybe not," said Whalen, "but I wouldn't be surprised at all if he does. Fact is, even your most hardened criminal is bound to neglect somethin' when it comes to disposin' of incriminatin' evidence, and I think you'd agree that the asshole we're dealin' with here is hardly a pro. As we already seen from the evidence we recovered, he's already been stupid and careless. And, as I'm sure y'all have already noticed, this is also a man who's both egotistical and arrogant; personality traits, I gotta say, which tend to give rise to a whole lotta stupid and careless."

"Be nice if you're right, and the gun *is* there," I said. "That would really seal the deal. So when do you go pick him up?"

"Any minute now, soon as we get us the search warrant." Reading my expression, he added: "No worries; we got a cruiser out at his house right now. He thinks it's to keep the gawkers and press offa him, but it's also there to make sure our boy don't rabbit."

"Obviously this means that the preacher's alibi for that day doesn't pan out, does it?" I said.

Looking slightly distressed, Whalen admitted, "Yeah, obviously. We dropped the ball there; passed over that one way too lightly. Shouldn't have." He shrugged. "But he wasn't exactly considered a real suspect, so at the time his alibi seemed sufficient. Now, when you take a closer look at it, it ain't no alibi at all. From the time stamp on the store receipts, to the afternoon counselin' session, there's almost a two hour window—even after allowin' for drivin' time from the crime scene over to Prineville."

At that moment Whalen's line buzzed. "Yeah? Great; we'll meetcha outside." He replaced the receiver, pushed his chair back, and stood; then looked at me. "Got it. Y'all want in on this, Cassidy?"

"You're kidding."

"Hell no," he said. "That's why we called y'all in here. In a way, it's your collar; you the one who noticed the crucifix. Without that, we might'a never made the connection."

I smiled as I stood. "Thanks, Detective, I'd love to."

"It's the least we can do," he said with a grin, "I'm kinda feelin' sorry for ya, there, Podnah. Once we get the preacher in custody, I think it's a pretty safe bet y'all gonna get stiffed on your fee."

Naturally that notion had already crossed my mind, and it hardly felt any better to have it expressed by someone else. So glad I'd at least deposited the retainer…

"Speaking of which," said Denove, suppressing a smile; "—and not meaning to pile on or anything—but I think it's also pretty clear now why the minister picked you over all the other PI's in town."

"Yeah, I figured that one out, too," I grumbled. "The asshole purposely picked me because I was a brand new PI with a fresh license and no apparent history in the field; precious little experience, few contacts and practically no resources. I'm sure he was convinced that I was such a complete loser that I'd be the least likely investigator in all of Central Oregon to make any headway on a difficult case. Meanwhile, the good Reverend got to boast, publicly, that he was pulling out every last stop searching for his boy."

"And oh yes," I said, elbowing the lanky detective, as we stepped into the parking lot, "thank you so much for not piling on—or anything."

"You're welcome." he said, shaking his head when I opened the front passenger door: "Uh-uh; you sit in back."

After sliding onto the rear bench seat of the vehicle, and shrugging off that odd, irrational sense of guilt one feels about riding in the back of a patrol car, I said:

"Of course, we're forgetting the minister's worst, most obvious mistake."

Whalen, driving the car, glanced at me in the rearview mirror. "What's that?"

"That he put the cross there at all."

The detective nodded. "Yeah, that's for damned sure; without that, we got no fingerprints, no tree bark evidence; no nothin', aside from one lousy .45 casing. Whydja think he did it? Arrogance?"

"That might be part of it," I said. "But I think the real reason is that, as pompous and egotistical as the guy is, and despite being warped enough to murder his own son, on some level J.T. Sayles still believes that he's a genuine man of God. I suspect that's the kind of incredible self-delusion you're bound to find at the core of any religious charlatan. Somehow, they've got to believe that, no matter what they do, it's always justified because it was done in the name of the Almighty."

"Messianic complex," said Denove.

"Right, and with that sort of mindset, Sayles couldn't just allow himself to walk away from Josh's unmarked grave—he had to commemorate the deed with some sort of sacred token; somehow twist a brutal, selfish act into something elevated and holy. So he brought the cross along. Of course the practical criminal in him also knew that placing the crucifix there could be grossly incriminating, so he carefully stuck the shrine on a different piece of land the other side of the road from the one the grave was in; which satisfied him that it was at least in the vicinity, while being safely stashed where he thought no one else would find it. He felt especially secure about this, since the killing itself was done in a particularly nasty, dense part of the forest, where he was reasonably certain the body wouldn't be discovered for years, by which time there'd be nothing left of that cross but a few crumbling pieces of gold-colored plastic."

"Yeah," scoffed Whalen; "best laid plans, right? Except that what he *don't* know is that the Forest Service's got its *own* plans for the place; and so trees get chopped, the body gets found, and then two kids stumble on the cross."

"That's some kind of bad luck," I said.

"Who knows," responded Whalen; "maybe whatcha *really* got here is a little divine intervention…"

We were silent, each plumbing his own thoughts about *that* one for a few minutes. Then Denove stirred.

"Of course," he said, speaking in his usual undertone, "you know what else that cross shows…"

Leaning forward to hear him better, I said, "What's that?"

"Premeditation. He might claim that it was mere coincidence the crucifix happened to be in his truck that day, but, with the way you're putting it, he'd have to have been planning ahead of time to carry it with him."

"Tough to prove in court," said Whalen.

Denove shook his head. "I'm not talking about court; I'm talking about my own impression of his intent. No matter what, the man's going down, and it'll be up to the District Attorney and the jury to decide for how long. But as far as I'm concerned, that cross tells me that this was a premeditated murder."

"Yeah," said Whalen; "that and the ATM withdrawals."

"So that was him in the videos," I said.

"Who else? And it makes sense, don't it? As his dad, he woulda helped his underage son open the bank account in the first place, showed him how to use the debit card. Wouldn't be too much of a stretch to figure that he also helped him select the pin number. And he certainly had easy access to the kid's closet, to grab him some clothes for a disguise."

"Which is why you won't be able to tie that one to him, either," I said; "the disguise—can't tell it's him."

"Likely," said Denove, "although with what we know now, we're going to be spending a lot more time poring over those tapes. With any luck, we'll be able to catch him slipping up somewhere."

"Funny," I said.

"What?"

"Well, by draining his son's account, Sayles was creating evidence which ran contrary to his argument that the boy wouldn't have run off on his own, had to have been abducted."

"So?" growled Whalen. "Y'all looking for consistency, here, Cassidy? The bastard's an amateur, for heaven sakes. Besides, if we ain't got him down as a suspect, then whatever theory he happens to be spoutin' while we're workin' the case is just gonna sound like a buncha noise to us. Who knows; maybe his original idea was to make it look like the kid *did* run off, and then afterward, for some sorta reason he decided it would make him look better if the boy got kidnapped."

That led to more silence, which continued almost to our destination. A few blocks short of it, though, I spoke up.

"You guys clear on a motive?"

"Ain't important to us," said Whalen. "Long's the evidence is solid, long's we got our man, y'all can leave the motive to the lawyers and the media. But if you gotta have one now; I'd say that you already supplied us with it."

"You mean, you think Josh warned his father that he was planning to go public with his mother's affair."

"Yeah," he said, "and the minister couldn't afford to have that kinda dirty linen aired—to be embarrassed like that just as he was about to do his first big telecast."

I leaned back. The detective was almost certainly correct: that J.T. Sayles was cold-blooded enough to murder his son just to prevent the humiliation of having his wife's affair go public.

But did that really feel right?

We pulled into the Sayles driveway.

Ah, well; not my problem.

Chapter Fifty

The street in front of the church compound was a zoo. Parked less than half a block down from the house were two TV transmitter trucks, their transmission masts competing for prominence with the nearby trees. The logos on the vehicles indicated that one belonged to a local TV station, the other, a network affiliate in Portland. In front of the minister's house, milling restlessly at the edge of the curbless country road, was a medium-sized gaggle of reporters, their weary, bored expressions suggesting that they believed, almost a week in, that they were stuck covering a declining story, and having to cook up some fresh angle out of stale bread for tonight's news broadcast or tomorrow's paper.

Hang in there, boys, I thought as I scanned the faces; *your by-line is about to change.*

Whalen frowned at the sight. "Looks like we got us a perp-walk."

"And you don't want that?" I said.

"No, actually, we don't," said Denove. "Not for the preacher's sake, though—the scumbag deserves every ounce of humiliation he gets. It's just that we can do without the spectacle; especially when something like this is bound to be running at least two dozen times on every cable news channel in the country over the next forty-eight hours."

"You think it'll play that wide?"

"'Prominent Oregon Minister Arrested in the Murder of His Own Son;' what do *you* think?"

As we were rolling to a stop, I could see two more Sheriffs' units, each with three uniforms inside, pulling into the church parking lot close to the house. These were followed by an evidence van, which lined up to the outside of them. Another cruiser, the one Whalen had mentioned back at the office, was already occupying a space next to the reverend's pickup, with a couple of uniformed sheriffs leaning against it. They pushed off from it and approached us as we rolled to a stop.

"He's not in there," said the taller of the two, gesturing towards the house as we emerged from the cruiser.

"Where is he?" asked Whalen.

The other one jerked a thumb over his shoulder. "In the chapel."

"What; still praying for his son? Making a show for the press?"

"Don't think so," said the tall one. "Way it sounds, he's been in there all day rehearsing his sermon for this coming Sunday—the one that's supposed to be televised."

"Ah, right; his big televangelism debut," Whalen said. "Y'all might say the asshole's about to be pre-empted."

"That'd suit me just fine," said the tall cop, with distaste. "Now that I know what's going down, I'm sick to death of the son of a bitch. He had a special service the other night, right? Now, I'm a Presbyterian, but I figured, as long as I'm around, I'd give it a shot; see what his spiel is. Wanna know what the theme was? 'Overcoming Personal Tragedy.' Can you believe that shit?"

There was a general shaking of heads.

"Where's the wife?" asked Denove.

"She's in the house with the social worker."

"Okay," said Whalen. "No need for us to bother her for the time being. But y'all might want to discreetly call the social worker out onto the porch for a few minutes and let her know what's what."

"Will do."

We then made our way around the side of the house and headed for the barn-shaped chapel. Whalen called all the other cops over from their cars and huddled with them near an angle of the school's play yard fence. One of them he assigned to the press, warning him to keep them from setting foot on the church property. "If they gonna film this thing," he grumbled, "y'all make damn sure they gotta use their telephoto lenses."

I glanced back as he said this, and saw that the flock of reporters, sensing that something fresh was afoot, had instantly morphed from pigeons into vultures. Straining to get a better view, they began to migrate, *en masse,* from the front of the house towards the parking lot, where they were then intercepted by the cop, who immediately trotted over and held them at bay with his arms spread wide.

Whalen then directed two other cops from our group to move around to the back of the chapel, to block any possible escape route. The last three and the crime scene techs were to accompany us to the building's main entrance.

"Keep your pieces holstered," he cautioned everyone. "This is a minister we're arrestin'—not John Dillinger. Let's do this thing as quiet as possible. Cassidy, y'all stay behind us. Okay, let's go."

When we reached the double doors of the chapel, we found them wide open. From the steps we could hear the preacher's booming voice, which, though un-amplified, was still loud enough for me to discern the words.

Whalen held up a hand. "I don't think it'd be proper bustin' a preacher inside his own chapel—especially with all them cameras out there. So, you fellas wait out here, and I'll go on in and wave him over. He's got no reason to know what we're doin' here, so there shouldn't be any trouble. Just the same, watch for my sign if everything starts to go south." He then disappeared into the reception area, while we stood waiting at the base of the church steps.

As we idled, I found myself fixing on the Reverend's words, which were riding a wave of stentorian excess out through the open doors. Though I'm hardly a biblical scholar, it wasn't difficult to recognize the passage:

"And they came to the place which God had told him of; and Abraham built an altar there, and laid the wood in order, and bound Isaac his son, and laid him on the altar upon the wood. And Abraham stretched forth his hand, and took the knife to slay his son."

"And the angel of the Lord called unto him out of heaven, and said, 'Abraham, Abraham:' and he said, 'Here am I.' And he said, 'Lay not thine hand upon the lad, neither do thou anything unto him: for now I know that thou fearest God, seeing thou hast not withheld thy son, thine only son from me.'"

Denove and I exchanged looks. Was *this* the text he was going to be using as the basis for Sunday's big televised sermon?

"Man," said the detective, shaking his head, wonderingly. "That is one sick, cynical son of a bitch."

The Reverend's voice continued to boom; now, if anything, even more energized and fervent as he plunged into the sermon:

*"But, my beloved friends, let me ask all of you: what if, at the last gasp, the angel had **not** appeared, to stay his arm? Should Abraham have backed away from that altar, thrown the knife to the ground and thereby refused to*

*submit himself to the will of **God?** Or should he have instead obeyed, and allowed the blade to continue on its downward journey, until, at the end, it plunged into the breast of his son?"*

*"I put it to you, Brethren, that as one of the righteous, Abraham would have had no other choice; Almighty Lord God hath **commanded,** therefore it must be **done.** So it is ever in life: once we have divined that which is God's will, it remains solely our mission to carry it out, no matter how personally painful the task may be; lest by refusing we rush ourselves to partake of the awful fires of **perdition!** The Lord sayeth—"*

His voice abruptly stopped, and I figured that at that moment the minister must've noticed Whalen waving to him from the back of the sanctuary.

A few minutes of weighted silence ensued, as I stood there wondering whether Whalen had said anything to J.T. Sayles which may have given him any reason to suspect what was happening. But when the two men appeared in the doorway, I could see that he hadn't: the Reverend was beaming—a man clearly very much at the top of his game--, and actually had a cordial hand on the detective's shoulder as he stepped out into the sunlight.

Then he saw the crowd at the bottom of the steps, and stopped; his face, panning back and forth as he took in all of the sober, resolute expressions, becoming painted with dawning comprehension.

A high, keening wail, so utterly unlike his normal baritone that it didn't seem possible, issued from the man's mouth; his strength failing him, he sank to his knees, as if collapsing under the crushing weight of suddenly-shattered dreams. With Whalen announcing his arrest and reading him his rights, one of the sheriffs stepped forward and put the cuffs on the wrists behind the back of the hunched over, defeated figure, who stared with wide, glazed eyes, at the immaculately stained and polished wood beneath him.

Upon completion of the recitation, and once the search warrant had been served, the evidence guys disappeared into the chapel. As they did so, Sayles was brought to his feet, and it was then that his eyes fell upon me. Immediately his face contorted into a snarl, which, frankly, did not exactly look threatening, particularly given the failure of his comb-over, which at the moment was hanging in an uneven cascade off of one side of his head.

"You bastard!" he hissed. "It was *you,* wasn't it?"

I wasn't sure what he meant, so I kept quiet.

"Thou art the foul spawn of Satan! Burn in Hell, accursed heathen!"

I should've let that one lie, but I just couldn't help myself. "I think right now you're the one whose horns are showing, Jeremiah. Jeremiah; am I wrong, or wasn't he the prophet that nobody would listen to?"

It was Sayles' turn to be silent.

"My guess is that when it comes to your fellow inmates you're gonna be having pretty much the same problem."

"Go fuck yourself!" he snapped.

"Whoa, Reverend!" I said, feigning shock. "I don't think I'm familiar with that particular gospel."

"Alright, Boys," said Whalen, not quite managing to stifling a laugh; "y'all can ship'im, now."

It was with an admittedly un-Christian sense of *schadenfreude* that I watched the minister, looking especially diminutive in the company of two much taller and more massive officers, receding down the path to the parking lot.

After a silent, amiable nod towards me, Whalen then followed the evidence team into the chapel. Their search, encompassing the church, the house, three vehicles and the surrounding grounds, would take several days; although, as it turned out, the two items of greatest interest would be found in the first half-hour, while I was still there.

Denove was the one to tell me, striding, with a particularly triumphant look on his face, out through the doorway.

"Found the kid's ATM card," he said.

"No kidding. Where was it?"

Displaying what for him must have been as close to a mischievous grin as he could manage, he said, "It was lying right next to the gun."

"The gun. You mean *the* gun?"

He nodded. "Expect so. Colt M1911A1 semi-automatic—Vietnam vintage."

".45 caliber," I said, shaking my head. "How about that. And the card, too. Where was he hiding them?"

His face and voice returning to their customary stolidity, he said, "Locked drawer in the pulpit."

"No kidding?" I said, shaking my head. "Man, talk about inappropriate..."

"Probably figured it was the last place anyone would look."

"And you're sure it'll match the slug and the casing."

"Please; let's wait for the lab results," he cautioned, then smiled again. "But yes, let's just say it's a fairly safe bet." He plunged his hands into his pockets. "I think you and I can leave now; the boys are going to be at this for some time, and there's no need for us to hang around. Whalen will stay, and catch a ride in with the others."

"Must be a happy guy," I said.

"He's ecstatic. If he didn't think it would be sacrilegious, he'd be in there whistling something saucy from Bourbon Street. Oh, and he says he owes you dinner."

"Pasta?"

"What else?"

Chapter Fifty-One

On the drive home, I called Cyrus Brooks, to whom I hadn't spoken since before my trip to L.A.

"It's about time," he snorted; "how'd it go?"

"Which?"

"Which? Our little sting operation, of course—that's the only thing I've got a personal stake in. So give: what happened with you and the lawyer at the hotel?"

I told him.

"No kidding," he chuckled, when I'd finished; "what a fortuitous mélange: an attorney with a drinking problem, an ego, *and* a big mouth. Sounds like you've got some good stuff. Care to send the recording along to me?"

"Of course," I said, knowing full well that by doing so I was breaking my word to Melcher. Fact is, I'd never intended otherwise. "I'll e-mail you the audio file. Though considering the way I got it, I doubt that it'll be anything you can use, legally."

"Never you mind," he said; "you just send it—I'll find a way to put it to good use."

"Whatever," I said, "just as long as he doesn't bother Kelly again."

He chuckled. "Sounds to me like he definitely won't. And you say you only had to slap him once?"

"I swear."

"Did you threaten to ice the motherfucker?"

I just smiled into the phone.

"Of course you did," he said. "How did Kelly react to all of this?"

"She left me."

"She did?" There was a pause. Then: "That's okay. Don't sweat it, man; she'll be back."

"She already is."

That brought a full-blown laugh from my friend. "I were you," he said when he'd calmed down, "I wouldn't take any more chances; I'd marry that girl right now."

"Cyrus," I said, "I think at the moment I'm just grateful to be halfway out of Kelly's doghouse. Besides, right now I don't think she'd be up for any proposals."

"Well, don't waste any time when you think she is. That Kelly is a hell of a woman; don't believe you could do any better."

"There *is* no better, Cy. And don't think I haven't been considering it."

"You have? Well now, how about that; looks like there might be a little hope for my boy after all…"

"Thanks."

"You're welcome. *Now* we can talk about your missing persons case. How's that going?"

"Pretty much over," I said, and then filled him in on the particulars.

"My-my," he said; "you *have* been at it, haven't you. But why did you say 'pretty much?' Aren't you through with it?"

"There's something that's still bothering me."

"What's that?"

"The motive: something about it doesn't feel quite right. I just don't think that fear of having his wife's infidelities aired in public would've been a strong enough reason to cause the preacher to murder his own son."

"People get killed for much less than that a hundred times a day."

"But not by the preacher—not this guy. Way I see it; he's much too smart, too calculating to have been panicked into shooting his son for something like that. I can think of at least a half a dozen ways he could actually have turned his wife's cheating into a public relations advantage, maybe portrayed himself as the unwitting victim or something."

"Okay, so let's say you're right. What *is* the motive, then?"

I was silent for a moment. "It had to have been something far worse; something so dark, so scandalous, that having it come out would have ruined him for sure."

"Any ideas?"

"Yeah, actually, I do have one."

"So what's the move?"

"Well," I said, slowly, "I've got one more card to play, just one; if it doesn't work, I'll forget about the whole thing, let the guy go off to rot in jail, and spend my days and nights doing my best to get back in my lady's good graces."

"And if it does?"

"If it does?" I said. "If it does; if I'm correct about what I'm thinking, then this case will be taking one gigantic turn for the weird."

"But you're not telling."

"Not until I know for sure."

"Sounds interesting. Keep me posted, Breh."

I closed my cell phone, and thought about that next move; the final card in my deck:

First a quick stop at the house to pick up it up.

Then one more trip to the Bluebird Motel.

Chapter Fifty-Two

Saturday, a week later, late afternoon.

Back at Franks, sipping wine with Nadine Sayles.

Restaurants, always restaurants, I thought; *no wonder all of the PI's I know look like "before" models for Jenny Craig...*

The last couple of weeks had not been kind to the woman. Where before, when I'd first met her, she'd looked decidedly young for her age, now the years seemed to have piled up in rapid succession: dark crescents underlay her eyes, worry lines creased her forehead, and her skin had taken on a pallid cast which, it seemed, no amount of makeup could mitigate. Even her once lustrous hair now seemed dull, faded—clearly neglected.

"The funeral's Tuesday?" I said.

"Yes." She spoke through tightened lips; her eyes on the table, hands compulsively kneading a paper napkin. "And it's going to be a *non*-religious ceremony," she added, with some fierceness.

"I'm not surprised," I said.

"Will you be there?"

"Of course."

She looked up briefly, met my eyes, smiled thinly, then looked down again. I wasn't sure she was pleased with my answer.

"Jennifer Longwell's been helping me with the arrangements," she said.

I knew that; I'd spoken with the girl earlier that day, on the phone.

"That's good," I said; "for both of you."

She sighed. "She really is quite a young lady."

"Yes she is," I agreed; "which kind of makes you wonder why Josh ever broke up with her."

Without lifting her head she said, "I...I really have no idea—"

"I think you do."

"What?" This time her head came up sharply, her eyes searching my face for answers, finding none. "I, I don't know what you're talking about," she said, guardedly.

"See," I said, "I was never quite able to buy into the idea that your husband murdered his son just to cover up your affair with Darryl Turnick. Sure, it would have been an embarrassment to him, probably cause a few murmurs in the back rows of his church; but it's not as if this sort of thing doesn't happen all the time to all kinds of people—including ministers. Besides, I think that a man as driven and clever as J.T. Sayles would have easily been able to turn something like that to his advantage. You know—man of God, so dedicated to his religious work, so self-sacrificing in his unceasing efforts for others, that, unwittingly, he has caused his own family to be neglected in the process, and has therefore suffered for it. In fact, it wouldn't be too hard to imagine him cooking up some sort of a Sunday sermon on the value of striking a balance between your responsibilities to your family, and your duty to The Lord."

Nadine was silent.

"So," I continued, "with that in mind, I decided to pay one more visit to the Blue Bird Motel."

Nadine seemed to flinch at the mention of the name, and then assiduously avoided my eyes.

"In my first visit there," I continued, "when the motel manager recognized your photo and told me about your relationship with Mr. Turnick, he also mentioned a couple of other men he'd seen you with, previous to that—"cowboy types," he'd called them—which suggested that your social life had been quite a bit more active than I'd first supposed. And while he was describing those two, he speculated that there might have been others."

Nadine said nothing.

"This notion of your having had a variety of previous lovers eventually gave rise to a possibility—farfetched, I'll admit—but one that seemed to jibe with my speculations about your husband having had a different, far more compelling motive for murder. So, as before, I approached the manager with a photo; only this time, I showed him a photograph of Joshua Sayles."

I paused, and looked at her; but she continued to study the wood grain in the table—although I could see that her body had tensed, as if awaiting a blow.

"Turns out the guy recognized him," I said; "had seen him a number of times at the motel, walking across the parking lot, carrying a bucket to or from the ice machine, getting a soft drink. But the manager never made the connection between the two of you because he never actually saw him entering or leaving a particular room, and therefore assumed that he must have been there with someone else. But when I asked him whether he'd seen *you* at the motel on any of those same days, he said: 'Now that you mention it, I'm pretty sure that I did—though I can't swear to it.'"

Her head was still hanging, but now tears began to trail down her cheeks. "You...you don't understand..."

"Oh," I said, "I really don't think it's all that difficult to understand, Nadine. You were having sex with your son."

This was thin—mighty thin—and depended heavily upon the very uncertain recall of a man whose character and reliability might be considered, at best, questionable. I fully expected my accusation to be met with a wall of anger, righteous indignation and vociferous denials; therefore I was completely unprepared for what came next:

There was a long silence. Nadine Sayles had shifted her gaze from the table, and now it rested on her lap. From the slight, rhythmic movements of her shoulders, I could see that she had begun to cry. Finally, without looking up, and in a small, watery voice, she spoke:

"Yes…yes I was."

There followed more silence. I realized, suddenly, that I didn't have the slightest idea of what to say. With what I'd learned in my second trip to the motel, I'd had but one thought: confront Nadine Sayles. But I had no plan at all for responding to such a meek, straightforward confession. As I wrestled with my reply, she looked directly at me and spoke:

"I know; you probably think I'm a monster. Well maybe I am, but maybe you don't have any idea what it's been like for me. For years—most of our marriage, really-—my life's been not much more than a prison: no friends, no relatives, no one to talk to, no one to…to touch me; a husband who thinks that I'm much too disgusting to share a bed with. And the whole time I've been expected to behave like this perfect little Christian minister's wife. All for the sake of my husband, all for the sake of his…*church*…"

She spat out the last word.

"And Josh?" she said, looking away, with her voice lowered. "He was so beautiful, so sweet, so understanding—mature for his age, too. I was lonely...so desperately lonely. I needed someone, and he..."

She shrugged.

"And besides, it...it was the kind of thing that I'd already known about much earlier in my life."

She fixed me with a significant, penetrating look.

"Your father," I said.

She nodded. "That's right; my father. He *raped* me, Mr. Cassidy. My father took me into the barn right after my twelfth birthday, threw me down on the straw; told me he was doing me a favor—'breaking you in,' he called it. And then he kept *on* breaking me in; two, three times a month, five long years; all the way until I was seventeen, when I finally got myself out of there and ran off with Bill...with J.T."

She stared at me, defiantly; daring me to respond. But I didn't. How could I? What could I have said at that moment, which wouldn't have sounded patronizing, or judgmental, or just plain banal and useless? Point out to her that using her past experiences as a victim to justify her own misdeeds was wrong? Looking at her face, I was sure that she'd already been beating herself up with *that* one for some time.

Seeing that nothing was forthcoming from me, Nadine shrugged. "So there you have it, Mr. Cassidy," she said; "that's how a young girl gets turned into a monster. That's how the idea of incest becomes an ordinary way of thinking, so that, when you commit it yourself, years later, it just feels like resumption of an old bad habit. You know that it's terribly wrong; that it goes against all the rules of 'decent' society; that in the end you'll despise yourself for what you've done." She shrugged. "But, you know what? It's what I *knew*."

"Besides," she said, staring at her glass, "it was the only option that was being left open to me…"

Left open.

At first I didn't quite get what she was driving at. Then I saw it in her eyes.

"He knew about it," I said; "your husband knew what you and Josh were doing."

She nodded.

"He did," she said. "He knew what was happening from the start, though he never said a word about it. It finally came to me, though, that in his own way J.T. was actually *encouraging* us: never asking questions about where we'd been, always making himself scarce at just the 'right' moments. Frankly, I think he was getting a sick sort of thrill out of it. Besides, I think he saw what was happening between Josh and me as a pretty neat arrangement; an easy way to keep the family together, all things considered, so long as no word of it ever got out."

"But it was bound to get out."

"Yes," she said; "it was—especially when I put an end to it." She paused, and again looked away. "When I got serious about Darryl."

"Right," I said; "and then Josh found out about that, blew up, and went to his father and threatened to tell the world what had been happening between the two of you."

She nodded. "Which would have destroyed everything for my husband: marriage, family, church, reputation," she said. "And of course it was mostly his church and his reputation that mattered to J.T."

"And that's why he murdered his son."

"Yes," she said, her eyes returning to the table; "that's why he murdered...*my* son." Then she paused, as if trying to summon her strength. I waited. At last, she looked up at me and spoke:

"So you see, Mr. Cassidy, it's really my fault that he's dead."

To reply to that would have been to lie, so I didn't. Instead, I said: "What will you do now?"

She looked at me, a plea in her eyes. "I guess that sort of depends. Are you going to tell the police about...about..."

"About this?" I said, and shook my head. "No, there's really not much point in that; with Josh gone, there's really no one to testify against you besides your husband and the motel manager. Believe me, that manager is hardly what I'd call a credible witness. And as for your husband, well, I'm pretty sure he won't be inclined to advertise his own participation in this...arrangement, if he has any thoughts at all about someday being able to gain parole and start over."

"What about you?" she asked. "*You* know."

"Me? Let's just say that this was a private conversation; no need for me to take it any further."

"Thank-you," she whispered.

"So again, what's next for you?"

Her gaze became distracted, unfocused. "I, I don't know. I've spoken to an attorney, but...well, I really don't expect that there'll be much money left for me after this is all over. Pretty much everything we've got is tied up in the church property, and we're already in the process of selling it to raise J.T.'s legal fees."

I didn't doubt that. Between the divorce and what the preacher was facing, chances were that most of their assets were about to disappear into the black hole of the legal system.

"And after *that*..." she continued, shrugging, "I...well, I guess I just don't know." Her head hanging again, she added:

"I have nowhere to go."

"What about Darryl?" I was immediately sorry I'd asked, because I knew, perhaps even better than Nadine, what the answer was going to be.

Her face growing even more defeated, she said, "He...he dumped me; said he's decided to go back to his wife."

She leaned back, leaving me to search for words of encouragement. I found none, sipped my wine instead.

We both knew that the conversation had now come to an end; but with neither of us seeming to be able to devise an appropriate exit, we continued to concentrate on our Merlots. Our waitress, who'd no doubt witnessed, from a distance, a good portion of what had been passing between us, had shown admirably good sense the whole time in not attempting to approach our table for a food order. But when our glasses were finally empty, I signaled to her for the check.

Once we'd passed outside through the double-glass doors of the restaurant, we both immediately zipped up our jackets. Dark clouds had pushed in from the mountains, blocking out the sun and making the afternoon look much more like late evening. Snow, blown sideways by a stiff, biting wind, had apparently been falling for some time; all of the cars in the lot had acquired a thin layer of white;

what the locals would call a "dusting"—although to me it meant that the drive home was likely to be unpleasant.

We hadn't spoken since leaving the table, but once we reached my car, which was several spaces closer than hers, Nadine turned to me.

"Well," she said.

"Well."

"Thanks for the wine."

"No problem."

She hesitated. "And...thanks again, for—"

I knew what she meant, and said, "Also not a problem."

She searched my face. "Wish me luck?"

It was a sign-off question, and even though I'd been clear about my intention to attend Josh's funeral the following Tuesday, I think we both knew that, aside from some sort of whispered condolence at the gravesite, these words here in the parking lot would be the last of any substance which would pass between us. Therefore I understood the weight of her request, and did my best to respond appropriately:

"I do wish it, Nadine. I hope that better days are ahead for you. You take care of yourself."

She nodded, smiling faintly, but, though she gave me a look which suggested that she thought it an impossible task, she said, "I will."

Then she turned and walked away, shoulders slumped; perhaps as forlorn a figure as I have ever seen in my life.

Chapter Fifty-Three

Since I'd returned from my meeting with Nadine Sayles without actually having eaten anything, Kelly and I opted to salvage the evening by throwing together a quasi-romantic late supper, complete with sunset and candles. While we prepared it—or rather, while *I* prepared it, with Kelly sticking to the table-setting and candle-lighting duties—I filled her in on the final, sordid elements of the Joshua Sayles case. At my feet in the kitchen sat Satchmo, who, disdaining the bowl of kibble I'd taken care to set out *before* beginning our meal prep, was watching me intently, obviously hoping for a little consideration, or at least, some sort of opportune food-dropping mishap.

"It's the ultimate vicious cycle," I said, tossing freshly-chopped vegetables and sliced Italian sausage into the hot, olive-oiled skillet, while I checked the linguini: "Husband shuns wife for the unforgivable sin of having been born to a sexual predator; wife reacts to the rejection by reenacting her father's behavior with her own son; son reacts to being 'dumped' by mother by threatening to blow the whistle; father, reacts to son's threat by shooting him in the back."

"Family destroyed," said Kelly, as she lit the candles. "Son dead; father jailed; church dissolved; mother..." Her voice trailed off, causing me to look up. Kelly was standing there, lighter poised over an unlit candle, a distracted look on her face.

"What?"

"Huh? Oh, I don't know...." She was silent for a moment. "It's just that...well, I suppose Nadine Sayles deserves what's happening to her—she certainly played a major role in how things turned out—but on some level I just can't bring myself to condemn her."

"Me neither," I said; "but in my case it's because I've gotten to know her a little. What's your excuse?"

"Me?" she said, her eyes drifting. "I don't...you know, I guess it's because I can't help but feel that she and I were in the same boat."

"Same boat...you mean both married to dominating husbands," I said. "I get it; but beyond that, the comparisons are kind of a stretch, don't you think?"

"Maybe," she said, doubtfully. "But what if the rest—the differences, I mean—are really just accidents of birth? Do you really think I would have done any better than Nadine if I'd been stuck with the rotten environment *she* grew up in?"

"Gonna go out on a limb here, Honey," I said, as I loaded our plates, and then carried them to the table: "I think you would have done much better."

"Oh, come on now, Cassidy," she said, frowning as she finally stirred herself to light the second candle; "what makes you say that?"

Placing the dishes onto their bamboo place settings, I said, "I've seen the two of you angry."

"So?"

"So a long time ago you told me you used to openly disagree with your husband."

"I did."

"A lot."

Her look was defiant. "Yes; a lot."

"And at times you got to be fairly vociferous, right?"

A half-smile creasing her face, she said, "Vociferous? I suppose you could use that word, though just plain 'loud' might be more accurate." She laughed. "Yeah, that was me: *vociferous*. I snapped at him. I yelled at him. Sometimes I screamed."—she cast a sideways glance at me—"believe me, you only got a small taste the other day."

I winced, nodded. "But I certainly got enough of a taste to guess what the full treatment must look like."

She laughed again. "Yeah, I'll admit I can be pretty fierce sometimes—a regular harpy, in fact." She shrugged. "But, so what? As I also told you, yelling at the bastard only made things worse for me."

"Maybe it did," I said; "but that's not the point, is it? The point is that you fought back—often, too. From what Nadine Sayles told me, she never disagreed with her husband; not once. And she sure as hell never raised her voice to him. Instead, she kept her head down and her mouth shut; dealt with her resentment by sulking in her bedroom like an adolescent, or moping about the grounds of their compound—or by sneaking off to the Bluebird to do the nasty with one saddle-bum or another."

"Or with her son," she added, distastefully.

"Yeah; or with her son," I agreed, then added, casually: "Kelly, did *you* ever cheat on your husband?"

"No," she said, her eyes flashing. "Of *course* I didn't. How could you—"

"Why not?" I said. "He cheated on *you,* didn't he?"

"All the time," she muttered, disgustedly.

"And yet you never even considered—"

"No, I never did. But, Hank," she insisted; "I also didn't *leave* him—and *that,* after all, is what I *really* have in common with Nadine Sayles: we both never left our husbands."

"Yes," I said, "that's right; you never left. But it's the *"why"* that really makes you different. Nadine Sayles stayed in her miserable marriage because she was too terrified to leave; too afraid that she'd never be able to make it on her own. You, on the other hand, didn't leave yours—not because you were afraid, but because it's just not in your nature to walk out on a commitment."

Kelly put the lighter down but remained standing, her thoughtful look and silence signaling confirmation.

"Jack got that about you, didn't he?" I said; "probably right away—back when the two of you were still in college. And, scumbag that he was, he learned how to use that knowledge to keep you constantly off-balance; to keep you with him, no matter what he did to you. Bottom line is that it wasn't fear or weakness in you that Jack was exploiting; it was your strength, your *resolve*. Actually, I think a better word for it might be *'integrity.'*"

She smiled. "Oh, come on now, that's *way* too lofty a word, Cassidy."

"No, it's not," I maintained; "it fits you like a glove. Integrity. And, frankly, I think that's also a big part of why you came back to *me*."

"Really," she laughed. "You're thinking that I've made the same kind of a commitment to you that I did with—"

I shook my head. "No, Honey. I don't; I should only be so lucky. Your marriage was obviously a much bigger deal for you. But, when you moved up here last year, as impulsive as it might have seemed at the time, I know that it was actually a huge step for you. Not the biggest sort of commitment—but pretty damn big, just the same. I just think it would take a lot more than one idiot blunder by me for you to bail on it."

"Oh?" she said, smiling, playfully; "and just how many idiot blunders do you think it would take?"

I returned the smile. "I don't ever want to find out."

Still smiling, Kelly circled the table to where I was standing, and put her arms around my neck.

"Cassidy, is this your extremely bizarre idea of a proposal?"

"Son of a bitch," I said, leaning back and slapping my forehead. "You know something? I think it just might be…"

She planted a long kiss on my lips, then pulled away, and patted my cheek, amusement dancing in her lovely dark eyes.

"Tell you what," she said; "I'll take it under advisement."

Then she turned and went back to her seat.

"Come on," she said, "let's eat. Food's getting cold and I am famished."

* * * * *

Made in the USA
San Bernardino, CA
05 September 2015